THE
YEAR *of*
COUNTING
SOULS

ALSO BY MICHAEL WALLACE

Crow Hollow
The Crescent Spy
The Devil's Deep
Victoria Crossing

The Righteous Series

The Red Rooster
The Wolves of Paris

THE
YEAR *of*
COUNTING
SOULS

MICHAEL WALLACE

LAKE UNION
PUBLISHING

Published by Lake Union Publishing, Seattle

www.apub.com

Amazon, the Amazon logo, and Lake Union Publishing are trademarks of Amazon.com, Inc., or its affiliates.

ISBN-13: 9781477823767
ISBN-10: 147782376X

Cover design by PEPE *nymi*

Printed in the United States of America

Chapter One

Louise Harrison was waiting at the waterfront to be evacuated from Manila when she discovered that one of her patients was missing, a young soldier from Los Angeles named Jimmy Fárez. She remembered him hobbling to the hospital door on his crutches, but couldn't recall seeing him climb into the back of the truck with the rest. Many of the men had already been evacuated by seaplane, but she was certain Fárez was not one of them, and he was not waiting on the waterfront, either.

"Where is Corporal Fárez?" she asked.

Nobody seemed to hear her over the crying children, the men shouting orders, the armed soldiers fighting back the press of civilians desperate to flee the city ahead of the Japanese army. The question had been directed at Dr. Claypool, who was assisting an injured man with a nurse in attendance. He didn't look up.

Dr. Claypool had the face of a meat packer and a brow that frowned in concentration, eyes intense beneath eyebrows as thick as hairbrushes, but his hands were delicate and clever. He bent over a groaning young man, re-suturing a thigh wound that had opened in the move from the hospital. His fingers danced above the wound like a pianist's moving over a keyboard.

Louise waited until he'd tied off the last stitch before tugging on his arm. "Dr. Claypool. Did you see Corporal Fárez? I don't think he made it down from the hospital."

"Fárez? One of the Pinoys? You know we couldn't take them all, they have to—"

"No, he's an American. The boy from Los Angeles."

Claypool groaned. "Oh, right. I saw him at the hospital. He was looking for that damn mutt. Must have missed the transport, the idiot."

"He's *our* idiot, though. I have to go back for him."

"What about the trucks? Could we . . ."

The doctor stopped and looked around him, and Louise wondered how he'd missed the army trucks rumbling off. They'd been mobbed by civilians trying to scramble on. Soldiers had pushed them away. Several hospital patients had left on the trucks.

"It's only six blocks back to the hospital," she said. "I'll be back in a jiff."

A seaplane, fully loaded with injured soldiers, nurses, and doctors, swung around from the docks and picked up speed as it pulled away from shore. Propellers churning, it lifted sluggishly from the bay, water streaming from its pontoons. A hush fell briefly over the crowd as eyes scanned the sky, watching anxiously for a pack of long, sleek Zeros to materialize. No enemy fighters appeared, and the plane disappeared in the direction of Corregidor Island. Corregidor was a small, supposedly impregnable island fortress in Manila Bay where troops could hole up while waiting for reinforcements.

Claypool looked away from the waterfront and met her gaze. "You'd better hurry, by God. The next plane should be here in twenty-five minutes. Five minutes to load, and then we'll be off. There might not be another plane after that, you understand? At some point they'll stop, and whoever is left will be stuck in the city when the Japs arrive."

"I'll be back in time."

Louise's heart was pounding as she ran up the street in her white skirt, hand on her cap to keep it from falling off. The muggy air wrapped around her like a hot, wet sheet pulled too soon from the wash, and sweat streamed down her temples and along her ribs from the exertion. She left the waterfront and its pungent scent of spilled fuel and dead fish. Grand old mansions and Spanish colonial buildings encircled the harbor, worn by the relentless sun and tropical downpours but maintaining a certain elegance. Palms flanked the streets, and every home seemed to have a garden overgrown with fragrant plumeria and bougainvillea.

Among the beauty and charm, the city showed evidence of three weeks of bombing: trees uprooted, buildings with windows knocked out, gutted vehicles in the street, a dead mule still attached to its harness that lay on the side of the road, stinking in the sun. A white banner strung across the street read "Open City—No Resistance."

Farther in, the streets were packed with fleeing civilians on foot and bicycle, women with crates of chickens, donkeys, and handcarts. An American truck loaded with Filipino soldiers rolled through the crowd, forcing people aside. The walls of the colonial fort and the spires of the cathedral rose ahead of her, and she used them for a guide when she was forced to detour around a bomb crater big enough to swallow a bus.

Louise arrived at the military hospital moments later. It looked gaunt and abandoned from the exterior, the gates open, supplies strewn about the street in front—looted or merely scattered in the haste to evacuate, Louise didn't know. A sound like thunder rolled in from the outskirts of the city, and the air was hazy with smoke that might have been cook fires except that it smelled of gunpowder and burning fuel. The Americans were torching gasoline supplies to keep them out of the hands of the enemy.

She rushed up the stairs and hurried down the hallway. A pair of Filipino orderlies dashed out of one of the patient rooms, their arms full of medical supplies, but Corporal Fárez's room itself was abandoned, only unmade cots, sheets tossed about, bedpans overturned. Abandoned crutches and piles of dirty clothes. Footlockers thrown open and hastily rifled through.

Louise kept looking. The hospital wasn't empty. There were still Filipino orderlies in the office, burning records, although many had abandoned their posts and fled into the city. No one had seen Fárez.

Other civilians were helping to evacuate the injured Filipino soldiers that the brass had decided to leave behind. There wasn't enough transport to get them all to safety, and so it was decided that some would be left to hide among the population and pray the occupying army didn't sniff them out. Wounded Filipino soldiers limped past her, bandaged and half-mad with pain or doped up with morphine. They'd shed their gowns for civilian dress.

"Miss Louise! Did you come back for me?"

She turned to see one of the Filipina nurses, a young woman named Maria Elena, whose slight build and pretty face always made Louise feel tall and gawky. Maria Elena's father had sent her to the American school, and she spoke excellent English. She was also a hard worker and covered full daytime shifts in the heat when the American girls were wilting. Never should have been left behind.

Louise cringed at the question. "There's no room on the plane, but the army will come back for you as soon as they can." The words felt hollow, and the other woman's face fell. "I'm looking for Corporal Fárez," Louise added stiffly.

"I saw him. He was chasing that dog. Come on, I'll help you look."

They walked down the hallways, checking each room for the missing soldier and his adopted pet. The hospital had 450 beds and numerous wings, and it was a laborious search. As they moved, Maria Elena made her case.

"I'm from Laoag, not Manila. I don't have any family to hide with."

"We're not evacuating for long. As soon as MacArthur gets his reinforcements—"

"And my father is with the government—he'll be arrested. I'll be arrested, too, maybe shot."

"I'm only a nurse," Louise said helplessly. "I had my orders."

"You could put in a word with the lieutenant. The one who evacuated us. He wasn't listening to me, but maybe if you told him . . ."

"I'll say something when I get back."

"Oh, thank you!"

Maria Elena's face lit up at this bit of false hope, which only made Louise feel worse.

They found the missing patient in the courtyard behind the hospital, where recovering soldiers came for exercise, in the shadow of a balete tree with its knotted, exposed roots like fingers thrusting into the ground. Fárez leaned on a crutch, a piece of rope with a noose wrapped around his fist. The other hand waved a stick.

"Come on, Stumpy," Fárez said. "There's a good boy. Don't you want to play?"

Stumpy was of medium size, with dirty brown fur and of average manginess for a Manila street dog. He was entirely unremarkable in appearance except that he'd lost half his tail in some accident. His temperament was mild, which was a good thing, as the mean ones didn't last long. Neither did the unwary, who were run down by vehicles or crushed by carts.

At the moment, the dog seemed suspicious of the corporal's attentions, but intrigued at the same time. His stump tail wagged madly, and he barked excitedly while staying just out of reach. The corporal lunged for him, and he scooted back with his tongue out in a doggy grin.

Fárez dropped his crutch in the attempt and grabbed the tree to keep from falling.

"Come back here!" He was near tears. "Those Japs will have you, don't you know? Fine, then. See if I care."

Louise understood why Fárez had adopted the street dog, or thought she did, anyway. The young man had lost a chunk of his left buttock in the bombing of Manila immediately following the Pearl Harbor attacks. The airfields and docks of Manila Bay had come under relentless assault, and hundreds of wounded poured into an army hospital previously occupied with appendicitis and malaria patients. Fárez and many others like him, facing the tedium of a lengthy recovery, needed something to occupy their time.

The dog seemed to appreciate the extra food but was otherwise indifferent. Why should he care? He enjoyed a rich, fulfilling life in the streets, where he spent his days off on some disreputable errand or other, only to return for meals. He wasn't Fárez's pet, so much as a freeloader who knew a good thing when he got it.

Louise picked up the corporal's crutch and took his arm. "Come on, we've got to get you to the waterfront. The plane leaves in fifteen minutes."

"I got to get Stumpy."

Louise stared at him, not sure at first that he was serious. He had the glazed look of someone on morphine; clearly he was a little loopy.

"Stumpy will be fine. Look at him—he's a survivor. Come on, Corporal."

Fárez pulled free. "I won't leave my dog. Stumpy! Come here, Stumpy. Good boy, a little closer. Darn you, no! Get back here, you."

A hysterical laugh threatened to rise up in Louise's throat. And a little anger, too, at his stubbornness, morphine or no. She had a farm kid's hard-hearted outlook on the comparative value between a human and an animal life, and this particular dog was indifferent to the corporal, she was sure. Meanwhile, the Imperial Japanese Army was overrunning the city.

"He's a street dog!" she said. "What the devil is wrong with you?"

"Please help me," Fárez said. "Just get him a little closer so I can get the rope around his neck."

And then what? Haul him down to the waterfront?

Louis exchanged a look with Maria Elena, and the two nurses moved to block the dog's retreat. But the moment they attempted to herd Stumpy, he danced back with a cocky bark. Louise lunged. Her fingers grazed fur but failed to catch hold. Stumpy's eyes lit up in a mischievous, almost-human expression. *Oh no, you don't!*

"I'll have one of the nurses look after him," Louise said, panting. "We don't have time. For Pete's sake, Corporal. Will you come, or do I have to leave you here for the Japs? The dog will be okay, but you won't."

"Please!" Fárez's brown eyes were pleading, and he looked so young, surely younger than eighteen, as his chart claimed. "Get the other nurses. If we all work together, we can get him. Once I've got hold of him, he'll be a good boy, I know he will."

Louise had been gesturing impatiently, but now her hands fell in exasperation, and she found the small bulge in the front-right pocket of her nurse's dress. It was a piece of cellophane-wrapped fudge from a C ration, given to her by one of the soldiers in the ward. The gift giver was a radioman who claimed he didn't like sweets. Louise thought he was slightly in love with her, and most of the other nurses as well. Put a boy in a hospital with a gunshot wound and he turned sentimental in a hurry. Louise could hardly say no to free chocolate.

Now she broke off a small piece and held it out. "Be still, both of you." She knelt. "Come here, Stumpy. Look at this. Bet it tastes really good, don't you think?"

The dog took a tentative step forward, tail wagging, nose twitching. The ground rumbled beneath their feet. Staccato bursts of small-arms fire sounded from the southeast. The enemy was in the city, an evacuation plane was about to depart and leave her behind, and here she was, trying to lure a street dog with chocolate.

Fárez and Maria Elena stood rigid while Stumpy came forward. The suspicion faded from his eyes, and he licked his chops. One final glance at Louise's face, as if searching for deception; then he came for the treat. He gulped it in one swallow, but not before she picked him up. He didn't struggle.

"Whew! You need a bath." Louise turned to the corporal. "We've got your dog. For God's sake, can we get out of here now?"

Once back inside, she tied Fárez's rope around Stumpy's neck and set him down, prepared for a fight. But the dog was placid now, sniffing at her apron. He smelled the rest of the treat. Perhaps if he was good, she'd give it to him.

Louise, followed by the hobbling soldier and the young Filipina nurse, led the dog down the hall and down the stairs to the street. The last of the hospital staff were fleeing into the city. More gunfire sounded to the north and the southeast. But it was still distant.

"You think they'll let him on the plane, right?" Fárez asked. "I'll carry him in my arms the whole way. He can be a mascot, you know. Raise all our spirits out there in the jungle or wherever they're taking us."

A mascot? He was fooling himself. They wouldn't let the dog on the seaplane, she knew that much. If they could carry thirty more pounds, it would be medical supplies.

For that matter, they'd probably send Maria Elena away. The ledger of the American forces in Manila had few credits and many debits; the equations were cruel and merciless. An American nurse would be evacuated, a Filipina nurse left to survive the Japanese occupation. Anyone who'd heard of the brutality in China these past several years knew what that meant.

But it wasn't for her to decide. So she led the dog by the leash and let the young nurse help Fárez walk, obviously with expectations of evacuation herself. Louise checked her watch. Five minutes left. Make it ten before they lifted off without her. They had time.

An artillery shell came shrieking in, and they threw themselves to the ground as it struck a block of apartments they'd just passed. Glass rained down on the street, and flames jetted out the upper window. A long, howling scream came from the building, and Louise sprang to her feet and made toward the noise, her nurse's training taking over. The dog's makeshift leash was wrapped around her leg, and he barked and jerked madly, trying to get free. She freed herself and handed the rope to Fárez as he climbed shakily to his feet. Then she remembered their more urgent purpose. She had to get to the waterfront. They were close now, with a view of the bay.

The cries continued from the building, and Louise felt twisted in two directions. *Every life matters. Go, help.*

Maria Elena grabbed her arm. "Look. Is that ours?"

In flew a seaplane, only a few hundred feet above the water as it approached for a landing. The angle was wrong to see any markings, but it had to be the US Army Air Forces flight that would carry her to safety on Corregidor.

Even as this thought coalesced in her mind, a roar of piston engines sounded above and behind her. She knew that sound.

Louise had lived more than a year in Manila and grown accustomed to the Curtiss P-40s roaring in and out of Clark Field north of the city. But for the last three weeks, the motorcycle-like rumble of Zeros, and the deeper, menacing sound of Japanese bombers had dominated the skies.

Louise turned slowly, staring into the brilliant blue sky to see three Japanese Zeros swooping low over the city. They made straight for the bay and the incoming seaplane.

Chapter Two

The red suns on the wings of the Japanese planes were like glaring eyes as they passed overhead. Louise caught a glimpse of a young man with a leather aviator hat staring down at her from the first plane, and then the enemy planes were past.

The American seaplane was too far into its descent to pull up and flee. It came in gracefully, skating over the water as it slowed. Soldiers on the waterfront aimed small arms at the approaching Zeros, who ignored them. Instead they trained their guns on the seaplane.

The first Zero overshot its target. Its bullets disappeared harmlessly into the sea, and it raced past, banking around for another attack. The second and the third, however, struck the American plane, and one of these shots punctured a fuel tank or engine. There was a muffled explosion, a geyser of flame, and the whole thing was on fire. The doors opened, and the crew flung themselves into the bay.

By the time Louise got to the waterfront, the burning seaplane was already slipping beneath the waves. The Japanese fighters had turned around and were coming in to strafe the people on the shore. Two Filipino soldiers with rifles took aim while an American officer shouted and waved to get people to shelter in the nearby buildings.

Suddenly the officer's body danced a grotesque jig, and all around him men and women were screaming and falling as bullets tore through them. Louise threw herself to the ground for a second time. The noise was terrible. The sick taste of fear came up in her mouth. And then the enemy was gone.

Not only had she forgotten about the injured civilians in the building, but she'd lost track of her companions. As she rose shakily to her feet, she saw that Maria Elena, Corporal Fárez, and the dog were all uninjured. Maria Elena was crying, and Fárez was still and pale, his brown eyes wide, as if he was in shock. The dog remained flattened on the ground, as if instinctively trying to make itself as small as possible.

Louise's heart was ready to hammer free from her chest, but she didn't have time to be terrified. She found Dr. Claypool, who was already at work trying to stop the bleeding of a man whose leg was torn apart in the attack. He called for help. A woman stood next to him but seemed not to hear his pleas.

The woman's name was Frankie Dover, and she'd been chief nurse at the hospital. Twelve years in the army, and an exacting, demanding head, but you wouldn't have guessed at her experience or authority the way she stood rooted in place. Her face was slack with fear as she searched overhead. The blood of the injured man was splattered like red paint across her face and white dress, but she didn't seem to notice it. She only had eyes for the sky, for the feared return of the enemy.

Louise pushed Frankie aside. She took off her cap and pressed it on the injured man's wound, allowing Claypool to remove his own hands and work. She didn't look at the wound, told herself it was just meat. Just flesh. A little blood didn't bother her at all. That's what she told herself as she put her hands into a wound that looked like something from butchering day on the farm.

The man writhed and screamed, tried to push her hands away. So much blood was leaking out, and the pain soon gave way to shock. By the time the doctor organized his instruments to enact an emergency roadside surgery, the wounded man was fading. There was nothing to be done for him, and he was soon dead in a small lake of blood. Soldiers came to ask if they could help, only to turn away, looking ill.

Two small miracles. First, the Japanese Zeros didn't return. They buzzed around over the city and flew south, where there was the sound of gunfire and artillery.

Second, the attack had done less damage than Louise feared. The three soldiers—the American giving orders, and the two Filipinos with rifles—were dead, as was the man she and Dr. Claypool tried to save. An older Filipina woman who nobody seemed to know, but someone thought might be the mother of one of the dead soldiers, had also died in the attack.

An army lieutenant by the name of Kozlowski took charge of the survivors. First, he organized a rescue of the aviators who'd escaped the burning seaplane; then he got a radioman to call for another evacuation. The radioman looked up after a tense, shouted conversation that seemed to involve someone incredulously squawking on the other end about the impossibility of sending in more planes. And trucks? Were they nuts? The bloody Japanese army was on the outskirts of town, and artillery shells were raining down all around.

The conversation continued, with Kozlowski unwilling to relent. At last he got the army to commit two trucks and a Jeep escort.

"Fifteen minutes," Kozlowski said. "The trucks will take us to Bataan. Essential personnel only. The doctor, nurses, injured Americans only."

Once more, that cruel ledger. Still, Louise was relieved. She'd been nervous about the plan to retreat to Corregidor. It seemed like a death trap. There was nothing to stop the Japanese naval and air forces from pounding the island night and day while they waited for the defenders to starve. Only a miracle would have got them off that rock alive.

Bataan, on the other hand, was salvation. She knew little about it except that it was rugged terrain, jungle, and crawling with American and Filipino forces. Soldiers had assured her that MacArthur could hold out indefinitely on the peninsula, while sailors promised it was only a matter of time before the United States Navy roared back into battle and sent the arrogant Japanese fleet to the bottom of the South China Sea.

The nurses used the delay to see to their patients. Many of them shouldn't have left their beds under any circumstances, but ugly rumors of enemy atrocities had circulated through the wards. So far it didn't seem that the Japanese were bayoneting prisoners the way they had in China, but nobody wanted to fall into their hands and sample the offerings of a Japanese POW camp.

Louise and her fellow nurses changed dressings, helped Dr. Claypool suture busted stitches, administered ointments, irrigated burns with saline, gave morphine, and handed out quinine pills to those suffering malarial chills. The war hadn't abolished the old tropical ailments, and in addition to malaria, patients suffered from dengue, dysentery, and yellow fever. So many miserable men—Louise's heart ached to see them sweltering under the tropical sun.

The young Filipina nurse, Maria Elena, fell in with her American counterparts, and there no longer seemed to be any talk of leaving her behind when the rescue came.

"It's been fifteen minutes," Miss Frankie said. Her tone held an edge of desperation. "What are they doing? Why don't they come here at once? We have to get out of here!"

Louise sized the woman up, surprised to see her still shaken. Frankie had been calm enough that morning during the evacuation of the hospital. They'd drilled many times, preparing for war long before the events of the "date which will live in infamy," as President Roosevelt called the attack on Pearl Harbor, but with more and more urgency in the last few weeks. Manila would fall; it was only a matter of time. How would they get as many patients and staff to safety as possible?

During the drills, Frankie had been her usual self, giving orders, bossing the younger nurses to the point of bullying. She got on fine with soldiers and doctors but had a more complicated relationship with other women. Clarice McGillicuddy, the fourth nurse in their little group, had once told Louise that the head nurse's bad attitude toward women came from romantic disappointment. She'd lost a man to a rival.

Army nurses were single by requirement, and Frankie was in her thirties and still unmarried, so it was reasonable to assume that in so many years she'd caught the eye of at least one man. Why hadn't she married him? Who could say? Louise's inner gossip had been awakened by the younger nurse's claim, and she'd pressed for details. Clarice had few.

Louise doubted the whole story, only knew that Frankie was driven, focused. Yet now, their first time seeing such danger firsthand, she'd been left rattled, irritable. Almost panicking from the attack of the Japanese Zeros.

Cries caught Louise's ear, the pleas of an injured man writhing on his cot. The commotion came from Private Higgs, lying on his belly beneath a canopy, squeezed in with three others to shield them from the sun. His back was badly burned from an attack on a fuel dump, and gauze enveloped his face. Louise struggled to control the churning in her stomach every time she had to change his bandages and inspect his injuries. Poor kid.

"Private Higgs," Louise told Frankie. "Do you know when he got his last morphine?"

"How am I supposed to know?" Frankie asked irritably, not even sparing a glance at the injured man. "We've got to get out of here!"

"Frankie!" Louise said sharply.

Maria Elena was over at the tent with the injured men and had looked over when Louise and Frankie began to talk. Some of the men were watching, too, expressions anxious.

Frankie looked around, seemed to catch herself. "I'm sorry, I'm sorry."

"When did Higgs get his morphine?" Louise asked again.

"I'm—I'm not really sure. Not too long?" Frankie shook her head. "We were treating so many people."

"He's in a lot of pain," Maria Elena called over. "He says it's been forever."

It was always forever when you were suffering. They had plenty of morphine, but Louise didn't want to kill him with an overdose. With Frankie paralyzed, should she hazard a guess?

Thankfully the older nurse seemed to get hold of herself before Louise was forced to make the call. "Let me think," Frankie said. "It was before the hospital evacuation. Let's call it an hour before we left."

Louise glanced at her watch. "That makes it at least four hours since his last injection. Probably five."

The soldier moaned again, and Maria Elena called for instructions.

"Give him a half dose," Frankie told her. "If that doesn't take, we'll give him more later."

Frankie grabbed at a passing soldier. "Where are those trucks? Why aren't they here?"

The man looked annoyed to be taken from his duties and snapped that he didn't know. The trucks would come when the trucks came.

Frankie looked ready to set off for Lieutenant Kozlowski, but just then the promised vehicles finally rumbled around the corner. There were two six-by-six US Army cargo trucks, together with a Jeep carrying four armed soldiers. There was saluting, some cheers, then a mad scramble for the vehicles as shells began detonating a few blocks away.

"Hurry up, you!" one of the men from the Jeep shouted at the stragglers, those too injured to hop into the truck without aid from the nurses and their fellow sailors and soldiers. "Damn Japs are in the city already. You don't get up here, you'll be left behind, so help me."

In all, it took a half hour from the destruction of the seaplane until the trucks were rolling away from the waterfront. Louise sat up front in one of the cargo trucks with the driver, a Filipino civilian with a cigarette hanging from his lips who shifted gears with the intensity of a man trying to wrestle a pig to the ground.

Maria Elena sat on Louise's lap, and Frankie squeezed in next to the window. They tucked their legs beneath them as crates of medical supplies ate up the rest of the space. Boxes of bandages and syringes piled against the window, reducing visibility out the front. The driver spoke heavily accented English and apologized to the nurses every time he hit an especially jarring pothole.

Louise's was the first truck behind the armed escort, and occasionally one of the men in the Jeep communicated back with the driver using hand signals. They changed course twice as they picked their way through the city, trying to get around burning vehicles and craters in the road. Then the Jeep took a right turn that the truck didn't follow. Louise glanced past Frankie at the side mirror. The other truck followed them, not the Jeep.

"Why aren't we following our escort?" Frankie demanded.

"They send us to pick up a government official, miss," the driver said. "We take a . . ." He stopped, searching for a word.

"Detour?" Louise suggested.

"Yes, detour. Government official is no longer this way. The Jeep goes to get the man—we meet again in a few minutes."

"They'll be killed," Frankie told the other two nurses. "*We'll* be killed. We need an escort. How are we supposed to find our way out of here? Stop the truck! Pull over. I want to talk to whoever is in charge."

Louise could no longer hold her tongue. "Oh, hush. Our driver is a native. He knows the city better than whoever was driving that Jeep."

"Actually, I am not from Manila, miss," the man said. "I am from the island of Lubang."

"You see!" Frankie cried.

Engaging the head nurse wasn't helping to calm her, so Louise decided to ignore her. Instead she called back to Clarice on the other side of the canvas, asking about the patients. All was well. What about up front, Clarice asked? Nothing to report, Louise said.

A few minutes later the truck hit the end of the macadamized road and rolled to a stop. They were still in the city. The second truck pulled up beside them, and the driver of the other vehicle leaned across his passengers to shout a question. The two drivers argued back and forth in Tagalog.

"Bet they're lost," Frankie said. She turned to Maria Elena. "You speak that jibber jabber, right? What are they saying?"

"We were supposed to meet the Jeep right here," Maria Elena said. "But it was going to get here first. Now they don't know what to do."

"I knew it! We've got to get out of here, we're going to be bombed."

"Please!" Louise said. "Let's all stay calm, shall we?"

She studied the drivers, wondering what was going to happen.

One of the passengers in the front seat of the second truck was Corporal Fárez. Stumpy sat on his lap, and when Fárez spotted Louise, he held the dog up and lifted its paw to wave. Louise shook her head but couldn't keep the grin off her face. Silly dog. And silly man—he'd done it, after all, managed to evacuate a common street dog in the teeth of a Japanese invasion.

An officer with a rifle came up front from the rear of the second truck. It was the same man who'd been directing traffic at the harbor, Lieutenant Kozlowski. He seemed to have kept his cool as he scanned the road ahead of them, and Louise studied him more closely, relieved by what she saw.

Kozlowski had a sharp, intelligent gaze, a square jaw, and a confident posture. The man simply *looked* like a fighting man. He wore khaki, but he could have easily dressed like a Roman soldier or a redcoat from the revolution, and he would have looked equally the warrior.

And a good thing, too. Without the Jeep, Louise felt stripped down and vulnerable.

Kozlowski nodded at the driver. "Keep going. We'll get another escort if we can."

"Sir, there is smoke rising ahead of us," the driver said.

"And there's smoke behind us, smoke rising at the bay, smoke to the south and east. Manila is an open city, but that doesn't mean the Japs are going to let us walk out of here. Only way out of it is straight ahead."

The two drivers had another brief exchange in their native tongue, and then Louise's driver said to the lieutenant, "But we have to head south, sir, to get north. The road ahead isn't open."

"Then go south."

"And if we judge wrong, sir, and we meet the enemy on the road—"

"I don't care how you do it," Kozlowski said. "Make for Route 3 and get us out of here. That's an order. And if you see the damn Japs on the road, you run 'em down. Now move!"

They were back in motion moments later. The high walls of the old fort and the cathedral towers receded behind them, and the buildings thinned into fields of long, stiff grass, rice paddies, and wallows for carabao, the water buffalo that were everywhere in the countryside. It wasn't raining at the moment, but the road was soft and pocked with ruts filled with muddy water. It splashed up on the hood when they churned through each hole. The driver had stopped apologizing, and hunched over the steering wheel, staring tensely out the windshield. The roads were suspiciously empty.

A man cried out in pain from the back, and Clarice called up for help.

Frankie scowled. "Better see what that's about. Doc gave us all the bad cases."

Of course he did. Why else were all four nurses in this one truck? Louise threw back the tarp separating them from the passengers in the back. Men were packed onto the two benches, legs held up against chests so that other, more seriously wounded men could lie down on the aisle between them. It smelled of sweat and blood, and eyes were wide with pain and fear. Clarice was tucked into a tiny corner, looking small and frightened.

Before Louise had a chance to see who was crying out in pain, shouts came from the front seat, and she whipped back around. The road had suddenly filled with bicyclists, and she thought at first that they'd overtaken a group of refugees fleeing the city. But they were all headed the wrong direction, toward their truck and the city, not away from it.

Japanese soldiers. Dressed in khaki and wearing helmets with canvas flaps to shield their necks from sun, each had a bedroll tied to the back of his bike, a rifle slung over his shoulder, and a canteen at his belt. It was an entire company of men, maybe a hundred and fifty in all. They were a mud-splattered, sweaty-looking bunch.

Maybe it was the exhaustion of riding their bikes in through the late-afternoon heat, or the surprise of seeing US military vehicles on a road they must have been told was clear of enemies, but the Japanese were slow in reacting. Some lurched to the side to get free of the lumbering trucks while a handful of alert men jumped from their bikes and fumbled with rifles. Others shouted and ducked for cover.

The trucks were almost through the enemy soldiers when they encountered a thick pocket of men who couldn't steer clear before the trucks hit. Their truck's driver was still accelerating, hitting every pothole with a bone-jarring shake, and he plowed into the men in the road. Bicycles crumpled and went flying. Soldiers rolled beneath the heavy tires or were dragged down the road.

They were almost through. A final man came straight at them on his bicycle. He flew up onto the hood and smashed into the windshield. His helmet fell off, and his face flattened grotesquely against the glass, blood running from his mashed nose. His face was only inches from

Louise's, and she turned away rather than stare at him through the windshield.

"Get him off! Get him off!" Frankie screamed, even as rifle fire chased them down the road.

Louise caught a glimpse of a Japanese soldier off his bicycle on the side of the road, shouting excitedly into a radio. Two men chased after the truck on foot, screaming a battle cry, but they couldn't keep up. More gunfire, this time spitting from the tall grass to their left. Bullets pinged off the door and spiderwebbed the glass next to the driver's head. Fortunately it was only rifle fire, not a machine gun, and none of it got through.

Then they were free and in open country again, no enemies on the road. The Japanese soldier was still lying limply against the windshield. His legs splayed out in front of the driver, obstructing the view, and his arms stretched overhead, hands dangling over the other side by the nurses. The driver hit the brakes to get him to slide off, but he stayed wedged in the gap between the windshield and the top of the hood.

"Don't you dare stop!" a soldier shouted from the back. "Get us out of here, dammit."

"I cannot see, sir! I'll drive off the road, sir." The driver turned to Louise. "Miss, can you help?"

Louise swallowed hard and nodded. She shifted Maria Elena off her lap and crawled over the top of Frankie, who unrolled the window for her. Louise leaned out. Thick tropical air rushed over her and tore her hair loose from the pins. It flapped and plastered against her face.

Louise grabbed the dead soldier's wrist and pulled. His hand was right in her face, and she could see the hairs on the back of his hand, read the time on the wristwatch with its brown leather band. A Zenith. It was the same watch her father gave her older brother when he graduated from Colorado A&M with a degree in agronomy.

How strange to see the same watch on the wrist of this dead Japanese soldier. And the man's face was all too human, not like the leering, slant-eyed sketches from propaganda leaflets. Just a boy far from home, struck dead while back home some family prayed for his safe return. Or whatever passed for prayer in that strange land.

The truck hit a pothole and jarred the body loose from where it was wedged. It began to slide off the side of the hood, when suddenly the man's hand shot out and seized her wrist. His other hand grabbed the top of the hood, and he struggled to keep his body from sliding off the end. Blood streamed from his nose as he lifted his head.

Louise cried out in shock, and vaguely, over the whistling wind and the sound of distant gunfire, she heard Frankie and Maria Elena screaming. They tugged on her legs and waist, but they couldn't get her free from the Japanese soldier's grip. She clawed at him, but he wouldn't let go.

The man fixed her with his gaze. He opened his mouth, and out came clear, unaccented English. "Please help me."

Chapter Three

The truck came to a halt, and Louise wrenched herself free at last. The Japanese soldier rolled off the hood and landed in a huge, mud-filled pothole. His legs were in front of the right tire, and as the truck rumbled back to life, it rolled slowly over them. The man cried out in pain as he was forced deeper into the mud.

Louise was more than halfway out the window, and they'd let go of her waist once the enemy soldier fell. The truck was barely moving. Instincts kicked in, and she couldn't help herself. Before she had a chance to think, she squirmed her way out the open window and flopped into the mud. Alarmed shouts came from her companions. Fárez's dog barked excitedly from the other truck, which rolled to a stop with squeaking brakes.

"Get in here, you idiot!" Frankie cried.

She'd already thought of the wounded Japanese soldier as a human when she saw the wristwatch and his boyish face, but the moment he spoke English, something more profound snapped into place. He was no longer a Jap or an enemy; he was an injured man, and she couldn't leave him here to die of his injuries.

The man was moving his upper body and his back, so she didn't think his spine was severed. He spat water and shook his head, then used his arms to drag himself out of the puddle as Louise helped. She turned her attention to his legs.

He may have survived being run over by the heavy transport—the truck had merely pressed him deeper into the mud and water—but his right leg was badly broken. Even without cutting away his trousers, she could feel a fracture of the tibia. The initial collision had left his nose streaming blood, but it didn't appear to be broken. Probing further, Louise discovered a gash on his abdomen. Between the blood and the tattered shirt and the mud, it was impossible to see the extent of it.

Men and women were still hollering at her. A hand rested on Louise's shoulder, and she thought it was someone come to haul her back.

She tried to shrug free. "Let go of me, I—"

"Miss Louise, it's me."

Dr. Claypool. He frowned beneath thick eyebrows, but she felt relief to see his expression. It was the probing, scientific look that crossed his face when he examined a patient.

Louise eyed the other men spilling out of the truck. They were injured soldiers and sailors, but they were all business now. They came limping over with intent clear on their faces. They meant to wrangle the doctor and nurse back into the truck so they could get off this long, straight stretch of highway. Here they were vulnerable to attack from the air and ground, with no friendly forces in sight. Louise was putting them all in danger, and she knew it. But she couldn't leave this man, not now.

Heavy drops of water fell from the sky, warm as bathwater, and splattered the back of her neck. It had been a brilliant tropical day, but now the lid was closing overhead, and as soon as it snapped shut, a deluge would inevitably follow.

Dr. Claypool reached out to feel the broken leg as his eyes roamed up and down the man's body, and Louise pointed out the gash in the man's abdomen.

"Ah yes. Good eyes." His expression darkened as he probed the wound. "Could be serious."

He glanced at the approaching soldiers. "No," he told them. "Give us a moment." Then, to the nurse, "Miss Louise, you know we can't."

The Japanese turned his head. "Please don't leave me here to die."

Claypool blinked. "My God, he speaks English?"

Fresh fear blossomed on the soldier's face as he spotted the soldiers glaring down at him from behind her. Louise turned, followed his eyes. The soldiers' expressions were ugly, weeks of frustration showing. One man had his sidearm out, and Lieutenant Kozlowski was there, too, his rifle leveled.

"Stand back!" Kozlowski ordered the others.

"Don't shoot me!" the Japanese soldier cried.

Hearing him speak English brought curses and shouts that they'd found a spy. The American soldiers—four in all—seemed suddenly determined to carry out their roadside execution. One grabbed Louise as she tried to shield the man's body. He yanked her away.

"Doctor!" she cried.

Nobody had touched Claypool, and indecision twisted his face one way and then the other. "No," he said at last. "We won't harm him."

"We can't take no Japs," someone said. "Ain't got no room, and none of the men would have him near if we did."

"He's right," Lieutenant Kozlowski said. "We're on the run, we've got to drive all day to get to safety, and we're stuffed full. If we had room, we'd have taken on some Pinoys, not a damn prisoner."

"Sir," Louise's driver called over to the lieutenant. "We're not safe here, sir."

"We can't be executing prisoners," Dr. Claypool said. "This man is injured and unarmed. Let Miss Louise give him some morphine, and we'll leave him for the enemy to find."

"Come on, Doc," Kozlowski said. "The Japs come up the road and he'll tell them what he saw and where we went."

Kozlowski had remained calm, but Louise no longer saw that as a good thing. No emotion on his face. Only a cold, calculated decision hardening in his eyes.

Louise pulled free of the soldiers and moved to shield the enemy soldier. "Don't you wonder why he speaks English?"

"He's a spy, obviously," Kozlowski said. "Or in charge of propaganda. An agitator. The kind that come in afterward and rile up the population to rat out the Americans. All the more reason we've got to take care of him now."

"I'm no spy," the man said. "I'm not any of those things, I swear it."

"Yeah, right. Anyway"—the lieutenant jabbed his finger at him—"you shut up. Stand aside, miss. I've got to do it, and it's not going to get any easier the longer we sit here jawing about it."

"What's your name?" Louise asked the Japanese soldier.

If only she could make the others see what she'd seen, he might have a chance. He was a man like they were, doing his duty. An *injured* man.

"Sammy."

One of the soldiers jeered. "If he's named Sammy, then so is my gram."

"He knows English," Louise said. "He might help us."

"What are you talking about?" Kozlowski asked. His expression had not softened.

"I mean he can tell MacArthur what the Japs are up to, where they're invading and the like. Can't you?" she asked the Japanese. "You've got all of that information, right?"

The man looked away without answering. It was a desperate attempt by Louise, and he hadn't helped matters.

"Just shoot the son of a bitch and be done with it," one of the soldiers said.

"No," Dr. Claypool said at last. "Miss Louise is right. We'll get him into the truck, make room for him somehow. Apart from the fact that he's injured and helpless, he might have valuable intelligence."

"You don't really believe that, do you?" Kozlowski said.

"It doesn't matter if I do or don't," Claypool said steadily. "That is my medical decision."

Unlike the nurses, doctors had an official military rank, and Claypool outranked the lieutenant. But maybe this was a battlefield decision, and Kozlowski could overrule him. The doctor and the young lieutenant stared hard at each other for a long moment; then Kozlowski grunted and looked to the others.

"You heard the doc. Get this ugly Jap into the truck. Search him first, make sure he's not armed. If he's got so much as a pair of chopsticks on him, that's it. Peterson and Balboni, change over to the other truck to make room. Now move it!"

The lieutenant loomed over the doctor and nurse, who'd knelt in the mud over the wounded man. "And if he does try something funny, it's on your heads. Got it?"

—————

Dark gazes and muttered oaths greeted the Japanese soldier in the truck, and there was a near riot when the other patients found out they'd have to move aside so he could be given their precious space and medical supplies. Only Kozlowski's shouted order and the respect they had for the doctor kept them in line.

Louise and Dr. Claypool had everything they needed but clean syringes for administering morphine. Those were in the other vehicle, and they'd set off so quickly there was no time to get any of it. Clearing out as much room in the back of the truck as possible, they laid their tools and instruments on the laps of the patients squeezed onto the benches on either side.

She took off the Japanese soldier's khaki shirt, which revealed the ugly abdominal wound. Doctor and nurse scrubbed their hands with alcohol, irrigated the wound with iodine, and then Claypool began exploring. The injured man hissed in pain. His face was pale.

This brought jeers from the Americans, most of whom had suffered painful injuries at the hands of the Japanese.

"Bloody Jap's a coward," one man said.

"Cut his balls off while you're at it, Doc. If he's got 'em."

"Will you monkeys lay off?" Claypool said. "We have a job to do."

"There's nothing for the pain?" the injured man asked in a thin voice. "Ether?"

"We're not going to put you under," Louise said. "Come on, where is that Japanese warrior spirit they're always going on about? What is it—Bushido?"

"That's not Bushido. Anyway, I never had it. Never had any of it—you'll have to talk to my brother if you want any of that."

She got a needle and sutures ready, but Claypool snapped his fingers impatiently. "No, no, the number-two sutures. The bowel is perforated, and I need to stitch it up first. Good, like that. Keep him talking, he moves less."

"Your brother is in the army, too?" she asked. His eyes drifted away, as if he either wouldn't or couldn't answer the question. She tried a different angle. "Is your name really Sammy?"

"Sachihiro Mori." He managed a clench-jawed smile. "In your country they called me Sammy. I figured that might be a better name to tell the soldiers if I wanted to stay alive."

This brought more mutters from the other soldiers.

"I knew it," Louise said. "Your English is too good to have learned it in school. Where were you living, San Francisco? I heard there are a lot of Japanese."

"Mostly Honolulu."

Her eyes widened as she thought of recent events. "Really? What were you doing there?"

Uncertainty flickered across his face, and his mouth closed. Claypool tugged on the thread to tie it off, and Sammy grimaced but didn't cry out.

"Of course he was in Honolulu," one of the watching soldiers said. "He's a damn spy. Probably waving in the Zeros as they came at Pearl Harbor. This one should be strung up, boys."

Kozlowski snorted. "Think that through, won't you?"

"What do you mean?" the soldier said.

"It's a pretty trick to be in Hawaii on December seventh and taken prisoner in the Philippines three weeks later."

"They must have flown him out right after the attack," the soldier said stubbornly. "Anyway, it don't mean he's not a spy."

"I'll wager he *is* a spy," Kozlowski said. "But let's not be ridiculous about it."

Louise was torn between sympathy for her patient and sympathy for those she'd been caring for the past few weeks. Broken, crippled men, bombed on their ships and in the docks. Gunned down trying to stop the Japanese landings at Lingayen Gulf and Lamon Bay. Shot, burned, bayoneted. Some they saved; others died horribly. She had no illusion what would have happened had one of her boys fallen into the clutches of the Japanese back on the road. Probably tortured mercilessly, then killed when he could no longer give information.

"Okay," Claypool said to Louise. "Now the number threes. Get the dressing ready." He grunted as the truck jostled. "Do you think the driver is trying to hit every last pothole?"

In spite of the bumpy road, they soon had Sammy's abdominal wound bandaged up and attended to the leg. Doctor and nurse shifted the broken tibia into place, while Sammy cried out in Japanese. They splinted it for now. Later they'd apply a plaster cast.

Once they were done, Claypool allowed the soldiers to throw open the tarps and let the breeze clear out the tight, close air in the back. They'd apparently found their way back onto Route 3 leading into the

Central Luzon Plain and were passing through a placid stretch of palms and grass-roofed nipa huts. There were Filipino civilians on the road, fleeing Manila, but little motorized traffic.

It was early afternoon when they came upon a major defensive position of Filipino troops who stopped the trucks on the road. Men set up Browning machine guns, muscled small field pieces into position, and hauled sandbags out of mule-pulled carts. They'd pulled down two of the huts to use their wood for a palisade and set others on fire to deny cover to the enemy.

It was a hive of work, but even Louise could tell that these men were green, untested. They were too clean, too fresh, with none of the battle-hardened, battle-shocked look of men who'd been in combat. They'd be facing veteran Japanese troops. Would they hold, or would they strip out of their uniforms and melt into the countryside?

There weren't any Americans about, and Lieutenant Kozlowski couldn't communicate with the nervous Filipinos refusing them permission to continue north.

"Where's that Pinoy nurse?" he asked Louise. "Bring her up front."

Louise found Maria Elena with Clarice as the two were handing out quinine pills and changing dressings in the second truck. She led Maria Elena up to where the lieutenant was still trying to communicate.

Some basic information came out at once. The Filipino troops were from the Fifty-First Division, tasked with holding the town of Plaridel. There was a tank battalion of Americans farther north in Baliuag.

"Baliuag is where the hospital is," Louise said. "How far is that from here?"

"No more than five miles," Kozlowski said.

Her heart lifted. Only five miles. What a horrible morning, and no doubt there would be more dangers in the days and weeks to come, but if they could only get to Baliuag, they could enjoy a respite. Safe, protected by American tanks and this strong force of Filipinos to the rear, they could get their patients settled into real beds. Get them proper treatment, with ample supplies and clean, modern operating facilities.

Kozlowski turned to Maria Elena. "Nurse, tell him we're going to Baliuag. He's got to let us through. We've got a prisoner, for one, a potential spy. And we've got injured men, we need that hospital. Make sure he understands."

Maria Elena translated, and the Filipino smiled in that obliging way that Louise had learned meant he was in disagreement without wanting to seem disagreeable.

"He advises that we continue toward Bataan, sir," Maria Elena said. "That we'll be safe there, that the Fifty-First is charged with holding the road against the Japs until Manila can be evacuated, sir." She looked nervous and cleared her throat. "And he wants me to remind you that he is a captain, and you are a lieutenant."

Kozlowski flushed, his calm wavering for the first time since Louise had met him. "I want a radio. Get me a radio, or so help me God . . ."

Maria Elena relayed this. Her tone sounded more conciliatory than the lieutenant's. The reply from the Filipino officer was just as even tempered.

The young nurse licked her lips before she translated. "Sir, he says he is unable to do that. He doesn't have an available radio at hand—they are all being used for military purposes."

"What the devil does he think this is?"

Kozlowski looked around at the men who'd climbed out of the trucks to stretch their legs and listen. His eyes narrowed. "Fárez, are you still messing around with that dog? Take that stupid rope off and let it go."

"But, sir!"

"That's an order, Fárez. Oh, for Pete's sake, will someone help him?" Kozlowski added as Fárez leaned on his crutch, trying to bend over. "Good, now get into the truck. That goes for all of you. We're going forward on this road one way or another."

Stumpy, released from his leash, trotted a few feet away and cocked his head at the corporal. Fárez looked crestfallen. He stared, frowning after the lieutenant, who was stomping back to the truck. Fárez licked his lips, then snapped his fingers at the dog. Stumpy, perhaps looking around at the unfamiliar surroundings, came trotting back to his would-be owner. The corporal scooped him up and gave him a hug. The other men were climbing into the truck, and Louise made her way over.

"You're not really going to disobey orders, are you?" she asked.

"No," Fárez said glumly. "Just saying good-bye. Anyway, the lieutenant is probably right. At least he's got a chance out here in the country. Away from all the bombs and guns."

Louise thought Stumpy would have survived in Manila just fine. He'd probably survive out here, too. Follow the road to one of the small villages and insinuate himself with the local pack of street dogs.

But what harm would it do to keep him around? Fárez and some of the other men had taken to tugging on Stumpy's ears and giving him bits of shoelace to wrestle. It was good for morale, took their minds off their injuries and the constant threat of enemy attack.

"Go get in the lieutenant's truck," she said. "Leave Stumpy with me."

Fárez grinned. "Yeah? What are you gonna do?"

"There's a crate of bandages that need washing. Stumpy can sleep in there, out of the way."

"And that humbug, Kozlowski? What about him? He'll find out sooner or later."

"You let me worry about Lieutenant Kozlowski. He'll lose his bluster when we get somewhere safe. Now hurry, before you get yelled at again."

Dr. Claypool raised his bushy eyebrows as Louise climbed into the truck with the dog squirming in her arms. "Ah, so now *you're* in charge of the mutt."

Stumpy licked her face before she could get him into the crate, and his breath was rank. She shuddered to think what filth he'd been eating. As soon as they got to Baliuag, she'd have him dewormed and treat his mange with carbolic acid.

Moments later they were in motion again. The head nurse was with Louise this time. Frankie complained of a splitting headache and declined to help Dr. Claypool when one injured young man started bleeding through his bandages. She told Louise to do it while she closed her eyes to rest.

As the two trucks and their evacuees from the hospital rolled north on the road, a Filipino soldier came into the road, waving his hands and shouting in English. They'd found their translator at last, but if he had anything useful to say, Kozlowski wasn't stopping to hear it. Somehow they made it through without being stopped by the Filipinos.

Their next destination was the American-held town of Baliuag. A company of American tanks held it. The Japanese were invading on bicycles. Surely the town was safe.

Chapter Four

Captain Yoshiko Mori stumbled into disorganized fragments of the unit he sought a few miles south of Manila. He ordered his driver to stop the truck and climbed out.

The Fourteenth. He'd found them.

Mori slipped his hand into his jacket pocket, where he felt the three thin sheets written in mixed kanji and hiragana in his brother's fine hand. Had they been mailed to anyone else, the sheets would have been inspected by the army's Monthly Postal Review Report. But Mori was Kempeitai, military police, and the mail got through. The ugly enormity of the letter was plainly evident, yet no censor's hand had touched his brother's writing. No other eyes had seen his words.

He's here. Are you ready for this?

Bicycles lay scattered about. Japanese soldiers sat smoking or drinking tea in the shade of a transport truck. Most carried the exhausted look of men who'd been up for days, fighting and clawing their way across Luzon toward Manila. There was still hard fighting to come.

A captain came over to shout at Mori to get his vehicle off the road but stopped when he saw the insignia and rank. He eyed the young adjutant accompanying Mori, with his white armband and the red kanji reading "Law Soldier."

The captain saluted Mori. It was not an impressive salute. His jacket was undone, his face red and sweaty from the heat, and there was mud on his trousers and under his fingernails.

"Is this the Fourteenth?" Mori asked.

"Elements of it, sir."

"Why the devil are you stopped here?" Mori asked.

"They say we're not ready. They say we've outrun our supplies."

When the captain took off his round eyeglasses to wipe off the mud, his eyes had a distant, myopic look. Mori pegged him as the bookish sort, a logistics man. Well, it took all kinds, but this one wouldn't be pushing the advance. It would take braver men, more dedicated to glory for the emperor and the rising sun, to secure the final victory.

"Supplies. What does that matter?"

"Sir?"

"The Americans are beaten," Mori said. "The Pinoys are cowards, coddled by the Americans—they won't stand and fight. A hundred men could take Manila."

The captain put his glasses back on and peered at Mori with a look of placid petulance. "It does little good to catch a thief and then look around for the rope to bind him."

"And so you have orders to stay here and wait for rope?"

"My orders were insufficient. I'm waiting for clarification."

Ah, so that was it. *Gekokujō*. The lesser ranks lead from below. Men who obeyed by disobeying. Someone had given the order to take Manila. Someone else had decided that to do so was to expose oneself to greater risk.

Not that *gekokujō* was always cautious; sometimes, the opposite.

Mori had seen plenty of it in the Kwantung Army in China, where he'd been serving until this recent folly. There, the Kwantung, openly defying politicians, and sometimes the entire Imperial Japanese Army, had set about expanding the war in China and fighting border skirmishes with the Soviets, dragging the rest of the country along with it.

He took in the dozens of men sprawling in the tall grass, stacking crates, pouring gas into trucks, dragging small field pieces into position with a lethargy befitting the tropical heat. A single enemy plane could have wreaked havoc, a single American tank could have rolled through and destroyed the encampment with little opposition.

Why are we here, anyway? We belong in China, not this sweltering hell. Not fighting Americans.

Like his brother, Sachihiro, Yoshiko Mori had lived several years in the United States. He didn't underestimate them as so many did, those who thought the Americans were soft and weak, who boasted that Japanese troops would take San Francisco by summer. That was foolhardy. He'd seen American energy and determination, knew their vast resources. It would be a long, costly struggle to defeat them. But this particular battle was won, or should be.

Mori removed a small notebook from the breast pocket of his uniform. The pocket opposite the one holding his brother's letter. "What is your name?"

The man's petulance faded, and now he looked worried. "Captain Soto. Why do you wish to know?"

"Because I am a law soldier, and it is my duty to ask questions. I am tasked with pacifying central Luzon, including Manila, and I must know who I am dealing with in the regular army." Mori turned to his adjutant. "How many Captain Sotos do you suppose are in the army?"

His adjutant looked thoughtful. "Hundreds, probably. It is a very common name."

The young man's name was Hiroshi Fujiwara, and he spoke in a cold, precise voice. Lieutenant Fujiwara was compliant and absolutely loyal to Captain Mori, and that showed in the earnestness on his face, his look of devotion as a boy might show to his father, although the two men were only about four years apart in age. The intensity of his voice tended to startle other men and make them all the more eager to answer Mori's questions.

"We arrested a man named Soto last week for cowardice under fire," Fujiwara added. "He was shot, I believe. Isn't that right, sir?"

"Beheaded." Mori rested a hand on the hilt of his sword. "There was no time for a trial."

"Yes, sir," Fujiwara said gravely. "I remember now."

This was all fabricated. All part of the game Mori and his adjutant played when dealing with stubborn IJA officers. Remind them of the power of the Kempeitai, the military police. The *secret* police, as most people thought of them. The beheaded man was a deserter by the name of . . . well, who could remember that now? The fellow had been mentally unbalanced, with a record of bizarre behavior. And Mori had not done the beheading, only witnessed it.

"What a strange coincidence," Mori said. "Two Sotos have come to my attention in the past week." He turned back to the captain. "Your full name? I wouldn't want to confuse you with the headless coward."

Soto licked his lips and blinked several times rapidly. "Captain Setsuko Soto."

"And what are you doing here, Soto? Why are you not pushing forward?"

"We're waiting for the Forty-Eighth to help us reach the outskirts of the city. The Seventh Tank Regiment is in the town of Baliuag. Once they break through the American lines, we can pincer the city from both directions."

"Baliuag? Where is that?"

"A small town north of Manila, toward Bataan, where the Americans are retreating. Here, I'll show you."

Soto reached into a pocket of his jacket and pulled out a map, which he started to unfold. Mori waved his hand dismissively, and Soto put it away with a frown.

"Anyway," Soto continued, "until the Forty-Eighth breaks the enemy lines, I will hold position here, then push forward. More companies are on their way." Soto stood a little taller. "If you have issues with that, you should speak to Colonel Matsui—he gave the orders, not me."

"Did he?" Again Mori thought of *gekokujō*. Did the resistance to orders go higher up? Apparently as high as this Colonel Matsui, at least.

"Yes, sir, he did."

Other soldiers had been watching the exchange with a mixture of caution and worry on their faces. Two more soldiers rolled up but, instead of joining the men lounging in the grass, stood astride their bikes, watching.

Enough of this. On the road behind, the Kempeitai was already setting up offices in captured towns to pacify the population. Mori had come ashore in Lamon Bay with crates of leaflets in English and Tagalog, urging partisans and abandoned rear units to surrender and promising humane treatment to those who obeyed.

Mori was allowing himself to be distracted; he had information to collect about casualties and supplies so that he could plan for the military rule of Manila. All of that was urgent. But first he must take care of this ugly business with his brother.

"I am looking for a Corporal Sachihiro Mori. He is in your unit, I believe."

Soto frowned. "Is he in some sort of trouble?"

"No. Where is he?"

It was clear from Soto's expression that he didn't believe that Corporal Mori was not in trouble, and these IJA units tended to protect their own. Mori expected that Soto would obstruct, and was not disappointed.

"I—I'm not sure. Don't think I have a man by that name, to tell the truth."

"Wasn't he hit by the Americans?" someone said. Mori turned to see one of the newcomers on bicycles nodding. "That's right," the soldier continued. "I'm pretty sure Mori was one of them."

"Hit?" Mori's mouth was suddenly dry. "What do you mean? An ambush? Snipers?"

"No, nothing like that," Captain Soto said. "A pair of American trucks came up the road and ran down some of our men before we could shoot them. They killed a few, injured some others. Mori might have been one of them."

"Your memory seems to be improving, Captain. Why don't you show me where this happened, if you can manage to remember."

"It was just up the road—didn't you pass through the field hospital?"

Mori hadn't taken note of it if he had. He'd been focused on reaching the vanguard of the advancing infantry. But now that he thought of it, he'd passed a rough tent encampment where surgeons were working on all manner of injured. Not far up the road.

He pointed to his vehicle and glared at Captain Soto. "Get in the truck. And button your jacket."

———

It only took a few minutes to get to the site of the incident. Several mangled bicycles lay heaped to one side of the road. They'd be collected later, repaired. Nearly as unceremoniously, four bodies lay in a neat line. Someone had put their steel helmets over their faces, and from a distance they appeared to be sleeping. But when Mori climbed out of the truck and approached, he saw that two were soaked in blood, and another's legs bent at strange angles.

Mori reached into his jacket pocket and felt his brother's letter. A cold hollow formed in his belly.

You were too American for your own good, brother.

His brother had kept the name Sammy instead of Sachihiro when the brothers returned to Japan after Father died. He played baseball and preferred checkers and chess to Go. Spoke poorly of the army when home on leave.

And yet, curiously, Sammy had clung to Japanese customs in Hawaii. He'd trimmed bonsai trees, helped Father care for the Shinto shrine in the yard with its torii gate, decorative stone lanterns, and purification font. He'd taught his little brother, Yoshiko, how to wash his hands and mouth, ring the bell, and pray. Made sure he read his lessons in Japanese. All things the younger brother had not appreciated at the time.

But if his brother were Japanese, truly and deeply in his soul, why had he done the horrible thing he'd confessed to in the letter?

Mori removed the helmets from the faces of the dead men one by one and breathed a sigh of relief when he didn't see his brother. He turned to Lieutenant Fujiwara and shook his head.

"The corporal is not here."

"He must have only been injured," Captain Soto said. He removed his glasses and polished them again. He put them back on, then immediately removed them to clean once again. "I suppose you could check the field hospital."

The field hospital sat on the side of the road a couple of hundred meters farther back. It was a pair of white tents, and Mori knew they'd have red crosses painted on top, although the warning was probably unnecessary, as the enemy air force had been chased from the sky by the heroic pilots of the Imperial Japanese Army Air Force. As if to underscore this thought, a pair of Mitsubishi Ki-21 bombers lumbered overhead on their way to bomb enemy positions to the northwest. No need for escort fighters. Mori wondered if they were on their way to Baliuag. If there was a tank battle brewing, air support might prove critical.

Mori, Fujiwara, and Soto made their way toward the tents. One of the native buffalo stumbled out of the waist-high grass, snorting a warning. Mori waved his hands and shouted for the beast to clear off.

"Careful," Soto said. "Carabao are dumb and mean. You'll get gored if you don't watch yourself."

39

Mori drew his pistol, scoffing. "It's an overgrown cow, and it's in our way."

He shouted again, and when that didn't work, fired his pistol in the air. The animal looked like it would wander off the trail, leaving them a path to the hospital, and Mori holstered his pistol and gave the captain a smug nod.

"You see. Like everything else in this miserable country—you need to show them you're in charge, is all."

Suddenly the carabao wheeled and charged. The three men scattered into the grass. The animal followed Mori, head lowered. The horns didn't look so cow-like now; they looked like curved spears. He fell as he was about to be overrun, and one of the horns hooked toward his face. It grazed past, and miraculously the animal didn't trample him as he lay helpless, but passed over and disappeared, snorting, into the grass.

Mori was unharmed, but his sword had slipped from its sheath and fallen in the mud. He was in a foul mood as he cleaned it with a handkerchief, and snarled at Fujiwara when the young man asked if he needed help. Captain Soto wore a barely concealed smirk, and Mori glared at him until it vanished.

His brother was not in the field hospital, which was taking on a more permanent shape. Even as doctors operated on patients, men hammered up boards for walls and replaced the tarp roofs with corrugated metal, gradually turning tents into actual buildings. A light drizzle drummed on the tent roofs, but the thickening sky threatened heavier rain.

Most of the injured were victims of snipers or mines, but Mori found three men who'd survived the incident with the American trucks. They lay stretched out on tatami mats while bare-chested carpenters constructed a wall behind them.

"Yeah, Mori was there," one man confirmed.

He spoke through a mouth stuffed with bloody gauze, as the collision with the truck had knocked out his front teeth. His eyes were puffy, nearly closed, and he pulled the gauze aside to spit saliva and blood into a chipped ceramic bowl.

"Went off with the Americans," he added.

"What do you mean?" Mori demanded.

"Took a ride in their truck." The soldier let out a gurgled chuckle, and he spit more blood before stuffing the gauze back into place. What came out next was garbled, and Mori wasn't sure he heard it properly. "Sammy Mori loves those Yanks."

Mori drew his sword. The injured soldier flinched, Captain Soto squawked, and Fujiwara stiffened. Mori waved around his pistol with slight provocation, but he had only drawn his *guntō* once in anger, and that had ended with blood. A Chinese peasant spat on a Japanese flag and lost his head for it. Fujiwara would be remembering that incident, too, and that made Mori pause, check his anger.

"My brother is not a traitor," Mori managed through clenched teeth. "I will kill any man who says he is."

And yet he is. Isn't he?

The injured man was trembling as he stared at the sword. He pulled the gauze from his mouth. "I beg your pardon, sir. Many, many pardons. I did not mean that."

He was trying to speak precisely, but he had an ugly country accent, and where his tongue slipped past his missing teeth, the words came out slurred and drunk sounding. The remnants of Mori's anger turned to disgust, and he lowered the point of the sword.

"He was on the hood of the enemy truck, sir. He flew up there when they hit his bike. They drove off with him stuck to the windshield. Nobody knew if he was dead or alive."

"Are you telling me the Americans got away?" Mori asked, incredulous, turning to Soto. "They drove through an entire company of your men and nobody bothered to kill them? How many trucks were there?"

"I'm not sure. Three?"

"Two, sir," the injured man said. "Yes, they escaped. We were told not to pursue them."

"Who told you that?" Mori demanded.

"I did," Soto said. "We have few trucks, and we couldn't have hunted them down with bicycles."

"Few trucks is different than no trucks. Did you radio for planes? Did you warn your colonel there were enemy elements behind your lines?"

"The Americans looped back around," Soto said. "Turned up along a country road so they could bypass the city and get north. Probably a mistake that they were headed this way in the first place. I wouldn't worry about them, sir. They seemed to be hospital trucks evacuating Manila."

"It's amazing how clear your memory has become," Mori said.

"Did you say he's your brother? I'm sorry to hear that. I didn't know that's who you were looking for." Soto seemed genuinely contrite, but Mori thought it was an act. "And I didn't know we'd never found him. Maybe he's up the road still. We could look. He might only be in the ditch, stunned."

Most of the traffic down the road since the incident with the Americans had been on foot or bicycle, except for a few light trucks carrying supplies or pulling carts laden with small field pieces. Mori was able to find the heavier tread of the American vehicles, and the scene of the mayhem when they'd barreled through the infantry. There were a few brass casings in the mud, but no evidence of a firefight. It was flat terrain and a straight road, and the IJA soldiers must have seen the trucks coming from a distance. They'd apparently managed no more than a few potshots before the enemy escaped.

"It was hot and starting to rain," Soto said lamely when questioned. "There were a lot of mosquitoes. We were singing a martial song to raise our spirits."

"Let me give you a lesson for the future," Mori said. "When you heap one excuse on top of another, the entire story begins to stink. Now what was it? What really happened?"

"I suppose we didn't expect the Americans to attack. When I saw the trucks, I thought they must have been ours."

"They were driving the wrong way. How could they have been ours?"

"That happens all the time," Soto said. "Trucks get turned around, men march in the wrong direction. The battlefield is confusion. We come in with maps, which we try to read under fire. Sometimes you shoot at the wrong people—have you ever been in a firefight with your own army? Have you ever been bombed by your own planes? Until you have, I wouldn't expect you to understand."

Mori's instinct was to bristle, but Soto was probably right in this case. Two lone trucks rumbling up the road, unescorted, wouldn't look like a threat. Not to a bunch of men on bicycles, heads hanging in the suffocating heat and tongues lolling like dogs'. The Americans might not have noticed, either, not until it was too late.

The three men were driving slowly up the road, following the tire tracks of the American trucks, when Fujiwara hit the brakes. It was raining harder now, the road sloppy mud, and they slid to a stop. Fujiwara jumped out, and Mori followed. The rain fell harder with every passing moment, but Mori didn't mind. It made him feel more alive.

He snapped his fingers at Captain Soto to follow, only remembering when he saw the man's confused frown that snapping was an American gesture. Something he'd carried with him from his time living among the enemy.

"Get out." Then, to Fujiwara, who was squatting in the road, "What is it, what do you see?"

"Look, sir."

Mori looked but didn't see at first what had drawn his adjutant's attention. "I see boot prints. Tire tracks. Are you saying the Americans stopped here and got out? How can you be sure?"

The lieutenant pointed. "These are big feet, and the pattern in the sole is different, see. These were Americans. For comparison, this is one of ours, over here. One of our soldiers got off his bike and stepped off the road, probably to take a piss. Do you see?"

"All right, if you say so. What's this?" Mori pointed to a long outline stretching through a muddy puddle—the tire tracks they'd been following since the field hospital crossed it. "What left this mark?"

"A body pressed in the mud. Here's the outline of a canteen. Looks like he was run over, whoever it was."

"Are you sure?"

"Yes, sir."

Mori stared hard but didn't see it. Not enough to be certain. Still, he trusted Fujiwara. The man's eyes were sharp, but more than that, his ability to detect patterns was incredible.

"He must have been carried along on top of the truck," Fujiwara said, "then thrown off. Then they ran him over."

Captain Soto grunted. He stood back a pace, trying in vain to clean his glasses even as rain kept falling. "You can't see all of that. Nobody could. If he was run over, where's the body?"

"That's right," Mori said. "There should be a body."

"Ah, look," Fujiwara said. He moved over a few feet and squatted again. His boots sank into the mud, but he didn't seem to notice. "A foot dragging here. Almost gone in this rain, but you can see it. Someone was helping him walk. Looks to me like they hauled your brother into the truck. He wasn't walking under his own power, but he wasn't carried, either."

"Then he's alive?" Mori asked. Mixed emotions twisted in his gut.

His adjutant stood up and gazed into the distance with a thoughtful expression. "That part is impossible to answer."

Yes, it could be that he was nearly dead, and they'd hauled his body into the truck so as to dump it later. Or it could be that they'd driven to some other location to shoot him and dispose of the body. That's what Mori would have done had the situation been reversed. The Americans would soon enough end up prisoners of war, and they wouldn't want to be tied to the incident on the road. Surely wouldn't want to be seen executing an injured man, even if they knew it must be done.

But Americans could be sentimental. They lacked the hard spirit so necessary in wartime. Like the time in Manchukuo when Mori had bloodied his sword on the neck of a Chinese peasant. He hadn't wanted to, but these things were necessary, even desirable so as to spread an important message. So perhaps Sammy Mori was still alive.

"You said the Americans turned around?" Mori asked Captain Soto.

"Just south of here. They were spotted later by a recon plane trying to make their way north again. There's another American hospital in Baliuag, and I figure that's where they were headed. Don't worry, sir, they'll soon be in our hands."

Mori remembered what Soto had said about the Seventh Tank Regiment. The fleeing Americans would be stumbling into an attack if they made it to Baliuag. He studied the man.

The captain had the look of a wet dog as the rain made his hair run in soggy strings down the side of his face. His glasses were mud splattered, and he'd finally ceased attempting to clean them on his wet jacket. He looked up the road toward his troops, as if desperate to be away from these Kempeitai officers and back to his job fighting the war. Or waiting around until someone told him to fight, anyway.

"This is a very grave situation," Mori said.

Soto turned. "What do you mean?"

"Your behavior has been shameful."

"I'm sorry about your brother," Soto said quickly, "but this is war, and these things happen. I've only been doing my duty, obeying orders."

"I've arrested many men who claimed they were only obeying orders. Men of higher rank and stature than yourself. I have broad powers, Captain Setsuko Soto, and I am going to exercise them now." Mori nodded at Fujiwara.

Fujiwara drew his sidearm and pointed it casually at Soto, who made a small sound in the back of his throat. He glanced desperately around him, but there was nobody on the road, nothing but Mori's small truck, its engine rumbling. Rain plinked against the hood, suddenly as loud as a martial drumbeat.

"All those men you have," Mori said, "lounging about while other soldiers fight and die. I'm going to put them to good use. *You*, sir, are going to put them to use."

"But Colonel Matsui ordered me to—"

"Feel free to complain once you've done your duty. Until then, your troops are mine, and they're going to escort me to Baliuag to find Lieutenant Mori."

As Soto bowed to show his obedience, Mori reached into his jacket pocket to remove the three folded sheets of paper. He moved them quickly to an inner pocket where they'd be safe from the rain that was threatening to soak through. Fujiwara returned a grim nod when Mori met his gaze. The adjutant knew about the betrayal. Knew the purpose behind his captain's search.

Sammy. Why had he done it?

You should have died on the road, brother, Mori thought. *It would have been better for us both.*

Chapter Five

Louise's first inclination that something was wrong in Baliuag came from the flaming nipa huts on the outskirts of the town, their grass roofs lit up like torches in the late-afternoon sky. But there was no crush of civilians on the road, and Lieutenant Kozlowski apparently decided that the town was safely in American hands and ordered them to continue toward the hospital.

They came upon American forces closer to the center of Baliuag, and here they learned the truth. Japanese tanks had rolled to the outskirts of town and were attempting to break through and sever the escape route to the Bataan Peninsula. Several buildings were on fire from supporting artillery fire.

General Jones had ordered the 192nd Tank Battalion to hold the town at any cost. A colonel found out the Manila evacuees had medical supplies, and ordered them to take cover and set up a mobile hospital for the inevitable casualties. What about the hospital itself, Dr. Claypool asked. No, it was already overrun.

That was the extent of their orders, so they were left groping forward into the center of town. The sound of shells and small-arms fire sounded both to their front and rear, and Kozlowski ordered them into a courtyard of sunken paving stones between two stucco Spanish-style buildings. They'd just parked the trucks when the battle started up in the street outside.

Louise and her fellow nurses evacuated the injured patients into one of the buildings, among them the injured Japanese soldier. A shell whistled in and detonated on the roof, and people threw themselves to the ground as plaster and broken tiles rained down. Clarice was shaking and crying, unable to get herself up without help, but Frankie finally shook off her whining and complaining and began ordering the other nurses around. There was some semblance to reason in her decisions, so Louise followed her lead, glad to have her back in command.

The existing men needed care, but they soon took on additional patients. One was a soldier with a gaping calf wound, followed shortly by three civilians who'd been caught in the crossfire. Frankie assisted Dr. Claypool in surgery while the other three nurses attended to everyone else. The most critical need was morphine. Louise and Maria Elena used a pressure-pumped Bunsen burner to boil water in the open courtyard, with which they sterilized needles, then used the hot water to dissolve morphine tablets. Clarice, white faced and silent, went inside the makeshift recovery ward to give injections.

The sound of battle grew louder until it was shaking the buildings. Frankie cried out for more gauze, and Louise went out to the rear truck to get some. The back of the vehicle was empty except for discarded boots and crutches, their crates of medical supplies, and a single duffel bag holding the few personal belongings the soldiers had been allowed to take from the hospital.

She found the gauze and hopped down from the back of the truck with her arms full. Only a few feet from the street now, she froze as a tank rumbled up with the clank of tracks and the stink of burning fuel and powder rolling off it. White letters on green: "USA." An American soldier crouched behind a machine gun at the rear, staring forward behind his gun shield.

Louise felt as though she were caught in a powerful magnetic pull, and she took five steps out to the gap between the two buildings protecting the courtyard, unable to help herself. There she stood on the edge of the street, arms laden with rolls of white gauze.

The building across the street burned. Two more wooden nipa huts lit up like torches farther down. A palm tree sprawled across the road, its trunk like a severed finger pointing at the sky. Electric wires sparked from a pole. The soldier on the back of the tank poured fire from his machine gun at something in the burning building. The tank turret rotated. There was another American tank coming up behind it, and its turret, too, was rotating in the same direction. Louise's gaze turned with them.

And there it was, another tank, somewhat smaller than the first, with a white star on it. No, there were two tanks. Three! All rolling in this direction, about seventy yards away, but closing. The farther American tanks fired at the newcomers. Then the closer one followed. Louise's eardrums ached at the earsplitting boom.

The first shell missed. The second smashed into the lead Japanese tank and exploded. Its top popped off, and flames shot out. Someone burst from the fire and threw himself to the ground. He was burning alive, screaming, but his agony didn't last long before the American machine gunner cut him down.

Then the Japanese were returning fire. One shell flew high and detonated in the second story of a nearby building, and a second slammed into the American tank but bounced off without exploding and flew into the wall of the building in front of Louise, some thirty or forty feet away. Only seconds had passed since she'd stepped out toward the street, and she remained fixed in place, like she was watching a movie or a scene from a dream. None of this was real.

How curious, she thought as she looked at the Japanese shell sticking out of the building. *A fluke of battle, one shell goes off, the other that fails to—*

49

The shell detonated. There was a flash of light, and Louise was flying backward. A moment of blackness, and when she began to come around, she was startled to find birds flying around her face, batting her with their wings. White birds, black birds. Birds on fire.

Someone shouted at her. Hands grabbed her. More shouting. The words sounded like they were coming down to her at the bottom of a well. Why were they so angry? The birds settled to the ground around her, and now she saw that they were gauze, blown out of her hands in the blast. Some of the pieces were burning.

A woman dragged Louise back into the courtyard, and though she was still stunned, she recognized Frankie's angry, frightened face.

"You fool. What are you doing?" Frankie still sounded muffled, like she was speaking through a pillow. Louise wasn't deaf; there was that to be thankful for.

Louise shook her head. She couldn't say. What had possessed her? What in God's name had made her step into the street to watch a tank battle and to stand there like an idiot, to stare at the Japanese shell, waiting for it to explode? If it had detonated against the American tank, she'd have been killed by shrapnel. If it had bounced in a different direction, there would be nothing left of her but red mist and bone fragments.

The battle raged in the street outside for several minutes before it moved on. A pair of infantrymen told her the American counterattack had been a complete success and had pushed the Japanese out of the center of town. But Baliuag was on fire, the hospital destroyed, and the Japanese would soon be back in greater force. They were ordered to evacuate toward Bataan as soon as the road was secure.

A few minutes before nightfall, a pair of Japanese planes came and dropped bombs. When the ruckus had died down, two infantrymen came to tell Lieutenant Kozlowski to prepare the trucks. The lieutenant had been trying to radio for orders during the battle but was unable to get to his superiors, and now he seemed pleased to be working again with a purpose.

The sound of men crying in pain cut through the evening air as they were hauled out on sheets of corrugated metal, planks of wood, and other improvised stretchers. American trucks and tanks prowled the streets outside the compound, and with them came voices calling out in English and Tagalog.

Once the lieutenant had ordered the ambulatory patients to begin reloading the trucks, he and Dr. Claypool stood in the courtyard having an urgent conversation in low tones. This continued for several minutes until the doctor called over his four nurses. Louise looked back and forth between the two men, curious as to what this was all about.

"Go ahead and tell them," Kozlowski said.

"We can't go to Bataan," Dr. Claypool said. "Most of these men shouldn't be moved at all. That burned fellow, for example. And there's that navy ensign in really bad shape—we're lucky he hasn't died already."

Louise nodded her agreement. "Plus the new patients. A couple of them are shot up pretty bad."

"So we're staying here?" Maria Elena asked.

"No," Kozlowski said. "Baliuag will be abandoned. Our side is only holding it long enough to keep the Japs from cutting the highway."

"But we don't need to go all the way to Bataan," Claypool said. "Not yet."

"We don't stay here, we don't go to Bataan?" Louise asked. "Where do we go?"

"There's an emergency field hospital and supply dump about twenty miles up the road in the mountains," Claypool said. "In a little village by the name of Sanduga."

"Never heard of it," Frankie said. "You say there's a military base there?"

"Not a base, no," Kozlowski said.

"A simple building and some medical supplies," Dr. Claypool said. "Hospital is probably too strong of a word, to be fair. It's a warehouse, really. But it's secure and hidden."

Kozlowski nodded. "We'll be safe from bombers for a few days while you get your patients stabilized. The Japanese will pause for a few weeks in Manila to consolidate."

"Do we know that for sure?" Louise asked.

"We don't know *anything* for sure," the lieutenant said. "For all we know, Bataan will be overrun by the time we get there. Or maybe it's not as defensible as MacArthur thinks, and we'll be captured anyway before reinforcements arrive to relieve us."

This seemed to Louise to be the most likely scenario. America was a long way away, half its fleet at the bottom of Pearl Harbor. Louise had no doubt that America would eventually prevail against this brutal enemy, starting here in the Philippines, but getting all of those men and supplies from America would take months, maybe longer. Did they have enough strength left to defend Bataan and Corregidor, as impregnable as they seemed?

The thought of falling into Japanese hands was terrifying, and getting to Bataan as soon as possible seemed the safest option. But Dr. Claypool was right: a protracted journey would kill some of their patients.

"How long would it take us to get to Bataan?" Claypool asked. "Two days? There will be thousands of injured men and few available beds. We'll be better off in the field hospital. And there's another thing about the village."

"Remind me," Kozlowski said.

"I stocked that hospital myself, and I saw the terrain," the doctor answered. "The road keeps going through Sanduga. I'm pretty sure it hooks through the mountains and comes around into Bataan from the back door. We'd have a way out even if the highway is cut."

"That is a good point," Lieutenant Kozlowski said.

Louise looked back and forth between the two men. There was something odd about this conversation she couldn't put her finger on, the way the doctor and the lieutenant kept glancing at each other before they took turns speaking.

"It sounds dangerous," Frankie said. "Up in the mountains . . . anything could happen."

"That's true enough," Kozlowski said.

"I'm a little confused," Louise said carefully. "We were ordered to evacuate Manila and go to Bataan. Then we were told to come to the hospital in Baliuag, and now we're being told to make for some mountain village. Or is some of this our own initiative?" It was put out there casually.

"Of course not," Kozlowski said. "We follow army orders."

"Then why does it sound like we're just now formulating this plan?" she asked.

"This isn't up for vote," Kozlowski said, "if that's what you mean."

"But I want to consult with my medical staff," Dr. Claypool said. "There's a choice to be made. Something the four of you can decide or not."

"I'll be honest, I didn't see much point in consulting," the lieutenant said. "You might have heard us arguing. That's what we were talking about."

"What do you mean by a choice?" Louise asked. She glanced at the other three nurses, who seemed confused. "Do we have orders or not?"

"We have general orders," Kozlowski said. "Getting specifics is another matter."

"This is now a medical matter," Claypool said. "And I'm offering a choice."

"So, a vote, after all." Kozlowski shook his head. "I don't agree with it, but go ahead."

"I still don't understand," Louise said. "Are you saying we each have a choice to either go with our patients into the mountains or to continue to Bataan?"

"More or less," Kozlowski said. "The doc says you'll all go with the patients if given a choice. I say he's wrong, that you'll evacuate to Bataan."

"What do *you* think?" she asked.

He tossed his head at Maria Elena. "This one isn't even an American. She can go back to her family while the rest of us are taken prisoner by the Japs. Why would she take her chances in the mountains? And Miss Clarice is all of, what? Eighteen years old? Terrified—look at her. She'll go to Bataan. You, on the other hand," he said to Louise, "are filled with romantic notions. You won't leave your patients. So you'll come with us."

She supposed that was a compliment, though she didn't like how he put it. Romantic notions? Her ears were still stuffy from the exploding tank shell. She'd seen blood and carnage, and there was a nervous clawing at her stomach that threatened to burst into full-blown panic. It sure as hell didn't feel like an adventure, if that's what Kozlowski was getting at.

"That leaves Miss Frankie as head nurse," Kozlowski added. "I expect as head nurse she'll go along with whatever her doctor says. That leaves two going to Bataan and two into the mountains. So why vote?"

"Prove it," Dr. Claypool said, tone stubborn. "Ask them."

"Fine. Girls, what do you say?"

"It's our responsibility to stay with our patients," Frankie said. "No, it's a *privilege*."

"You see," the doctor said to the lieutenant.

"But it's nuts to go into the mountains in the first place," the older nurse continued. "We'll be stuck behind the Jap lines. If we really care about these men, we'll take them to Bataan, where they'll be safe."

"Miss Frankie," Claypool said sharply. "That part is not up for discussion."

"We'd all be on Corregidor Island by now if that plane hadn't been shot down," Frankie continued. "Safe. Well, what's the next best thing? Get to Bataan. Don't make us carry these wounded men into the mountains. We'll all be killed up there."

"Thought you said it was our privilege to look after them," Louise said.

"You be quiet and remember your place," Frankie said. "I saw what you did, running back into the city for Fárez, then helping that Jap, then standing out in the street watching that tank battle like it was a tennis match—you have a death wish. I won't be taking your advice, you can safely assume that much."

"The lieutenant was right about me," Clarice said. "I want to go to Bataan."

Her voice was thin, and this was the first time she'd spoken in the conversation. Louise studied her, surprised. She'd assumed that the lieutenant was wrong and Clarice would stay with the doctor and the patients. Or at the least, follow the consensus of the other nurses.

"Miss Maria Elena?" Dr. Claypool said.

"I don't want to be captured—that much is right. You're Americans, and the Red Cross will come looking for you if you're taken prisoner. Not me. The Japs will treat us Pinoys like they're treating the Chinese. And I can't fade into the population—I'm not even from around here. I'd be safer in Bataan."

"Then we've lost three nurses." Claypool sighed. "I assume you're with me, Miss Louise?"

"I'm not finished," Maria Elena said. "I know I'm at risk if the enemy gets us. I know what they'll do to me. The Japs are animals." She shuddered. "But there's a reason I was still in the hospital when Louise came back for Corporal Fárez. I was doing my job, I didn't walk away. I won't walk away now. These men need our help. We can't let them die. I'm going with you into the mountains."

Dr. Claypool let out a deep breath. He looked more confident now. "Miss Louise? Your official word?"

Louise chewed her lip. What kind of choice was he giving her? Stay behind enemy lines and maybe face the enemy? She didn't want that. God, no. But if she left for Bataan to save her own hide . . .

"I'll stay with the injured men," Louise said at last. "I don't think I could live with myself if men died because I was a coward."

"What about that Jap we picked up on the road?" Lieutenant Kozlowski said. "You want to save him, too?"

Louise's head swiveled to one side as a man was carried past her on one of the makeshift stretchers, crying for morphine and water. His eyes were bandaged.

"Even the Japanese soldier," she said. "If we're caught, he might save our life."

"That's ridiculous," Kozlowski said. "The Japs won't care. They'll probably bayonet him first thing as a deserter. Unless he's a spy, and then everything we've said will be twisted against us."

"In that case, we save Sammy Mori because he's our patient and that's our job," Louise said. "Anyway, it's just for a few days, until we get the men stabilized. Then we'll go to Bataan anyway. Right, Lieutenant?"

"Right," Kozlowski said, but he wasn't looking at her; he was looking at the doctor. Again something was passing between the two men.

"I'm changing my mind," Clarice said. All eyes turned to her, and she looked away quickly. Louise couldn't see it in the darkened courtyard but imagined Clarice's face was flushed, as it did when she got excited. "I was wrong. I'll do my duty. If Dr. Claypool says to go into the mountains, I'll go into the mountains."

"So that's three staying with me and the patients, and one going," Claypool said.

"I don't believe this," Frankie said. "Dr. Claypool, really. Why are we even having this discussion? Let's all go to Bataan."

"You're on your own, apparently," Claypool said.

"No, I'm not on my own!" Frankie's voice was frantic. "I won't be left behind while the rest of you go off to wherever. Who knows what will happen to me? I might be . . . Damn you all, I'll go."

At that moment a pair of Filipino soldiers came running into the courtyard from the street outside. The road was clear; there were no enemy aircraft in the sky. The hospital evacuees were to travel back down the road in the direction from which they'd come, lights out. When they reached the highway, they would drive all night toward the Bataan Peninsula.

But the local units didn't know their true orders. Five minutes later the hospital evacuees were on the road, only they were not going to Bataan.

Chapter Six

The hospital evacuees started in the direction of Bataan, but ninety minutes later they turned off the highway and onto a small dirt road. The sign marking the road had been pulled down so as to slow the enemy forces rolling across the countryside, but Dr. Claypool remembered the spot, or said he did. Louise didn't know how he could be sure. It was dark, and they were running without lights, except when they were turned on to briefly inspect some landmark or other.

The dirt road turned into a rutted, muddy track. They crawled into hill country through a mist so thick that the lights couldn't have cut through it even if they'd dared to use them. Kozlowski turned on his flashlight, shielded it from the sky with his helmet, and probed ahead on foot to find the way.

Louise and a few others got out to walk. It was so cramped in the back, the air sickly from ointments, dirty bandages, and the smell of the engine. Walking relieved boredom and exhaustion and eased the frustration at not being able to help the injured men under her command.

She walked up next to Kozlowski. He flickered the light onto her face to see who it was.

"Shouldn't you be keeping an eye on the patients?"

"Nothing to be done at the moment. We're out of sterilized needles for morphine, and we can't do much of anything in the dark."

"What about the Jap? Giving you any trouble?"

"Rest easy, Lieutenant. He's in pain and immobile."

"What's to keep the other men from tossing him out of the truck while you're out here? Thought you'd want to keep an eye on him." His tone was sarcastic.

"He's just another injured man—nobody's going to kill him."

"Every one of those men is a victim of Japanese aggression, and don't think they'll forget it."

"I'm not asking them to forget it. I'm asking them for simple human decency toward a fellow sufferer."

Kozlowski only grunted at this, and they stopped talking. The jungle filled the silence with the hum, buzz, and chirp of countless insects, a shrieking call somewhere in the distance, and creatures crashing through the underbrush.

"How much longer?" another voice asked from the darkness. It was the soft voice of Corporal Fárez.

Kozlowski turned the flashlight briefly on him, and he blinked in the light. Fárez limped with his crutch while a cord wrapped around his free hand. The light trailed down and reflected off a pair of eyes near the man's feet.

"Fárez!" Kozlowski said. "For the love of . . . Do you still have that mutt? I told you to get rid of it. More than once."

"Don't blame him, blame me," Louise said.

"You?"

"I picked up the dog and brought him into the truck. It might be useful for therapeutic purposes."

"Therapeutic?" Kozlowski said. "Right, sure."

Others shortly joined them in walking ahead of the slowly moving trucks. Some had no business being out, and Louise sent them back with a stern word. She wouldn't have them busting stitches. Clarice and Maria Elena came out, too, but the noise of the surrounding forest seemed to unnerve Clarice, and she soon returned to the truck. That left six or seven men on the road, plus Louise and Maria Elena, hiking up the hill along the muddy, rutted trail while the trucks rumbled behind them.

About an hour later they stumbled upon a pair of nipa huts that flanked the road on a steep hillside. More grass-roofed huts and shacks with corrugated-metal roofs appeared. Soon an entire village emerged ghostlike from the looming, vine-strangled trees. Not a sound or light, not so much as a barking dog to greet them. Had the people heard the trucks and fled into the night, thinking it was the Japanese? Would they be shot at by frightened villagers?

Kozlowski ordered them back into the trucks. He questioned Claypool about the village, but the doctor said this wasn't Sanduga. Then where was it? Claypool said he was sure they were on the right road, that it wouldn't be long now. Probably by morning. A few groans greeted this pronouncement.

They crept forward. Claypool admitted his doubts about an hour later when they were all back in the trucks and moving at a slightly faster pace. The road crested a hill and followed a ridge for about two miles before dipping into a bowl-like valley and ascending again. The doctor said he couldn't remember the terrain.

"Great plan you gave us, Doctor," Kozlowski said. "I'm sure your patients won't mind losing several hours. Especially those with critical injuries."

"Shh, these men need to rest," Louise said. She was glad Frankie was in the other truck, or the lead nurse would be ratcheting up the alarm. Clarice, too. No need for the girl to panic.

"Sorry, you're right." The lieutenant sighed. "Which truck are we in? The one with the English-speaking driver? No? Let me get out and talk to the fellow—we'll turn around and stop losing time."

"Hold on now," Dr. Claypool said. "This *might* be the right road. It might *not* be, that's all I'm saying."

"And when will you know for sure? Doc, we're losing time."

"Give me another mile. Let's see." Claypool's voice sounded like it was floating in the dark air, unattached, but Louise could hear the worry in it and could easily picture the thick eyebrows drawn together.

But it wasn't another mile before they stumbled into another village. This one was even smaller than the previous one, a small collection of huts and shacks on stilts, together with a patchwork of rice paddies that crawled up and down the hillside. A long, warehouse-looking building made of cement block stretched alongside the road, and when Kozlowski's flashlight illuminated it, Claypool cried out for the trucks to stop. He climbed down, calling for Louise to follow him.

"And turn on the truck lights," the doctor said. "Let's see what we've got."

Moments later half the evacuees were out of the trucks and looking around doubtfully. This was it? A dozen nipa huts, as scruffy-looking as street dogs, two wooden shacks with rusted corrugated-metal roofs, and a cement building that looked about as enticing as a Japanese prison?

"It's a fully functioning hospital," Claypool said. "Or it will be soon enough." He looked around at the patients. "I want everyone who can walk out here. We've got work to do."

Lieutenant Kozlowski waved his flashlight. "You heard him, boys." If he was feeling doubts, they didn't show in his voice. "Move it."

———◆———

There was a small electric generator and three buried tanks of oil to supply it, and Kozlowski soon had the building lit, including blue vapor lights for the surgery. Louise and the other nurses inspected the building while the men put blankets over the windows to maintain blackout conditions.

The place was filthy, with a thick layer of dust, a moldy smell, dead roaches lying on their backs, and live ones scurrying to the corners. Every visible piece of metal was rusting. Water had leaked through the roof, leaving a big puddle in the middle of the largest room.

"What do we do first?" Dr. Claypool asked. "Cots? Fix the roof?"

He directed the questions to Miss Frankie, but the head nurse was looking around her with a bewildered, anxious expression and seemed not to have heard.

Claypool turned away from Frankie. "Miss Louise?"

"We're not bringing patients in until we've scrubbed this place down. So I say brooms and buckets and mops first. Did I see a cistern? Good, we'll need the water. And fire up the Bunsen burners, because we'll need the water hot."

"Good. You'll lead the work."

Anyone who could work did, and shortly they had the worst of the filth cleaned out and one small corner scrubbed enough for Dr. Claypool and Miss Frankie to attend to some minor surgeries. The older nurse began to rally from her earlier confusion and worked alongside the doctor without complaint or hesitation. Maybe she just needed to get settled and she'd be fine.

The cots had been stacked in one room, packed in ten-year-old copies of the *Manila Times*, but this hadn't kept them from rusting. Louise ordered the cots hauled outside and set soldiers to work with steel wool to scour off the rust.

The hospital was stocked in some ways, deficient in others. Surgical instruments were packed in petroleum jelly as protection against the rust and would need to be cleaned with ether. There were large quantities of gauze and bandages, as well as plenty of linens, towels, swabs, and other necessities, but no electrical sterilizer.

Instead there were steel-lined pressure cookers that could serve the same purpose.

As for medications, the field hospital had been stocked with a mountain of all manner of trivial drugs, but little of the most critical medications. How much aspirin and bicarbonate of soda would they possibly need? Where was the quinine, the morphine, the sulfa powders? It was good that they'd only be here a few days. Hopefully their rescued supplies from the hospital would serve until then.

The doctor and the lieutenant seemed to have patched up their differences and had come together for several whispered conversations throughout the night. At one point Louise caught them talking about the radio and figured that Kozlowski must have news from Manila. His face was grim, whatever he'd heard.

By morning, Louise was exhausted. Two nights with little sleep, clearing out one hospital and setting up another. Then there was the drive, the nerve-rattling battle at Baliuag, and the final crawl into the hill country. Some evacuees were sleeping on the floor or outside in the truck, but others, like Kozlowski, Dr. Claypool, and the other nurses, had worked all night alongside her.

Louise made a final inspection of her patients and stumbled outside. The clouds had cleared, and as her eyes adjusted to the brilliant tropical light, she took in her surroundings. What she saw made her draw her breath.

Rice paddies layered up and down the hillside like a glittering quilt of green squares. Mist shrouded the surrounding mountains, which towered like sentinels all around. Brilliant red and gold birds with long tail feathers flitted across the sky between the surrounding jungle and the trees in the village.

Sanduga was bigger than it had appeared last night, with more buildings visible through clumps of trees that had appeared as jungle in the darkness. In all there were about twenty nipa huts on stilts, half of them clustered around a small stone church with a cross, and flanked by the hospital on the opposite side. The corrugated-metal roofs of the hospital and church contrasted with the grass roofs that hung like shaggy blankets from the village houses.

The road hooked around the hillside and disappeared on the other side, but it was impassable at the moment, blocked by the two army trucks. They'd been covered with palm branches as rudimentary camouflage, but this hadn't stopped curious villagers from coming out to investigate. Some thirty Filipinos gathered around, watching and discussing in low voices. Children stood next to the elderly. Naked toddlers nursed at their mother's breasts while twisting their heads to stare at Louise.

The sound of birds squawking from the trees competed with the steady thump of someone pounding rice. Roosters crowed, and a pig snorted and snuffled alongside one of the rice paddies. A pair of village dogs trotted up, and Louise wondered what they'd make of Stumpy when they met him. The dog was inside, sleeping at the foot of Fárez's cot.

She didn't spot Dr. Claypool at first. He leaned against the wall of the hospital a few feet away, smoking a cigarette. He'd taken off his smock, but flecks of blood had dried beneath eyes baggy with sleep, and he looked old and exhausted. He raised his eyebrows at Louise, as if inviting her to speak but not insisting.

"Happy New Year," she said.

"Ah yes. I suppose it is." He nodded toward the surrounding bowl of mountains. "Not exactly what I had in mind, but it's hard to imagine a more scenic place."

"It's beautiful, isn't it?" she said. "Almost makes you forget there's a war out there."

"Almost."

"Let's hope 1942 brings happier times than 1941. Maybe it will all be over by the end of the year."

"Don't count on it, Louise. At this point, I'd say 1943 is looking pretty grim, too."

"Well then," she said, "we can at least look forward to either being rescued or reinforced. Back behind friendly lines on Bataan—that would be something."

Claypool glanced at the hospital door. "Where are the rest of the girls?"

"Clarice is on duty. Frankie and Maria Elena are sleeping. I should be, too, but I'm wound too tight." She put her hands over her stomach. "Feels like a ball of snakes squirming in my belly."

"Are you sure it's not intestinal parasites?" He winked. "Might have picked them up from that mutt."

"Wish there were something I could do for the nerves."

"Bet if you ask the villagers, they brew gallons of the stuff for just that purpose. And they'll happily sell it to you, too. Cheap!"

Louise smiled, cheered by the doctor's weary good humor.

Lieutenant Kozlowski came around the corner of the building, carrying a crate. He'd stripped to his undershirt, which revealed bulging arms and shoulder muscles, and Louise frowned to realize the crate held weaponry of some kind, based on the markings and its weight. Mines or grenades or bullets. That didn't leave her reassured, knowing that he was preparing a defense.

Kozlowski glanced at her as he trudged past, then gave Claypool a more significant look. The doctor returned a nod so slight that Louise might not have caught it if she hadn't been studying them so carefully. There was something between them, a secret of some kind. She was sure of it.

"We're going to lose a patient," Claypool said, which brought Louise back to the moment.

Her stomach fell. "Private Higgs?"

"His burns have become infected. I've treated the infections with sulfonamide, but he's not fighting it off. I expect he'll be gone by nightfall, but he might linger. They often do."

One of the last things she'd done this morning after getting her patients settled was to unpack personal belongings, those few things stuffed into a duffel bag upon evacuating the hospital. Small details were so important for the men to remember what they were fighting for, and by that she didn't mean the war. She meant fighting on the long, painful road to recovery. A favorite book, a baseball and mitt. Playing cards, a jackknife for whittling. A letter from Mom.

One of these belongings was a picture of Higgs and his best girl on some beach. Louise had only seen a man with his face melted off and didn't recognize the handsome boy in the picture. It was only the name on the back that told her who it was. Higgs had a broad, happy grin in the photo, and the pretty brunette clinging to his arm looked up at him with an adoring expression.

"We knew we might lose him." Her voice felt as soft as jelly when it came out, and she composed herself before speaking again. "What about Private Smith?"

"He'll pull through. Therrien, too. He looks bad, but he'll recover if we can keep him otherwise healthy. The young Jewish boy—what is his name?"

"Rubens."

"That's right, Rubens. He's my biggest worry after Higgs. It's too soon to say if his spinal injuries will heal, but moving him around so much didn't help." Claypool finished his cigarette. "You're from Colorado? What part?"

"Southern Colorado. Near Durango."

"Isn't that desert? I thought you were a farmer's daughter."

"It's dry country, but you can farm with irrigation. In happy times, you can make a go of it."

"And were they? Happy times, I mean?"

"My father got an agricultural degree and tried to build a scientific farm. Took out a big mortgage from the bank in early 1929 to try out his theories."

Dr. Claypool winced. "Ouch."

"Yeah, bad timing. Didn't lose the farm, though. One year we lived on eight dollars, cash. Everything else we grew, milked, slaughtered, or salvaged."

The thing that drove her crazy was the uncertainty of it all. It wasn't the hard work—that would have been bearable if it paid off. But so often it didn't.

You got your seed in the ground only to see drought hit, or an early frost that wiped out the crop. Or maybe there was a bumper crop, but the price of wheat collapsed due to a glut. All your lambs might die of a mysterious illness.

"Tell you the truth, I had enough of the farm life by the time I finished high school," Louise said. "I was happy to get out of there."

"Must have taught you some good lessons in life, though. How to survive, how to be resilient."

"I know how to get by. And I suppose it prepared me for death. There's a lot of that on the farm." Louise hesitated. "Or so I thought."

"It's one thing to see an animal die, another to watch a man go."

"I was certainly naive when I got to Manila—I'll never forget losing my first patient. But after six months of malaria and dysentery cases, I figured I knew what was what."

"They said war was coming," Claypool said. "Guess none of us really believed it. I know I didn't—not until I saw the Japs flying over to bomb our airfields." He studied her face. "And did you? Know what was what, I mean."

Louise managed a short, ironic laugh. "Yes, I think after three weeks of poor, mangled boys, now I *really* know." She caught his wry smile. "You don't think so, do you?"

He shook his head. "There's another layer of naiveté to strip off yet. There's always another layer."

She eyed him curiously. "Miss Frankie said you were in the Great War."

He continued as if he hadn't heard her. "I grew up in farm country, too. Iowa, but we weren't farmers. My father and my older brother were country vets back when that was mostly draft animals. Thanks to motorized tractors, my brother works with cats and dogs these days. Small-animal practice is the future."

Louise was surprised by the personal turn to the conversation. The doctor was serious about his work and had never shared such things before or questioned her. But she supposed it came from having been under fire, a bond that wouldn't have been possible between a young woman and her mature superior under other circumstances.

"Yes, I was a doctor in the Great War," he said, shifting directions. "I'd tell you about it, paint a picture with my words, but you've had a taste of carnage. You can imagine easily enough without me saying a word about the trenches, about operating in an underground bunker while dirt shakes from the ceiling with every shell. You don't need to hear the screams of dying men to imagine them—you've heard them yourself. Maybe I could tell you about men bleeding from their lungs or convulsing when they've been gassed, but I don't think you need it. Isn't that right?"

"I'm already picturing it. No need for more."

"Ten days of artillery bombardment, you haven't slept well in months, and your hands are shaking. But a man needs his leg amputated or he will die. What do you do?"

"Grit my teeth and carry on."

"It's Miss Frankie's job, too. She is older, has more experience, and is your superior. Yet she is on the verge of a nervous breakdown, and you are not. Why?"

"Maybe I am and I don't know it yet. I figure I keep doing my job, maybe it will keep me going." She shrugged. "And hopefully save the lives of these boys while I'm at it."

"What if the life is that of a wounded Japanese soldier?"

"That's my job, too, isn't it?"

Somewhere in this, Lieutenant Kozlowski had stopped his work after being approached by a pair of villagers: a woman and her young, shirtless boy, his skin well bronzed from the tropical sun. She had a basket of eggs, and she combined her gestures with the pidgin English of her son to negotiate their sale to the lieutenant.

The woman and her child soon left with a few coins. The lieutenant kept the basket of eggs, which he carried over a few feet and set it down as he joined the doctor and nurse in the shade beneath the roof.

"Has Manila fallen?" Louise asked him.

"I wouldn't know."

She gave him a sharp look, but he was staring down the road toward the jungle beyond the village and didn't catch it. But when she turned toward the doctor, he'd been studying her, and now looked away.

"Weren't you on the radio during the night?" she asked Kozlowski.

He turned back to her. "I reported our location, got yelled at. You know."

"Is the way still open to Bataan?"

"The highway? For now. We probably have a few more days before the main road is cut, but maybe not."

"So we might need to use the back road out of here, after all," she said. "So what about Manila? Why didn't they tell you? Why didn't you ask?" "I didn't need to know," Kozlowski said. "That is a good rule of thumb in military situations." He glanced at Claypool, who met his eye, then looked away.

"You're hiding something, both of you." Louise looked back and forth between the two men. "What is it you're not telling me?"

For a moment it looked like they would answer the question. First Dr. Claypool moved his lips as if preparing to speak, and then it shifted to Lieutenant Kozlowski, who cleared his throat. But that was all he did. A second, even briefer look passed between the two men.

"Nothing beyond the usual doubts and fears," Kozlowski said at last. "We're safe enough up here for now. Now come on, we all have work to do."

Chapter Seven

Sammy Mori woke in something that felt like a trance. Even drugged he knew it was morphine hanging about him, sending him visions. But he let it hold him down, aware on some deeper level that what he would find when he awoke fully would not agree with him at all.

The morphine had an accomplice: the smell of plumeria flowers. It washed over him on a warm breeze, a heavy, perfumed scent, and it seemed to activate some deep part of his brain. He knew he was deep in the Philippine wilderness, injured and a prisoner of the Americans, and yet the smell took him back to Hawaii. There he found a memory that floated in his brain like a *kami* spirit lingering around an old Shinto shrine.

It was a Saturday in early 1932. Sammy was sixteen, and his brother Yoshiko was fourteen. They were on Waikiki Beach, resting in the shade of a bent palm with their long wooden surfboards thrust into the sand nearby. Pearl Harbor swept around to their right, while behind them the rugged volcanic fin of Diamond Head cut a slash against the blue sky. The surf crested and broke into white froth that rolled toward shore in a continual rumble. A handful of surfers bobbed in the waves, occasionally riding one of the larger ones in.

Sammy was watching for pretty girls walking along the beach while his brother, who hadn't yet started to notice such things, complained about Father. Specifically, how he'd told them to sand the floor of the shrine when they got home. The shrine itself was an embarrassment. And why did he hang paper lamps at the gate? They blurted to any passersby that the occupants of the house were Japanese.

Yoshi's embarrassment at being Japanese had bloomed since Japan had started a dumb war in Manchuria. There were Chinese kids at school, and plenty of haole—white—kids who looked for an excuse to argue with the brothers about Japanese aggression. Not that there was anything to argue. The Mori family was Japanese, yes, but they were not so fond of Dai-Nippon Teikoku, the Empire of the Rising Sun. Even his father had compared the incursion in China to a small dog attacking an elephant. The dog may be fierce, the elephant old and sick, but it was still an elephant.

But the whole thing would obviously pass. The only reason it mattered at all was because they had family still living back in Japan. Sammy and Yoshi's two older brothers were serving in the Kwantung Army.

"It's going to take all afternoon to sand that floor," Yoshi said.

"Next week is the anniversary of Grandfather's death. Father wants it cleaned up before then."

"I don't see why. Grandfather didn't die in Hawaii, so what's the point? And if we're living in this country anyway, why can't we act like it? And another thing: I'm sick of trying to learn my *kanji*. There's no end to them. Why does the stupid Japanese language have so many letters? Why couldn't they make it all *katakana* or something? There's forty-something letters there alone. That should be enough."

"And how would you read the poets without your *kanji* and *hiragana*?"

"Who cares if I read them or not?" Yoshi asked.

"Father cares. At the very least, he won't be satisfied until you know a few poems from the Great Four."

"A bunch of dead old men."

Sammy sighed. He was about to explain—again—that they weren't going to be here forever. Father worked for a *zaibatsu*, one of Japan's large, family-controlled businesses, exporting silk and tea to America. They'd spent three years in San Francisco and four now in Hawaii, but there was always the rumble in the background that they'd be returning to Tokyo. If not this year, then next. Yoshi seemed to have only scattered memories of living in Japan and was living in denial that they would ever return. Let him go back to Tokyo semiliterate, stumbling through shrines and temples like a dumb *gaijin,* and see how he was treated.

But before Sammy could say as much, he glanced up to see their father standing at the edge of the sandy beach, hand shading his eyes as he looked out to the waves. Twenty or thirty boys were in the water, trying to catch the swells as they broke, but Noritaka Mori didn't seem to know that his boys weren't among them.

For a long moment Sammy watched his father undetected. Father was a small, thin man with a mustache and a pinched face. With his bowler, his dark suit, and his eyeglasses, he looked like an accountant. Father's family had been from the samurai class before the Meiji Restoration set Japan on the course to modernization, but there was nothing of the warrior in his appearance. Sammy didn't have it, either. He'd noted that glumly many times looking in the mirror as his face matured in a not very samurai-like direction.

"Look!" Yoshi said. "It's Father. What is he doing here?"

"Looking for us, obviously." Sammy grinned. "Maybe he wants us to paint the torii gate, too."

Yoshi's face crumpled into a scowl. Sammy now studied his brother, suddenly seeing a resemblance with pictures of Grandfather in his army uniform. Wait, was it possible that *Yoshi* would turn out to have the samurai face?

Father at last noticed the two boys, who rose to their feet, obedient and reluctant at the same time. They grabbed their towels and surfboards and made their way across the sand. From Father's rigid posture and furrowed brow, it seemed as though he was angry. But why? He'd known they were going to surf before doing their work on the shrine.

Father spoke to them in Japanese. His tone was stiff and flat. "Sachihiro, Yoshiko. You will both get dressed and come with me, please."

Sammy and Yoshi exchanged looks. After changing in one of the beach cabanas, they hoisted their heavy wooden surfboards over their shoulders and followed their father down Kalakaua Avenue. It was a long walk to the quiet residential street where they lived, and there was a streetcar that could have dropped them off two blocks from home, but the conductors yelled at them if they tried to enter carrying their nine-foot boards.

Father said nothing the entire time, only walked with his hands clasped behind his back, studying the sidewalk in front of them. Every once in a while, a hand went to the breast pocket of his jacket, where he tugged at a piece of paper, though he never actually pulled it out. By the time he unlatched the gate and they entered the small courtyard in front of the house, Sammy was more confused than ever about his father's strange mood.

The brothers leaned their surfboards against the inside of the fence next to the gate and set their bundled towels and bathing suits on the stairs to the house, then joined their father by the purification font. Sammy thought the trickle of water from the bamboo pipe into the bucket was a mellow, soothing sound. His brother always said it sounded like someone pissing.

Using the scooper, Father washed his hands, swished water in his mouth to cleanse it, then rinsed the handle of the scooper before waiting for his two sons to do the same. When all had washed, they made their way to the small shrine in the corner of the yard, where they removed their shoes before approaching to pray. All the while, Yoshi kept rolling his eyes when Father wasn't looking.

Sammy didn't have time for it. He was worried. Something was wrong.

"Boys," Father said in a low voice. "Your mother doesn't know anything of what I am about to tell you. She is so delicate now, and her nerves won't take it. For the time being, this must stay between the three of us."

His hand went into his breast pocket again. This time Sammy caught a glimpse of the top of a piece of paper, and the familiar letters of "Western Union" across the top, and he began to guess what had left Father agitated. A telegram had come from Japan with news. Bad news.

"What is it, Father?" he asked.

"Your brothers. You know they were serving in Manchuria."

Brothers. Not brother, but brothers.

"Did they—?" Sammy asked. "Are they—?"

His father answered with a *jisei* from Bashō, a death poem, written not for himself, but for a poet and friend he was mourning.

Move the gravemound
My wailing voice,
The autumn wind.

———◦———

Ten years later Sammy came up from his morphine dream like a pearl diver with burning lungs and black spots floating before his eyes.

He still smelled plumeria. It came on a breeze from his right. He looked in that direction, where a small square of light was framed by shadow. Gradually he saw that it was a window in a wall of whitewashed cement block. A lizard crept along the wall, stalking what looked like an elongated cockroach with waving antennae.

Sammy's mind was still swimming, and a partially formed haiku in English came to him.

Green lizard creeping

Hunter of the unwary
Tiger of scales and—

No, that wasn't quite right. There weren't tigers in Hawaii, and so the metaphor fumbled. Or was this Hawaii? No, he was in the Philippines, and the poem should be in Japanese because he was a soldier now. His loyalty—

Pain interrupted that thought. It came first as a sharp, stabbing sensation in his abdomen, followed by the dull throb of his broken leg. Someone was touching it.

He looked down to see one of the American nurses wrapping his leg in linen while another mixed plaster with water in a ceramic bowl. The one mixing was the one who'd saved his life. Others had wanted to leave him or worse, but she'd fought until they relented. The young woman was tall and would have been considered homely in Japan, all bony limbs and angles like a crane fishing for frogs. Put her in a bathing suit in Hawaii, on the other hand, and the boys would stare.

A soldier sat on a stool in one corner, a rifle and a crutch propped behind him on the wall. He had dark hair and brown eyes, and Sammy was still disoriented enough that at first he thought the man was Japanese. Only gradually did he realize the man was Spanish looking, not Japanese.

A dog with half a tail sat on the man's lap, sniffing at pockets as if looking for a treat. The soldier stared toward the window, one hand idly scratching the dog's ears. Nobody seemed to have noticed that Sammy was awake.

The larger and older of the two nurses jerked his leg to get some of the linens around it, and Sammy gasped at the pain. The two women looked at him, looked at each other. The soldier dumped the dog and climbed stiffly to his feet. He reached for his rifle.

"He's all right," the younger woman said. "You can sit down, Corporal. This one won't cause us any trouble."

It was all coming back to him now. He'd been riding toward Manila with other men of his unit, trying to block out the conversations around him. For soldiers supposedly on their way to combat, they'd been surprisingly jovial, passing crude jokes and anecdotes. Two yokels had been relating their experiences in a Korean brothel. Another man described what a white woman looked like naked—not from experience, mind you, but from something his brother had told him. Other conversations were more mundane: about the relative merits of udon or soba noodles, about the sights of the Philippine countryside, and whether or not one's backside or leg muscles were more sore after a day on a bicycle.

Then the American trucks appeared. One barreled toward him like an enraged, three-ton metal carabao. Other men threw themselves away, but Sammy looked up, staring, not moving his bicycle off the road until it was too late. He thought he'd be crushed, tossed under the wheels and mangled. Instead he found himself plastered to the windshield as the truck rumbled on.

You could have moved in time. Why didn't you?

For the same reason he'd written that letter to Yoshi in the Kempeitai. That's why.

The woman who'd saved him was now studying him with her blue eyes. "It's Sammy, isn't it? How are you feeling?"

"Don't talk to him," the other woman said sternly.

"He's just an injured boy," the younger one said.

"He's a dirty Jap soldier, and the less you tell him, the better. Corporal Fárez, go tell the lieutenant that the Jap is awake. No, wait. Stay here." She licked her lips nervously. "I'll go myself. Someone needs to guard him at all times."

The remaining nurse sighed and kept working on the plaster as the older woman left the room. "Don't mind Miss Frankie. She's not as hard as she seems."

Sammy thought she was *exactly* as hard as she seemed, maybe harder. There was a difference in the way she'd been jerking him around, as if he were a bag of rice, and the way this other nurse was gentle with her touch.

"You can forgive Frankie for being a bit testy," she continued. "It's been a long few days. A long month, to be honest."

Her expression hardened as she said this last part, as if she was only now remembering who he was.

"My belly really hurts," he said. "Whatever you gave me before is gone."

"It doesn't hurt enough," she said, then seemed to catch herself. "What I mean is that until you're crying out, you're not getting any morphine. We've got to ration what we have, and you're . . . well, Japanese."

"Doesn't make it hurt any less."

"Maybe you people should have thought of that before you sent your army ashore."

She may not have had the immediate antagonism toward him as the other nurse, but Sammy recognized risk when he saw it. A man lived and died in the army by what he noticed or didn't. He remembered how the woman had asked his name, and knew why. The same thing could work in his favor.

"I thought I was a dead man, and I'm awfully grateful to you for saving me, Miss—?"

"You don't need to know her name," the injured soldier said. He put down his gun and settled back into his seat with a wince but kept the weapon within reach. "You can call her nurse. That's good enough for you."

"It's all right, Corporal Fárez," she said. "My name is Miss Louise. I don't bear you any ill will, but you are the enemy, and I have no illusions about what would happen to me had I fallen into your hands instead of you mine."

"You mean we're monsters who would torture you for fun?" Sammy shook his head. "Your typical Japanese soldier isn't so different from an American kid. Not too bright, a little crude. Basically good-hearted."

"Oh, really? I've never heard of American boys bayoneting Chinamen for sport, have you?" She turned her back to him and scrubbed the plaster from her hands in a basin of water.

He'd been readying a joke, something about drunk tattoos and brothels, that would have proven the point about the commonality of your average soldier, but her comment was like a punch to the face.

"No?" she said, her back still turned. "Weren't you in China? Haven't you heard the rumors?"

"I was in China," he said, his voice quiet.

He'd been there, his brother had been there, his commanding officer, too, and most of the soldiers of his company were veterans. The best, most battle-hardened troops of the operations now seizing all of Southeast Asia, from Singapore to the Philippines, had sharpened their swords in China. Sometimes literally, after having used those swords to kill so many people that frequent sharpening became necessary.

Some men—those with a sense of shame—didn't speak of what they'd seen or done. Others did. It might come out with braggadocio, but mostly with an air of the inevitable. Like a man who is forced to kill to defend his home.

Sammy didn't mean to speak the words aloud, but they came out before he could stop them. "A man doesn't *want* to kill Chinese, he is forced to by circumstances."

"You tell yourself that if it makes you feel better," Louise said.

She'd missed the irony, hadn't heard the lead weight hanging to his sentence, the ugly, deformed, and burned history behind it.

Sammy studied the ceiling while she finished washing up. The lizard had apparently caught his roach and retreated to the shadows to digest its meal. At the very least, it showed no interest in the other bugs crawling across the ceiling. He composed a better haiku and spoke it aloud to cleanse his mouth and his mind.

Green lizard napping
Ignores a feast of vermin—

Belly full, you sleep.

Louise turned around, blinking. "What?"

Sammy pointed at the ceiling. "The lizard has eaten his fill and now seems indifferent to the fact we're being overrun by bugs. Doesn't it know it has a job to do?"

The edge of her mouth turned up in a smile, as if she couldn't decide whether to be amused or irritated. Sammy understood. She hadn't forgotten what he'd said moments earlier. He was an enemy, and though she'd treated him well so far, she was only doing her duty.

The door opened, and in came a tall young soldier with a hard face. Sammy recognized this one, too. He seemed to have been charged with evacuating the hospital staff to wherever they were now. What was his name? Kozlowski, that's right.

The older nurse, the one Louise had called Miss Frankie, followed him in. She fixed Sammy with a look that reminded him of a weasel studying a chicken coop. He licked his lips.

"Corporal, you will stay," Kozlowski said to the man with the dog. "Miss Louise, you will leave. You only slept a few hours this morning— you're no good to us if you don't get some rest."

"But, I—"

"That's an order. Go." As soon as Louise was gone, the lieutenant turned his wolflike gaze to Sammy, whose mouth felt suddenly dry. "And now, soldier, you and I have some things to discuss."

Chapter Eight

Louise didn't think she'd be able to sleep in the small, sweltering room that had been set up for the nurses. There were bugs, for one: giant cockroaches that didn't bother to flee in the light, ants marching about as relentlessly as columns of Japanese soldiers, and mosquitoes that had somehow found their way through the netting hung up at the windows. She swatted as many of them as she could but always found new bite marks when she searched.

And then there was her worry about her patients. Seaman Therrien had taken a turn for the worse, two men had come down with dysentery, and she couldn't stop thinking about the vengeful look on Frankie's face when she'd come in with Kozlowski to interrogate the Japanese soldier. Kozlowski was a serious man, willing to take serious measures, but she didn't think he'd hurt Sammy Mori to extract information. But she wasn't sure.

And what about Frankie? Would she harm their patient? Surely not.

All these thoughts and fears were churning through Louise's mind, but when she lay down on her cot, they faded into a feeling of pure exhaustion.

Hours later Louise woke in the gray of early dawn, still sleepy, but with a full bladder insisting that she get up. A rooster crowed, a man called out in the lilting tones of Tagalog outside the window, and there was what sounded like a clanking bell—all in the distance. The chattering birds were closer at hand, and frogs and insects carried on their usual racket.

Louise dressed and made her way down the darkened hall of the hospital. Coughs and snores sounded nearby, but there were no men crying out for pain relief. Whoever had worked the night shift had done her job.

She was fully awake by the time she finished her business at the latrine, and enjoyed the quiet that had settled into the mountains. So much to do today, starting with sharpening needles and sterilizing bandages, but she didn't have to begin yet. May as well have a look around, as there might not be another chance today. Once she started, the work would continue relentlessly until she collapsed again onto her cot.

Louise walked past the army trucks camped on the edge of the road with camouflage netting and grassy "roofs" on top. A familiar face poked out from behind one of the tires, tongue hanging from a grinning mouth.

"You again?" she told the dog. "Did they throw you outside, or did you climb through the window?" She raised an eyebrow as Stumpy fell in beside her. "I hope you're not making a nuisance of yourself in the village. These local fellows will get jealous if they catch you sowing your wild oats with their ladies."

Stumpy barked twice, and someone moved behind the open shutters of the house to her right. It was the largest of the nipa huts in the middle of the village, standing on long stilts in a way that made Louise think of a daddy longlegs balancing on the hillside. Someone said that Kozlowski had paid the villagers to use two of the houses, and she guessed from the mosquito netting at the window that this was one of them.

Louise wanted to be left alone, so she stayed quiet as she kept walking. So did Stumpy, bless his mangy little heart. He trotted a few steps ahead of her, swaggering, as if he couldn't wait to show her his new domain. Woman and dog followed the road in the opposite direction from which they'd arrived the night before last.

A dull rumble vibrated like distant thunder. Louise had heard that sound before. Artillery shells, bombs. The sound could carry for many miles, depending on the weather and how it bounced off hills and mountains. It might be ten miles away, it might be fifty, but there was fighting raging somewhere. Men were dying.

The road hugged the hillside as it wrapped around to more terraced rice paddies. Above there were only two more houses, and then unbroken jungle to the peak of the mountain, draped with gauzy mist. Louise stopped, blinking in surprise as she took in the road ahead.

There wasn't one.

Or rather, what had been a narrow ribbon just wide enough for a truck turned into a footpath when it reached the far end of the village. The path curved up the hill in a series of switchbacks, rising higher into the mountains behind. There must be other villages up there, more isolated even than Sanduga.

But those villages wouldn't be reached by vehicles. And they weren't on a road leading to the Bataan Peninsula and MacArthur's army. The trail was going into more rugged terrain still, and she had no doubt that it ended altogether somewhere far above them.

A scuff of dirt made her turn around. Dr. Claypool and Lieutenant Kozlowski stood on the road behind her. Kozlowski wore an undershirt, khaki pants, and unlaced boots. The doctor held a cigarette at his lips and scratched at his gray stubble.

Louise studied their expressions. The doctor was thoughtful, eyes serious beneath those thick eyebrows. The lieutenant's gaze was sharp and questioning.

"There's no road," she said.

"No," Dr. Claypool said.

"No back door out of Sanduga for the Bataan Peninsula. No way out except back down the mountain the way we came."

"That's right," he said.

"You've been here before. You knew already."

"I did. I knew it all along. This was a one-way trip."

She glanced at the lieutenant. "And you knew, too? Or did the doctor lie to you as well?"

"Dr. Claypool told me before we left Baliuag," Kozlowski said. "Before we spoke to the nurses, in fact. I knew already. I received my orders, Claypool and I consulted, and we decided to lie to you girls."

Louise remembered the urgent words between the two men before Claypool called them over. The significant glances, the feeling they were hiding something.

"I don't understand. Why would you lie?"

"The lie wasn't for your ears so much as the other nurses'," Claypool said. "You were an innocent bystander caught in the crossfire."

"What are you talking about?"

"Think about how Miss Frankie acted out. Her attitude was poor. Self-centered and cowardly. Now imagine if she knew there was no back door out of the village that would get us to Bataan, that once we got up here there would be no escape. How would she have responded?"

"Not very well," Louise said.

"She'd have had a mental breakdown at a time when we needed calm," Claypool said. "That's why we lied to her and carried on that charade about letting the nurses have a say. To a lesser extent, we were lying to Miss Clarice and Miss Maria Elena, too."

"You could have told me," she said. "Why didn't you?"

"We think you can be trusted, but we're not sure," Kozlowski said. "Can you?"

"What do you mean, trusted? Trusted with what?"

"Not to panic," Kozlowski said.

"I'm not the panicking type. What are we doing here? Will one of you tell me what's going on?"

"I'd have said that about all of you a few weeks ago," Dr. Claypool said. "None of you were given to panic."

"That was before Pearl Harbor," she said, "before the Japanese started bombing the Philippines. We didn't really expect war."

Lieutenant Kozlowski grunted. "Men, planes, artillery, full tank battalions—that's just what the army sent us since September. What did you think, it was all for show?"

"Deterrence," she said. "So the Japs wouldn't get any ideas."

"The evidence was there," Kozlowski said. "You'd have to be blind not to see it."

"Anyway, that's no excuse for what I've seen," Claypool said. "Look at Miss Frankie. Head nurse, years of experience, and she's right on the edge."

"She's still good in surgery," Louise said.

"And a mess the rest of the time. As for the others, Miss Clarice is a child, Miss Maria Elena is a Pinoy, and every day she'll be thinking she can slip away and hide herself in the civilian population."

"No, she won't. I'll concede the other two, but Maria Elena is steady."

"Maybe she is, maybe she's not," the doctor said. "But you're the one I'm going to, the one to keep your head, to make sure the nurses work, the men stay comfortable, and the hospital is clean. All of the dozens of things that I need to keep functioning."

"I can manage the girls," Louise said. "But as for keeping the hospital functioning, we don't have a fraction of what we need. Quinine and morphine for a start. We have a little bit—whatever we shoved in the truck—but it won't last. We've got mounds of aspirin and bicarbonate of soda, for all the good that will do us."

"Take a closer look at those jars next time you're digging through supplies," Dr. Claypool said. "The useless stuff is mislabeled on purpose, in case the enemy got to it. You have everything you need to run this hospital for months."

"Months." Her voice sounded hollow. "Months?"

"Maybe longer. Let's call it indefinitely."

"I still don't understand." She looked at the doctor, then to the lieutenant. "Why? Please tell me."

"War was coming," Kozlowski said. "We've been fortifying the islands the best we could with what little the army gave us. But we knew what would happen if the Japs came, and we've made contingency plans."

"You don't think Bataan will hold?" she asked. "Corregidor? They're fortresses, they can hold out for reinforcements. That's what everyone says."

"How long do you suppose it will take to build a navy to replace the one at the bottom of Pearl Harbor?"

"I have no idea."

"Neither do I, but it won't be soon, Miss Louise," Lieutenant Kozlowski said. "And until that happens, there won't be any reinforcements. That means Bataan falls, Corregidor, too. Even if they don't fall, we have our orders."

"What orders?" Louise said. "I want to know what and why. That's all I'm asking. Stop holding back information. What are we doing here?"

"We're a hospital," Dr. Claypool said. "We heal the wounded. For now, the men we brought with us, but in the future . . ." He shrugged.

"In the future?" She was still confused.

"Partisans," Kozlowski said.

"There are partisans already?"

"There will be," he said with a nod. "Filipino soldiers, Americans caught behind enemy lines. Even bandits, if they'll kill Japs for us. Anyone taking to the mountains to stay out of the reach of the enemy. We'll give them support, get the wounded back into the fight."

"I see." Her thoughts ran over her patients and stopped at Sammy Mori. "What about the Japanese soldier? He's immobile with that cast, but he'll heal. What will you do with him?"

"We can't let him go," the lieutenant said. "I'm sure you know that."

"We can't kill him, either." She looked at the doctor. "Right? Dr. Claypool?"

Claypool looked troubled. "Our job is to heal the sick and injured. I won't do any killing, if that's what you're worried about."

"We're not permitting others to do it, either. That's pretty much the same thing. Lieutenant? Promise me you won't hurt him."

The expression on Kozlowski's face was harder to read. "The Jap is no threat for now. When Mori can walk again, we'll see."

The two men fell silent, and she turned away from them, her mind churning. Stumpy had found something nasty in the grass lining the road and was gnawing it with great relish.

"So," the lieutenant said after several long moments. "I hope you won't be any trouble."

Louise remembered the poem the Japanese soldier had recited. Or composed—she wasn't sure which. He'd been studying the lizards and insects on the wall. Noticing. She could notice, too.

When Mori can walk again, we'll see.

"We have our orders," she said. "Assuming you're telling me the truth, I will do my duty."

Both men nodded, and the doctor said, "I told you we could count on her," to which the lieutenant grunted but looked satisfied.

"We can't hide this from the others," Louise said. "Not for long."

Kozlowski eyed her. "No, we can't. But I'm not ready for everyone to know, not yet."

"You know them best, Miss Louise," Dr. Claypool said. "Any suggestions?"

"The first step is to keep them from coming out this far. They're not stupid. If they see all this"—she waved her hand at the road where it turned into a cow path—"they're going to figure it out in a hurry. Could you make up a story about the road being mined or something? That might hold them in the village."

"Not a bad idea," Kozlowski said. "Let me think up something."

There were so many other questions she wanted to ask, but at that moment a familiar whine came from the sky, and the three of them hurled themselves into the grass.

Louise was lying face-to-face with Stumpy as the airplane approached. The dog kept working at his prize, a pig's foot and the lower part of its leg bone. He nosed one end of the leg toward her, as if offering her the other side to chew on.

"You're too kind," she said. "But no thanks."

The engine grew louder, and Louise looked skyward. A slow-moving scout plane flew overhead. On its wings, the familiar and hated round red spot, like a fried egg. She held her breath as it passed over the village, waiting for it to spot the trucks beneath their camouflage netting, but it flew on without slowing or wheeling back around. Lieutenant Kozlowski let out his breath beside her.

They were apparently safe for now, but it was a taste of what was to come. Retreat into the mountains and take their place among the partisans and more of the same would follow. Hiding in the grass, waiting for that inevitable moment when the Japanese discovered them.

Chapter Nine

Baliuag stank of defeat when Yoshiko Mori entered the town several days after the battle. He'd finally dismissed Captain Soto's men and sent them back to terrorize Manila, which was under Japanese control at last.

For two days, he'd tried to push his way to the small town where his brother was presumed to have gone, only to be turned back by enemy snipers, by petulant Japanese commanders, and even by muddy, impassable roads. Of these, the opposition from his own side was the most galling, and he'd finally radioed his superiors to complain. Still more stonewalling. The trail felt cold when Lieutenant Fujiwara finally drove them into the village, except for word of a promising Filipino prisoner who had fallen into army hands.

As for Baliuag, Mori was unimpressed with the strutting soldiers holding it. Not with so many dead tanks remaining in the streets, their turrets blasted off, their tracks slipped as they were hit by enemy rounds. One lay on its side like a dead buffalo, and smelled just as bad, too; apparently nobody had bothered to remove the charred soldiers inside, and they were now rotting in the tropical heat. Mori counted eight destroyed tanks, all Japanese.

The rising tide of imperial power had been sweeping across Southeast Asia for the past month, but here it had met resistance. The

Americans had held long enough to keep their lines from being severed while they fled west toward Bataan.

Mori stopped at the Spanish-style building at the center of town where the commanding officer had made his headquarters. It was the most impressive structure in Baliuag—or had been at one time. Three stories with a tile roof and an upper balcony. Now the shutters were blown off, the balcony half-collapsed, and the rising sun flag hung limply, waiting for a breeze.

A squat, toad-like officer with the insignia of major stood outside smoking when the truck pulled up. This must be Major Noguchi, the one who'd been delaying him. There was a large bamboo tub of dirty water in front of him, and two soldiers were drowning a half-naked young man in it. They let him up when the two Kempeitai got out of the truck. One of the locals. The man jabbered in Tagalog, eyes wide with terror, until the soldiers pushed him back under.

Other soldiers, not paying much attention to the drowning Filipino, sat on mats on the side of the street, drinking miso soup and shoveling rice and fish from their bowls with chopsticks.

The major eyed the newcomers as they approached, fixing especially on Fujiwara's armband reading "Law Police." He turned to Mori.

"Captain Mori, I suppose?"

"That's right. Major Noguchi?"

"*Hai.*" The major waved his hand at the soldiers. "Bring him up again. We don't want him dead. Not yet."

He chuckled at this, as if it were a rather clever joke, and there was something in his narrow, stupid eyes that made Mori instinctively hate the man. He had no idea why they were torturing the prisoner, and assumed there was more to it than petty cruelty, but the pleasure in it was unseemly, like a child sneering as he pulled the legs off a grasshopper.

"The rest of you, get inside." Noguchi waited until the grumbling soldiers had collected their mats and bowls and gone into the building, then turned back to Mori. "So you're looking for your brother."

"That's right. I have reason to believe he came this way."

"So do I, Mori. So do I. That's why I let you through, even though I should have turned you back for your own good. This is a war zone, after all, and not safe for your kind."

"My *kind*?"

Noguchi chuckled, clearly delighted to have irritated the Kempeitai officer. Was this another case of *gekokujō*, the ignoring of proper chain of command?

"Yes, your kind, Mori. We're fighting Americans here, not terrorizing dumb peasants. You don't understand war—you'll only put yourself at risk." The major sighed in an especially patronizing way. "But one has a duty to one's own brother, I suppose."

Noguchi was wrong, of course. It wasn't looking after his brother that had brought Mori; it was the opposite. It was about stopping that brother before more of his stupidity spread to the wider world. That was both Mori's duty and what might save him from the repercussions of Sammy's behavior.

The major glanced over at his men, who were holding the half-drowned young Filipino without showing the least bit of initiative. "Well, what are you waiting for? Give him his bath." Then, to Mori, "What do you think it's like, fighting Americans? You think it's a stroll in the cherry blossoms?"

Mori gave a significant look at the burned-out Japanese tank across the street. "It looks like the Americans gave you everything you could handle."

Noguchi grunted. "You'd have been pissing your trousers if you'd been here. There's not a one of you law police who knows how to fight. Bunch of cowards."

There was no point in arguing the matter, of explaining that both Mori and his adjutant had seen brutal fighting in China. Noguchi would only point out that this fight was different, that these were Americans, or otherwise belittle Mori's combat experience in an attempt to side-track him from his objective.

"Lieutenant Fujiwara," Mori said. "Major Noguchi has made an interesting observation, don't you think?"

"Yes, sir." Fujiwara took out his notebook and began writing in it. "Unusual, but illuminating."

Noguchi's eyes narrowed. "What's he scribbling there? What's this about?"

"The corporal is recording your thoughts. They might prove helpful later when we're asked about your cooperation. Now about this information you supposedly have."

Mori had been hoping that the major would prove as pliable as Captain Soto, but Noguchi seemed uncowed. He put his hands on his waist and stared piggishly.

"I'll help you, but it will cost you."

"What do you mean?"

"I mean I have information. You're looking for your brother. This is no important mission, it's about your duty. Well, I respect that, Mori. I really do. But you're asking me for army resources to clear up a family matter. And I need some resources in return to pay for it. We're short on critical supplies, and I need your help."

"I have no access to armaments," Mori said.

This was not entirely true. The military police had broad powers, especially in occupied areas, which Manila had officially become. They'd captured numerous fuel depots and ammunition dumps. If Noguchi needed something to keep pressing toward the Americans on Bataan, Mori could make it happen, assuming his commanding officer, Colonel Umeko, allowed it.

"I'm not short on armaments," the major said. "Those aren't the supplies I need."

"What is it, food, clothing?"

"Oh no, we've got all of that. Well, supplies are adequate, at least." He turned to his soldiers, who were dunking their prisoner with a little too much enthusiasm again. "You idiots, you're going to kill him. That's right, bring him up, let him breathe."

The two men held up the young man, who was slumping, nearly unconscious. One of them struck the prisoner on the back, and he coughed up water. The soldiers slapped him and shouted until he steadied himself without falling.

"Morale is slipping," Major Noguchi said, paying no attention to the abuse of his prisoner. "That's the truth. Three weeks of hard fighting, and we've barely had a rest. I'm sure the boys in Manila are having a good time and all, but it's tough out here on the front."

"Not as good a time as you would think," Mori said. "There are plenty of foreigners in the city, Red Cross observers and the like. They're watching. We can't have any incidents like in China. That's the official word. So the men must be kept in line."

"I suppose so. But a good hunting dog needs to be thrown a bone now and then."

"What is it you're looking for?" Mori asked cautiously. "Comfort women for your men?"

"No, not that. We've got a brothel. Only four girls, but we're putting them to work. Little brown things, boy, do they know how to . . . Look, Mori. Here's the truth. I want some whiskey, and I want you to get it for me."

"You want whiskey?"

"Something high quality, you understand, not that coconut slop. What do they call it? *Lambanog*. Tastes like distilled rubber sap. I need the good stuff."

"I'm not sure getting your troops liquored up is going to help the war effort," Mori said.

"Not for the common soldiers, only the officers. High quality, you understand. From what I understand, there were a bunch of foreign clubs down on the waterfront. Now, I've heard from General Homma that they kept the troops out and saved what they found for the officers. I want you to get me some of it."

Mori's first reaction was disbelief, followed by outrage. How dare Major Noguchi make such demands? The Kempeitai had broad powers, and when a man like Mori declared that he was on official business, these common soldiers had better stand aside if they knew what was good for them.

On the other hand, Noguchi was right, at least to a certain point. This business was personal, a search for his brother. It was a detail he'd let slip to Captain Soto, and now this major knew it as well. A hand touched the letter in his jacket pocket.

"I think I could manage four or five bottles of whiskey," Mori said.

"Twenty bottles. Not just any whiskey. Scotch. I'm partial to Ben Nevis, if you can get it. Or Glenmorangie. That's good, too."

Noguchi butchered the pronunciation of these Scottish brands, but it was clear he'd said them before and wasn't just repeating what someone had told him were good scotch labels. Mori knew nothing about whiskey but assumed it was high quality and hard to come by.

Mori clenched his teeth. "Twenty bottles of scotch. Now where is the Pinoy with the information?"

Noguchi made a face that Mori supposed was satisfaction but looked like a man straining to move his bowels. "Why, he's right here. Let him up, boys. It's time to give him a breather."

"That's him? That's the informant? You almost drowned him!"

"Oh, don't get worked up—he's fine. I was softening him for you, is all."

"I thought he approached *you*. I thought he was a willing informant. That he's a—how do they say?—a Sakdal."

"Well, sure," Noguchi said. "We pay the Sakdals for good information when they've got it. But this one was trying to extort us. Petty thugs and criminals, deep down that's all they are."

Mori raised his eyebrows. "Extort? Was he asking for scotch?"

"No, nothing like that," Noguchi said, obviously missing the irony, although his two men didn't. A slight smile passed between them behind the major's back. "I offered twenty pesos. He said a hundred. I told him forty, but no more, and he swaggered off. So now he gets nothing except a free bath."

The young man wasn't showing any swagger now. His head hung low on his bare chest, which heaved as if he'd never get enough air into his lungs. Perhaps the major was right: this one wouldn't give Mori any trouble.

"I'll need an interrogation room."

"Easily done. He doesn't speak Japanese, only a very little English and the local gibberish. I'll lend you my translator."

"No need for that," Mori said. "Lieutenant Fujiwara speaks Tagalog."

———

The interrogation room Major Noguchi gave the Kempeitai had been used to billet troops, and they'd left it filthy. Mori refused to work under such conditions, demanded that the major clean it up first. Soldiers hauled out tatami mats, bowls filled with half-eaten suppers squirming with maggots, and soiled clothing. Once that was done, the major sent in a pretty young Filipina to scrub the floor on her hands and knees. She didn't look older than sixteen or seventeen, although it was hard to tell with these native girls. She might be twenty-five and the mother of three, for all Mori could tell.

"I wonder if this is one of the 'little brown things' Noguchi was talking about," Mori said to Fujiwara while the girl worked.

"I believe so, sir," Fujiwara said. "She looks very young."

"The lack of discipline in Noguchi's troops is appalling, don't you think?"

"Quite appalling. He was rather insolent, too. His demand for liquor as the price for doing his duty . . . I was surprised you would do such a thing, sir."

"Who says that I will?" Mori asked. "Ah, here we are at last."

The woman left with her pail. The floor was still damp, and cobwebs hung in the corners. The windows were either broken or filthy. Mori supposed his brother would have had a poem or a saying from a Chinese philosopher about the matter, but for him it was clean enough.

Fujiwara brought in the prisoner and put him in a chair. The young man was trembling and wouldn't look at the two Japanese secret police.

"Tell him what we need," Mori said. "Advise him that there will be no second chances if he doesn't answer truthfully."

Fujiwara had warned that his Tagalog wasn't perfect, claimed that he frequently missed nuances or misunderstood, but every time the corporal spoke it seemed fluent to Mori's ears.

Then again, when Mori spoke in English, he couldn't even hear his own Japanese accent, only knew that people in Hawaii had noted how curious it was that Sachihiro Mori, the older brother, spoke English perfectly, while Yoshiko, the younger, did not. Certain words gave him away. That had grated on him.

The semi-drowning had softened the Sakdal and would-be extortionist. The man answered Fujiwara without hesitation. Indeed, he babbled on after every question, giving more information than had been requested.

The Filipino had apparently been working for the Americans before and during their defense of Baliuag, acting first as a spotter, then as a cargador, loading and unloading supplies. Naturally, he claimed to have been working for them under duress. Mori scoffed at this. A Sakdal had no loyalty. He'd work for anyone, anywhere, so long as it put silver in his palm.

Fujiwara questioned him some more, then turned to his commanding officer. "He says there were two trucks that arrived before the battle carrying sick and wounded soldiers. One of the injured men was Japanese."

"What did he look like?" Mori asked.

Fujiwara asked, but the prisoner had no good answer. He seemed to think that one Japanese soldier looked like another. But the man's injuries had seemed consistent with a crash on the road, including a broken leg that had not yet been set, only splinted.

"The Japanese was evacuated with the rest," Fujiwara translated. "There was an argument—some of the Americans wanted to abandon him, others thought they had a responsibility."

Mori eyed the Filipino suspiciously. "I thought he spoke only a very little English. How did he pick up on that?"

Fujiwara questioned some more. "He admits he speaks better English than he let on. He didn't tell Noguchi at first so as to gain an advantage in haggling for money. Then Noguchi started torturing him, and it was too late."

"Do you believe it?"

"I'm not sure, sir. I think he's telling the truth, but you can never tell with these vermin."

Mori supposed he could speak in English to test the man, but he was reluctant to do so in front of Fujiwara. The adjutant didn't know the extent of Mori's contact with the language, or that he'd lived among the Americans for so many years—few people did. Mori was already walking beneath a cloud of suspicion and would be until he settled matters with his brother.

"But here's the interesting thing, sir. The hospital trucks weren't evacuating to Bataan. Not right away, at least."

"What? Are you sure?"

"*Hai,*" Fujiwara said with a nod. "He overheard an American officer speaking to one of the drivers. There's apparently a hospital closer to here, in the mountains. And a back road to Bataan if they're cut off from the highway."

Now that was interesting. The army was going to have a devil of a time rooting out the tens of thousands of Americans and Filipinos holed up on Bataan behind MacArthur's defensive lines. The peninsula was rugged and hard to attack from either land or sea. But if Mori could get hold of his brother before he escaped—even better, if he could discover this back road to Bataan that cut down through the mountain passes . . .

Mori now had his justification for finding his brother. Get to Sammy, take him prisoner while killing or capturing the injured Americans, then turn over his valuable information to the army.

But could he be sure? What if the Sakdal was inventing the whole thing? Major Noguchi knew about Mori's brother and might have let it slip to his prisoner. The prisoner, desperate to squirm out of the trap he was in, might have concocted a fantastic story to free himself.

"Sir?" Fujiwara asked.

"I'm half inclined to hire this man to lead us into the hills to find the missing soldier. Pay him a reasonable sum of money and see what happens."

"That sounds dangerous, sir."

"Of course. There's all kinds of risk in it. We might spend the next two weeks romping pointlessly through the jungle, looking for something that doesn't exist. But there's no real choice—we have to hire someone."

"I suppose so," Fujiwara said, his tone doubtful.

"*Several* someones, in fact. They'll all be crooks and traitors. And the mountains are dangerous, full of partisans, and will remain so until we can pacify the population. But you're a clever man, Lieutenant. Surely you see the opportunity."

"In finding a back road to the American army on Bataan, sir? I do, sir. But . . ."

"But what? Speak freely."

"I'm not so worried about the tromping through the jungle, sir," Fujiwara said. He glanced at the Filipino, who stared dumbly at the wall while the two secret police spoke in Japanese. "I'm worried about outright treachery and ambush. This man worked for the Americans—how do you know he isn't still loyal to them? The whole thing might be an act."

"Might be, but I doubt it."

"One thing is for certain," the lieutenant said. "The prisoner is not loyal to *us* and never will be. Major Noguchi saw to that with his pointless brutality."

"Hmm, a good point. Torturing the man made him our enemy. He might very well look for a chance to shove a knife in our kidneys when we aren't expecting it."

"So we'll let him go and find another guide, sir?"

"We'll find another guide—there must be all manner of weasels in these parts who can show us the roads into the mountains—but we won't let this one go." Mori sighed. This may not be pointless brutality, but it still felt unnecessary. If only the major hadn't bungled matters. "We can't. He's a talker, and we don't want him talking about this. We have secrets to maintain, including from the major and his kind."

One of them being the secret of my brother.

Mori didn't say this last part aloud, of course. Instead he said, "We'll say the prisoner was killed trying to escape. There's no need to make it look like an accident—nobody will question us. Nobody even needs to believe it. Just shoot him, and we'll be off."

"Yes, sir. Now, sir?"

"Now, Lieutenant."

Mori turned toward the door, not needing to see the look of horror in the Sakdal's eyes as he saw Fujiwara draw his pistol. No need to see the bloody mess, only brace himself for the gunshot in the close confines of the interrogation room.

But the words were barely out of his mouth when the prisoner sprang from his chair and hurled himself at Lieutenant Fujiwara, whose hand had not yet drawn his weapon. Fujiwara could only throw up his arms as the prisoner barreled into him. The two of them flew to the ground, and the prisoner fumbled for Fujiwara's pistol.

You fool, Mori silently berated himself. *He understood everything.*

Mori drew his *gunto*. It was a standard-issue officer's sword, modeled on the old samurai weapons, and it felt long and deadly in his hand. Fujiwara was struggling for the gun, but his smaller opponent already had it and was turning it on its owner.

Mori swung his sword from the shoulders, an angry grunt at his mouth. Angry with himself, angry with the treachery of this place. Angry with the war.

The blade could have trimmed the hairs on the back of the Filipino's neck, it was so sharp. Brought down with all of Mori's strength, it nearly severed the man's head. He fell down, and the gun skittered away across the floor.

Mori was shaking as the enormity of his blunder sank in. He'd already known the man was a liar; the Sakdal had lied about his English ability when speaking with the major. Mori had accepted this without imagining that he might also have lied about his ability to speak Japanese, too. It was well known that these people were clever with languages, that many spoke four of them: a village dialect, Tagalog, English, and the Spanish that had once been common throughout the islands when the Spaniards held it as a colony. Surely some of them also spoke Japanese. And what kind of man would be the first to approach the Japanese army? Someone who was confident he could communicate.

The Sakdal must have been listening to the entire conversation between the two Japanese. Weighing his options, cooperating so long as he thought the secret police would let him live. Maybe, in his more optimistic moments, he'd returned to scheming not just for his life, but for money.

And then Mori had given his adjutant the order to execute the prisoner. The man had had nothing left to lose.

Mori looked down at the dead body. A hysterical, nervous laugh threatened to come out, but he fought it down. He moved slowly, deliberately, as he removed a handkerchief and wiped off his blade. The handkerchief came away only a little bloodied. It had passed too swiftly through the man's neck.

Fujiwara shoved the body off himself and climbed up, spitting the Sakdal's blood from his mouth and wiping at his face. He looked a mess.

"I am all right," Fujiwara said. "I am not injured."

"That is obvious enough."

"Sorry, sir. I was clumsy and careless."

"The error was mine."

A bowed head. "Thank you for saving my life, sir."

"There is one good thing to come of this," Mori said. His hand trembled as he slid the sword back into its sheath. "We no longer need to lie about how the prisoner died. Killed trying to escape—for once, it is absolutely true."

Chapter Ten

Louise helped Lieutenant Kozlowski and Dr. Claypool maintain their fiction for several days after arriving in Sanduga, but she worried that the secrecy would break down. As soon as the patients had all been stabilized, the less injured men began to clamor for an evacuation to Bataan.

That same day, two more badly injured soldiers arrived, one a Filipino and the other an American. The so-called bamboo telegraph had carried news to Sanduga of a firefight in the lowlands and a pair of injured soldiers being hid by the locals. Kozlowski and the two truck drivers went down from the mountains to rescue them. The injured men were carried on litters for miles through the forests and mountains until they arrived in the village, where the doctor and his nurses set to work saving their lives. Lieutenant Kozlowski quashed talk of evacuation until they were ready to be moved.

Occasional bits of news reached them in the mountains, and it was uniformly bad. The Japanese advanced on all fronts. MacArthur had completed his evacuation to Bataan, but no reinforcements had come to relieve him. No American naval forces had arrived.

The two Filipino drivers disappeared one day. Louise didn't know if they'd talked to the villagers about the back road and learned the truth or if they'd gone ahead to scout, but their desertion came as a blow and set the injured soldiers talking, as did additional rumors coming into the village. And soon enough the bamboo telegraph wasn't their only source of information.

Claypool forbade using the generator for anything but medical purposes and Kozlowski's radio communications with the army, and the lieutenant was tight-lipped about what was happening in the war, but an enterprising young sailor put together a simple crystal radio, a so-called cat's whisker receiver. He used a piece of galena—lead crystal—to receive the signal, a capacitor, a coil of copper wire to adjust the radio, and additional wire for the antenna. The crystal set didn't need outside power but was powered by the radio signal itself. That limited its range.

At first, they could only pick up the Voice of Freedom being broadcast by the US military from Corregidor, but someone else came up with the idea of making a generator powered by an old bicycle, mounted and stationary. This allowed them to receive weaker stations from farther away. At night, when the signals traveled farther, they could even hear the distant, thin sound of KGEI out of San Francisco, broadcasting on shortwave.

Late on the afternoon of January 9, Louise came out of surgery to find several soldiers and nurses outside clustering around the radio. One of the men pedaled the bike. The signal came in and out of focus, with an excited correspondent on the other side reading war news in that strange announcer accent. There was something about German U-boats spotted off the Carolina coast, followed by news of the inexorable Japanese advance on British-held Singapore.

Lieutenant Kozlowski stood a few paces off beneath the corrugated-metal awning, his arms crossed and his expression serious. He caught Louise's gaze and shook his head.

The radio cut into static, and the men groaned. Miss Frankie stood with them, making worried comments to Maria Elena. The radio came back on after a few seconds.

". . . the Philippines, where our heroic boys continue their struggle against the Jap menace. Reports have the enemy crossing the Abucay Line onto the Bataan Peninsula." The signal broke down again, then sputtered briefly to life. "Wainwright and MacArthur insist—"

The signal died again. A voice came through the noise that sounded like a radio broadcast in Chinese, and then pure static.

"What happened?" Frankie said. "Pedal harder!"

"It ain't the pedaling," the sweating man on the bike grumbled as he kept at it. "Give it a try if you don't believe me."

"That's enough," Kozlowski said. "Those of you who are well enough to pedal the radio or stand around shooting the breeze can make yourselves busy. The sun is going down, and I want some work out of you men before it's dark. Understood?"

"But sir," one man protested, "what about Bataan? The Japs are gonna overrun the whole of it before our reinforcements arrive."

"You trust the news from the other side of the ocean?" Kozlowski said. "Bataan will hold. Don't you worry."

"They can't be *that* wrong," another man said. "What about the Abucay Line? Is that wrong, too?"

"Where is the Abucay Line?" Frankie asked, her voice high and nervous.

"Bataan," the man said. "Japs gotta cross it to get at MacArthur and Wainwright. And we gotta throw 'em back. Means the enemy is already trying to advance on the peninsula."

"Then we're cut off!" Frankie said.

"Miss Frankie, please," Kozlowski told the nurse, tone exasperated.

"We're all going to die here!" Frankie's voice rose even higher. "The Japs will find us, and since we didn't surrender in time, they're going to give it to us good. Oh, it's fine for you men. We're women, and you know what they'll do to us, right, Louise? Tell them!"

"We're not cut off," Kozlowski said. "There's an unexploded bomb or two in the road. Once it's time to go, we'll disarm the ordnance and be on our way. We'll come around the back side into Bataan, and nobody will be the wiser."

He glanced away as he said this, and to Louise it was obvious he was lying, but nobody else seemed to notice it.

"Now get to work, all of you. Johnson, I want that new latrine dug. These villagers are complaining about the old one draining into their stream. Nalty . . ."

Louise studied Miss Frankie as Kozlowski sent the men off in one direction or another. The woman kept wringing her hands, looking around her, as if the rising mountains were a prison. She was breathing too hard.

"As for you nurses," Kozlowski said with a sharp look at Louise, "I recommend you get back to work. Too much worrying does nobody any good."

Louise grabbed Maria Elena as the young woman turned toward the hospital. She looked up at her quizzically, but Louise didn't speak until Frankie was inside.

"I need your help."

"You mean with Miss Frankie? She shouldn't talk to the lieutenant that way, miss."

"That's only the last straw. I was already worried."

Maria Elena nodded. Her dark eyes were solemn, her pretty mouth pursed. "I'm worried, too. She only makes it worse the way she talks all the time."

"We have to keep an eye on her. Calm her down. She's a risk to herself and others. She's all right when she's busy," Louise said. "That's the key. Keep her occupied, lost in her work."

"I understand."

"Don't take her work. Don't do too much—it doesn't do any of us any good."

Louise glanced up to see the hospital door open and Frankie stick her head out.

"What are you two mumbling about over there?" Frankie asked. She came out. "It's about me, isn't it? Are you two complaining again?"

Maria Elena shrank back, but Louise ignored the intrusion and said smoothly to Maria Elena, as if continuing an ongoing conversation, "But I wouldn't deworm the patients on a suspicion. Verify that it's parasites first. Examine their stools under the microscope."

The Filipina nurse seemed to recover her balance. "Yes, miss."

"For one, we've got a limited supply of medications. For another, I'm not convinced the intestinal issues aren't caused by a change in diet. From city food and army rations to rice and mungo beans. Plus all the tropical fruits. Too much at once if you ask me."

"I know what you're doing," Frankie said. "Trying to push me aside. You think because Dr. Claypool favors you that you're suddenly above me. That you can give orders to the other nurses and shove me out of the way. And I saw you flirting with Kozlowski so he'll favor you, too."

Louise bristled, face on fire. "Flirting! That's strictly against regulations, and . . . and that's not the point! Our job is to calm these men, not get them worked up. You need to get hold of yourself."

"Worked up? What do you mean, worked up?"

"Exactly what I'm saying. Worked up! You get them all agitated, Frankie. Well, guess what? These men are sick and injured, and they need rest. That's physical *and* mental rest. What do you think our job is here? It's not to argue with the army, it's not to second-guess our orders, it's to do our damn job."

Frankie's voice climbed. "So they're worked up. They need to be. We never should have come up here, and you know it. What are we doing, anyway? We can't save all these men here, we need to get them to a hospital, not keep taking in more patients. For the love of God, we need to go. We need to get out of here. We can't wait to be bombed, to have the Japs come and take us captive. For God's sake, do you know what that means? You must know!"

Frankie was actually shouting now, and a few men passing with shovels looked their way, alarmed. A young Filipina girl from the village, barefoot and carrying a basket of rice on her head, stopped with eyes wide. Fárez's dog materialized, barking excitedly.

The corporal himself came limping outside with his crutch, wincing as he called out Stumpy's name. He took in the scene, frowning. "Is everything okay?"

"Everyone needs to calm down," Louise said.

It was more to herself than to Frankie. She'd pulled Maria Elena aside precisely to stop the head nurse from reacting this way. That sort of hysteria could easily spread to the injured men, many of whom were eighteen, nineteen years old. Boys, really. Instead Louise had let the other nurse goad her into an argument.

But Frankie wasn't done. "I won't calm down! This is crazy, this whole thing. Look at us. We'll be trapped up here if we don't take the back road. Why aren't we taking care of those bombs? Why aren't we sending for help?"

"Please, Miss Frankie. Let's all, everyone, calm down. You, me, everyone." Louise took a deep breath. "It was one radio broadcast. We don't know if it's true, and we don't know what it means."

Frankie's breath was coming so quickly now that she seemed to be hyperventilating. She wobbled on her feet, and looked ready to swoon, and that seemed to be the only thing cutting her off from a panicky scream. Louise and Maria Elena caught her arms.

"Oh my God," Frankie said. "Someone help me. My heart is giving out. I'm going to die."

"Take her inside," Louise told Maria Elena. "Tell Dr. Claypool what happened. How bad it was. If he could sedate her—"

"Don't sedate me!"

"Corporal, help us, please," Louise said.

Fárez stepped forward to help Maria Elena lead Frankie inside. Louise thought maybe she should follow, but she needed to be away from them. She, too, was shaken by the news from the radio, by the sense of inevitability. By Frankie's panic. There was no back road out of here. The Japanese had already seized the populated areas of Luzon outside the Bataan Peninsula, and surely they would penetrate the mountains to attack rebellious pockets, to cut off supply lines, to force villagers and tribal people to submit to imperial authority.

The bamboo telegraph flowed both directions. It seemed impossible that it wouldn't also carry news down to the Japanese. The villagers had warned of Sakdals: bandits and thieves who were already working for the enemy. A bounty of a hundred pesos for every American turned in, dead or alive. Fifty pesos for Filipino soldiers in hiding.

"Miss Louise, are you all right?"

She turned to see Corporal Fárez studying her in the dying light. He must have come back outside while she was standing here, stunned. He leaned against his crutch, and his young face was earnest, worried. Stumpy had wandered off to sniff at the brush, no doubt looking for another rotten treat. The dog was limping, and she thought she should have another look at him, see what other ailments he had now that the mange was clearing up and he'd been dewormed.

"You should be in bed, Corporal. We can't keep stitching you up again because you can't be bothered to let yourself heal."

"I was worried."

"Stumpy can take care of himself. He already rules the village." Louise smiled. "Have you seen how the village dogs follow him around? He struts through Sanduga like a king."

"Worried about *you*, Miss Louise. You lost your temper. You don't do that very often."

"More than you think, believe me. I'm sorry, Corporal. I was wrong, I let her get to me. There's really no excuse."

"Please don't you apologize to me, Miss Louise. She deserved it and more."

Louise glanced at Stumpy, who was still sniffing around in the grass. He lifted his leg to mark the spot, and when it came down again, he hobbled off.

"He's limping, Corporal. Did he injure himself?"

"Um, yeah, I saw that. He's all right, don't worry about it."

Something about Fárez's tone made her curious. "Did he get in a fight? What is it?"

"It's, well, kinda funny. I took Stumpy to the doc, but he didn't have time for a dog right now. Said to come back in a few days when he's not so tired. Claypool's an old man and all and needs his rest when he's not working, which is most of the time."

"Bring him here, and I'll take a look. I've got time right now."

"Well, I don't know exactly, it seems like maybe not the right thing for you to look at."

"Huh?"

Fárez looked away, and though his skin was too tanned to show it, she heard a blush in his voice. "Miss Louise, it's kinda embarrassing, but it's not something you can take care of. He's not right back . . . you know, back *there*."

"Back *there*? You mean his groin? Or does he have an abscessed anal gland?"

"Miss Louise, please!"

"Corporal Fárez, I'm a nurse. You must know what things I've seen on men. A dog's ailments aren't going to embarrass me."

Fárez must remember that she'd seen him undressed, having attended Dr. Claypool when he was operating on the corporal's gluteal muscles, not to mention draining pus and cleaning him up when he couldn't get himself to the bathroom. So Stumpy was limping a little—how bad could it be?

"Call him over here. I mean it, Corporal," she added in a mock-stern voice when he didn't immediately obey.

Fárez complied. Or tried to. Stumpy, for all his limping about, was spry enough to play a game of tag with the corporal. Every time the man bent to grab hold of him, the dog danced out of the way with a delighted bark. Louise stood casually, watching out of the corner of her eye, as if disinterested. When Stumpy came her way, she grabbed for him and took hold before he could squirm free and make a run for it.

It was getting dark, so she carried the dog back to where light was bleeding out from behind the blankets hung in the hospital windows. There she had Fárez hold the dog's front quarters while she inspected the rear.

Louise found the source of the dog's discomfort and his owner's embarrassment. One of Stumpy's testicles was swollen to the size of a small apple. She prodded it, and the dog didn't protest but kept licking the corporal's face. Its limping was apparently caused by movement of the oversize object, not by pain from the testicle itself.

"Is it bad?" Fárez asked.

"A tumor, I think, but it's hard to say for sure. Probably not aggressive, but we'll need to have the whole thing taken off regardless."

"Taken off!"

"Don't worry, I'll put him to sleep, stitch him up again. He'll barely feel it."

She set Stumpy on the ground, and he set off with a trot that was only slightly less jaunty than usual. Fárez stared after him.

"Just one of them, right?"

"Just one."

He looked back at her, still frowning. "But he'll still wake up being only half as . . . you know."

"Half as manly?"

"Miss Louise!"

He sounded so anguished, so earnest, that she couldn't help but laugh. "I'm sorry, I shouldn't make fun, only it's . . . He'll be fine with one testicle, Corporal. In fact, he'd be fine without both of them, would never notice it. I've done it before."

"You've done what? Wait, really?"

"Castrated dogs. Yes, of course. We always had dogs on the farm, and you know what happens if you let nature take its course. They breed without restraint, and you end up needing to put down puppies. That's far more cruel than castrating a few male dogs. It's not an invasive procedure, just a cut and then you draw the testicles out and—"

She stopped when Fárez dropped his crutch and had to catch himself against the wall. He looked gray, like he was going to throw up or faint. How this man had gone through battle and injury and watched other men die was a mystery.

Louise steadied him and picked up the crutch. "Are you okay, Corporal? Do you need the smelling salts, the fainting couch? Is your corset too tight? We could loosen it a bit."

He managed a chuckle at this. "I'm sorry. It's silly, I know."

"I'll take care of Stumpy, don't you worry. He'll never know it happened."

"What about the other dogs? What will they think of him?"

"What will the other dogs think of him?" She patted the young man's shoulder. "Why, I promise they'll respect Stumpy just as much as ever, even with only one testicle."

Fárez was quiet for a long moment. "Well, okay," he said at last. "But could you do me a favor? Don't tell me when it's going to happen. I don't want to know."

"Corporal, if Stumpy is my patient, and I'm acting as the doctor, that means I'll need a nurse."

"You mean Miss Clarice or Miss Maria Elena?"

"They're far too busy. I mean you, Corporal."

Chapter Eleven

Sammy lay motionless when Miss Frankie and Miss Clarice entered the ward to do their rounds. Frankie made Clarice empty bedpans while she checked on the patients. Sammy feigned sleep as they worked their way toward him.

Feigning sleep was something he did a good deal of these days. He interacted with the others as little as possible. He'd all but stopped talking to them after the lieutenant interrogated him last week, tired of the overt hostility from Kozlowski and from Sammy's fellow patients. He'd hoped that cooperating would help, but it hadn't.

Kozlowski had blustered plenty, but when Sammy said he didn't have information, knew nothing about Japanese troop movements beyond the order to seize Manila, the American hadn't struck him or harmed him in any way. Merely threatened. Sammy wasn't afraid of the lieutenant; in fact, he wanted the man around as much as possible so the injured soldiers wouldn't attack him.

But Miss Frankie was another matter. When the other nurses were not around, she engaged in petty cruelties, like poking roughly at his bandages, or moving his bedpan so he had to get up and grope in the dark. Once, he'd nearly soiled himself.

Frankie wouldn't give him morphine those first few days and made Miss Clarice bathe him, saying he was too disgusting to look at. Under other circumstances, Sammy would have complained to either Miss Louise or the doctor, but he knew it would get back to Miss Frankie, who would no doubt make him pay.

Tonight Sammy's fellow patients had seemed especially agitated. They'd caught bad news on the radio, although it wasn't clear what. Something about the Japanese army advancing or lack of resupply from their own side. When they saw Sammy watching, they turned their abuse to him: he smelled bad, he looked like a monkey with buck teeth, he had yellow skin. It was all stuff he'd heard before, but concentrated tonight. Aggressive and real.

Finally someone told the abusers to lay off, and that set off an argument that only died down when Miss Louise came in with a stern word. Sammy, who'd remained silent through all of this, sent quiet thoughts of gratitude in her direction.

When the lights went out, he struggled into a position that both kept his legs straight and didn't put pressure on his abdominal wound. It was impossible to get comfortable. He worked on a poem he'd been composing for the past couple of days, hoping it would put him to sleep.

Sammy's cot was in the corner, out of reach of the other patients. Also, farthest from the door and on the opposite side of the room from the window, perhaps to prevent him from escaping should he decide to take his chances in the jungle.

Now, as Frankie approached his isolated spot, he wondered what she intended. Not to empty his bedpan—Clarice had already seen to it. His bandages had been changed that afternoon, and his leg was immobilized in plaster. He was facing her and let his eyes crack open as she approached. She stood over him, a dark, watching shadow. There was something in her hands, but he couldn't pick it out in the dim light filtering in from the hallway.

Frankie was a tall woman, big boned. With her strong features, she'd have been considered ugly in Japan, like all of them but the little Filipina nurse. Otherwise, there was nothing inherently unpleasant about her face that Sammy could see. She seemed to be aging well, anyway. A couple of the older soldiers in the ward even included Frankie in their talk about the nurses and their relative attractiveness.

But that was when the ugly look didn't creep over her face, as Sammy had seen several times. When she poked too hard at Sammy's wounds, there was a cruel upturn to her lips that rendered her whole face as unpleasant as an *oni*, an ogre from Japanese folklore. She wore that look now, a sneer, a glint in her eyes.

Frankie glanced over her shoulder at Clarice, who was leaving the room with a bucket of waste from the emptied bedpans. When the younger nurse was gone, Frankie turned back around, and now Sammy caught sight of what she held in her hand. His stomach turned over.

It was a syringe.

Let her. The thought came unbidden to his mind. *Let her stick the needle in, let the sleep wash over you. Think of a suitable death poem, and let it end.*

Frankie stood over him for a few moments, then dropped the syringe into the pocket of her nurse's dress. She wasn't going to do it. Perhaps she hadn't meant to at all.

Sammy moved. He propped himself on an elbow and yawned loudly. "A little morphine would help."

"What?" Frankie asked. She sounded startled.

"Morphine. Isn't that what's in the syringe? It would deaden the pain. I wouldn't mind."

Her lips curled. "I'm not going to waste morphine on you." Other men stirred around them at her raised voice.

"Ah, well. My mistake."

Sammy made a show of trying to get comfortable but didn't close his eyes until she'd moved off. In a moment, she'd left the room, and he allowed himself to breathe more easily. His fellow patients settled back down with grunts and shifting about.

He couldn't shake the feeling that she'd been standing above him with a lethal dose of morphine, concentrated enough to stop his heart. A little prick in his sleep, hardly detectable above the background discomfort of fleas and mosquitoes.

Until that moment, Sammy hadn't seriously considered trying to escape. For one thing, how? Hobble into the jungle and attempt a lengthy trek to the lowlands while his enemies searched for him? He'd be fortunate if the Americans recaptured him instead of the Filipinos. American soldiers may hate him, but they had rules and generally followed them. The Filipinos would be all too happy to take their revenge for the atrocities of the Japanese army.

And then there was his own army. If he came staggering out of the jungle with the evidence of American medical care about him, how would that go over? The Kempeitai would have him. He'd be forced to give up the location of the people who had, after all, saved his life.

Never mind his own brother. Armed with Sammy's letter, Yoshi might very well be searching for him right now. Come to arrest him for his treachery.

But seeing that syringe in Miss Frankie's hand had changed everything. He couldn't stay here and worry that he was going to be murdered. He had to get out of here. Now, tonight, while the woman was disoriented, wondering if Sammy had discovered her plan.

He eased himself from his cot to the floor, the broken leg outstretched and stiff in its plaster cast. None of the other men in his room were moving, but low voices came from the adjacent room, and he knew that nurses were out and about. He'd have to leave through the back door, into the rice paddies behind the hospital.

Sammy had two choices: hop loudly or scoot across the floor on his backside until he had a way to move himself. He opted to scoot. The movement hurt his injured belly. The cot nearest the door was Jimmy Fárez's, and Sammy had planned to steal the man's crutch. But when he got there, he found the cot empty and the crutch gone.

He silently cursed himself. Fárez was a restless sleeper and frequently up and about when the others weren't, which was why his cot was close to the door. He was probably out with his dog again or trying to bum a cigarette from whomever was on guard duty. Now what?

Sammy grabbed the door frame and got himself to his feet. Maybe out back he could find some villager's hoe or tool and use it as a makeshift crutch. The thought of hobbling into the jungle like that brought a desperate laugh that threatened to burst out and spoil the whole escape.

But no other alternative presented itself. He could steal one of the trucks, but how could he manage the clutch and brake with a broken leg?

Maybe he could take a hostage and force him to drive out of the mountains to the Japanese army. Where would he get a weapon to take a hostage? What would he do if the man refused—kill him and try again with someone else? How ridiculous.

His escape lasted all of five minutes and twenty feet. He'd reached the hallway but now stood helplessly looking at the back door, knowing he would only turn around and crawl back to his cot, hoping nobody spotted him returning. Hoping that Frankie left him alone.

The door to the surgery opened before he could move. Out came Fárez, hobbling on his crutch. Louise was behind him, carrying Stumpy, who wasn't moving. The dog seemed dead.

"With any luck, he'll sleep until morning," she told Fárez. "Make a bed for him beneath your cot, but be sure to tie him up. He'll wake up disoriented and—"

The corporal spotted Sammy standing beneath the bare bulb in the corridor and came to an abrupt halt. Louise bumped into him and nearly dropped the dog.

Fárez balanced on one leg and swung his crutch around, holding it out like a club, ready to bash Sammy over the head.

Sammy leaned against the wall and held out a hand. "No, don't."

"What are you doing out here?" Fárez demanded.

"I couldn't sleep. I wanted some air, that's all."

The man glared, clearly disbelieving. But as he took in the cast, the way Sammy couldn't support himself, Fárez seemed to note the ridiculous futility of an escape attempt, and the notion dropped from his face. Of course Sammy wasn't trying to escape. That would have been ridiculous.

Louise's sharp expression took longer to fade. "Go on, Corporal. My arms are getting tired. Let's get the two of you settled."

"What about him?" Fárez asked, gesturing with his crutch.

"Sammy isn't going anywhere. I'll see what he needs when we're done."

They disappeared into the room with the dog, leaving Sammy standing awkwardly in the hallway. Louise made soothing noises once she got inside, reassuring the other men that there was no excitement, to go back to sleep. Sammy waited, sure that one of the other nurses would soon come out and see him standing there, which would only complicate matters. Nobody did.

Louise emerged a moment later and told him to wait. She went to the supply room with her key in hand and returned a few minutes later with a pair of wooden crutches. "We should leave through the back door, don't you think?"

Sammy followed her outside. Hope stirred in him, unfamiliar after these days of pain and worry. The rain was fading into a drizzle, and the clouds scattered from the night sky to reveal stars and a half-moon, but it was still plenty dark. Louise warned him to watch his footing, then helped as he got settled under the awning, back leaned against the wall for support.

She rustled in the pocket of her dress. "Would you like a cookie?"

"A cookie?"

"A snickerdoodle, to be precise. They're stale—the cookies came in the mail from my mother over a month ago, before all this started. But they taste okay if you haven't had anything sweet for a while."

"And you've been saving them all this time? That's some self-discipline."

"It's the last one."

"I couldn't eat your last cookie."

"Half a cookie, then." She groped for his hand and pressed it in.

Louise was right. It *was* stale. Not only that, but these last years in Japan and then the army had changed his tastes, and a treat had become a rice cake filled with red bean paste or sweet, chewy *dangos* on a stick. The half of a cookie didn't appeal.

But the small, kind gesture brought a lump to his throat. So much cruelty in this war. He'd stepped over dead bodies so badly mangled that he couldn't tell if they were Japanese or Chinese, men or women. He'd seen his own troops cut down as they were ordered cruelly to charge fixed gun positions to gain some small advantage in a larger assault. Sometimes, he wished he'd been among those ordered to sacrifice themselves in the name of the emperor.

"Are your parents alive?" Louise asked.

The question surprised him. He hadn't yet reached the point of thinking of his mother and father, but his thoughts had been sliding in that direction, and it was as if she'd sensed the turn of his mind.

"Yes, last I heard. My mother is in weak health, so you never quite know. I hope she's all right. How about yours?"

"Alive and still working the farm," Louise said. "My dad will do it until the day he dies. My mom is . . . tired. It's a hard life, and she's been ready to sell the farm for years. She encouraged me to leave. Pushed me out the door, practically, to get me off the farm. Dad wasn't too happy when he heard my plans."

"Domineering sort?" he asked.

"Not at all. Well . . ." She hesitated, seemed to turn it over. "I love my father, you've got to understand that. He's a gentle man, rarely raised his voice and never hit us. Loves his kids. But, well, he has his expectations. You should have seen his face when I told him about the nursing training, my plans for the army. What did he think, that I wanted to be a farmer's wife like my mom? But I hated disappointing him."

"Disappointed parents—sounds very Japanese."

"Are your parents like that?" she asked.

Sammy sensed that she was starting to dig, to look for something else, and he fell silent, worried what that would be. As the rain ceased, insects hidden in niches beneath the awning started up their nighttime calls.

"Sammy," Louise said in a quiet voice. "Where were you going just now?"

"Going? Oh, nowhere. I wanted a little fresh air, is all."

"There's nobody else around, Sammy. No need to lie."

"Lie? About what? Are you saying I was trying to escape?" He affected a laugh. "I'm crippled, I'm miles from the Japanese army. They'd shoot me as a deserter anyway if I somehow managed to reach them. Nah, I was going out for a breath of fresh air, I told you."

"Are you going to make me report it to Lieutenant Kozlowski?"

"Report that I was trying to escape with a broken leg? Like I said, that would be crazy."

"I know what I saw, and I know Kozlowski will believe me. Go on, Sammy. Give me a reason, something that doesn't sound like you finding your buddies and ratting us out."

The only answer was the buzz of insects, now rising to a crescendo.

"I'm going to die here," Sammy said at last. "You know that, don't you? I won't survive this war."

"Don't be morbid. You have as good a chance as anyone."

"I doubt I'll survive this camp, but if I do, I'm probably dead anyway. And you know something, it might be for the best. I have no country, I have no people."

"Sammy, what are you talking about?"

He didn't answer, couldn't. Not for a long moment, and then he wanted to tell Louise everything. It wouldn't change the past, and it couldn't alter his future, but telling her would be like removing a stone from the pit of his stomach.

"Let me tell you about Nanking," he said at last.

Chapter Twelve

We Japanese have been born in a country of no mean blessings, and thanks to the august power and influence of His Majesty the emperor our land has never once, to this day, experienced invasion and occupation by a foreign power. The other peoples of the Far East look with envy upon Japan; they trust and honor the Japanese; deep in their hearts they are hoping that, with the help of the Japanese people, they may themselves achieve national independence and happiness.

"Read This Alone: And the War Can Be Won"—pamphlet given to soldiers of the Imperial Japanese Army as they were sent into war

December 13, 1937, Nanking, China

Four years earlier, Sachihiro Mori had stood with a company of troops on the outskirts of Nanking. His heart was pounding and his mouth dry. The towering stone walls of the city loomed above them and in another era must have seemed as immovable as a mountain range. But they had crumbled under the relentless artillery bombardment of the last few days. Smoke trailed into the sky inside the city, and word had it that departing Chinese forces had lit half of Nanking on fire as they departed.

Sammy's troops had come under heavy fire last night as the Chinese opened a breach in the Japanese lines to flee the city. Many Chinese had not made it. The bodies of drowned soldiers and civilians clogged the Yangtze. Their war was at an end.

The Chinese army had supposedly abandoned Nanking to its fate, but the Japanese artillery kept pounding through the night and into the morning. Even now, small-arms fire sounded from both inside and outside the city walls, although Sammy's sector was quiet. Men were chanting eagerly around him, and the shouts of officers rose above the din, warning soldiers to check their ammunition, to make sure their bayonets were fixed.

Outside the walls, telephone wires dangled from drunk poles, and the abandoned buildings looked like mouths filled with rotten teeth, with their gaping windows and gutted storefronts. A dead horse stank nearby, squirming with maggots. The badly burned body of a Chinese woman dangled from the window of a charred car overturned on the side of the street.

"Get ready, men!" an officer cried.

The soldiers around Sammy started shouting *"Tenno heika banzai!"*—long live the emperor!—as well as other chants and slogans to the emperor and the homeland. Sammy mouthed the chants, but his throat was dry, and no sound came out. A feeling of doom had been spreading for days, and now it felt like he'd swallowed a live grenade that was about to explode.

The Japanese were ordered to advance into the city. It was disciplined, in formation, but there was a restless energy all around Sammy. These men had been fighting since Shanghai, had suffered casualties, deaths, forced marches on empty stomachs. They were angry, frustrated, and triumphant in turn—this was all somehow palpable at once, and dangerous.

There was no opposition as they entered Nanking.

Debris littered the road inside the gate: discarded uniforms, abandoned guns and knives, overturned carts and military field pieces. A sniper took a shot at them—the first resistance—while they were dragging away a burned truck blocking the road, and for the next twenty minutes they shot at the surrounding buildings while women and children tried to escape under fire.

Sammy and five others were sent to clear out another building. Inside they found a man frantically trying to strip out of a policeman's uniform. Someone bayoneted him.

They found an old couple in one of the upstairs apartments. Sammy feebly protested while his fellow soldiers bashed the old man over the head with rifle butts. The woman wouldn't stop screaming, so they threw her out the window.

Back in the street, Sammy went to Lieutenant Soto and told him what had happened. The men were out of control, and they needed to be brought back in line before it got worse.

Soto scowled at the complaint. "And what do you expect me to do about it, Mori? The buildings must be cleared of hostile elements."

Rifle fire punctuated his words, and Sammy and the lieutenant looked across the street as several crying, begging Chinese men were led out of another building, shoved against a wall, and shot. A boy of about twelve ran screaming from a building, and a soldier casually lifted his rifle and fired. Not only did he miss, but he'd also fired in the direction of another group of soldiers, who were coming out of a building on the opposite side of the street, and they took umbrage. The shooter's fellows came to his defense, and the two sides stood screaming at each other while the boy escaped, dodging overturned cars and abandoned field pieces.

Sammy dragged his gaze away from the spectacle. "'Hostile elements.' What does that mean?" he asked Soto. "We're going to kill every male in the city? Is that what you're talking about?"

"Of course not. But we must first establish order, wouldn't you agree? And until order is established . . ." Another shrug.

Order? Men were wandering off on their own with every block they progressed into the city. Their officers either followed as one of the pack or stood around helplessly like Soto. Heaven help them if there were actual organized Chinese troops in the city, the way discipline was collapsing minute by minute.

That night Sammy found himself bedding in an abandoned house with four other soldiers, who all seemed alarmed by or even terrified of the destruction going on around them. None were from his unit, but such niceties as regimental organization seemed to have broken down throughout much of the occupied city. Through the window came the sound of individual rifle shots. Again and again and again. This was punctuated by shouts, laughter, shrieks, and screams.

The next day was worse. Three times soldiers burst into the home where Sammy and his fellow nonparticipants were bivouacked, wild-eyed men with violence on their minds. Someone from his group set out to rejoin his troops but returned a few hours later. He was white faced and refused to say what he'd seen.

On the third day, twenty or thirty soldiers marching past in formation convinced Sammy that the anarchy had ended. He ventured into the city to look for his regiment. The electricity was out across Nanking, with fires burning everywhere. Bodies lay in the street, often maimed. So many dead men, but perhaps the Chinese males weren't getting the worst of it. Twice, bands of sloppy-looking soldiers grabbed Sammy, grinning, urging him to join their search for "prostitutes," which seemed to be any woman or girl foolish enough to be caught by the Japanese.

Pay the prostitutes? Of course not. The Japanese had already paid with blood and sacrifice. The filthy Chinese whores would be lucky if they were left with their lives.

Sammy escaped this group and others wanting him to join in looting and random destruction. He was encouraged when he found his regiment, or part of it, anyway, and even more relieved when Soto had them marching off to the so-called safety zone, where the international community huddled in terror, waiting for the situation to stabilize.

This must be when it stops, Sammy thought. Three days of anarchy, but it would come to an end now. The foreigners were watching, and that would shame the Japanese into behaving better.

What a deluded fool he was in those days.

———o———

"Please stop," Louise said. Her stomach had been twisting in knots, and now she felt sick.

"I haven't been sharing details," Sammy said. "Only showing you the outlines. A bare sketch. The violence went on for weeks. The army was a mob, a horde, no better than the barbarian tribes that used to cross the Great Wall from Mongolia. In late December, our generals declared an end to the violence. They declared an amnesty for former Chinese soldiers who confessed. Hundreds did. They were promptly executed. And the killings and rapes and robbery went on and on. Another month, longer."

"Why tell me these things, to make me hate you, hate the Japanese? Why, Sammy?"

"So you'll understand."

"Understand what?" she pleaded. "I know about the Rape of Nanking. The whole world does."

"Yes, and part of the reason you know is because of me."

His voice had been distant while he told his story, as if he were floating in the darkness above his body, telling a story about someone else, but now it took an intense edge.

"I began to write what I saw in a small notebook. I wrote it in English, kept it hidden, ready to destroy it at a moment's notice. The foreigners were huddled, terrified, in the safety zone. They saw plenty of atrocities—our men didn't respect the zone and would drag out Chinese who tried to hide in it—but nothing compared to what I witnessed. Later I made a contact with a man from the German embassy, and—"

"A German!" Louise said with a bitter laugh. "May as well have thrown your notebook on the fire as give it to a Nazi. As if they care about such things as rape and murder. Do you know what they're doing in Poland? In Russia?"

"This was 1937, and they weren't all Nazis in the embassy, not here in Asia. I trusted this one, and only gave him a copy, just in case."

"And what did he do with it?"

"Large excerpts were published in European and American newspapers, so he didn't burn my report. I knew he wouldn't—he was horrified by what was happening, no matter what the Germans have done since then.

"It was well known that the source of the information was a Japanese soldier," Sammy added. "There was talk of traitors and defeatists. If it had got out to the Kempeitai that the account had been written in English—"

"The Kempeitai is the secret police?"

"Right, if it had got out to the secret police that the account was in English—and not told to a foreigner, as my German friend made it sound—they'd have found me easily enough. There weren't that many fluent English speakers in the Japanese expeditionary force that took Nanking. My own brother is secret police and would have no doubt arrested me. He has become a fanatic. Can you imagine that? A boy who wouldn't study his letters, who scoffed at everything that was beautiful about Japan, who said that he wasn't a Japanese, he was an American. Who grew up in Hawaii, with his feet in the sand and a surfboard by his side, caring nothing for his homeland. Now Yoshi would see the whole of Asia burn and Japan stand astride it, dominating until the end of time."

"It's an ugly thing you've fought for, Sammy Mori," Louise said.

"I know."

"A legacy of violence and destruction. China was a great country and civilization, and the Japs dismembered it. What possible justification do you have? Tell me, Sammy. What possible reason?" She had a bitter taste in her mouth, a physical, tangible thing, and she was so angry that a tremble worked down her limbs. "The world would be better if Japan never existed, if a giant earthquake blasted the islands to the bottom of the sea."

"Look up at the sky," he told her.

There was something solemn in his voice that made her look up. A warm breeze murmured through the leaves of the nearby trees. The air was thick and moist. The clouds had cleared, and the stars glimmered in the vast black bowl of the night, vibrating, moving against each other.

"A night in summer," Sammy said, his voice quiet. "Even the stars whisper to each other."

"What is that? Did you write that?"

"Me? No, of course not. That is a famous poem from my country. Kobayashi Issa, a great poet. Miss Louise, you haven't been to Japan, or you wouldn't have said that. Let me tell you something. I took a trip to Kyoto two weeks before they shipped me to China for my first taste of war. It was my last leave before the nightmare that was to become my life.

"I went to see the beauties of Kyoto: the Golden Pavilion, the Pure Water Temple, the Path of Philosophy. The Inari torii gates stretching like a line of red sentinels up the mountainside." Sammy's voice glowed like that of a man describing his lover's naked body. "What you see there is sublime. An understanding of what is beautiful and pleasing to the eye that speaks to your ancestral soul. I would say it is purely Japanese, but foreigners feel it, too."

"And yet there is the Rape of Nanking," she said.

"And yet." His sigh contained a deep anguish that seemed to come from his bones. "Miss Louise, how is it possible that those two things come from the same source? How is it possible?"

"I don't know." Her anger had faded, and now she felt only sadness. "Germany is the land of Goethe and Bach, after all."

"Here is another poem from Issa, Miss Louise, if you will allow me to indulge myself."

"Go ahead."

A carp dying in his basin
Spends his last moments
Thrashing the water with his fins.
So man wastes his short life
In senseless agitation.

"Okay," Louise said tentatively, turning the words of the poem over in her mind.

"Since Nanking, my soul has been in a state of turmoil. Senseless agitation? I don't know, maybe. I can't change what I saw, and I can't take responsibility for it, either. I did what I could—my hands are clean, as Christians say. But I was raised to believe in Japan. My brother struggled against it in Hawaii, but in those days, *I* was the fanatic. But now I've seen things that can't be unseen. And so I engage in senseless agitation. I engage in self-destructive behavior."

"Like tonight?"

"Like tonight," he said. "When I was about to set off into the jungle to escape. Miss Frankie came on her rounds, and I thought for a moment she had a syringe filled with morphine."

"What are you talking about?"

"Nothing, it was a fantasy. A fantasy that Frankie would give me a lethal dose of morphine and I would slip away to somewhere calmer. She was standing over me with a syringe in her hand, and I thought, 'I'll just lie here, pretending to be asleep. In a few minutes it will be over.'"

"That's ridiculous. Miss Frankie would never do that."

Yet shivers danced down Louise's spine. She pictured Frankie's dark silhouette standing over Sammy with a syringe. Ugly thoughts would be running through Frankie's mind. She had condensed her fear and hatred into a syringe filled with a lethal dosage of morphine to take her revenge on one Japanese soldier.

"I know she wouldn't," he said. "Like I said, it was a fantasy. But that put other thoughts into my mind. I would crawl or hobble into the jungle and set off toward the Japanese army."

"You'd never have made it, Sammy."

"I know. That's the whole point. I'd either be shot by enemies or collapse to die of thirst or snakebite. And if I did somehow reach the Japanese, I'd be killed because of another moment of senseless agitation."

"*Another* moment?" She smiled gently. "How often do you suffer these lapses, soldier? Is this a daily occurrence, or weekly?"

"I'm not a strong man, not mentally. And you need to be to survive this madness. I can't look away while they cut the ears off a screaming prisoner. I can't see my comrades blown in two, come across the bodies of the dead lying in heaps. There's an expression in Japanese—*ashita no kougan, yuube no hakkotsu*—a rosy face in the morning, white bones in the evening. Life is so fragile, so easily destroyed. Once I saw a child sucking at his mother's breast. Five minutes later he was facedown in the mud, dead, while men had their way with his mother."

Louise felt immediately guilty for the flippant remark that had stirred these memories in him. "Don't tell me any more. I don't need to know."

"I'm sorry, I'm sorry." Sammy swallowed loudly, and continued a moment later. "The point is that I'd seen it all in China. This invasion would be more of the same—more killing, more horrors of war. It wouldn't surprise me if the army is doing right now in Manila what they did to Nanking. We were warned, of course, told to maintain our discipline, so maybe not, but that's what I was expecting."

"Then it's a good thing you're here with us instead of in Manila."

"You know what I think? I think maybe I threw myself in front of your truck. I don't remember the exact moment, but maybe I had a flash of courage and did it on purpose so I wouldn't have to face the rape of Manila."

"I was watching when the truck hit you," she said. "You had a look of surprise on your face. If you did it on purpose, it wasn't through any forethought."

"Ah, well. I should have known." He sounded disappointed in himself.

"Did you do something else? Is that what you're talking about?"

"Yes."

"Sammy?"

"I sent my brother a letter. I confessed to everything, told him that I was the one who'd written the reports of Nanking that were then shared on newsreels around the world."

"Your brother in the secret police?" she asked, aghast. "Why would you do such a thing?"

"So he'd arrest me, of course."

Chapter Thirteen

Yoshiko Mori was quickly disabused of the hope that he would quickly find his brother. After leaving Baliuag, he and Lieutenant Fujiwara came down to Route 3 so they could find the road into the mountains taken by the American evacuees. But army roadblocks stopped them twice, and Mori had to call back to headquarters to get Colonel Umeko to force matters.

The second time, the colonel sounded agitated. "Mori, what the devil is this about? I don't have time for this nonsense."

No, obviously not. That's why it took so much blasted time to move forward. If Umeko would spend a few minutes on the radio himself, he could open the path for Mori all the way to Bataan.

Mori gritted his teeth and ignored the chuckles from the IJA soldiers in the guard post who could hear Umeko's tinny shouting, even though the receiver was at Mori's ear.

"It's important, sir, part of my forward base for cutting off partisan activity. We spoke of it, remember?"

"Right, but you said nothing about needing an armed escort. You think the army can spare the men when they're fighting Americans? There's fifty thousand enemy troops still at large on Bataan."

"But we're taking fire, sir. There are snipers and deserters and villagers with guns. The two of us can't go alone into the mountains."

"And you know what else? I'm getting word from the IJA that you're mucking around with their prisoners and threatening their officers."

"They were obstructing. Is that a problem, sir?"

"Dammit, Mori, yes. In this case, it is. You apparently promised Major Noguchi thirty bottles of scotch, and I had to pay it out when you failed to deliver."

"It was *twenty* bottles, and I never planned to pay out. The bastard was extorting me, and I told him I'd do it so he'd give me what I needed." Mori shook his head and shifted the radio receiver to the other hand. "I can't believe you paid him."

"Mori!" Colonel Umeko's voice roared over the radio, scratchy with static, but full of fury.

"Sorry, sir. My apologies, sir."

"Noguchi isn't any old major. His cousin is a general in the Forty-Eighth, and he can cause us trouble if he wants."

"I need to get past one more roadblock and I'll be able to get into the mountains. I haven't seen Noguchi since Baliuag and don't plan to interact with the man again. I'm almost to the front, sir."

"Not for long, you're not. Get your ass back to Manila—it's a mess here, and I need you to sort out these foreign civilians. They keep yelling about their rights and privileges, and I don't have time for it. I'm trying to stop the bloody looting."

"But, sir—"

"No, Mori. That's an order. You can chase down partisans when you've got things settled here. I'll see you tonight in the Manila Polo Club. Got it?"

"Yes, sir."

Mori handed the radio to the operator, who wore a large, buck-toothed grin like something out of American propaganda. Other IJA soldiers stood around the shack that was headquarters for the signal corps, and there were grins all around. Mori took Fujiwara outside.

"That was a disappointment, sir," Fujiwara said.

Mori glanced toward the truck. Their new driver sat on the hood, smoking a cigarette. His shirt was off, and grease smeared his face. The sky was closing over again, and it seemed like it would rain some more.

What if he ignored the colonel's order? What if he got in his truck and kept going? He was only a mile or two from the road that must be the one taken by the Americans. He could enact his own personal *gekokujō*. A little insubordination in service of the greater cause, which was recovering a traitor and wiping out an untidy nest of partisans before it had a chance to establish itself in the mountains.

No, he couldn't do that. But maybe there was an alternative, so the trail wouldn't get too cold.

"Do you remember that village we passed through about a mile back?" Mori said.

"The one with the Christian shrine to their virgin queen, sir?"

"That's right, it was named Santa Maria, wasn't it?"

Soldiers, thinking they were being clever, had uprooted the statue of the Virgin Mary from her shrine, carted her out to the road, and hung a sign in Japanese around her neck, reading: "This Way to the Christian Brothel."

"It would be a good place for a Kempeitai post. It's off the main military highway, but close enough to both the Central Luzon Plain and the mountains to keep an eye on both."

"So we're not going back to Manila like the colonel ordered?" Fujiwara asked.

Was Mori imagining it, or was there an element of doubt in the lieutenant's voice? What would he do if ordered to disobey Colonel Umeko? Where would his loyalties fall?

"He didn't order you to Manila, he ordered me."

"That is true, sir." Now Fujiwara sounded relieved.

"I'll go back and sort out this mess with the foreigners. You'll take position in Santa Maria and establish our post. Don't worry, I'll send support. More law soldiers so you won't be abandoned and vulnerable. And money to pay informers. Give me five days, then I'll be back in person."

It wasn't five days, unfortunately. The situation in Manila wasn't as chaotic as what he'd seen in China, but the city struggled with electricity, with looting, with random fires and occasional murders of Japanese civilians and soldiers. These killings were paid back tenfold, and by official decree.

Mori distributed a proclamation to the newspapers as they resumed publication:

Anyone who inflicts, or attempts to inflict, an injury upon Japanese soldiers or individuals shall be shot to death. If the assailant or attempted assailant cannot be found, we will hold ten influential persons as hostages who live in and about the streets where the events happened. The Filipinos should understand our real intentions and should work together with us to maintain public peace and order.

He kept hidden that he'd written this notice himself, not wanting to expose his knowledge of English when it was unnecessary.

Mori then set about with other secret police to round up foreign nationals in the city. With the exception of a few Germans, all the whites—Europeans, Americans, Canadians, and Australians—were shipped to the University of Santo Tomás for internment. A rock wall already surrounded the university, and Mori had it topped with barbed wire. A wrought-iron fence marked the front of the university, and Mori had it blocked off with woven bamboo mats to cut down on communication and smuggling to the internees.

Most of the foreigners complied with the orders to surrender to the new authorities. Some even seemed relieved to gather in one place where they could presumably be safe from Japanese soldiers. A handful tried to hide or escape the city. These were dragged off and occasionally beaten as an example to the others. Regrettably, a few foreigners died in the roundups, as well as several dozen Filipinos shot or hung for helping them.

Unfortunately this all took time. And then Colonel Umeko had Mori interrogating locals to serve in the new administration. There were plenty of volunteers—that was never a problem in an occupation—but by definition such people weren't very loyal. Mori sent a few men up the road to Fujiwara, as well as supplies, but grew increasingly anxious to return to Santa Maria as the days dragged on. This was tedious business, mopping up in an increasingly tranquil city while the surrounding countryside and mountains teemed with uncaptured enemies and Filipino partisans.

Finally, in mid-January, the colonel allowed Mori to leave the city, but with conditions. He was only given three more secret police to join the four already in Santa Maria, not twenty armed men, as he'd requested. Ten thousand pesos to pay for supplies and buy off the locals, not forty. And he couldn't use the main highway, which was still clogged with military equipment for the army pressing into Bataan to fight the Americans. Back roads only.

Mori left in the middle of a tropical downpour and got stuck three times in the mud. The last time, he bullied some villagers into lending him their carabaos. Remembering his encounter with one of the buffalo a couple of weeks earlier, he kept a wary distance as Filipinos roped the surly beasts to his vehicle. The truck came out sullenly, like a rotten tooth. Mud and water had flooded the engine, and it needed to be cleaned.

It took a full day and a morning to travel the twenty miles to Santa Maria. It was raining so hard, mud and water splattering onto the windshield, that the driver almost passed right through the village without seeing it. The driver hit the brakes hard, cursing, to avoid hitting a person standing in the road.

But when the driver stopped and revved the engine to get the person to move, Mori realized it was the statue of the Virgin Mary with the sign hanging around her neck. What he'd thought were trees on the side of the road was a row of dilapidated nipa huts.

Mori left the others behind and came dripping into the only building in the village with a corrugated-metal roof instead of leaky cogon grass. The metal roof leaked just as badly. Wooden buckets collected the drips. Lieutenant Fujiwara bent over a crude table, writing furiously by lamplight.

He gave a relieved look when he saw Mori, put down the pen, and crumpled the paper.

"I was expecting you yesterday, sir."

"The roads are bad," Mori said. "We spent the night in an open shed fighting off pigs trying to muscle their way out of the rain. What were you writing?"

"I was going to radio the colonel to tell him you never arrived. I was preparing my thoughts, making sure they were well organized."

Mori brushed the water from his clothes. The place seemed to be the lieutenant's home as well as his headquarters, with *patatis*—woven reed mats—laid out in the best approximation of tatami, Japanese-style. He'd set up a small stove on one side of the room, with a pot of half-eaten rice, a cot in the corner, and a few personal belongings in open cupboards to keep them out of the dripping water.

Mori removed his muddy boots before passing the threshold. The two men sat cross-legged opposite each other on one of the mats and shared information. Mori's was sketched only. His lieutenant didn't need the boring details of the Manila operations, and Mori was anxious to hear what Fujiwara was up to.

"The Sakdals weren't cooperative at first," Fujiwara said. "I threatened them, their livelihood, their families. Nothing seemed to work. But I thought of the old saying, 'What brings profits, brings people.' Instead of breaking thumbs, I decided to bribe them to be cooperative."

"You'll catch more flies with honey than vinegar," Mori said, nodding.

Fujiwara blinked. "That's clever, did you just think of that, sir?"

"I'm not sure, but anyway, it doesn't matter," Mori said with a wave of a hand. He was pretty sure he'd dredged it from English, now that he thought of it. "Go on."

"The bounty is a hundred pesos for an American, alive or dead. But what if I paid a few of them ten or twenty pesos first, in advance of any information? That brought the bandits out of the hills, let me tell you."

Mori couldn't help but chuckle. "And how much money did you waste this way?"

"Almost a thousand pesos, sir."

That much? He'd expected a hundred or two. A thousand meant Fujiwara had paid off somewhere between fifty and a hundred different men, by his own admission. Free money, and nothing in return. Fujiwara was lucky he hadn't thrown it all away. Give it a few more weeks and no doubt he would.

Yet there was a confidence in the lieutenant's posture and voice that said he was pleased with the results. Mori bit back a sarcastic retort and nodded for the other man to go on.

"Most of it was wasted, that's true enough. Some of those Sakdals slipped away and haven't been heard from since—doubtful they'll be seen again in these parts. One of the men I paid off was later caught with American rifles and several hundred rounds of ammunition stuffed beneath a grass mattress. He was tied up in the sun for two days and then shot."

"Yes, yes. But what came of it? Anything at all?"

"*Hai.* The Sakdals unearthed an American pilot who'd been hiding for the past two weeks in a nearby village. We sent the pilot to a camp and took care of the Pinoy who was hiding him. There were a pair of British nationals—a mining employee and his wife—who ran for the hills. We caught them. They're off to Manila as well."

"So, one pilot and two civilians. That hardly justifies the expenditure of a thousand pesos."

Mori was already thinking gloomily about how Colonel Umeko would react when the report came his way. Too much money, not enough result. Time to abandon the effort.

Fujiwara was not done, however. A slight upturn to his lips gave away his secret before he spoke it.

"Oh, and I might know where your brother is, sir."

Mori stiffened. "Well?"

"News flows through the rural areas, mouth to ear, mouth to ear. The village head calls it the bamboo telegraph. So keep in mind this has passed through four or five retellings."

"Quickly, Lieutenant. I'm growing impatient."

"Some Americans went into the mountains, all right—three different people told me as much. A white doctor and some female nurses, together with injured soldiers, both Americans and Pinoys. They're in a village called Sanduga or Sanbuga—something like that—and they're apparently still there. Not easy terrain to traverse, but if the Americans did, we can, too."

"This is good information," Mori said. "Get the doctor, the nurse, and the wounded soldiers, and it will be worth the money, for sure. But what about my brother?"

"Ah yes. Apparently there's a Japanese man with them, sir. A soldier. He has a broken leg. I only found this out yesterday, when I was expecting you to be here. And get this: he speaks English."

"Yes, that would be my brother." Mori's voice came out flat, yet his emotion kept boiling beneath the surface.

So Sammy was still alive. That was both welcome and unwelcome. Mori had been dreading the news that the hospital evacuees had been killed, or that he'd find the Americans only to discover that they knew nothing of his brother. Or that he'd died in surgery. And he was relieved to discover that Sammy wasn't in the hands of the enemy army on the Bataan Peninsula, ready to broadcast his treasonous remarks over the radio.

But if Sammy had been killed, even if he'd disappeared without a trace like so many others in this war, so many problems would have been resolved.

"What have you done about it so far?" Mori asked.

"Nothing yet, sir. I was waiting for you to arrive before acting. But I continued making my inquiries, and I have more information."

"Good. Tell me."

"You know the road we were trying to reach before the army turned us back?" Fujiwara shook his head. "That's not it, sir. That continues up to the side of the Bataan, and we'd only run into the American army if we tried."

"No worries of that. We'd be stopped by General Homma's troops long before we reached the front. So how do we get there? Colonel Umeko still won't let us move forward from Santa Maria."

"We don't have to go forward, sir. The road *north* out of town will take us to the mountain pass, and on we go. We could get there in a day's march, but we'd need at least twenty armed men to do it. The mountains are infested with bandits and partisans."

"We don't have twenty men," Mori said. "And won't until this business on Bataan is settled, and that might take weeks. We have eight law officers, counting the two of us. You say we need twenty?"

"To be honest, sir, I'd suggest thirty. To be sure."

Mori gritted his teeth in frustration. The enemy was near. Not deep in the mountains, where they'd be hard to root out, but close enough that a strong enough force could finish them in a single blow.

A plan began to form in Mori's mind. With a few more seconds of thought, he knew what needed to be done.

Chapter Fourteen

After two straight days of rain, Louise was so relieved to see the sun that the heat almost didn't bother her. She and her fellow nurses worked in the shade cast by a row of trees that grew along the dike between two rice paddies behind the hospital. The mountains loomed green and mist-shrouded against a brilliant blue sky. Birdsong filled the air like a hundred flutes and whistles all playing different tunes.

The nurses were sharpening needles on stones, which had dulled again from constant use. The pressure cookers sat on wood fires in the open, far enough away to keep from passing along heat, but close enough to take advantage of the wood smoke, which kept away mosquitoes and other bugs. Louise was grateful for that; two more men had come down with malaria, and they were going through quinine at a rapid rate. But it wasn't easy to maintain stove pressure burning wood, so the fire needed regular attention.

Stumpy had followed them outside. His swollen testicle was gone, and he'd recovered quickly without losing his swagger. Now he was nudging around the women, hoping to be fed. Louise shooed him off, and he trotted away with his nose in the air before settling into the shade of a banana tree. He gave a loud and aggrieved sigh.

"The silly thing probably smells our lunch," Maria Elena said. "I don't know about the rest of you, but I'm still hungry."

Louise tried to remind herself to be grateful against the gnawing, hollow ache in her belly. "It was nice having a little chicken in the rice for a change, don't you think?"

"I wouldn't mind some pork," Clarice said. "There are a couple of pigs in the village—do you think Lieutenant Kozlowski could buy them?"

"Chicken is good enough," Louise said.

Clarice sighed. "I suppose so."

"I don't care about chicken, I refuse to eat any more rice," Frankie said sourly. "When it's grainy, it looks like insect eggs. When it's sticky, it's like glue. And it's always tasteless. Why can't we have bread?"

Because there was no flour, of course. Anyway, there was no point in answering, as Frankie was just looking for an argument. But Louise was tired of the complaint, of all of Frankie's complaining. It only made things worse.

Anyway, it didn't take a genius to inventory the supplies and see that it was only a matter of weeks before they were down to a diet of rice and mungo beans and whatever else the villagers happened to bring their way. For now, they may as well enjoy the good old staples: canned tuna, beef, pork and beans, and evaporated milk. They wouldn't last long. At least the coffee would hold out for a while. And if a real chicken happened to find its way into the pot once a week, they should take it and not complain.

"When are we going to Bataan?" Clarice asked.

The youngest nurse among them complained less than Frankie, but she couldn't leave this idea of Bataan alone. It was a miracle that Lieutenant Kozlowski and Dr. Claypool had kept their secret hidden so long. It was over two weeks now since Louise had figured it out, but both Frankie and Clarice were still in the dark. Surely Maria Elena knew—she spoke Tagalog, and one of the villagers must have said something—but if so, she hadn't let on.

"We're not going to Bataan until we can move all of the patients," Louise said. "That might be another week."

"We'll never get there, if that's what it takes," Frankie said, "because they keep bringing us new wounded. They're not even Americans anymore."

"Every soldier gets the same care," Louise said.

Frankie snorted. "You're telling me we're going to stay here because some Pinoy kid was stupid enough to take a shot at the Japs and that makes him a soldier?"

"If the lieutenant says he's a soldier, he's a soldier. And once they arrive it doesn't matter anyway. If a man needs medical care, we give it to him."

"Even a Jap?" Frankie said. "Yes, we know you love them all."

Louise ignored the barb. "Anyway, don't get so anxious. We're safer here than on Bataan. Those guns you hear at night aren't fireworks, they're killing people."

She put away the needle she'd been working on and helped Maria Elena unload one of the pressure cookers. The two women heaped the heavy, wet linens into a basket; then the Filipina nurse put the basket on her head and walked around the hospital to hang them to dry on the lines they'd strung between palm trees.

"And we need to remember," Louise said when she took her seat again and picked up the sharpening stone, "our job is to help *all* these men: Americans, Filipinos, and even Japanese soldiers. Every soul counts."

Frankie let out an exaggerated groan. "And you really believe that?"

"And what do you propose? Kill the ones we don't like? Put them out of their misery?"

"I'm working as hard as you are in there, putting in the same hours. Don't try to set yourself up as an angel of mercy."

"I'm not saying you're not," Louise said, frustrated she was being drawn into a pointless argument, yet unable to help herself. "But could you do it with less bellyaching?"

"It's time to face the obvious, that's all I'm saying."

"Really? And what's that? Please tell us."

"It's time to surrender," Frankie said.

"Surrender?" Louise gave her a sharp look. "Where did that come from?"

Frankie's voice rose in pitch. "No, I don't want to do it, of course not."

"You're the one who mentioned it."

"We're going to get caught here, you know we are. And the Japs will be angry because we hid when we were ordered to surrender, and then you know what they'll do!"

Louise shook her head, disgusted. They were going to surrender because the enemy was "angry"? What kind of nonsense was that?

"I don't want to surrender," Clarice said in a small voice.

"Ignore her," Louise told Clarice. "Frankie's trying to get us riled up so we'll go to Kozlowski. Maybe if we all complain, she can get her fantasy of going to Bataan and wait to be rescued."

"It's better than your fantasy of living with the mountain people in peace and harmony," Frankie said. "Louise loves it here, Clarice. She never wants to leave. She loves rice and mungo beans and filthy street dogs and Japs and Pinoys and naked kids peeing in the street. Miss Louise loves it all."

"That isn't fair," Clarice said. "She never asked to be here any more than you did."

Louise felt herself spiraling into a dumb argument with Frankie. She couldn't take that path, or soon enough they'd all be divided, complaining, unhappy. She turned back to her work sharpening needles.

"Fine, ignore me," Frankie said. "See if I care."

"I'll tell you what has me concerned," Louise said a few minutes later. "It's dysentery. Six patients have it already, and now Dr. Claypool is sick, too. Either our water supply isn't clean, or there's something wrong with the food preparation."

"Couldn't it be something else?" Clarice asked.

"Could be, I suppose, but those are the most likely causes. Anyway, we've been lucky that it hasn't hit someone already down with malaria." Louise had been giving the matter some thought. "We've been bathing upstream from the camp. You don't suppose we're contaminating the water supply, do you? How are they filling the cisterns, does anyone know?"

"I'm not moving our bath," Frankie said firmly. "That's the only place we can get any privacy around here."

"We'll have Corporal Fárez and Private Johnson rig us something below the hospital. If they put up a fence with burlap for privacy—"

"No way," Frankie said. "I'm not going to bathe down by the village. It's not just the soldiers staring, or the village kids peering in through your so-called fence. The water is cool up above, and I can stop thinking about blood and surgery and death and the stupid Japs and all of it. Why would you take that away from me?"

Louise sighed and was about to point out that they'd only consider moving the nurses' bathing area after looking into everything else first, when movement from the road caught her eye.

A Filipino came running up the road as it climbed into the village. He was a teenager, thin, wiry, and bare-chested, his lungs heaving, his feet stumbling with exhaustion. Louise recognized him as one of the cargadores who the alcalde—the village head—sent into the lowlands to buy goods to smuggle up to the Americans. Normally he went with his two older brothers, but there was no sign of the brothers, nor was the boy carrying goods.

The boy stopped in front of the nurses and let out a stream of Tagalog between gasps. This brought Stumpy springing to his feet from where he'd been dozing in the shade of the banana tree. Louise shushed his excited barks and tried to make sense of what the boy was saying.

"Oh, for heaven's sake," Frankie said. "What does the Pinoy want now?"

The boy kept shouting, and Louise picked out one word. "Haponese! Haponese!"

"Clarice," Louise said. "Get Maria Elena. Quickly, now."

"Did he say Japanese?" Frankie said. She rose to her feet. "I think he did. What's he going on about?"

Maria Elena hurried back from around the building, her sleeves still rolled up from hanging linens. Clarice came after her, chewing her lip and making worried noises in the back of her throat.

Maria Elena made calming sounds to the young man, who started in again, this time more slowly. Fear lit up the Filipina nurse's face as she listened. Louise forced herself to stay quiet while the man finished, even though her heart was pounding.

At last Maria Elena turned to her. "The Japs have found us. They're coming."

———

Lieutenant Kozlowski and Dr. Claypool met with the nurses in front of the hospital a few minutes later. The village's alcalde was there, too, as well as the young cargador, who was named Diego. Maria Elena translated.

Diego and his brothers had strolled into one of the lowland villages without realizing it was occupied by the enemy. The Japanese seized the two brothers, but Diego escaped into the woods with bullets zipping past his head. As soon as he was safe, he crept back to look for his brothers and see if they could be rescued.

That was when he saw several Japanese and numerous Filipinos armed with machetes and rifles loading into a pair of army trucks. They rolled out of town toward the mountains where the Americans were hiding. Diego came running for home.

"If they have trucks, they'll be here any time!" Frankie said.

"Calm down," Lieutenant Kozlowski said. "The roads are impassable—they'll have to abandon the trucks. Otherwise Diego wouldn't have beat them on foot." He nodded at the boy. "I went down with this one and his brothers a couple of weeks ago. We took out bridges and diverted streams across the road."

Frankie stared, eyes narrowing. The wheels were spinning in her head, Louise could see. Two weeks ago was not long after they'd arrived in Sanduga. The nurse would be wondering why Kozlowski had closed down the road before the Japanese had even arrived.

"Go on," Dr. Claypool urged Diego.

The boy didn't have much more, and they were left short on information. Most importantly, how long until the Japanese arrived? The alcalde thought they might arrive as soon as nightfall, but Kozlowski scoffed at this. You had to think like a military man venturing into unknown and hostile territory, he said. They'd move slowly and camp somewhere safe. There was another village between here and there, and the Japanese would need to secure it. That left the medical camp all day and night to evacuate.

"Tell the alcalde we'll hire every man in the village to haul our goods," Kozlowski said to Maria Elena. "As many cargadores as we can get. And his own people should get ready, too. The villagers have been helping us—they won't want to be caught here when the Japanese arrive."

Louise had been fighting down panic since Diego came running up the road, and now it returned like a stab to the gut. "Some of our patients can't be moved, Lieutenant. What about them?"

"Why not?" Frankie said. "We'll be loading into the trucks, right? Why can't we just drive out of here by that back road? We came in by truck, we'll leave the same way. It can't be worse than the trip up here. How long until we get to Bataan?"

"Miss Frankie," Dr. Claypool said. "Take Clarice. Bundle up the essential supplies, but don't put them into the trucks yet."

"What about them?" Frankie asked Kozlowski with a nod at the two remaining nurses. "Why aren't they helping?"

"I need Maria Elena to translate our needs to the villagers," Kozlowski said smoothly, "and Dr. Claypool has some questions for Louise about the patients."

"Hurry, Miss Frankie," the doctor said. "There's no time to waste."

Maria Elena left with Diego and the alcalde while Frankie and Clarice disappeared into the hospital to set the evacuation into motion.

"She's going to find out soon enough," Louise said to the doctor and the lieutenant.

"And she'll have plenty of time to panic when that happens," Kozlowski said. "Let's see how much work we can get out of her first."

"You're right about the patients," Claypool told her. "We've got a big problem. What's to be done about them?"

"I have no idea." Louise couldn't help a glance toward the village, where people were already scurrying about. "I really don't. Some of those men won't survive a hike through the jungle, even carried on litters. And supposing we get to the next village. What do we do with the survivors? What do we do without our equipment?"

"I've scouted the road already," Kozlowski said. "Stay ahead of the Japs and we'll be okay. We'll lose them on the mountain trails—it's a maze up there. The deeper in we go, the harder it will be for them to get at us."

"But you haven't answered my questions," Louise insisted. "We can't haul everything out of here by hand. We'll have to leave cots and bedding. Heck, what about our pressure cookers? How will we sterilize anything? Wherever we go, we'll have nothing, not even lodging. Is it nipa huts for the lot of them?"

"All of this is a challenge," Dr. Claypool said. "But it's not as bad as you think. There's another stopping point set up."

"You mean another hospital?" Louise asked. "Really?"

"Well, no. It's an old missionary school. Run-down, I'm afraid. Makes this hospital look like Massachusetts General."

"That's hard to imagine."

"Anyway," the doctor continued, "we cached a few things before the war, so the situation isn't hopeless. We'll be challenged with cots and bedding—that's true enough. Challenged with everything, to be honest, but we can make it."

"How long to get there?" she asked.

"It will be a slog," Kozlowski said. "At least two days. Maybe longer."

"Two days." The words hung in the open air, and Louise studied the two men. Their faces were grim. "We've got injured soldiers who can't be hauled two *hours* through the open air, let alone two days."

"I count three men we'll have to leave behind," Claypool said. "Rubens worries me the least. He's an American—he'll be okay. They'll take him as a POW."

"No, they won't," she said. "He's paralyzed. The enemy won't carry him out, and they won't leave him here alive, either."

"And the other two are Pinoys," Claypool added, as if he hadn't heard her objection. "I don't know what to do about them."

"You know *what* to do," Kozlowski told the doctor. "You just don't want to do it."

"I can't believe we're having this conversation," Louise said. "This is nuts. Dr. Claypool, tell him. It's crazy."

"Miss Louise, there's no other choice," Claypool said. "The lieutenant is right. There's no way to keep them from the Japanese, and they won't survive in the woods."

"They'll have to be left behind," Kozlowski said.

"Left behind," she repeated dully.

The lieutenant's face had been set into its usual stern, unsentimental look, like a farmer steeling himself to slaughter his hogs, but now it softened a little. "Maybe we're wrong, and the enemy will turn around before they get here. But if not, we'll make sure all three of them have the means to end it. It's either that, or they fall into enemy hands. This is the best way to save the most men. I know it, the doctor knows it, and you know it, too."

Louise took a deep breath. Her gut twisted in knots, but she managed a nod.

"Now, let's discuss the Japanese prisoner," Kozlowski said.

"The Japanese *patient*, you mean." Louise thrust out her chin. "Sammy Mori is in my care, and he's injured. So if you're suggesting we do something ugly on our way out of here, you can forget it."

"Don't get soft, Miss Louise," Kozlowski said. "You're a war nurse, and you know what happens when an enemy soldier falls into our hands. He's a prisoner, not a patient. I never begrudged you medical people from giving him care, but don't you forget that he's the enemy and always has been. A prisoner, do you understand?"

"And we have obligations to prisoners, too. Right? Or are you suggesting that we do what the Japanese would do? Have him killed?" She felt herself trembling with agitation. "Are *you* going to shoot him? Or tell me to give him a lethal dose of something because you can't face it, knowing you're murdering a man?"

Kozlowski blinked. "That's what you think this is about? Heavens, no."

Dr. Claypool put a hand on her arm, a fatherly gesture of concern. "Sammy Mori is well enough to be let loose," he said. "His abdominal injuries are healing nicely, and his bone is set. There's nothing left for him to do but recuperate. We thought you would consider your duties done and suggest leaving him here for the Japanese to find."

"That's the part I can't allow," Kozlowski said.

"Oh. Yes, I see."

"I wasn't suggesting we kill him," he added, "only warning you that he couldn't be left for the enemy."

"I'm sorry, I don't know why I thought that. It's this war, it's so cruel." Louise managed a short laugh. "I know how these things go. You can't be crying over every death or you'll never survive—you'll have a nervous breakdown."

"We can't turn him over to the Japs," Kozlowski said, as if he was still trying to convince her. "For one, he knows plenty about us. He might give them something useful. For another, he's one more soldier out of commission. We send him back, and he'll have a gun in his hand soon enough. We do that and we might be responsible for more American deaths."

"I understand," she said.

The truth was, Louise wasn't thinking about leaving him to the enemy. Sammy wouldn't want to go back—that's what these two men didn't know. They didn't know how he'd reported the Rape of Nanking, or that he'd confessed to his brother, the military police.

"So we have to take him with us," the lieutenant said. "Question is, can you keep Mori quiet during the evacuation?"

"Miss Frankie has complained about you," Dr. Claypool said. "Most days, in fact, she has something to tell me. Something you've done wrong, something you've said that she doesn't like."

"That doesn't surprise me. You don't put any stock in it, do you?"

"Of course not," Claypool said with a wave of his hand. "Miss Frankie is a complainer by nature. She'll complain about anything. The point is, she says you're too close to this soldier. Fraternizing with the enemy. Now hold on, don't protest. I know it's nothing—you're being kind to him the same way you are to Fárez and Rubens and all the rest. The point is," the doctor added, "you have some rapport with the man, and that makes you most suited to manage him."

"Manage in what way? What do you think he'll do?"

"Maybe nothing," Kozlowski said. "Or maybe he hears what's going on and tries something."

"What sort of something?"

"Could be anything," Kozlowski said. "Sabotage, starting a fire to send up smoke. Escaping into the woods. Grabbing someone's gun. Anything he thinks will help him get back to his own side."

"Oh, I don't think he'll do that," Louise said. "In fact, you're reading him exactly wrong. Sammy is a very depressed man. He blames himself for what he's seen and done. He doesn't want to go back to the army. His conscience is hurting him."

Kozlowski snorted. "Conscience? You think a Japanese soldier has a conscience?"

"We're all born with a conscience, Lieutenant."

"Maybe," Kozlowski said, sounding doubtful. "But if a Jap ever did, if he was born that way, it was drilled out of him. You know they make their officers test their swords on prisoners, right? It's one of their rules. They sharpen it and behead some innocent villager. Proves their sword, proves their manliness. That's how they behaved in China, and it's no doubt how they're behaving here, too."

"That sounds like propaganda," she said. "I'm not saying it doesn't happen, I just can't believe they're mostly that way. Anyway, Sammy's not an officer. He's only a corporal."

"Can you take responsibility for him?" Dr. Claypool asked. "That's the only thing that matters here."

"I think so."

"You need to do more than think it," Kozlowski said. "You need to pull on those farm-girl boots and be hardheaded about it. If Mori pulls anything, if he *tries* to pull anything, you've got your eye on him, right?"

"Yes, sir." She said it more confidently this time.

"Good," the lieutenant said. He gave a curt nod. "Now, enough of this chatting. We've got a camp to evacuate. We don't do that, you'll get to see if I'm right about head chopping with your own eyes."

Chapter Fifteen

They had the hospital camp and the entire village working. Everyone who was capable, from the youngest Filipino children to injured American soldiers, went to work. The nurses identified the critical medical supplies, which the workers hauled into the open air to stack and organize.

Filipino men loaded the supplies into huge baskets, slung them onto their backs, and trudged up the road as soon as they were ready. This was a great sacrifice, as half the village was planning to evacuate with them, and this meant abandoning many of their own possessions so they could carry material from the hospital.

Other villagers carted off barrels to bury in the rice paddies in case they were able to smuggle them out later. Miraculously, nobody had yet asked about the trucks and the back road to Bataan, but Louise knew it was only a matter of time.

Shortly after midnight, they had everyone who could move or be moved out of the hospital into the open air, and a good portion of their supplies out as well. Several men lay on cots, heavily bandaged, missing a foot or leg, or otherwise too sick or injured to walk. The three men who could not be moved remained inside. Louise tried not to think about them.

Kozlowski gathered the nurses. "I'm sending Miss Louise and Miss Frankie ahead with the most badly injured men. With the slowest, who need as much advance time as possible."

"The trucks aren't traveling together?" Frankie asked.

"You're not riding in the truck," Kozlowski said. "There's no room for passengers. Please, no argument. Miss Louise will explain when you're on the road."

Louise said nothing, but inwardly she groaned. She understood well enough why the lieutenant was doing it. Frankie would start arguing, and with the evacuation commanding all of their attention, this was the worst time and place to have this discussion.

The lieutenant cast a glance at Sammy, who leaned against the exterior of the building, away from the men. It was almost dark, and the enemy soldier's face was hidden in the shadows.

"We're taking the Jap?" Frankie asked.

"We can't very well send him back to the enemy," Kozlowski said.

"We should have left him on the road," the nurse said. "Never should have helped him in the first place."

"But we did," Louise said. "So there's nothing to be done for it now."

"Sure there is."

"Will you be quiet and listen to the lieutenant?" Louise snapped.

"Maria Elena spoke to the alcalde," Kozlowski said. "His men will lead you in the dark and carry those who can't walk."

"What about Rubens and the two Filipinos?" Louise asked. "Has anyone spoken to them yet? I should maybe do it before I go."

The lieutenant's expression turned grim. "I did it already. They understand why they can't go, and what to do if they're found." He glanced around at the gathered soldiers and nurses. "That is all. You have your orders. Move."

Louise's advance company consisted of herself, Frankie, four men on litters, eight Filipino litter bearers to carry them, another Filipino carrying a basket strapped to his forehead and an army flashlight in hand to lead them, plus five men on crutches, including Corporal Fárez and Sammy Mori. One scraggly dog with a half tail, a rope around his neck and the other end held tightly in Corporal Fárez's fist, marched along with the ragtag group.

Louise and Frankie inched out of town on the road, hobbling along at the pace of the men on crutches. The cargadores would carry the litters ahead, stop to rest while the others caught up, then set off again.

The two nurses carried bags slung over their shoulders heavy with food and water for their small company, and each had a flashlight. But only Louise had hers on, which she used to illuminate the path ahead.

"I can't believe it," Frankie said. "We're taking that Jap with us and leaving our own men to die. There's something wrong with that. And what about the trucks? Why should we have to walk all night? It's not fair to us as nurses."

"It's going to be a long night if we worry about what's fair and not," Louise said. "Anyway, let's not get the patients worked up, okay?"

"I'm not complaining, I'm only pointing out facts."

They'd passed the stationary trucks about ten minutes ago, but this was the first time that Frankie had mentioned the vehicles aloud, although she'd been sighing loudly since they set out. Louise carefully kept her flashlight trained on the road immediately in front. They were coming to the end of the part that was wide enough for vehicles, as would have been obvious had Louise swept her light from side to side.

Some animal crashed in the brush to their right. Stumpy let out a series of startled barks while Fárez tried to hush him. The dog let out a final, satisfied bark and stopped.

"Keep him quiet, Corporal," Louise called back. "You promised."

"Sorry, Miss Louise. I'm sorry, he'll be a good boy." Then, to the dog, "Why, I've had enough of you. You be good, now."

"Dumb dog," Frankie said. She let out another exaggerated sigh. "Oh, why not? We've got a Jap with us—what's one more mangy animal?"

This brought grumbles from the other men on crutches, not just Fárez, and Frankie stopped, seeming to understand that she'd overstepped herself in criticizing their mascot. Or maybe they'd begun to warm to Sammy. The Japanese soldier wasn't constantly whining, for one.

They trudged along in merciful silence after that, and the older nurse didn't even complain about the mosquitoes. They'd shared a bottle of 6-2-2 No-Bite to rub on their skin, but that didn't seem to do much to keep the bugs away, only made the lot of them smell like repellent.

Finally the jig was up. They came upon the litter bearers resting, and this brought the customary greeting of unintelligible Tagalog and flashlights illuminating the newcomers. Flashlights swept across the road, which was nothing but a thin trail at this point, with a towering, vegetation-choked hillside both above and below. The "road" was a narrow ribbon hugging the hill, wide enough for foot traffic, but nothing else.

"Wait a minute," Frankie said, and Louise braced herself. "We're lost!"

"We're not lost. These villagers know where they're going."

"No, I mean it, we must have taken a wrong turn. Look, the road is gone. It's completely missing. We're on a pig trail or something. You can't get a truck across this."

The injured soldiers came hobbling up to where Frankie had planted herself. Louise tugged her arm, but the other woman wouldn't budge.

"It's not a pig trail," one of the soldiers said. "It's cut right into the hillside, you can see plainly enough."

"You didn't know?" another man asked.

"Guess she *didn't* know," Fárez said. "The rest of us figured it out about an hour ago. You saw it, didn't you, Miss Louise?"

"I'll bet even the Jap figured it out by now," the first man said. "This ain't no road. There never was no road here."

"What are they talking about?" Frankie demanded. "How are the trucks going to pick us up? How are they going to carry us to Bataan?"

Now Sammy joined them, hobbling up last of all. "The trucks aren't going to Bataan," he said. "That was never the plan, was it, Miss Louise?"

The Japanese soldier's voice was flat, his emotions hard to read. A defensive strategy, Louise thought, to hide what he was thinking from these people who would just as soon see him dead. But what did he think of the plan?

Frankie wheeled on Louise. "You knew?"

"I did."

"And you never told me? What's going on here? We can't walk all the way to Bataan with these injured men. It's impossible. And you're telling me it was our plan all along to abandon the trucks? I can't believe that, it doesn't make any sense."

"Oh, shut up, you dumb broad," a voice called. This was one of the men from up front, who was being hoisted up by the litter bearers, ready to set off again.

"Don't you tell me to shut up! You'd be dead if it weren't for me."

"If you don't shut your piehole, you're going to make me wish I were," he said, to laughter from the others.

"Hush," Louise told Frankie, feeling her face flush. "You're making us seem ridiculous."

"I'm going back. That's all there is to it. I'm going back, and I'm demanding that I travel with the soldiers who can walk. If I have to walk all the way to Bataan, I won't be stuck with these cripples."

Her flashlight came on, and she trudged off the way they'd come. Louise started to say something, then thought better of it.

"You're letting her go?" Sammy asked, watching as the light bounced along in the direction from which they'd come. It vanished around the corner.

"She'll figure it out soon enough, even if she has to walk all the way back to Sanduga." Louise set off again, slowly enough for the Japanese soldier to keep up with her. "We can't have gone more than two miles."

"Feels like twenty," Fárez said, coming up behind her. Stumpy sniffed at Louise's feet and pulled on his leash.

"She'll get back to Kozlowski, who will yell at her, and then she'll have to hurry to catch us again. By then she'll have it figured out." Louise shrugged. "If not, I'm sure she'll hector me into telling her the rest."

"Call me a dummy," one of the other men said, "but what is it exactly we're trying to figure out?"

"That we're not going to Bataan," Louise said.

"Yeah, I figured that out, but there's something else, right?"

"We never were. There was no other road out of Sanduga, and both the doctor and the lieutenant knew it when they brought us there. None of these trails lead to Bataan."

"We're a field hospital behind enemy lines," Fárez said. "Is that it? There's some other hospital in the mountains that we're supposed to find, is that right?"

"Yes, Corporal, that's about the shape of it," she said. "There's not going to be a rescue of Bataan and Corregidor. The Philippines are on their own, and that means they're going to fall to the Japanese. At least so far as I understand it. We've been sent out to help the resistance. Once you boys are healed, I imagine you'll go out and join the natives in raiding and the like. I'll stay behind and fix you up when the enemy shoots you full of holes."

"Wonderful," someone grumbled. "Nobody asked us."

"You expected the army to give you a vote?" someone else said.

This brought chuckles, but they were strained, and Louise heard pain and worry in the men's voices as they kept up their banter. She called a temporary halt a few minutes later to check them over. More of the same: stitches breaking, wounds leaking blood, and slings in need of adjustment. She gave out half doses of morphine to two of them. They were no good to her crying out in pain, but she had to conserve her morphine and couldn't give them full doses.

The miles trudged on and on. The green curtain grew thicker and thicker. There was no rain, but the air was so warm and humid that she was drenched with sweat. They drained their canteens, she filled them with stream water disinfected with halazone tablets, and they drained them again. Louise's legs ached from the constant up and down of the trail, and she had blisters on her feet, but anything she felt would be suffered tenfold by the men on crutches, so she kept her mouth shut. The flashlight batteries died, and she replaced them.

Three hobbling soldiers with lesser injuries overtook her company in the middle of the night. One was Private Johnson, who'd been healthy enough to dig latrines and do carpentry but was now shaking and sweating with malaria and could barely keep up. She ordered him to slow his pace and continue with them.

And then Frankie reappeared. She was with two cargadores, trudging along with their impossible burdens.

"What a nightmare," Frankie said as she fell back in with her original companions. "Stupid me, putting extra miles on my feet on a night like this." A loud sigh. "I guess you know the truth. Guess you know everything and have all along."

"That we're not going to Bataan? I'm sorry I didn't tell you earlier. I was ordered not to."

"Because of my reaction—that's why they told you to keep it from me. They thought I'd react badly."

None of this came out as a question, but as a flat statement. Subdued. Louise had never heard Frankie so discouraged. She must have been yelled at, told to act her part, do her duty. This was the army, and she was no schoolgirl. Time to grow up and do her job. That's what Louise would have told her, anyway, and she couldn't imagine either Dr. Claypool or Lieutenant Kozlowski going more easily on her.

"Well, I won't react badly," Frankie added. "Mark my words, I'll do what must be done, and without complaining."

Louise glanced at her. If only she could be believed.

———————

Morning brought a spectacular vision of deep mountain gorges and craggy, mist-covered hillsides. The trail snaked around mountainsides, over gushing streams, and past towering moss-covered walls. The air was thick and dense with the smell of trees and wildflowers. White cockatoos soared overhead, along with other birds that filled the air with their calls and screeches.

A rumble came from deep in the mountain range, sounding like the distant boom of guns. But it was thunder, nature's artillery, and the rain began to fall. A drizzle turned almost at once into a deluge just as they were crossing a rope-and-plank bridge. The men on crutches struggled across, and Frankie began to sob, sounding so miserable that Louise felt sorry for her in spite of everything. The trail on the other side was a muddy current they had to wade through.

At the moment when things couldn't seem worse, they stumbled upon a grass-roofed shack on the side of the trail. Cargadores had taken refuge inside, and urged the newcomers to join them. They had a smoky fire going and were chewing betel nuts.

One of the cargadores handed them sweet, sticky rice balls wrapped in banana leaves. Louise had never cared for their gummy texture, but they tasted wonderful now, as they'd trudged all night with little to eat. The other Americans accepted theirs gratefully and shared cigarettes in return. Only Frankie turned up her nose at the food.

Louise attended to blisters on hands and in armpits caused by hobbling on crutches for hour after hour. She gave more quinine to Johnson, who collapsed on a woven reed *patati* and shivered uncontrollably. As she worked, more refugees from the village and its hospital kept joining them, until the shack was packed and people were practically sitting on top of each other. Among them was Maria Elena and several more of the wounded.

"How are they doing?" Louise asked Maria Elena in a low voice after taking a quick glance at the newcomers. The three nurses had tucked into one corner, knees drawn against their chests to leave more room for others.

"Some better, some worse. Private Zwicker is in bad shape."

Louise frowned, surprised. "I thought he was on the mend. Don't tell me his wound is infected."

"Dysentery," Maria Elena said. "It hit him just after you left."

She looked about but didn't see the man. "Where is he?"

"Outside, I think. He can't go long without taking a break, if you know what I mean."

Poor fellow. Pouring rain outside, and he was squatting miserably in the jungle, voiding his bowels. She didn't have anything to give him, either. Just then, he limped in, looking as pale and feeble as an old man. The only place to sit was near the entrance to the shack, where the water left the ground muddy, but Zwicker looked relieved to be in position to get back outside in a hurry the next time his bowels opened up.

There were two good things about the rain. First, it gave a break to exhausted men and women, and second, Louise figured it would slow the Japanese, too. Maybe the last group leaving Sanduga would enjoy a few more hours to haul out goods, to rest, and to attend wounds and illnesses.

The rain thrashed the hut for another couple of hours. And then, as quickly as it had started, it was over. One minute Louise cocked her head, wondering if the rain was pounding with less ferocity on the roof or if she'd grown accustomed to it, and the next it was a light drizzle. Five minutes later it had stopped entirely, and five minutes after that, the sun peeked through the dispersing clouds.

Unfortunately the two sickest men had only grown worse. Johnson was barely coherent, stricken by malarial chills, and Zwicker was too weak to get up and had fouled himself. The nurses cleaned him up as best they could.

"You go on ahead," Zwicker told Louise. He licked his lips. "There will be others along for me and Johnson."

All the others were moving again, except for Sammy Mori, who stood just outside, visibly reluctant to leave her protection, and Fárez, who stood scowling at Sammy, as if not trusting the Japanese alone with the nurses.

Stumpy stood next to Fárez with his half tail wagging and his mouth panting around a muzzle caked with mud. He cocked his head at the two prone men and whined, his expression seeming to say, "Come on, guys! Get up, let's go!" So much fun to be had on the trail, after all.

"Someone should stay with you," Louise told Zwicker. She glanced at Johnson, who kept his eyes squinted shut.

"Nah, you don't worry," Zwicker said. "I'll take care of Johnson." He winced and put his hand on his belly.

"Don't be ridiculous. You can't take care of yourself, let alone anyone else."

"I could stay," Fárez said. "Me and the Jap—I'll keep an eye on him, too. You go on ahead."

"I'm not doing that, either," Louise said. "You and Sammy are both continuing on the road."

She was torn between her desire to stay with the sick men and to catch up with the other nurses and the multitude of patients already pressing ahead. She should go, she decided at last. Roughly half the hospital crew was still behind them on the road, including Miss Clarice and

Dr. Claypool. It's not like she'd be abandoning Zwicker and Johnson to their fate.

"Okay," she said reluctantly. She squatted and put a hand on Private Johnson's sweating forehead. "Private Johnson," she said in a soothing voice. The malarial patient's eyes flickered open, and he managed a nod. "I'll be . . . soon as the quinine . . ."

"Take care. Both of you drink plenty of water, and don't either of you start on the road until you're told. I know you might start feeling better, but I don't want you out there alone."

Both men agreed with that, and Louise rose with a sick feeling in her stomach that she wouldn't see them again. She turned toward the door.

Fárez grabbed for his crutches, relaxing his grip on the leash. Stumpy took the opportunity to pull loose, and he came trotting back into the shack. He shoved his muzzle under Zwicker's chin and whined.

"Come on, Fárez," Zwicker grumbled. "Keep your mutt away from me."

Nevertheless, he rubbed at the dog's head, and looked away when Louise picked up the end of the rope and tugged Stumpy along. The dog whined one last time, and somehow that made her feel worse than ever.

Chapter Sixteen

The journey was more miserable than ever. The sun was blazing hot, and the air felt like damp cotton balls as Louise drew it into her lungs. The trail was one big puddle where it wasn't crossed with muddy streams. Fárez occasionally spoke to the dog, but otherwise the three traveled in silence. Louise wanted to enjoy the quiet, knowing they'd soon catch up to the others, and her responsibilities would multiply, but her thoughts and worries were more oppressive in the silence.

"Tell us some poetry," she said to Sammy when she couldn't take it anymore. "One of your nature poems."

"Between the blisters, the heat, and the mosquitoes, I'm not feeling an affinity for the natural world at the moment."

She smiled. "Neither am I, which is why I need a reminder that we shouldn't burn the whole wretched jungle to ash."

"Okay, then here's an appropriate one."

Mosquito buzzing at my ear—
Does it think
I'm deaf?

Fárez groaned. "That's not a poem, that's reality."

"True enough." Sammy fell silent, and Louise was settling back into her thoughts, when he spoke up again. "Here's one you might like more. Or maybe not."

The man pulling radishes
Pointed my way
With a radish.

Fárez stopped briefly, and an odd expression crossed his face. "That's . . . There's something about that. I don't understand it, but I like it. Could you say that one again?" Sammy did so, and Fárez nodded. "He's a man picking radishes, but he doesn't think about what he's doing."

Sammy looked pleased. "That's right. What makes Issa's haiku satisfying is something mundane looked at from a strange angle. It's startling, it makes you think. Do you see the question? Every man can pick radishes, but what kind of man points with them?"

The poem had seemed simple at first, almost pointless, but now Louise gave it some more consideration and thought she understood. "The kind of man who gives no more thought to the radishes in his hand than he does to his index finger."

"That's exactly what I meant," Fárez said excitedly. "Only I didn't have the words to say it."

"You did well enough," Sammy said. "Of course that's not the only meaning to the poem, but it's a good one. It's deeper thinking than my brother ever did. Yoshi always scoffed at Japanese poetry."

At mention of his brother, Sammy's face darkened, and his mood seemed to be swinging shut. Louise hurried to put her foot in the door before it closed altogether.

"This is the brother who is looking for us?"

"Yes." Sammy hesitated a moment, and Louise thought he was done speaking, but then he added, "When we lived in America, he was purely American. Not Japanese. That's the funny thing.

"He was younger than I was when we came to America, and barely even remembered living in Japan by the time we returned. Maybe that's why he never took to all the Japanese stuff. Never saw a point in learning how to read his native language. He said our art and poetry were simple, didn't care about praying or any of it. Didn't eat his rice with chopsticks."

"That last part seems reasonable," Fárez said. "Who can pick up rice with chopsticks?"

"Any Japanese person over the age of two," Sammy said.

"Oh," Fárez said.

"So when we went back to Japan, and he couldn't use his chopsticks well, when he could barely read, when his vocabulary was as sophisticated as a seven-year-old boy's because he'd never wanted to keep it up, you can imagine how that affected him. So much for hating Japan. Now he loved it."

Louise wasn't sure she understood. "I'd have thought he'd hate Japan all the more. He'd be like a fish out of water when he got home."

"We were still kids—there was no choice but to dive back in. I was sixteen, and Yoshiko was fourteen. We had to go to school, had to interact with kids who saw us as practically foreigners. School was . . . ugly."

"How do you mean?" Louise asked.

"A school is an unnatural place if you think about it. If you think how people used to live, everyone on farms, children learning from their parents, from their brothers and sisters. The village elders. Maybe they would study for a few hours a week, but they didn't sit with other children while an overworked teacher tried to keep them all from running wild. Japanese kids are quieter and more disciplined than what you see in America, but there's a cruel struggle going on at all times. Every kid is bullied, and every kid is a bully. You find your place in society, and you torment those below while you get tormented from above." Sammy grimaced. "That's how it was in my school, anyway."

"Mine, too," Fárez said, "and I grew up in Los Angeles. Maybe it's that way everywhere."

"It's good preparation for the army," Sammy said.

"Isn't it, though?" Fárez said. "Gets you used to the abuse."

166

"It explains everything about my brother. Yoshi learned his lessons—how to bully, how to be bullied—and when he joined the army, he took them with him. Became fanatically devoted to the emperor, devoted to spreading Japanese power. He joined the Kempeitai, the military police, although *secret* police is more accurate. They catch traitors, punish the disloyal, force military rule on civilian populations through bullying and terror. That's my brother. That's the ugly face of Japanese culture."

"But what about you?" Louise asked. "You must have faced the same thing, but it didn't turn you into a monster."

"My brother learned one lesson, and I learned another," Sammy continued. "He turned outward, and I turned inward. We both became authentically Japanese, I suppose. Each in our own way."

"And the army?" she asked. "Why did you join?"

"No choice. I was conscripted and sent to China. After all these years, I'm still a corporal, so I obviously didn't thrive in the military. I'm not sure I'd thrive in any environment, to be honest."

Louise wasn't so sure about that. Sammy was intelligent and sensitive. He reminded her of an artist or an artisan. A writer, a musician. If he'd been Catholic, a priest or a monk. Someone who lived a solitary, contemplative life, unless he took on students. Or maybe simply a poet with a garden, like one of the men Sammy was always quoting.

"Is that why you wrote a confession to your brother?" Louise asked. "You wanted to get out of the army?"

"I suppose I could have shot myself in the leg. But that seemed like the coward's way out."

"What confession?" Fárez asked.

Louise glanced at the Japanese soldier, her eyebrows raised in asking his permission. Sammy managed a shrug as he kept levering himself along on his crutches.

"Corporal Mori witnessed atrocities in Nanking. He wrote what he saw in English and shared it with the international community of the city so the world would know."

Fárez let out a low whistle. "That takes guts."

"The Japanese knew it was one of their own," she said, "but never figured out who. A few weeks ago, Sammy wrote a letter to his brother in the secret police to confess."

"You must have a death wish, buddy," Fárez said.

"Maybe I do," Sammy said.

"What's wrong with you, anyway?" Fárez asked.

Sammy cast a dark look over his shoulder.

"I mean it," Fárez pressed. "Why would you do such a dumb thing? I don't mean telling people what you saw—that was brave—but confessing to the secret police. What kind of idiot does that?"

"If you'd seen the things I have, felt the things I have, you'd understand," Mori said.

This only set off Fárez more. "You think you're the only one with problems? You think you're so special, so fragile, so damn sensitive that you deserve special consideration? Let me tell you something, you crazy Jap. You're not. You're like every damn soldier who has ever lived. We're all terrified, we all see things we were never meant to see. What do you think war is?"

Louise stared at Fárez, surprised to see such fire coming out of him. This was the same man who'd blushed at the thought of removing one of his dog's testicles.

"And I'll tell you something else," Fárez said. "There's none of us fighting this war for glory. Maybe a few, but they're the scary ones, the ones who order you to charge a machine-gun nest when you're out of ammo. The more of the glory kind you get, the more likely you are to have stuff like what you people did in China. The rest of us are trying to stay alive, and we're trying to keep our buddies alive. You wanted something to fight for, that's it. You fight to keep your friends from getting killed. That's good enough."

Mori didn't answer but scooted along, pace quickening, though how he managed after so many hours on the road, Louise didn't know.

He all but disappeared ahead of them. The other two let him go for a stretch, and soon enough he slowed. Sammy resisted for a while, but Louise and the corporal finally reeled him in like an exhausted fish played out on a line.

Sammy stopped, panting and leaning against his crutches. Fárez handed over his canteen, which the other man took without comment. He drank half and handed it back. The American took his turn drinking. Neither soldier said anything for a moment, and Louise stayed silent, too, feeling something pass between the two men.

Stumpy was off his leash at the moment and came to nose at the three companions to get them moving again. He started with Louise, then moved to Fárez, and finally pushed insistently on the back of Sammy's leg. The Japanese man smiled and reached to scratch the dog's head.

"You can't fool a dog, you know," Fárez said.

"Sorry?" Sammy said.

"If Stumpy will vouch for you, I guess you ain't so bad." Fárez grinned. "For a Jap."

Sammy shook his head, a smile at the corner of his lips. He plucked something from Stumpy's coat. "You got yourself in some burrs, friend." He picked again and showed it to the other two. "Look, they're all over him."

"So he did, the little stinker," Fárez said, starting in on the burrs. Stumpy didn't want to be groomed and tried to get away, but Louise had learned this trick by now, and got hold of him long enough for Fárez to put the leash back on.

When the three had cleaned the dog of the worst of his burrs, Louise took the leash. The dog whined and pulled to keep going. She allowed her patients one last pull on the canteen, then pressed them all into motion. Nobody spoke after that for a long time.

They stopped that evening in a nipa hut crowded with evacuees, with more arriving throughout the night. Other patients and villagers, she supposed, were strung out all along the trail both ahead and behind. Louise was the only nurse in this particular shack and had few medical supplies, so it was fortunate that she didn't have any critical injuries to care for.

But it was hardly a comfortable night. The pounding rain leaked through the roof and dripped on their heads. She huddled with a village woman and her two children, while around her men struggled to sleep. Morning came as a relief, though she was exhausted. Someone cooked up some rice, and she ate a cup of it with a pinch of salt before she was back on the trail with Fárez, Sammy, and their stub-tail mascot.

The evacuation was fluid, with soldiers and cargadores passing them and being passed in turn. By late afternoon, Louise had caught up with Maria Elena and Frankie, and they re-formed their original group with a few additions. They were trudging painfully along when they came upon three Filipinos with ancient rifles standing by the side of the road. The men watched with sharp expressions.

Louise didn't recognize them from Sanduga, and her heart pounded, thinking she and her companions were going to be robbed or worse, when the men suddenly broke into smiles, showing teeth stained red from betel-nut juice.

"Ang mga Amerikano ay mabubuting tao," one of the men said.

Maria Elena translated: "Americans are good people."

Their faces darkened when they spotted Sammy Mori, but Fárez glared them down, and Louise interposed herself between the Japanese soldier and the Filipinos until they'd left the men behind.

"I suppose those are our partisans," Fárez said with a final glance backward, as if worried they were being followed. "Not much to 'em, is there?"

"We're lucky we weren't murdered," Frankie said. "Or worse."

Shortly after that, another man with a rifle directed them onto a small side trail that climbed a steep zigzag up the mountainside. Roots and jutting tongues of stone made steps of sort, and they inched higher with the injured patients.

They found themselves in a high, bowl-like valley, surrounded by peaks. A tidy grid of rice paddies and vegetable gardens spread out from about a dozen shacks. The village had a small Catholic church built of wooden planks and a grass roof like all the rest, and the early arrivals were already busy trying to make it suitable for a hospital. A few supplies had been cached on site, but they were even more meager than in Sanduga.

The place was named Cascadas, a Spanish word referring to the swiftly flowing mountain stream that passed through the center of the village. The villagers seemed related to the refugees from Sanduga and, like the people of the lowlands and hill country, knew all about the arrival of the Haponeses. They'd promised to help the Americans and their Filipino allies. Still, Louise couldn't help but notice the worry on the faces of village elders and the anxious glances of mothers with young children at their breasts.

Louise spotted two women who looked out of place: short, black-skinned people who looked more like Papuans than Filipinos. Negritos, she learned, an ancient tribal people of the mountains who sometimes came down to help with the rice harvest in return for cigarettes or a bottle of *lambanog*. They were safe enough if you encountered them in the village, she was told, but don't wander too far into the jungle, or they're liable to cook and eat you.

Maria Elena told Louise this, translated from an earnest old man with stubby teeth stained red by betel nuts. He was animated in his gestures when he talked about cannibals, but the whole thing seemed fanciful. He warned her about cobras and wild boars as well.

The last of the hospital refugees didn't arrive until the next morning. Dr. Claypool was with them. Louise had snatched a few hours of sleep, but spent most of the night attending to a sickly group of patients. Now she met the doctor outside the hospital. The view of the little valley and the surrounding mountains was spectacular in the early-morning light, everything glittering and green. It was cooler up here, too, thank God.

"That's everyone," Claypool said. "The only one we're missing is Kozlowski, but he has business on the road. He and the alcalde are disguising a couple of the side trails we took to get here, making them harder to spot. And, well, there's someone else we left behind."

Louise guessed with a sinking feeling who that was. "Private Johnson didn't make it, did he?"

"You heard?"

"I inventoried the patients this morning, and there was one man missing."

"Kozlowski and the locals are digging him a grave." Claypool's heavy eyebrows furrowed in a look of pain. "Blast it, he was doing fine. He was well enough to be on work duty just a few days ago."

"Digging a latrine, if I remember. That's probably when he got the dysentery. Bet he touched something and didn't wash his hands."

"Spread the word," he said grimly. "I want the men to know why Johnson is dead. Get it through their thick skulls. Disease is as big a threat as enemy bullets. That means sanitation, that means mosquito nets. We've got plenty of malaria and dysentery to go around—we don't need any more."

"The journey didn't help matters," Louise said. She held out her arm to show dozens of little red marks. "There's not one of us who didn't get chewed up by mosquitoes every step of the way. I suspect we'll be seeing a lot more malaria and dengue over the next couple of days."

Claypool sighed long and hard. "We've lost four already, Miss Louise. Three we left in Sanduga, plus Johnson." The doctor looked exhausted, defeated, vulnerable in a way she couldn't remember seeing before. "Somehow we've got to carry on. I just, I don't see how we can manage it. We left our food, we left most of our supplies, we have no electricity." He drew in a single great breath and let it out into another sigh. This one held what sounded like a shudder. "Miss Louise, I can't do this, I can't hold it together."

"I don't see as you have a choice."

"I never said I did, but I wouldn't be the first man to break down under pressure, you know. That's all I'm saying, that I . . . that I feel . . ."

"Just keep doing what you're doing," she urged. "Somehow we'll manage. *You* will manage."

"Do you believe that?"

"I do." Louise put a hand on his wrist. "Don't lose faith."

"You're right." He let out his breath and drew it in slowly, and this time sounded calmer, like a man settling himself. He looked stronger, more confident when he was done. "I'm sorry, Miss Louise. I had a bad moment, that's all. Don't tell the other nurses, please."

"No worries, Dr. Claypool." She gave what she hoped was an encouraging smile. "There's nothing to tell."

Chapter Seventeen

Yoshiko Mori and his men left Santa Maria by truck and made excellent time at first. Eight Japanese secret police, plus seventeen Filipino Sakdals, all armed and ready to snuff out any resistance they encountered on their way to Sanduga.

But they slowed under an onslaught of heavy rain and slowed even more when Lieutenant Fujiwara's sharp eyes detected disturbed ground on the road where the Americans had mined it. Or so it seemed at first. They couldn't find a way around the mines, so Mori appropriated two carabao from a nearby village and drove the buffalo down the road to detonate them.

Nothing happened to the carabao. There were no mines; it was only a decoy. Fujiwara's vigilance had cost them at least three hours. Worse, a few minutes later they hit a legitimate trap. The enemy had sabotaged a short bridge over a muddy stream, and the truck fell off and broke an axle.

They abandoned the truck and continued on foot. The rain turned from heavy to torrential. Floodwater washed out the road in multiple places. Elsewhere it seemed intentionally damaged. More sabotage.

Japanese and Filipinos alike were in a foul mood by the time they came upon Sanduga. Three days had passed since leaving Santa Maria in the lowlands. They were hungry, footsore, and covered with bug bites and fungal infections from damp socks and boots.

Sanduga was mostly empty, and those villagers who remained were slow to cooperate. There was some shooting that may or may not have been in response to hostile action by the locals. The only casualties were an old woman and a couple of pigs. The dead pigs would be put to good use, of course, but the dead woman only served to drive the rest of the villagers into the brush.

Mori took stock of his conquest. Americans had been here; there was no doubt of it. The largest building had been a hospital made of cement block and was now a mess of overturned cots and smashed bottles of medication. The enemy had destroyed their generator and dumped their fuel into the ground on their way out.

It smelled ugly inside the hospital, a stench of dirty bedpans and used bandages infested with maggots, and so he covered his mouth and led Fujiwara back outside without inspecting the entire building. Let his men see to that.

Mori shielded his eyes from the sun. "They can't be far ahead of us."

"It's my fault, sir. If we hadn't wasted so much time getting past those fake mines, we might have arrived in time."

"Your skills of observation could have easily saved us had those mines been real," Mori said.

"They didn't spot the sabotaged bridge."

"True," Mori conceded. "You deserve blame for that."

Fujiwara hung his head in shame.

Mori looked around, instinctively disliking the close, jungle feel of the surrounding mountains. Sanduga itself was shabby, ramshackle, nothing like a tidy Japanese village. It was dirty; it smelled bad. These unruly mountain peasants would no doubt resist the Japanese until they were driven out and forced to settle in towns and cities to be civilized.

The Sakdals were busy looting the village but seemed unhappy with what they found and soon started to set the buildings on fire to amuse themselves. Let them. Mori didn't intend to stay, and the destruction of Sanduga would send a message to other villages that were tempted to side with the conquered instead of the conquerors.

Meanwhile, one of his secret police had set up the radio to communicate with headquarters, and now he came running up, breathless, to say that Colonel Umeko wanted to speak to him.

"What the devil are you doing up there?" the colonel demanded when Mori picked up the receiver. "I thought you were in Santa Maria."

"I was, sir. But remember what I said about partisans?"

"No, I do not remember, Mori. What are you up to?"

"We found an American hospital, sir, recently abandoned. They're trying to set up to support the partisans, but we'll sniff them out, sir. We can't be more than a day or two behind."

"Where?"

"Up here in the mountains. We'll have to keep moving. I've got enough armed men to take them, and if they're carrying their wounded, I'll overtake them without trouble."

"Don't you have better things to do than muck around in these little villages?"

"No, sir. This could be important."

A gunshot rang from the hospital, and Mori jumped. He dropped the radio receiver and sprang to his feet. He and Fujiwara rushed inside with pistols drawn. They moved slowly from room to room, then more quickly when they heard a groan and a cry for help in Japanese.

Mori ducked his head into one of the rooms and withdrew it quickly as someone fired at him. He'd seen enough in that brief glance to understand. There was an American on a cot with a pistol. Another man lay on the floor nearby, a Japanese soldier.

"Damn my haste," Mori said to Fujiwara. "We didn't check the whole hospital."

"One of the Americans, sir?"

Mori gave a sharp nod. "Too injured to move, apparently. He can't even hold himself up. But he managed to shoot one of our men."

"Who did he get?"

"I didn't see. We'll figure that out later. For now, we've got to take care of that American." Mori thought it over. "The man's cot is against the back wall. We'll both go in, you to the right, me to the left. Watch out for the body on the floor. Ready?"

"Yes, sir."

The two law soldiers came into the room, firing as they spread out. The injured man on the cot got off one more shot, but it was wild, and the Japanese emptied their pistols into him. He cried out, then was still.

Breathing hard, Mori studied their enemy. It was an American, all right, missing his right leg and his right arm, but that hadn't kept him from using what he had left to good effect. Mori had to respect him for going down shooting instead of surrendering.

He was so focused on the dead American that he didn't notice the other two enemies until Fujiwara hissed a warning. Mori would have shot them, too, if he hadn't already emptied his pistol. He drew his sword and rushed the nearest cot before seeing that neither man was a threat.

These two were Filipinos, also severely injured. One had something white and frothy about his mouth, and his breathing was low and shallow. He seemed to have swallowed something. The other man, badly burned on the face and neck, stared through eyes wide with terror and pain. He had something clenched in his hand, which Fujiwara pried loose. Looked like morphine tablets.

Mori held the man's gaze. *You should have swallowed these when you had the chance.*

"Help me," the injured Japanese said from the floor.

Mori spared him a glance. It was Yamaguchi. The bullet had caught him in the thigh, but the wound didn't look serious.

"Put your hand on it. That will slow the bleeding. I'll see to you when I can."

"Yes, sir," Yamaguchi said through clenched teeth.

"So they couldn't move everybody," Mori told Fujiwara. "They gave these three a lethal dose of morphine and left them behind."

"A hard decision, sir," Fujiwara said, "but a necessary one."

"*Hai.* I'd have done the same thing." He glanced at the remaining soldier, who continued to stare. Mori couldn't help the twinge of sympathy for the injured man. "Too bad this one was too cowardly to follow through."

"But good for us, sir."

"Good for us," Mori agreed.

Yamaguchi groaned. Mori supposed he'd better see to the man's injury. He stayed with the Filipino while Fujiwara went to fetch the medic.

Fujiwara came running back a few minutes later with two Japanese soldiers. The second man was the radioman, who was frantic for Mori to attend to the colonel.

Mori had completely forgotten about the conversation with his superior, and when he got back on the radio, he cringed as Colonel Umeko roared at him. He tried to explain, but the man cut him off.

"Listen up, Mori. I'm going to give you orders, and I want to make this very clear. Are you listening?"

"Yes, sir, I am list—"

Mori didn't finish the word. Instead he ended the call. Then he pulled off the panel cover and disconnected the leads to the receiver. Fujiwara and the radioman were both staring at him when he finished.

Gekokujō.

The lesser ranks lead from below. A strategy that had always set Mori's teeth to grinding, an excuse for incompetence and insubordination. Yet here he was, doing the same thing.

"Sir?" Fujiwara asked.

"I didn't actually hear the colonel's orders."

"No, sir, but I'm not sure that answer would satisfy him."

"You are right, Lieutenant, it would not."

Indeed, Mori could already imagine the colonel raging in his office, shouting at subordinates and throwing things. Heaven help the Filipino in Manila today who crossed the man's path; he'd get his head lopped from his shoulders if he dared frown in the man's direction.

"So what will we do?" Fujiwara asked.

"It's temporary for now. If we don't find what we're looking for, we can always reconnect the radio and give a suitable excuse." He glanced at his adjutant, then to the radioman. "I'm sure we all agree that a small falsehood would be justified in this case."

"What kind of falsehood?" the radioman asked, tone cautious.

"We lost the radio due to a technical problem," Mori said. "Now it's back, a few hours later. Again, this lie is only necessary if we don't find what we're looking for."

"And if we *do* find what we want, sir?" Fujiwara asked.

"Then the radio stays disconnected. We go into the mountains to find the traitor, to capture the Americans. Once that happens, it won't matter if we disobeyed orders or not."

"In that case," Fujiwara said, "we'd better get started interrogating the prisoner. That is what you intend, isn't it, sir?"

It was indeed, although it was not without some reluctance that Mori led his adjutant back into the hospital. He was not naturally a cruel man, after all, though he could be firm when needed. Perhaps if he was lucky, there would be no need for it.

Two of his men carried out Yamaguchi, who had one hand on his wounded thigh and the other on his face in an attempt to cover a grimace. The incident would be humiliating for the young man. Good. It would serve as a lesson.

One of Mori's men had tied the injured Filipino's wrists and ankles to the cot, but this looked unnecessary. The man was heavily bandaged and also shaking and pale. The bandages smelled of decay, and it seemed as though his wounds were infected.

"Translate for me," Mori told his adjutant. Then, to the Filipino, "You must know why we're here, and what we're looking for."

Fujiwara translated this into Tagalog, but the man just stared.

Mori continued in a calm voice. "The Americans, the others who were here with you, where did they go?"

Again there was no answer. Mori didn't show anger or emotion, but he removed his sword from its sheath. The Filipino blinked hard, then closed his eyes tightly.

"I know the common opinion in the army," Mori said, "but I don't believe it. I think the Japanese are wrong about this."

"What opinion is that, sir?" Fujiwara asked.

"That's for you to translate, not for you to answer."

"Oh, sorry, sir. I misunderstood."

Once the lieutenant had translated it into Tagalog, Mori continued. "People say the Pinoys are cowards, that they'll only fight when the Americans are standing there shouting at them. I don't believe this. Maybe you people don't have training, and maybe not all of you are fighters, but plenty are brave enough. Look at you, closing your eyes while you wait for me to cut off your head. You're not begging for mercy. And yet you weren't brave enough to kill yourself when you had the chance. That shows you have a breaking point. Or maybe you're just a Catholic and couldn't kill yourself because it's a mortal sin. We'll find out."

He took the tip of his sword and caught the edge of the injured man's bandages. Among other wounds, the man was swathed from ankle to thigh in bandages that may have once been white but were now blotched and dirty where they'd bled through. The man's eyes flew open, and he winced when the blade cut through the dirty linen.

"You should have taken the morphine," Mori said. "If not enough to kill yourself, then to deaden the pain."

The Filipino had remained stoic, feigning indifference, though he must be terrified. Any man would be in his situation. Now, however, his eyes moved to Fujiwara even before the adjutant began to translate Mori's words. Anxious to know what was being said, to learn his fate. His eyes widened slightly; then he looked away again.

Once he had cut through the bandages, Mori used the tip of the sword to peel them back from the wound. The flesh on the calf and thigh had been stitched together in three different locations, two of them ragged, and the third in a straight line, as if someone had cut in with a scalpel to repair internal damage. A fine hand had stitched them up again, using sutures that looked impossibly small.

Mori had spent time in a field hospital in China and watched Japanese surgeons at work. Speed was paramount, getting as many men back on their feet as fast as possible. A soldier without a gun in his hand was worthless. In contrast, the American doctor who'd operated on this man had worked with an eye that looked beyond function to aesthetics. And with the Filipino's extensive burns to the upper body, it was possible that a Japanese doctor would have determined the case hopeless from the beginning.

Unfortunately the wound on the thigh had turned gangrenous. The flesh was swollen until it made the sutures ooze, and a sickly greenish color radiated outward into uninjured tissue. It smelled like a dead animal.

"This man needs his leg amputated," Mori said. "You don't have to be a doctor to see that."

"If we do that, how will we get him down to Santa Maria?" Fujiwara asked. "You can't cut off a man's leg and then force him to march out of the hills on foot, sir."

"No, I suppose not." Mori paused with his sword tip just above the man's thigh. "Tell the man he has one more chance. Tell us what we want and he won't hurt anymore. We'll get him morphine and medical care."

Of course, the two secret police had just agreed that medical care would be pointless. In any event, Mori's small company had a medic, but no doctor.

The Filipino didn't respond, which forced the law officer to make good on his implied threat. He took the tip of the sword and plucked at the sutures. They broke apart like the stitches of an overinflated ball. Pus and blood ran out.

The man's stoicism vanished at the first touch. He bucked and threw his head back with a loud groan. His hands fought with the restraints the Japanese soldiers had fastened to his wrists and legs.

Mori poked and prodded with his sword tip, lancing the infected wounds on the upper thigh. Soon enough the stubborn prisoner was babbling for mercy. Mori stopped and asked again for information, even while he kept the blackened, dripping tip of his sword near the wound.

This time the prisoner talked. He didn't have a lot of information, but he had enough.

Chapter Eighteen

Louise's conversation with Dr. Claypool left her worried and feeling alone. Frankie had been on the verge of a breakdown since Manila, Clarice and Maria Elena were young and frightened, and now the doctor seemed to be cracking under the strain. She needed him to hold it together.

But she soon had worries other than the doctor's mental state. Within a few more days, her predictions came true, and disease swept through the camp. Three men went down with dengue, which the soldiers called breakbone fever, because it felt like someone had taken a hammer to every bone in the body. Several others suffered from malaria, and while Zwicker's dysentery was passing, two other men suffered the same ailment. One of these men also had malaria, giving him a one-two punch that pushed him to the verge of death.

And then there were the injuries. One man's wound, which had seemed on the mend earlier, turned gangrenous. Dr. Claypool set up a debriding table. Louise attended the surgery, which saw the man's left foot amputated, and flesh on his calf debrided, or cut away, so as to allow healing of what remained. Claypool looked exhausted at the end of the surgery. He went to lie down and rest, but Clarice soon brought word that he was down with malaria himself. Out came the quinine.

Fortunately the nurses remained healthy, as did Lieutenant Kozlowski, who kept the camp functioning. He had cots made and helped her scrounge pots from the village so they could sterilize bandages and surgical equipment. He also brought her something unwelcome: three more injured men carried from the lowlands.

All three were Filipinos injured in a firefight with Japanese soldiers, men who'd kept resisting after the enemy overran their positions. Some of the Americans in the hospital camp had scoffed to learn that they were expected to treat injured partisans. The Filipinos would fight only so long as Americans were around to lead them, it was claimed. The local units had dissolved in the face of enemy fire, as men abandoned fixed positions, threw down their rifles, and stripped from their uniforms in the hopes of blending into the civilian population. But others fought to the end, as evidenced by these three.

The Filipinos were dehydrated and suffering heatstroke from their long journey into the mountains. One man was carried by the other two, and he soon died of his injuries, but the other two could be helped. Dr. Claypool roused himself from bed long enough to operate on the more serious injury but collapsed soon after.

Frankie got in a fight with Clarice and Maria Elena during supper, and Louise told her to go outside until she cooled down. Frankie stormed off, muttering, her shoulders hunched and a glare on her face. The other three nurses were playing a quiet game of rummy by lamplight in the hospital ward, sitting on *patatis*, surrounded by sleeping men, when Frankie returned.

"It's over," Frankie said in a loud voice that made some of the men stir. "It's all done."

Louise set down her cards and stood. "Will you hush? There are men sleeping."

"I will not hush. I'm done hushing. Maybe if I'd spoken up earlier we wouldn't be in this position." Her voice was louder than ever.

"Play without me," Louise told the other nurses. "I'll deal with her."

"You'll *deal* with me," Frankie said as Louise took the older nurse by the elbow and led her outside. "Isn't that lovely? You'll deal, will you? And how will you deal with me?"

"Listen up." Louise turned the other woman around to face her. "I am sick and tired of your nonsense. We have a job to do, and you know it. Now what's this about?"

Fárez was on guard duty, sitting on a stool beneath the eaves with his rifle across his lap. He rose to his feet and leaned against his crutch, watching the two women. Sammy came hobbling outside on crutches, also apparently drawn by the commotion. Frankie sniffed at the two men and put her hands on her hips.

"We're out of food," she said. "No pork and beans, no powdered milk, no sugar, no canned beef or salmon, no hard biscuits, nothing. What do you think about that?"

Louise's stomach growled at the mention of those foods, but complaining wasn't going to materialize the supplies they'd abandoned in Sanduga.

"We'll eat what is available," Louise said.

"Rice and salt. You call that eating? Rice for breakfast, rice for lunch. There's not even a piece of stringy chicken. If we're lucky, we get mungo beans and a banana."

"Lieutenant Kozlowski paid for some food to be brought in," she said. "We should get a little meat next week. Some eggs, too."

"Listen to yourself. Next week. By then we'll all have beriberi." Frankie's voice was a near shout. "You think these men will survive on rice? They're going to die. We're all going to die."

"Please keep your voice down. Men are sleeping, they need their rest."

"Oh, so now I'm hysterical, is that it? We've been lied to. *Lied* to! And you're calling me hysterical?"

"I didn't say that."

"You did!"

185

Frankie pushed Louise, who staggered backward, shocked. Fárez growled a warning at the older nurse.

"And you're the worst of them all!" Frankie was screaming now. "You're a liar. I'll bet you found something to eat, that's why you don't care, and I know what you did to get it. I'll tell you what I think—"

Louise slapped her across the face. Frankie fell back a pace.

"Corporal," Louise said to Fárez. "Please go and wake Lieutenant Kozlowski. Tell him that Miss Frankie needs to be confined for her own good and the good of our patients."

A malicious look passed over Frankie's face. "Go ahead and tell him. He won't hear you, he's delirious. That's right, Louise, he's sick, too. We're on our own now."

———

Louise left Frankie with Fárez and Sammy, instructing them to take her somewhere quiet in the village where she couldn't disturb the patients. Frankie fought and shouted, especially when the Japanese soldier took her arm. She called him "a filthy Jap" and swore she'd tell the men he'd tried to rape her if he didn't let go. Louise was not worried about this; the patients had soured on Miss Frankie to a man and wouldn't believe a word she said.

Carrying the lamp ahead of her and swatting away the cloud of insects it attracted, Louise picked her way along the dike between two rice paddies to the house Kozlowski had set up as his home and head-quarters. Fear and anger warred within her.

Frankie's rants only mirrored the worries of everyone in the camp. They were low on food, under continual threat of discovery by the enemy, and trying to save lives with limited medical equipment. But they needed calm, they needed unity. Frankie's outburst was the last thing they needed.

When she saw Kozlowski, she had new concerns. He lay on a mat in the corner, still in his uniform. Shivers worked through his body.

"Lieutenant," she murmured as she squatted next to him. She touched him, and he shivered so hard it was almost a convulsion.

"Go away, Frankie."

"It's me, Miss Louise."

"Oh, I thought Frankie was coming to complain again."

"Has she been bothering you? No, never mind. Look, we have to get you to the hospital."

"Just let me die."

"You're not going to die," Louise said firmly. "You need quinine, and you need good nursing care." She pulled on him. "Come on, there's a cot right next to Dr. Claypool. The two of you can suffer together."

She got him up, helped him down the stairs, and steadied him as he wobbled along the dike. He fell to his knees in front of the hospital and this time couldn't be lifted. Louise called for help, and two men came out to get him inside.

Once she had some quinine in him, she felt better, but then she turned to Dr. Claypool, who she'd supposed would be sleeping. Instead he was turning deliriously.

She fetched Clarice, who stood wringing her hands while Louise questioned her about treatment.

"I gave him his quinine not twenty minutes ago," Clarice said.

"You're sure? And he hasn't missed any doses?"

"No, Miss Louise."

Then why wasn't he getting better? Quinine was hardly a miracle cure. A man could still suffer malaria with it, fighting the disease over an extended period of time as illness and medicine vied for control. But quinine should knock it down eventually. After that, much depended on whether the patient continued to be exposed to malarial mosquitoes.

Sammy returned to say that he and Fárez had calmed Frankie down with *alak*—rice wine—given them by a villager in a bamboo flask. They put her by herself in a nipa hut. The corporal and his dog stood watch outside her door to make sure she didn't leave.

The three remaining nurses rotated their shifts throughout the night, two working and one sleeping. By morning they saw improvement in many of the men. There were two exceptions: one man who was stricken with both malaria and dysentery, and Dr. Claypool.

Kozlowski was up and able to eat some guava and rice with a bit of what the Filipinos called calabaza, some sort of squash. It wasn't much, but it was the best breakfast in the camp. Rice and salt for everyone else.

After he'd eaten, the lieutenant looked over the ward. He was drawn and pale. His eyes rested on Claypool, then turned to Louise, who'd been watching him carefully as she and Clarice emptied bedpans, which were really just bowls scavenged from the village. Between the wood, which held the smell, and the dysentery, the task was more unpleasant than usual.

"Where's Miss Frankie?" Kozlowski asked.

"Under house confinement."

"This was your idea?"

Louise tapped out another bedpan into the bucket and stacked it with the others. "There was nobody to give me permission. She was harming morale and keeping us from our duties. I had to do it."

"Understood. How are you feeling?"

"Exhausted, hungry. Worried."

"But not sick?"

"Not sick," she said.

"Thank God for small favors," Kozlowski said. "If you go down, we're in trouble."

"Lie down and rest. We can't lose you, either." Louise sent Clarice out with the bedpans and the bucket and glanced around the room, searching for anyone who needed her attention. When she looked back, Kozlowski was still sitting. "I mean it, Lieutenant. You need your rest."

"I've got work to do."

"Not today, you don't."

A smiled stretched thinly across his face, but it was followed by a violent shiver, and he obligingly stretched out on his cot, which was really a bamboo plank elevated a few inches off the floor on stubby feet. He squinted his eyes shut, and she continued about her work. Louise came back a few minutes later to check on him, and he seemed a little stronger.

"I'm taking three of your patients," he said. "Sending them off on a mission."

"A mission! I like that, spread the word of God to the heathen villages of the mountains. Do we have enough Bibles to go around?"

"Funny girl. You know what I'm talking about. For the war."

"Who are you taking?"

"Fárez, Zwicker, and . . . that Pinoy who lost part of his ear. What's his name?"

"Bautista. What do you mean, 'taking them'? Not one of those men is in any shape to leave the hospital."

"They're well enough. Even Fárez. I caught him hobbling along without his crutch yesterday."

"Against my orders," Louise said. "He needs a crutch, and if you saw him put it down, it's only because he's still got blisters on his hands and armpits from our trek to Cascadas."

"If Fárez's biggest complaint is blisters, then he's well enough to fight. I have a job here, and that's to win a war."

"I thought our job was to heal the sick and injured."

"That's *your* job. My job is to fight the Japs. I'm sending those men out with a guide from the village. There's a small group of partisans to the west of here—bandits, really, but they hate the Japanese more than they like stealing. Only, they have no military experience, and they're short on ammo. We give them three trained military men and one of our arms caches, and suddenly you've got a real headache for the enemy when they enter the mountains."

Louise looked in frustration at Claypool, but the doctor was still senseless. Why couldn't he be awake for this? Surely he'd push back against Kozlowski's unreasonable request.

"Can we at least wait until we're on top of the malaria?"

"None of those men have it, so that's irrelevant. If you want to send them with a few pills, go right ahead. Whatever other supplies you can spare."

"Lieutenant, please. If we can just wait until Dr. Claypool is better."

"No." His face hardened. "I'm sorry, Louise. Those are my orders, and I expect them to be carried out."

The lucky three limped off that afternoon in the company of a village boy of about twelve, who was acting as their guide to find the bandits/partisans. Fárez left Louise in care of Stumpy, and both dog and owner seemed to know that there was a risk of permanent separation. The corporal held Stumpy a little too tightly, and when he passed the dog to Louise, the animal whined and squirmed in her arms, trying to jump down and follow. She kept him tied up for the rest of the day so he wouldn't run off.

Kozlowski ordered Frankie released. The lieutenant was still bed-ridden and ordered the nurse brought to him, where he dressed her down in front of the entire hospital. She listened without comment and nodded sullenly when asked if she'd behave herself. Apart from a poisonous glance at Louise, she seemed subdued and compliant. She obeyed Louise's orders, but spoke to nobody as she worked, except when necessary.

Claypool got worse, and it wasn't just malaria. When Louise did her morning rounds the following day, he pointed wordlessly at his bedpan. There was blood in his stool. If the stool was harder, she'd have thought maybe his anus had fissures from constipation caused by too much rice and banana, but the consistency seemed normal.

There was no microscope, but she dewormed him as a precaution and sent Maria Elena out to get fruits and vegetables from the village, no matter how much she had to pay, badger, or threaten. Claypool seemed marginally better that afternoon, but by nightfall he was in the grips of another malarial attack.

The sound of gunfire woke Louise in the night. At first she thought it was her dream or thunder over the mountains confused as the sound of battle. But then the shooting started up again, the distant snap of a rifle. One shot, then two more.

Clarice was sleeping next to her in the shack that the nurses made their home. The other two women were on duty at the hospital. Now Clarice sat up on her mat. Her breathing came fast and shallow, and she reached out to touch Louise, as if needing confirmation that Louise was with her.

"Maybe it's just hunters," Clarice said.

"At this hour?"

"Bandits, then. Or Corporal Fárez teaching the partisans how to shoot." Clarice's voice was high and tight, and she sounded desperate. "There could be other explanations, not all of them bad."

"Maybe," Louise said doubtfully. The two women sat in the darkness, listening.

The gunfire continued. Sporadic fire, followed by moments of silence. Finally chattering bursts of what could only be a machine gun, and now Louise's stomach clenched. Clarice whimpered.

This was not target shooting or even a skirmish between rival clans of bandits. This was a small battle, and it was taking place only a mile or two away from the village.

Chapter Nineteen

Louise and Clarice threw on clothes and rushed to the hospital. It was already in turmoil, with Kozlowski ordering the patients out of bed, putting rifles into the hands of men who could barely stand, and shouting at Frankie and Maria Elena when they didn't move quickly enough.

Louise took this in with alarm. "What are we doing?"

"The Japs are almost here," Kozlowski said. "Another hour, tops. A few villagers went down the mountain with rifles, but they won't hold them for long. We've got to get as many people out of here as possible." He turned to shout. "Nalty, get your butt in motion, I don't care if you're dying, I want you ready in five minutes, so help me God."

"You're sure it's the Japanese?" Louise asked. Kozlowski gave her a withering look. "I'm sorry," she said. "Of course you know. But we can't . . . Lieutenant?"

He'd turned away again, shouting more orders and shoving a sick man through the doorway.

"Lieutenant!"

"I don't have time for you, Louise. Go help the others. We leave in twenty minutes."

"We can't go, Lieutenant. We'll never make it."

He wheeled on her, grabbed her shoulders, and gave her a little shake, before he seemed to recognize what he was doing and let go.

"What would you have me do? For God's sake, they're here. Last time we did it, last time we evacuated, last time—"

"Last time we had a day and a half. This time we have an hour." She stopped as the sound of gunfire returned. "Where is Dr. Claypool?"

"I can't get him up, it's helpless. Blasted malaria. We'll have to leave him."

"Leave him and you won't have a field hospital to run."

"I'll have you, won't I? That will have to do."

"I won't allow it."

He blinked. "What?"

"The doctor is down, and that leaves me in charge of the hospital. And I'm telling you I won't allow it. We left three men in Sanduga and lost another on the road. If we run off in the night, we'll lose more, and the enemy will catch us anyway."

"What would you have me do? Surrender?"

"No, I want you to leave. Take Mailer and Nalty—they can walk. You'll have a chance. The rest of us will throw ourselves on the mercy of the Japanese."

The lieutenant said nothing for a long moment. It was probably only a few seconds but given the situation seemed to stretch on and on. At last he nodded.

"We'll go. You'll come with us."

Louise was prepared for this. "No, I'm staying. These men need me." She held up her hand when he started to protest. "Please don't order me. I'll only disobey."

"I need a nurse," Kozlowski said. "Mailer and Nalty can walk, but they're still sick and injured."

The other three nurses had gathered around and were listening with varying degrees of panic visible on their faces. Clarice, who'd never left Louise's side, could barely hold herself up, she was shaking so hard; Frankie looked stricken, her hands slack by her sides; and Maria Elena was crying quietly.

"Take Frankie," Louise said. "She's healthy, she—"

"I'm not going! You can't make me, I won't do it."

"But Frankie," Louise said, "if you stay, you'll be taken prisoner with the rest of us."

"I don't care, I won't go. I can't take it anymore, I can't do this. I want it all to be over, I want it over *now*."

"You think being a prisoner will make it over?" Louise asked.

"I—I'll go," Clarice said in a small voice.

Louise nodded. "Fine. Lieutenant, you have Miss Clarice."

"What supplies should I bring?" Clarice asked.

"Whatever you can carry. Be sensible." Louise turned to Maria Elena. "Help her get ready."

"Am I going, too?" Maria Elena asked.

"No, I need you here with me. Only Miss Clarice will go."

"That's really helpful," Kozlowski said sarcastically when the two youngest nurses had rushed off. "Miss Clarice. Wonderful. What would I do without her?"

Louise ignored him but addressed Frankie instead. "As for you, you can stay, but only if you do what I say. Is that understood?"

"All right," Frankie said. Some of her old sullen tone came through, but at least she'd said the right thing. "I'll do what you tell me."

"Good, start by getting the rest of those men back in their beds. Clean up what you can. I don't want it looking like men went rushing off, I want it to look like we have nothing to hide. Go, hurry."

When she'd gone, Louise turned back to Kozlowski. "Take your men and your nurse and go. Leave the rest of this to me."

"You're not in charge here, Louise."

"This isn't a military matter anymore. It's medical. Nobody else is around to make a decision, so until Dr. Claypool is up, that leaves me. And I'm making the call. I'm authorizing you to take Mailer and Nalty. You took Fárez, Zwicker, and Bautista already. Nobody else is well enough to leave. That's final."

Kozlowski looked at her, not budging. More gunfire. It wouldn't be long now. Finally his face softened. A decision in his eyes, followed by something that looked like relief.

"Okay. Good luck, Louise. These men are lucky to have you. Keep them alive if you can."

She took a deep breath. Claypool was down, Kozlowski soon to be gone. That left Louise in charge. But it needed to be done—it would save lives.

"And you, Lieutenant. I expect to see you again someday, alive and well."

"You've got yourself a deal. Take care, Louise."

He held out his hand. She returned the strong handshake of a farm girl.

And without another word he turned away. Five minutes later Lieutenant Kozlowski disappeared into the darkness with Mailer, Nalty, and Clarice.

<hr />

The villagers did their job and delayed the Japanese for three full hours. Far longer than Louise could have hoped. By then, she had the men back in their beds. She hesitated over Sammy for a long time.

"Please don't worry, Louise," he said, looking up at her from his cot. His face looked even more solemn than usual in the lamplight. "Nobody will think you abused me."

She'd already made him look as bedridden as possible, then, when it was clear they had a little more time, changed his bandages and fit his bed with the only set of sheets in the entire hospital. Make him look well cared for.

Louise glanced around. Scattered groans, coughs, and movement came from the darkness, a few asking for morphine or water but all staying relatively quiet. Waiting. She knelt and touched Sammy's hand.

"That's not my worry."

"I know."

"You're still my patient. I'll protect all of my boys, don't you worry." He took her hand and squeezed it. "You've done what you can," he whispered. "I'll take my chances with the rest of you."

Her heart ached to think of what might happen. The Japanese army was notoriously cruel to any who stood in their way, whether they were defending their homeland or not. Would they see Sammy as a coward for surrendering to the Americans? Would they learn of the letter he'd sent to his brother?

"Louise," Maria Elena said in a small voice. "What about the nurses?"

"What will they do with us?" Frankie asked. "Louise, I'm scared."

Louise rose to her feet. "Stay in the back, the both of you. At least until we know the enemy's intentions."

She also felt the cold dread that every woman in a combat zone faced sooner or later, that they'd fall into the hands of brutal soldiers intent on rape and other abuse. But somebody had to greet the Japanese and offer the surrender, so Louise gathered her composure and went outside to wait in the darkness.

The minutes crawled by. No gunfire now, only the croaking, squeaking, chirping countryside, the rush of the nearby brook, and the buzz of mosquitoes in her ears as they continued their relentless search for blood. Finally, at dawn, the enemy reached Cascadas.

The first to arrive were Sakdals, who swaggered into the village at first light. They were about fifteen in number, and Louise's first thought was that Kozlowski had made a huge mistake, that it hadn't been Japanese at all. Only a well-armed group of bandits who were taking advantage of the collapse of law and order in the wake of the invasion. In that case, it was a mistake for the lieutenant to have fled. A well-organized defense would have driven them off in search of easier prey.

Some of the swagger diminished as the men approached, and they looked about warily, as if watching for threats or perhaps simply places to loot and people to terrorize. One of the men spotted Louise where she stood in front of the hospital door. She froze in place as two of them approached, grinning. Her instincts cried for her to flee inside. There were soldiers in the hospital, and sick or not, they'd rise to defend her.

No. You are their last line of defense.

"This is a hospital," she said firmly, pointing to her armband with its red cross. "I am a nurse. This is a *hospital*. Do you understand?"

They didn't. That was clear from their expressions.

Wasn't the word for hospital the same in Spanish, which a lot of Filipinos still spoke? Maybe even Tagalog, too. She repeated the word with her best attempt at a Spanish accent.

The men turned to each other and grinned. One reached for the military badge on her collar and ripped it off. The gesture jerked Louise forward, and she cried out, startled. The men laughed at her discomfort. She regained her balance and shrank back against the hospital door.

"We surrender, but you must respect that this is a hospital. The men inside are injured, do you understand? They must not be harmed. They have rights as prisoners. This is a hospital!"

More laughter. For God's sake, why hadn't Louise kept Maria Elena with her instead of tucking her into bed? The Filipino nurse could have translated, could have insisted that the Sakdals obey the rules of war.

As if that would do any good. Thugs, that's all these men were. They wouldn't respect the men inside or any attempt to surrender. And one could only guess what they'd do with the women, starting with poor Maria Elena herself. Being a Filipina wouldn't help her; it would only make it worse.

And then a uniformed man pushed through the Filipinos, and such was Louise's fear that her first glimpse of the hated Japanese who'd pursued them into the mountains brought a flood of relief.

He was taller than she expected, thin and with sharp facial features. His eyes were hard and piercing, and he studied her like a hawk on a branch would look down on a rabbit sitting frozen with terror below. The man looked young, only in his early twenties, although she wasn't entirely confident in that assessment. But he carried himself like a captain or a major, with an arrogant confidence. He wore a sword on one side, a pistol in a holster on the other.

A second Japanese man came up, this one shorter. He had a pistol, but no sword, and wore a white armband with red Japanese letters. If not for the uniform, his round face and eyeglasses would have made him look like a schoolteacher. He asked a question of the first man, who responded in short, clipped tones. The second man gave a short bow and said something else. Both men sounded harsh and angry to her ears.

Meanwhile, the two Sakdals were leering at Louise. One reached out a dirty finger and stroked it along the side of her face, and she shuddered. His other hand went to her waist, and his companion laughed.

"Please," she said to the Japanese, unsure if they could understand. They would certainly understand her tone. "I am a nurse, and this is a hospital. Don't let these men inside."

Miraculously, her voice didn't shake, though she was weak with fear. She swore it wouldn't show on her face. She must appear confident.

The last defense. There is nobody else.

The Japanese man with glasses said something in Tagalog, and the two Filipinos pulled back, grumbling. But they seemed afraid of him and wouldn't look him in the eye.

The Japanese with the sword stepped forward. Between his sword and the way the other man deferred to him, she guessed he was in charge.

"Where is your commanding officer?" he asked. "Why isn't he here to speak to me? Is he a coward?"

Louise stared. He spoke in English, the accent so good that if she'd closed her eyes, she'd have thought him an American. There was a halting nature to it, though, like a car engine starting up after sitting unused in a garage.

"Answer me at once!"

She stammered getting the words out. "I . . . I'm sorry, I was surprised to hear English. We have no officer. He died of his injuries. There are only sick and wounded men inside. Prisoners of yours now, and you have responsibilities not to mistreat them."

After her initial shock, she knew whom she was looking at. Yoshiko Mori. Sammy's brother. She couldn't see a resemblance in his face, except for the general way that all of these Japanese looked alike to her untrained eye. But it must be him. Who else would speak English so perfectly?

"Who is in charge, then?" he asked.

"I am, sir."

He laughed, and anything American in his features disappeared into an expression that seemed utterly foreign and barbaric.

"It's true," she insisted. "We have a doctor, but he is sick with malaria. There's nobody else but us nurses. I'm the head nurse."

"And so you, a woman, are in charge?" He turned and said something to his adjutant, and the two men shared a cruel, mocking laugh.

Louise bristled inside but managed to keep her face calm and her voice even. "There is nobody else, sir."

"I don't believe your officer died, I think he's hiding somewhere. We'll find him, don't worry. Meanwhile, are there armed men inside?"

"No."

"Good. If there are, they will pay for it. As will you."

Mori, if that was indeed who it was, said something to his adjutant, who in turn gave instructions in Tagalog to the two Sakdals. These shouted back toward the other Filipinos.

These men had been rampaging through the village, kicking in doors and shouting. Many of the villagers had fled during the night, including the poor refugees from Sanduga, who'd been put to flight twice now for the crime of harboring Americans. But many remained, and there were cries and protests. A gunshot. An anguished woman's scream. Louise's stomach churned, but she kept her eyes on the Japanese officer.

Several more of the Filipino bandits came when they were called. Also, two more Japanese soldiers approached, lugging a machine gun between them, which they put down on a blanket and began to assemble. They moved slowly, faces pale and sweating, and even from a distance Louise could see that they were suffering from some ailment, most likely malaria.

Once five more Sakdals had arrived, Mori gestured at the hospital and shouted an order. His assistant translated, and the Filipinos came at her, grinning.

Louise blocked the door with her body. "No! Don't send in your thugs—I don't trust them. Please just go in yourself."

"And stumble into a trap?"

"There's no trap! I'll go with you. You'll see."

Mori put a hand on his sword hilt. "I'm warning you, woman."

Despairing, she tried one last time. "Before I let them in, tell them not to mistreat these injured men. For God's sake, I'm begging you."

"You have nothing to negotiate with, unless it's the hiding place of your commanding officer. Where is he?"

"I told you—"

He shouted something, which was passed on in Tagalog. The Sakdals dragged her out of the way. Her heart sank as they burst inside, shouting and jeering. Protests, cries of pain from those inside. Louise tried to go for the door, but more men held her against the wall.

A gunshot. Shouts and overturning cots inside.

"Leave them alone!" Louise cried. She struggled but couldn't get free.

Chapter Twenty

In the moments before the Sakdals entered the hospital, Sammy had been lying on a cot covered in a sheet, motionless, his ears turned toward the commotion outside like a radio antenna in search of a signal. Louise's voice came through, and though he couldn't pick out the individual words, she sounded remarkably calm. There were voices in Tagalog, which he didn't understand, plus Japanese and English. He heard someone say they were searching the village for Americans, and a man saying in English he was going to search the hospital, but nobody had entered yet.

Those inside were silent, listening. Some men muttered curses, others prayers. Maria Elena stood to one side, gnawing her fingernails, while the other remaining nurse, Frankie, made herself as small as possible in the corner. Moments earlier, she'd been complaining loudly.

Frankie had wanted to leave with the lieutenant. Why hadn't they let her? Except that everyone heard Frankie refuse to go. She didn't seem to remember that part now.

Louise had changed Sammy's bandages before going outside and told him to look both well treated and completely bedridden, whatever those things meant. Bedridden was to protect him from the Japanese soldiers, and well treated was to protect the nurses and Dr. Claypool. He meant to do it, if he could. More likely, his presence would only outrage the Japanese, who would see him as nothing but a traitor.

Isn't this what you wanted? Isn't this why you sent Yoshi that letter? You wanted to be found, and you wanted to suffer.

Well, yes. But that was then, and this was now. What did the suicidal man feel when he put the gun into his mouth and pulled the trigger? Was there a moment of regret, a split second of dismay between when the finger depressed and oblivion came? A terrible, awful feeling that a mistake had been made?

Sammy was feeling that awful regret now. But the moment between the finger tightening on the trigger and the sweet oblivion of death was dragging on and on. Weeks, in fact. The self-doubt and worry was crippling.

He reached out for Stumpy, but the dog wasn't there. Sammy had been caring for Stumpy since Corporal Fárez left for the bush to take up arms with the partisans, but he'd turned him out during the night. Stumpy would be safer with the other village dogs, where he'd be ignored by the occupiers.

If he were spotted inside the hospital, he'd be identified as something important to the wounded men. Their mascot, something to boost their morale. That would make the dog a target for abuse. And so Sammy had opened the window about an hour ago and pushed him out. Stumpy had stared back at him, tongue hanging out, then seemed to give a little shrug and trotted across the rice paddy toward the village. Off to attend to his doggy business.

The front door of the former church swung open. Voices in Tagalog came through the blankets that divided the wide-open space into separate rooms. A hand reached around the blanket and yanked it down from where it had been hung on a line. Several grinning Filipinos looked in.

There were about twenty patients in the room, counting the doctor, who was delirious, plus Sammy and the two nurses. Nobody moved or spoke or tried to resist as the newcomers strode in, holding rifles and looking for all the world like they'd overthrown some great military base instead of a small field hospital. There was nothing professional about them. They were nothing but Sakdals—thugs and bandits.

One of them stopped at an injured man and jabbered excitedly. The man on the mat answered. It was one of the four wounded Filipinos in the hospital. They dragged him to his feet, or what would have been his feet if he hadn't been missing them. They'd been blown off by an artillery shell a month ago now, and he'd been recovering ever since. He cried out as they balanced him on his stumps and jeered at his pain. After tormenting the man for several seconds, they dragged him toward the front door.

"What the devil?" one of the Americans said. "Let go of him, you sons of bitches." The man struggled to rise, but one of the Sakdals shoved him down.

The Sakdals found another Filipino moments later. This one saw what was coming. He threw back his blanket and tried to push past the men for the door. A man swung his rifle butt and caught him across the jaw. He went sprawling. The wounded Filipino was struggling to get back up when another Sakdal pointed his rifle at the man's back and fired. The gunshot was deafening in the enclosed space.

This was enough for the rest of the hospital patients. Shaking with fevers or grievously wounded, they were in no shape to resist the armed invaders, but this didn't stop them from trying. Someone called for Claypool, but the doctor was unresponsive. Others struggled to their feet.

"No!" Sammy cried. "Don't do it!" They hesitated. "Don't fight them! We don't know what's going to happen. But don't resist—that will get us all killed."

The Sakdals had spotted the near revolt, and they shouted to each other as they huddled in a defensive position. Two had dragged the man without feet outside, which left four more inside. Was Sammy wrong, had he made a mistake? Maybe the injured men would have overwhelmed these four, taken their guns, and mounted a counterattack against the ones remaining outside. No, that was pure fantasy.

He heard Louise crying out, begging for mercy. A man shouted at her in English.

Several more Sakdals entered the room, and the immediate crisis passed as the sick and wounded settled back, resigned to their fate. The search continued. The Sakdals found the other two Filipino soldiers and hauled them outside. A Sakdal spotted Sammy and came toward him. He seemed to think he'd spotted another Filipino, but confusion spread on his face as he approached.

At that same moment, someone discovered Maria Elena. This brought the attention of all the Sakdals, and Sammy was momentarily forgotten. They pressed her against the wall while Frankie went slinking in the opposite direction rather than come to her fellow nurse's aid. One of the Sakdals said something, and Maria Elena answered in a high, frightened voice. This brought laughter, and they groped her.

"Help me," she said in a small voice. "Somebody."

Once more, injured men started rising, pushed too far. This time the Sakdals had two men with rifles leveled at the prisoners. Two more were returning from dragging away the last of the injured Filipinos, and they had their guns aimed in from the far side of the room. It would be a bloodbath.

"Enough!" Sammy shouted. "Don't touch her, you animals."

He said this in Japanese, and the Sakdals froze at his voice, turning toward him. He grabbed his crutches and rose to his feet.

"I demand to see your commanding officer." Again, this was in Japanese. "These men are prisoners, this woman is a nurse, and you will stop abusing them at once. Am I clear?"

None of them understood Japanese; that much was clear by their blank expressions. It didn't matter. Neither did the specific commands. He could have been reciting the steps to make soba noodles, so long as it was in Japanese and his tone of voice commanding.

There was a moment of consultation, and then two of them went running for the door. To fetch the other Japanese, no doubt. Well, there was no sense waiting here to be discovered. No sense in feigning grievous injury.

He glanced at the injured Americans, expecting to see hatred and distrust. *Now,* they would be thinking. *Now he sells us out. He's been waiting all this time, and now is his chance.*

But what he saw surprised him. There was distrust in some faces and worry, certainly. But no hatred. And in others he saw hope, even admiration. These men knew what he was doing, or what he was trying to do, anyway.

Sammy could only do his best. If he died, so be it. Outside, all was shouting: English, Japanese, Tagalog. He couldn't pick out any of it.

He came out on his crutches, eyes blinking in the bright sunlight of early morning. A glorious day had dawned on the mountainside, with the clouds gone, the mist dissolving on the surrounding peaks, and everything a shimmering green. The outstretched wings of a hornbill soared overhead. Its massive beak was knobby and red, its neck plumage burnt orange. Sammy could almost picture the scene in the simple lines of a watercolor, how it would be painted for the viewer.

That was the wider view. Everything close at hand was fear and horror.

One of the injured Filipinos was already dead. He lay facedown with his head bashed in. A second sat in front of three Japanese soldiers, who were all shouting at him at once while he cried out in his own language, hands over his head. The Sakdals had the man without feet and were pushing him back and forth between them, jeering and spitting. When he fell, they slapped him and dragged him back up.

Louise was protesting all of this, but two Sakdals pinned her against the building with their forearms. She spotted Sammy and cried out for help.

"Leave them alone!" he said in Japanese. All eyes turned toward him. The mob parted.

And there he was, Sammy's brother, standing in the middle of the commotion. Yoshiko Mori. Older, more mature than when Sammy had last seen him, three years ago. He wore a captain's stars over red and orange stripes and carried his sword naturally, as if the *guntō* were a part of his body, like an arm or a leg. The samurai ancestry was evident on his face, proud and unyielding.

Yoshiko's expression didn't change but remained fixed in place like a mask from a Noh play as he came over. "So, I've found you."

"I'm asking you to leave these men alone. They're soldiers, they've surrendered, and they deserve to be treated as prisoners of war."

"The Sakdals are working out their frustrations. They've been cursed, shot at, crippled by malaria and dengue."

"Those things happen in war," Sammy said. "One doesn't need to become an animal."

"And now they must have their moment. Someone will bear the brunt of it. If not the injured Filipinos, then the Americans. I'm sure you would agree that would be worse. Once they have taken a little revenge, I'll bring them back into line."

It sounded both monstrous and reasonable at the same time. It was the sort of argument that Sammy had heard in China four years ago. The poor Japanese soldiers had suffered, and they must not be chastened too harshly for what they were doing in Nanking.

"You came for me," Sammy said. "Not for these men. They've done nothing to you."

To this point, the brothers had been speaking in Japanese, but this was delivered in English, and Yoshiko answered in the same language.

"Father would have been proud of me," Yoshiko said. "One should always look after one's brother, after all."

"You received my letter."

"I was . . . disappointed. And angry. Furious. What you did was"— a pause as he seemed to search for the right word—"treacherous."

Yoshiko glanced at Louise, which brought Sammy's attention, too. But if the nurse was listening to their conversation, she didn't show it. Instead she stared ahead, eyes glinting fiercely as she watched the Sakdals holding her against the wall.

"You know why I did it," Sammy said. "You must."

"You saw the whole thing through your American eyes, and you felt guilty. All of that garbage they taught you in school." Yoshiko's English was coming faster now. "You believed it. What a fool. What a damn fool."

"That's not American, Yoshi, that's human nature. That's *Japanese*! We're Buddhist and Shinto, and there's nothing there to justify the brutality of our armies."

"Stop playing dumb," Yoshiko said. "You know what I'm talking about."

"No, I do not," Sammy said. "Are you trying to justify what happened in Nanking? That was the army working out its frustrations, as you put it? You know what they call it in English? The Rape of Nanking."

Yoshiko said nothing.

"Listen to me," Sammy said. "This is Japanese, what I'm doing. It isn't me being an American, it's me loving my country."

"You're speaking English. That's proof enough."

"I switched to English to protect you. So we could speak frankly in front of your men. And you answered in English—you could have switched back at any time. As Bashō said—"

"Spare me your poetry," Yoshiko said. This was in Japanese. "Fujiwara, come here."

A young man with a "law police" armband came over. He was sweating and none too steady in his bow to Yoshi, and Sammy wondered if it was the heat, or if he'd been hit with malaria.

"Send off the Sakdals. They're to leave the Pinoys alone."

"Yes, sir."

But before Sammy could breathe a sigh of relief, his brother added, "We need those men alive to interrogate. After that, it doesn't matter what becomes of them." Yoshiko turned back to Sammy. "Where is the commanding officer?"

He and Louise had worked out the answer to this question earlier, and the lie came easily. "He died on the road. We left Sanduga in a hurry, and not everybody made it."

Yoshiko glanced at Louise. "That's what she said. Where are his papers?"

"I don't know anything about that. He probably didn't have any. They've been on the run."

"We took prisoners in Sanduga. An American and two Pinoys. We interrogated them. According to the men, there was a commanding officer and he was well and healthy when he left Sanduga. If he died, then where are his papers, his radio?"

Sammy figured his brother was bluffing about the prisoners, just as Sammy had been about the death of the lieutenant. There had been three men left behind in Sanduga, but they were to have killed themselves if the Japanese arrived. And so he shrugged.

"I don't remember any radio. Anyway, the officer wasn't healthy, he was dying. He barely made it five miles. They buried him by the side of the road."

Yoshiko smiled, and he switched to English once more. "Nice try, big brother." Back to Japanese. "His name is Lieutenant Kozlowski. He was uninjured, and he had a radio. Is he in the hospital feigning illness as he hides among the others?"

And just like that Sammy's lie was left in tatters. He only just avoided looking at Louise.

"Very well," Yoshiko said. "Don't answer the question. You've proven yourself a liar and traitor. Fujiwara, we'll be here a little while. Let's see if we can find suitable quarters for Corporal Mori."

Chapter Twenty-One

There was more violence that afternoon as the Sakdals ran through the village. They burned two houses, killed a man who fought back when they were harassing his daughter, and three of them came at dusk, drunk, trying to muscle into the hospital. Louise had remained standing at the hospital door all day, and ordered them to leave in the same tone she used when chasing Stumpy out of the garbage. To her astonished relief, they wandered off and left her alone.

When night finally came, she retreated inside, exhausted. Someone handed her water, which she gulped. She ate a little rice.

After that she felt well enough to work. She enlisted patients in nailing boards over the door to barricade it for the night. Then she organized herself and the other two remaining nurses. One was to stand by the door and listen for approaching enemies. Another was to serve patients. The third would sleep. Every three hours they would rotate responsibilities.

Dr. Claypool was still delirious, but many of the men had made slight improvements now that they'd being given quinine and other medications and been allowed to sleep and recuperate without the constant moving. Nature's remedies of time and the body's natural healing abilities were still the best medical care of all.

The enemy returned at dawn. Louise waited up front alone as two Japanese kicked down the makeshift barricade of boards. Captain Mori and his assistant stood to one side, waiting. Mori gestured for her to step outside. She obeyed.

Mori gestured for Fujiwara and another man to go inside, giving them instructions in Japanese. When she protested that her men were hospital patients and should not be abused, Mori said, "I am looking for Lieutenant Kozlowski. I have reason to believe he escaped into the woods with several other men, but I will check the hospital myself."

"You'd better not touch my patients," she said. "Those boys are sick and injured."

"Perhaps."

"Anyway, I told you that the lieutenant died. You won't find him inside."

"It would be better for you if you did not lie. And if a lie is the only thing you are capable of saying, then I'd suggest keeping your mouth shut."

"Where is your brother? Sammy is my patient, too, and I need to see to him."

Mori ignored the question. "You claim you are in charge. Very well, then you will be responsible for the behavior of all. Let me tell you the rules. First of all, you will be given the rice paddy behind the hospital as a yard. Your men will erect a fence around it to mark its limits."

"You can't put them to work in the sun. They're too sick for that."

"If they leave the building and the yard, they will be killed. If they have unauthorized contact with the villagers, they will be killed. If they strike or touch a Japanese soldier, they will be killed."

Mori ran through a list of offenses, several of which carried a death sentence, but other infractions would be punished in seemingly arbitrary ways. There would be morning calisthenics according to the style of the Japanese army, regardless of the weather. Those who were too ill or injured to participate would forfeit breakfast. Those who did so in a

slovenly way—whatever that meant—would be staked under the direct
sun for four hours. Fail to bow to any Japanese or fail to bow in the
correct way? You would be whipped or struck, depending on the whim
of the Japanese soldier you had insulted.

"Now I will teach you how to bow."

"I know how to bow," she snapped. "This is preposterous. These
men are prisoners. They have rights. The Japanese have promised to
obey all appropriate conventions."

"They will have their rights. Soon enough we will march them out
of the mountains. In Manila, there are camps, and they will enjoy all of
their privileges as prisoners of war. Packages and letters from the Red
Cross. The right to organize themselves as they see fit."

Louise stared. She let the hostility rise to her face.

"But for now we are in the mountains, and there are bandits all
around."

"Most of them working for the Japs, of course."

He ignored this insult. There was something professional about
him, even in his cruelty.

"Until the fence is constructed, nobody will leave the building
except as part of an organized labor crew."

"And what if we say no to your demands?" she asked.

"You won't."

"The devil, you say."

"You won't for long, I suppose I should say. You might try. Look
at me, Louise Harrison—yes, I know your name. Look into my eyes. I
am not playing a game. I will kill those who resist until I have complete
compliance. If necessary, I will let the Sakdals have their way with them
first. Injured men, your sick doctor, even the nurses—everyone must
comply or face the same consequences."

"You're a cruel, terrible man."

"I am a soldier at war. I have a traitor to deliver and enemies to kill
and capture. A population of sullen locals who must see the wisdom of

cooperating with the Japanese in throwing off the American imperialists. I will do what I must."

Louise had no doubts that he was serious and not bluffing, but she couldn't let this happen. She pitched around desperately for some way to soften the blow.

"Now I will teach you how to bow," Mori said. "Learning it properly will save you pain and humiliation later."

There was plenty of humiliation *now*, as he showed her how to do it and then corrected her multiple times. He put his hands on her head to force it down, and she bristled at his touch. But she couldn't fight this small battle when she had bigger concerns. She must get them resolved, or men would die.

Fujiwara came out during the bowing lesson, which stopped while the two secret police had a short, sharp discussion. They hadn't found Kozlowski, of course, because he wasn't inside. Louise braced herself to be interrogated again, but Mori sent Fujiwara off on some errand or other. The adjutant dragged himself off.

"Your man is sick," she said.

"Yes, many of us are sick. This cursed climate doesn't suit Japanese people any more than it does the Americans."

"I don't think it's malaria, luckily, but he's picked up something. He should be seen to. Probably all of you should be treated."

"You will, of course, use all available medicines to treat Japanese first, Americans second. If there is anything left, the Pinoys can be treated."

"No."

"Yes, you will. Japanese first, Americans—"

"No, I won't treat Japanese at all. You want to see your men treated, you'll take them back to your army and ask your own doctors. I won't do it, and neither will the other nurses."

"You'll do what I tell you, woman, or I will kill your patients one by one."

213

"And then I will kill yours. The first injection I give will be a lethal one."

Mori struck her across the face with an open palm. Her head rocked back, and her hand went to her stinging cheek, but she didn't cry out. She slowly lowered her hand and stared at him, though tears stung her eyes. Angrily, she willed them down. She would not cry.

"I can hit harder," Mori said. His hand went to his sword hilt. "Or if you refuse to use your hands for the purpose for which they were designed, I could take them off for you."

Fujiwara returned. He stood rigidly, staring. His hand was on his pistol. Louise looked at him, then back to Mori. She steadied her voice.

"I will help your men. There will be conditions."

"No conditions."

"Then there will be no help."

"I said no conditions!"

Louise didn't answer this. Instead she stayed still and rigid, waiting to be hit again. Her heart hammered away, her knees buckled, and her head floated as if she were about to swoon. She was more frightened than she could remember in her life. But she had to do this; she had to be strong.

A dog barked somewhere in the village—it sounded like Stumpy. Mori turned and seemed to notice the staring Japanese and Sakdals for the first time. They'd gathered around to watch the confrontation between the Japanese officer and the American nurse. He snarled at them, and they scurried off.

Only Fujiwara remained. He fixed her with a look that was even more terrifying than Mori's, because it was cold, impassive, without his officer's passion and fury. It was the look of a man who would commit atrocities when ordered to do so.

"Nothing unreasonable," Louise said. She couldn't keep the quaver from her voice and didn't continue until it felt under control. "Only requests of the most humane sort. If you do that, I'll help your men. You'll see that I can be compliant."

He said nothing, and that encouraged her to press on.

"You must return the two injured Filipinos to the hospital."

"They are inside already," he said.

"I mean they must be treated like the other prisoners. They can't be abused because they're Pinoys and you think they mean nothing. I know why you're doing it, I know what you're thinking, and I'm saying if you want my cooperation, you won't hurt them. The Sakdals answer to you, and if you tell them not to kill, not to harm them in any way, they'll obey. If they don't obey, then you have no control over them at all."

"And that's your demand?"

"They won't touch my Filipina nurse. Won't bother her in any way. And they won't abuse the villagers, either. They are innocent, and they had no more choice to house the Americans than they have in helping the Japanese now."

That wasn't true, of course. The Filipinos had been all too willing to help the Americans, whereas they held special fear of the Japanese. Dump as many leaflets as you'd like on Luzon—the people would never believe the invaders had come to liberate them.

"Very well. You have your conditions. I expect you to obey me in every way if I give you these things."

"I'm not finished. My men won't be digging a trench around the property or be putting up a fence. They are too sick and injured."

"They are prisoners of war. They must be confined until we leave the mountains."

"I'll see that it's done."

"You? A woman? A nurse?"

"Yes, me. I'll explain to them. You say they can't leave the building or the rice paddy behind. I will tell them. Any man found venturing away will be unprotected, will face severe punishment." Louise took a chance. "Only the nurses will be allowed to leave the property, and my men will know that. You'll see, they'll obey. And I'll see that they do their proper bowing when they must, that they show you proper deference, that they don't resist in any way your reasonable requests."

Mori spoke to his adjutant, who responded, then bowed, then spoke and bowed again. Mori grunted and turned back to Louise. Again she took this as acceptance, or as close to it as she would get.

"Finally—"

His eyes widened in disbelief. "There's more?"

"One final thing, assuming you allow us other reasonable accommodations—sufficient food, the ability to bathe, safety from reprisals for inadvertently misunderstanding your culture."

"Well?" he demanded. "What is it?"

Louise took a breath. "I need to see your brother."

"Ha! No. That is too much."

"He's injured, and I must be allowed to treat him."

"Impossible. You will not see him again." Mori said this with an air of finality. "Now, will you comply, or will I have you killed and deal with another in your place?"

She hesitated. He had given her almost everything she'd asked for, including the part she'd slipped in about allowing the nurses to leave the hospital. As much as she wanted to help Sammy Mori, he was out of her hands, and she couldn't sacrifice the rest of them for his sake.

Be patient. You'll have your chance.

Louise bowed as she'd been taught. "Yes, I will comply."

The Japanese that Louise treated in the hospital suffered the same tropical ailments as the Americans. She gave out quinine and deworming pills, passed them insecticide powder to help prevent scrub typhus caused by biting chiggers, and gave strict instructions for proper foot care; many suffered the so-called creeping cruds from spending too much time in wet socks and boots.

The Japanese didn't want to be near the American patients, and the Americans didn't want to be near the Japanese, so she treated the enemy soldiers in a small corner of the hospital with blankets for walls. Neither Maria Elena nor Frankie would help at first, both terrified for their own reasons, but she insisted.

The only real injury was a thigh wound, inexpertly bandaged by a Japanese medic. It was recent—must have happened during the Japanese march into the mountains. She stripped off the dirty bandage, cleaned the wound, and rewrapped it. The man grumbled irritably the whole time she was working on him.

When the Japanese had left, Louise explained the new rules to the hospital patients. The Filipinos practically wept with relief to hear that they would no longer be targeted, but some of the Americans reacted badly.

"I ain't bowing," one man grumbled. "Let the bastards kill me, I ain't gonna do it."

"It's a gesture," Louise said. "It means nothing."

"The hell it don't. I never would have bowed to my own general, and I sure ain't gonna do it to a Jap."

"It's like a salute to them," another man said. "It doesn't mean anything."

"I don't care," someone else said. "I'm not saluting, either."

"You want us to get killed over a bow?" came another man's opinion. "Don't be an idiot."

They carried on like this for several minutes. When the argument grew too heated, Louise told them to keep it down. She stood with her hands on her hips, waiting for it to burn out.

"You'll bow," she said. "That's all there is to it. I got everything else I wanted. Well, almost everything," she said, thinking of Sammy. "You fight the bowing and maybe you'll live, but the Pinoys won't. You'll have them killed over a bow?"

She nodded at the two Filipinos, and finally the Americans settled down. Grudging assent across their faces.

"Miss Louise is right," Frankie said.

She and Maria Elena had been bandaging the stumps of the Filipino without feet who'd been forced to dance for the amusement of the Sakdals.

"We're prisoners now." Frankie sounded surprisingly calm, and more reasonable than she had in weeks. "We have to swallow our pride and obey the enemy if we want to stay alive. That's our responsibility now. To obey without question."

"I wouldn't go that far," Louise said. "But let's pick our battles. And let me fight them, okay? Until Dr. Claypool is better, I'm in charge of all of your care. I need to keep you alive—that's the most important thing. Please, I'm begging you, don't make my job any harder."

That settled, she looked to Dr. Claypool. He was worse. The nurses got him up and moved him around a little bit, worried about bed sores and constipation. Louise gave him more quinine, but when she asked him for medical advice about a couple of patients, he muttered incomprehensibly and rolled over with a groan.

"Why isn't he getting better?" Frankie asked after they'd put him back down to rest. "The quinine should be working by now."

"He's older than these boys, and he was already run-down from all the work getting us into the mountains—that can't have helped. Give it time," Louise added with more confidence than she felt. "I'm sure he'll recover."

<hr/>

The Japanese wasted no time in enforcing their bowing rule. They arrived that afternoon and forced everyone to line up in the hot sun, even Dr. Claypool, who could barely hold up his head, and the various amputees. Captain Mori stood by, watching sternly, while Fujiwara showed the prisoners the proper way to bow. It came from the waist, with the head held just so, eyes in the correct position. When someone didn't do it properly, he was slapped across the face.

Mori kept his hand on his sword hilt, as if daring someone to respond to the provocation. Two other Japanese stood nearby with bayonets fixed to their rifles. Louise held her breath every time Mori punished one of her men, but though there were dark looks and mutters, no one was foolish enough to test him.

As the instruction went on and on to the point where it became obvious that it was more about establishing dominance than bowing technique, villagers were digging a trench around the hospital. Others built a guard station on stilts like a small, open nipa hut. Every villager seemed to be working, from children of four or five to the very old, even if they could barely drag a plank or carry a bundle of cogon grass.

The prisoners and guards alike were wilting in the heat by the time Mori called a halt to the bowing lessons. Nobody had been allowed to leave, no matter how ill. Some had soiled themselves, others were shaking violently. Dr. Claypool was barely conscious, held up by two other men.

Night was a blessed relief from the heat, but the nurses' work had only just begun.

Chapter Twenty-Two

Louise didn't leave the hospital grounds for three days. Already, after only a couple of weeks in Cascadas, they were running out of many basic medical supplies. She had no adhesive left for dressings, very little morphine, and the quinine was going down at a rapid rate, thanks in part to the demands of the Japanese. More urgently, they'd run out of vegetables and beans and were down to rice and salt—breakfast, lunch, and dinner. Captain Mori was nowhere to be seen, and there was nobody to translate her needs.

When Louise finally left the hospital, she did so alone. She didn't trust Frankie to behave, and she wasn't convinced the Sakdals would leave Maria Elena alone. Bring the pretty young Filipina nurse out of the hospital and they might forget their orders and start harassing her. How firmly had Mori put it, anyway?

One of Louise's shoes had completely worn out, damaged by all the trekking through the mountains and endless days on her feet. In place of shoes, she wore a pair of *bakya* like the locals, which were wooden soles tied with hemp cords to keep them in place. Her dress was hanging out back to dry, and in its place she wore a pair of men's trousers rolled up at the cuffs. They wouldn't have fit under any circumstances, but given how the weight was melting off her body, they hung tentlike over her bony hips and legs and would have fallen right off without the length of twine she used as a belt. In one pocket, she carried Sammy's book of Japanese poetry.

She meant to return it if given the opportunity, but with what motive, it was hard to say. Surely if he were a free man he'd have retrieved it himself or sent someone for it. That he hadn't meant he was a prisoner. Or worse. Louise's fear was that Mori had held a sham trial for his brother and ordered him shot.

A pair of Japanese soldiers sat beneath the open hut the villagers had built for a guard station. It sat about thirty feet across from the hospital door in a drained rice paddy. They were negotiating with a boy holding a bunch of bananas, but sprang to their feet when they saw her. One of the men shoved the boy aside with a sweep of the arm, and the two men grabbed their rifles.

One of the guards was the man whose thigh wound she'd treated a few days earlier, but from his glare, she didn't think he was remembering the treatment. Ingrate. He'd have gangrene if she hadn't treated him.

Louise bowed deeply. "I am going into the village. We have nothing but rice, and I need food for the hospital." She pointed to the boy and his bananas. "Like that. We need more food."

She started for the trail that led across the dike between two rice paddies, but had only taken two steps before one of the men blocked her progress. He looked irritated to be driven out of the shade and into the hot sun. He said something to her that was either an order or a question. Who could tell?

"I need food from the village," she repeated. She pantomimed eating. "Captain Mori said I could leave when I needed to. Yoshiko Mori—your officer. He said I could."

This seemed to spark something in the men, and they began to discuss the matter. Mori's name was repeated several times. Louise thought it better not to wait for their verdict, so she stepped around them and kept walking. She expected to hear a short, angry retort, the Japanese equivalent of "Halt!" But they didn't stop her.

Louise walked until she reached the shade of a tree between two village shacks, where she stopped to catch her breath and calm her thumping heart. Sweat trickled down her ribs and between her breasts.

She wasn't the only one to take refuge in the shade. Three village dogs lay dozing around the tree trunk, one of them Stumpy. He lifted his head and thumped his half tail, but the heat was too much to get him to stand up. He was her patient, too, in a way, and she couldn't help but see how he was doing.

"Look at that," she said. "Your mange is back. You need to keep better company than these mutts. Bet you have worms again, too, with all that garbage you're eating."

His tail thumped again, and he gave her a look that seemed to say, "Yes, and I don't really care. It's delicious."

She thought he'd stay napping in the shade, but when Louise moved on, he rose to his feet and followed several paces back.

"You're better off on your own," she warned him. "You know that, right?"

Stumpy paid her no attention but kept following. She thought about shooing him off, worried for his safety, but he was probably okay. The dogs were safer than anyone else in the village. Americans had died of injuries and illness; villagers suffered under the rampaging Sakdals. The Japanese soldiers risked partisans, tropical ailments, and even their own officers, from what Louise could see.

No, being a village dog wasn't the worst thing in the world, given present circumstances.

Louise's destination was a villager named Nola, who had sold them food before the Japanese arrived. The woman kept several chickens at her home on the edge of Cascadas and sold the eggs for exorbitant sums to the Americans, who were desperate for them. For a more reasonable price, the nurses had acquired lard for cooking, as well as squash, corn, and a spinachlike plant called Talinum.

What Louise really wanted, what she'd have given anything for, was fresh bread with butter. But it was all rice here, meal after meal, day after day. That was acceptable if you could find something else to go with all that rice.

She found Nola squatting outside her hut, roasting bananas on a stone over a little fire. It was the most delicious thing Louise had ever smelled, and her stomach clenched greedily.

Nola was slender and flexible, and her figure looked girlish squatting in front of the fire, not like the grandmother she was. One of her daughters had moved to a nearby village with her husband, who was a trader of sorts, and it was through him that Nola got some of her supplies. Her husband was dead, but one son still lived with her, and if Louise made the purchase, he'd haul the goods to the hospital.

Louise cleared her throat. "Excuse me."

Nola looked up, startled, and her eyes widened when she saw the nurse. She glanced around with a worried expression and waggled her finger in a warning.

"There's nothing wrong," Louise said in a calm tone. "The Japanese let me out. I only want to buy some food—eggs and vegetables. We'll need more rice. Bananas, too. And eggs, did I say that already? As many as you have." She pantomimed cracking eggs.

"Food no. Today no. Not give. Not have."

From the fearful look on the old woman's face, it seemed that the Japanese had already been here, had no doubt taken what they wanted. Louise looked to make sure there were no Japanese or Sakdals around, then pulled out bills and coins from her trousers, about twelve pesos in all.

"Don't worry, I'll pay. I won't steal from you."

The smell of roasting bananas combined with the mere mention of eggs to make her almost faint with hunger. It was all she could do not to reach down and help herself, burned fingers be damned.

"*Mabuting tao ang mga Amerikano,*" Nola said. Americans good. This was followed by something else in Tagalog that Louise didn't catch, and finally, "No food. No give. Haponese!" Another fearful look around.

"They took everything? Even fruit? How about that?" Louise pointed to the roasting bananas and pantomimed giving money. "I'll take it."

Nola pushed away the offered money. "Haponese no food Amerikanos." She clicked her tongue and drew her index finger across her throat.

Louise finally understood. Nola wasn't saying she didn't have food; she was saying that the Japanese had forbidden her from selling to the Americans. With more than twenty men under his command, Captain Mori would be demanding everything for himself.

"A little bit, then." Louise held up two fingers. "Two eggs. And some rice." She pantomimed pouring grains of rice through her hands. "And the bananas. Please. Just a little."

But nothing would budge Nola. She grew more agitated the longer Louise tried, finally waving her arms and speaking rapidly in a high voice. Worried that the noise would draw attention and put them both in danger, Louise threw up her hands in defeat.

"Fine, refuse to help us." Desperation made her sound shrill. "We have two days of rice and almost nothing else. Do you hear me? Nothing. For God's sake, if you don't—"

And now Louise was the one who would attract attention. She had to get hold of herself, had to pull herself together. She straightened her clothing, turned around, and walked away. Stumpy had been watching the whole exchange with a slightly puzzled expression and fell in behind her.

Louise felt more exposed and in greater danger than ever walking through the village, but her heart sank at the thought of returning to the hospital empty-handed. There had been few complaints about food—except for Frankie, of course, who would complain about anything—but given how Louise's mouth had watered and her stomach growled at the roasting bananas, they must be ravenous by now.

Rice and beans every meal, and now only rice. She had to get something, if for no other reason than to fend off beriberi and scurvy. Venture to the edge of the rice paddies and see if she could scavenge fruit? What about wild game? Could she convince Captain Mori to let her men out hunting? What if she promised to share the meat with the Japanese? No, what a ridiculous thought. Mori would never allow it.

In fact, she was putting herself at risk simply by walking around the village. Venture toward the forest and they might simply shoot her. But she had to take the risk. There was fruit in the trees on the edge of Cascadas.

But when she cleared the last of the village houses and reached the brook, she stopped in dismay. A Japanese soldier was bathing in a pool beneath one of the series of cascades that gave the village its name. He was short, with broad shoulders and a thick neck. Built like a wrestler, with a prominent scar on his back. Fortunately he was turned and didn't spot her.

Louise thought he was one of the men she'd treated for malaria earlier, although he seemed better now. At the very least, his chills hadn't stopped him from washing in the cool mountain stream. He scrubbed himself so vigorously with a bar of soap that it looked like he was trying to peel off his skin. It was easy to read something into that, but she'd once seen Sammy washing his hands and face with that same enthusiasm, so it was probably a Japanese habit.

Stumpy kept trotting forward even as Louise backed away. For a moment she thought the dog was going to go up and say hello to the soldier and then she'd be discovered, but he stopped and looked back at her. She gestured urgently. Miraculously, the dog returned to her side.

Louise gave him a stern look once they were back in the relative safety of the village. "I think it's time you and I parted ways, don't you? I've got to find my way out of the village, and I can't have you sniffing soldiers or barking or whatever."

He looked up, panting. Looked worn out from the heat, but he kept following.

"Go on, then, you heard me. You'll be happier in the shade, and I don't have a single thing for you to eat if that's what you're hoping for. I mean it. I'm putting you in danger, too, you know."

It was then that she realized something odd. Since getting past the two men at the hospital, she hadn't seen a single other enemy soldier until now. Her mind had been fully occupied, or she would have noticed it earlier. There were only seven or eight Japanese soldiers in all, so that part wasn't so strange, but what about the Sakdals? Where were they?

She was more observant as she backtracked through the village. It was quiet, few people out and about. A naked child of three or four stepped out of his house and looked up at her with wide eyes. A woman emerged after him, her expression fearful as she dragged the child back by the arm. Her face grew more fearful still when she saw Louise.

"Food not give. Not have." The woman vanished with her child.

"Yeah, I get it," Louise said. "You're all scared and won't lift a finger. Fine."

In any event, if the rest of the Japanese had left, along with their thuggish helpers, she had only to avoid the bathing man and the pair guarding the hospital and she could keep searching for food. There were some banana trees next to the alcalde's house, which Mori had taken over as his headquarters. If he was away, she could risk stealing some.

The exact situation was uncertain enough that her heart was pounding as she worked her way down a tiny alley between the hillside and three village homes. When she reached the last one, slightly larger and less dilapidated than the others, she stopped and listened. Voices came from one of the houses, but they were two women speaking in Tagalog and a baby crying. Nothing from the alcalde's house. It seemed abandoned.

You could go inside.

The thought came to her unbidden. She realized as she'd been walking through the village that she'd been unconsciously searching for Sammy Mori. Far from pocketing his little book of poetry just in case, she'd fully intended to find him and return it.

Before she could reconsider, Louise took the three steps to the porch of the shack and pushed aside the mosquito netting to let herself inside. It was clean and tidy, with a rolled-up mat in one corner that must serve as Captain Mori's bed. A shorter bamboo mat sat in front of a stubby makeshift desk, and there were a few papers on it with Japanese writing. The papers were stacked, with two pens lying side by side. A wooden bowl sat with a pair of chopsticks on top of it. Both clean.

There was nobody inside. Wherever they kept Sammy, it wasn't in his brother's house.

For a moment Louise thought about setting the book on the table. Let Captain Mori return and see his brother's poetry book. Maybe it would prick his conscience. Maybe he'd carry it to Sammy and the two brothers would have a moment of reconciliation.

But no, she decided. It was too risky. The Japanese officer would know how it got there. If he thought she was searching his house while he was away, he'd withdraw her privileges. Maybe worse.

Disappointed not to have found Sammy, Louise came outside and went to the banana grove. There were no ripe bananas, but she spotted several clusters that looked almost ready to eat. Take them back to the hospital, hide them for a couple of days while they ripened, and share them out. It wouldn't be much, but it would be something. Now, how to get them down from the tree?

She'd climbed many trees in her younger days, but the slippery trunk of the banana tree was something else. She kicked off the *bakya* and dug her toes into the trunk as she tried to hoist herself up. Maybe a few weeks ago she could have managed, but her arms were weak, the muscles melted away through disuse and sorry nutrition.

She had greater success with another tree. Its bananas were higher up, but it grew next to the hillside, and she was able to use the hill for leverage as she scaled the tree. When she got up, she realized they couldn't simply be plucked off like apples. What she needed was a machete to hack down the entire stalk. She wrenched and twisted and finally got some of them loose, which she dropped to the ground. She shimmied down.

So far, so good. Now she just had to get past the guards at the hospital, who hopefully wouldn't question her about the origin of the inexpertly harvested bananas.

Stumpy barked as Louise was slipping on her *bakya*. She turned to hush the silly thing, but the dog wasn't barking at her. Instead something beneath the house had drawn his attention. Like the other nipa huts, it sat on stilts a couple of feet above the ground. This kept the buildings dry from the constant rains, as well as kept out snakes and other animals. Of course, this also provided an ideal hiding place for various crawling things.

Stumpy squirmed his way farther in until only his rump and tail were exposed. He'd probably found a cobra. Didn't a street dog have better sense than to go in after it?

"Get back here right now," she whispered.

Stumpy whined, then barked again, this time more agitated. Good heavens, he was going to get her caught. She eyed the bunch of bananas at her feet, tempted to snatch them, leave the dog, and run.

"Stumpy!" she said. "Stop that."

And then a voice came from the darkness beneath the house. "Miss Louise? Is that you?"

Chapter Twenty-Three

Louise froze in shock. Sammy? Had Captain Mori been so cruel as to chain his brother up beneath the house, as if it were a dungeon? It had been three days already, and Sammy must be dying down there in the mud and rotting leaves.

She grabbed for Stumpy to pull him out of the way. He resisted, whining.

"Did they put you down there?" she whispered.

"No, I'm hiding."

"What?"

Stumpy escaped from her and squirmed into the hole. He barked again.

"Keep quiet, you dumb mutt," the man said. "Go on, get. I'm trying to hide here."

That wasn't Sammy's voice. It was Corporal Fárez.

"What are you—Jimmy, is that you?"

"Shh, yeah." Then, in a different tone. "Stumpy, will you please . . ."

Fárez's hands emerged from the hole, pushing a filthy dog ahead of him. Stumpy shook off clumps of dirt and leaves, trotted a few paces away, and flopped down with an aggrieved sigh.

Louise straightened and looked around. When she was certain she was alone, she turned over the bananas as if studying them. She didn't look at the house or the space beneath it.

"What are you doing down there?" she asked.

"Waiting until night. I got here before dawn and have been hiding here ever since. As soon as it got dark, I was going to come to the hospital and find you."

"What? Why? Did you know you're hiding under the house of the Japanese commander?"

"Huh?"

Louise turned over the bunch of bananas again, as if it were the most fascinating thing in the world. "This is Captain Mori's house."

"Mori?"

"Sammy's brother. He's military police."

"Figures. I didn't know. It was the best place I could find. Most of the houses are too open underneath, too easy to spot someone hiding there."

"You're lucky he's not here."

"I know he's not, 'cause he's out in the jungle looking for us. I saw the Japs with my own eyes. Five of 'em, together with a bunch of those Filipino bandits. Don't know how they found us so quick. Must have been Sammy. He must have told his brother."

"He wouldn't do that."

"Sammy is back with his kind now," Fárez said. "He's one of them again, and I'll bet he told 'em everything."

"How would he have helped, anyway? Sammy didn't know where you'd gone. None of us did."

"Bet he told his brother we'd escaped. That put them on the trail."

"Captain Mori already knew," Louise said. "He spotted the missing radio. He didn't believe me when I said that Kozlowski had died—he's no idiot. And his adjutant is plenty clever, too. Then there's the locals, always talking and spreading the word. I'm sure that's how Mori tracked you down."

"However it happened, they found us, all right. We were about twenty miles from here in another village. Well, five huts and a church with a collapsed roof—not much of a village. Someone warned us the Japs were on the way."

"Mori must have heard through the bamboo telegraph. It's hard to keep secrets up here."

"It helped us in this case," Fárez said. "We got word and made a run for it. You've got to hand it to that Mori guy. He's relentless. We came down the hill to find the enemy coming up the other way. Had a little firefight—I think we got two or three of the Sakdals, but they hit Kozlowski."

"Really?" Louise licked her lips. "Was he . . . is he . . . ?"

"No, he's not dead. I brought him partway down, but he can't travel anymore. Anyway," Fárez continued, "we got into the jungle, and the Sakdals didn't want to go in after us. Don't blame them, really. Mori shouted at us in English. He said he had all of you prisoners at the hospital."

"That's true enough."

"The guy's English is perfect. Like his brother's. Sounded like a Yank yelling at us. Anyway, he says we can turn ourselves in and we'll be taken care of. We keep fighting, and he'll have us shot 'cause we didn't stop when we had the chance."

"Did anyone want to surrender?" she asked.

"Hell, no!"

"Tell me about the lieutenant."

"Koz is alive. He needs Claypool, but I think he'll pull through if he gets seen in time."

"What are his injuries?"

"Got hit in the gut, but I don't know anything more than that. That's why I came for the doc. Was going to wait until night, then go around to the hospital and see if I could get someone's attention. The doc could sneak out with me and be back by morning."

"Dr. Claypool can't help. He's deathly ill."

"Then you'll have to do it. Come hide down here until dark, and we'll go out."

"That's no good," Louise said. "The Japanese do a check every night and another check every morning. They'll see I'm missing. Besides, two guards saw me leave. They'll expect me back before dusk."

"I can't just let him die!"

"Shh, quiet. I'm not saying that. Let me think."

Louise had been lucky so far. Nobody had come to challenge her. There hadn't even been any villagers out. Some of that was the heat, some no doubt their fear of the Japanese and the Sakdals. But with Mori and his men gone, there were apparently only three enemies left in the village: the two guards and the man she'd spotted bathing at the cascades. Where was the bathing man now?

And where was Sammy? Between his leg cast and his brother's suspicions, she couldn't see a scenario by which he was out slogging through the hills looking for partisans. He must be around here somewhere. An idea came to her. Risky, but no riskier than standing here talking to Fárez when being caught would mean both of their deaths.

"How are you doing down there?" she asked.

"I'm all right."

Something in his tone gave her pause. "You're sure?"

"It's wet, it's hot, it's cramped. Some darn thing or other crawled past my leg."

"You're not sick, though? Your injuries are still healing up?"

"I'm fine. Got no complaints."

No complaints! Stuck in a filthy hole beneath the home of his enemy, but no complaints. These men. Whenever Louise felt sorry for herself, she could look to their example. She didn't feel brave, but then again, Fárez didn't sound that way to her ears, either. She'd always thought bravery was a feeling—confidence, surety of purpose—but maybe she was wrong. Maybe the brave were just as terrified as anyone else. Maybe *more* terrified. Because they wanted to cower and hide but knew they must put themselves in danger or they'd never live with themselves.

"Can you hold out until night?" Louise said. "Let's say an hour after dusk. I'll come get you."

"If I have to. What if Mori comes back?"

"If he does, sneak out and meet me at the cascades. Do you know where that is?"

"Yes, Miss Louise. How you gonna do it? How are you going to get past those guards?"

"I don't know that yet. But I've got an idea. I'll work it out some more, don't worry."

"Okay. One other thing. Can you do me a favor? I'd sure appreciate it."

"What is it, Corporal?"

A dirty hand reached out from the gap beneath the building, holding something in its grasp. "I brought this for Stumpy, but I didn't think he'd leave if I gave it to him just now. Could you?"

She took it. It was a ham bone wrapped in a banana leaf. Fárez had been shot at, had fled through the jungle with his injured officer, and had come back here to hide in a filthy crawl space for hours on end. And all that time he'd been carrying a bone for his dog.

———

Louise cast Stumpy a skeptical look as he sprang to his feet and followed her out of the alley.

"And where's *your* loyalty, hmm? The only thing you're loyal to is the smell of a ham bone in my pocket. Sorry, but you're not getting your greedy little paws on it. Not yet."

Stumpy licked his chops and panted.

She'd thought about leaving the bananas behind but decided that when she made her way back to the hospital it would look more suspicious with her hands empty than carrying the pilfered fruit. And then there was the ham bone. Fárez didn't know how hungry his fellow soldiers had become since he left Sanduga, or he might not have trusted her with the bone.

The village was just as quiet as before, but Louise didn't feel complacent. Her biggest worry was the Japanese soldier she'd spotted washing himself in the cascades. He was surely finished bathing by now and was who knew where. There could be Sakdals, too, or merely informers who'd be happy to say that they'd spotted one of the American nurses skulking about.

The bananas were her defense. At worst, she was on an unauthorized scavenging mission. And that much was true. Or had been. She had a different object in mind now.

Louise stepped down another alley, this one behind a single ramshackle nipa hut that looked in danger of sliding down the hill. An old woman peered out from the doorway, lips pulled over toothless gums in an expression that made her look like a withered doll. She didn't look like an informant, and Louise decided to take a chance under her gaze instead of out in the open.

She turned her back on the woman without waiting to see if she'd go back inside and took out Sammy's book of poetry. She held it under Stumpy's nose.

"Now I know you're no bloodhound, but I bet you can smell that and know who it belongs to."

The dog casually sniffed the book; then his nose jabbed at the pocket holding the ham bone. She pushed his snout away.

"I'm serious, Stumpy. We need to find Sammy. Come on, take another smell." She put the book in his face.

He sniffed it a little more and pulled back with what looked like the dog equivalent of a shrug. She studied his face, searching for some evidence that he understood. And saw none. He looked as carefree and unconcerned as ever.

"You're an opportunist, do you know that? You may have everyone else fooled, but not me. You weren't whining because you missed Fárez, you smelled his bone, didn't you? Well, guess what? You're not getting it if you don't help me find Sammy. I'm serious. I'm going to drop it in the rice water and boil that darn thing until there's not a scrap of flavor left, and I'm giving the broth to my men. And then I'm going to toss your bone in the latrine. What do you think about that?"

Who was she fooling? Negotiating with a dog. First of all, nothing would get his little walnut-size brain off the ham bone until he'd eaten it. Second, she wasn't so hungry yet that she'd steal Stumpy's treat. Not when she'd promised Fárez. He'd end up gnawing it to pieces when all was said and done.

Stumpy trotted ahead of her, and hope rose that he understood and was off to find Sammy. He sniffed at a rubbish heap in the space between two houses. He rolled in it. Another dog came out from the shade where it had been resting, and the two dogs sniffed each other's backsides.

"No wonder you need another deworming," she muttered.

Well, this was pointless. Time to go back to the hospital with the bananas and think of another plan. How was she going to get to Lieutenant Kozlowski?

She started to turn around, but Stumpy and his friend finished their snout-to-rump visit. Stumpy trotted ahead with a glance over his shoulder, as if curious whether she was following. His half tail gave a quick, encouraging wag.

"Oh, all right. I'm coming. I know it's pointless, though."

Louise emerged from the alley, glanced either way to make sure the unaccounted-for Japanese soldier was nowhere to be seen, and crossed to another alley on the other side. There were three more grass-roofed shacks on the left, while on the right, paddies terraced down toward the forest. Two women thrashed sticks at bundles of rice to separate the grains but didn't look in her direction. The village simply wasn't very large, and this was the last unexplored corner. Sammy might very well be around here somewhere, in which case she'd already walked past his house. Short of calling out his name, how was she going to find him?

As if in answer to this question, Stumpy trotted up to the middle house and stood at the bottom of the steps, staring. She took a closer look. A Japanese-style army shirt hung on a line on the porch, together with socks, undergarments, and several other articles of clothing that were evidently not Filipino.

The clothing wasn't Sammy's. Kozlowski had taken the man's uniform weeks ago in Sanduga and given him a pair of pants and a white shirt from the hospital supplies. The Japanese uniform had been irritating the other patients. The drying clothing must belong to another Japanese soldier.

Stumpy looked back at her, then turned and stared hard. He looked like a bird dog pointing into the brush. It must be the right house. Either that, or both nurse and dog were idiots, and that couldn't be ruled out.

Heart pounding, Louise walked up the three steps to the open doorway. She peered into the gloom. There was movement, a man coming toward the door.

"Sammy? Are you in here?"

An angry Japanese voice responded.

Chapter Twenty-Four

Louise shrank back and turned to run. A Japanese soldier followed her out and grabbed her arm. He was thick faced and squat, but strong, and he spun her around and knocked the bananas out of her arms. His breath smelled of fish and pickled vegetables.

"I'm sorry," she said. "I was looking for your officer. Mori. Yoshi—I don't remember. Yoshiko Mori! The captain. Ouch, let go of me, you animal."

He kept yelling at her as he shook her, and she kept protesting. Stumpy came up the stairs, barking. The soldier kicked at the dog, connecting with his bare foot, and Stumpy ran off with a yelp.

A second voice spoke up from inside, and the man who'd grabbed Louise looked back and answered. A brief argument broke out.

"Louise, is that you?" It was Sammy. His voice was anxious, worried.

"Tell him to let me go. Sammy, please." She squirmed in the man's arms, but he kept shaking her.

"I'm trying!" More angry words in Japanese.

The soldier dragged her inside. Her eyes adjusted, and she saw Sammy sprawled on a *patati* on the floor, wearing nothing but his skimpy Japanese loincloth. She was so relieved to see him that she almost rushed to his side with a cry.

He and the other man kept arguing, but Sammy seemed to be getting the upper hand. Finally the other soldier stopped, crossed his arms sullenly, and stared. Louise got a better look at him. He was the man Louise spotted bathing at the cascades.

"I treated him for malaria," Louise told Sammy after taking a closer look at the other man's face. "You'd think he'd be a little more grateful."

"That's probably why you're still alive," Sammy said. "Oto isn't the sort you want to cross."

The other soldier seemed to recognize his name, and he glared at Sammy, who said something back. Oto glanced at her. His expression was unreadable.

Sammy reached for his clothes and began to put them on, starting with his trousers. His cast was gone, and he moved his leg stiffly to get it in the pant leg. That worried Louise, but she had more immediate concerns.

"What did you tell him?" she asked.

"That you've come to check on his malaria."

"He's not going to believe that. How would I even know he was here?"

"Presumably, the same way you figured out *I* was here. Anyway, it doesn't matter. My brother left him on guard duty for a reason. Oto is as stupid as he is mean and ugly. Pretend to examine him. We'll keep talking—you can tell me what this is all about."

Louise took a tentative step toward Oto. The man glared back. Veins stood out on his neck. He glanced to one side, and following his gaze, she saw his rifle against the wall. He was thinking about going for his gun.

Then he must be scared of you, too.

When she'd treated him in the hospital, he'd initially refused to take his quinine. Only when Captain Mori yelled at him had he done it. Oto must have thought she was going to poison him. He was apparently still afraid. This boosted her confidence.

Louise spoke in soothing terms, as if trying to comfort him, though her words were directed to Sammy, whom she didn't look at. "Where is your cast? Why did you take it off?"

"That was my brother's idea."

"Your leg is still healing. You should have worn it another three weeks."

"I know. That's why he had it cut off. He's trying to immobilize me."

"Oh, I see." She put her fingers on Oto's throat, as if checking his pulse. The man closed his eyes rather than look her in the face. "This man is healthy. I wish Dr. Claypool would recover like this."

"What are you doing here?"

"I came to look for you."

"Louise."

He sounded like he was going to say something else but stopped. Unlike Oto, however, he didn't look away, but held her gaze. Louise took a breath, and for the first time she felt something for this man. Not merely a nurse for her patient.

"I would have come for any of my boys."

"I know." Sammy stopped, and she thought that he was going to turn away from whatever had been on his tongue a moment earlier. Then he said in a soft voice, "That is what makes you special, Louise."

Something moved inside her breast, a feeling so physical and unde- niable it was like watching a green shoot rise from the warm spring soil. But before it could leaf out, Oto opened his eyes and scowled.

Louise forced herself to speak in a normal tone. "What is your brother going to do to you?"

"Turn me over to his colonel. I don't know if he's told his colonel yet, but he'll know soon enough."

"Would your brother really do that to you?"

"He would." There was no uncertainty in Sammy's voice. "It's just a question of getting me down to headquarters. Then they'll have their way with me, I suppose."

"But he's your brother."

"My brother is a loyal subject of the emperor and the Imperial Japanese Army, and happy to prove it. We'd have returned already except for the matter of Kozlowski, Fárez, and the rest. They were spotted at another village not far from here, and my brother set out to bring them in. Yoshi wants a total victory."

"How did he know about the partisans? Did you tell him?"

"Of course not!"

His voice was too sharp, and Oto pulled back. He said something to Sammy, and the two men argued again. It ended with Oto grunting and looking displeased.

"I told Oto he needs more quinine," Sammy said. "He says he doesn't need it."

"He's right. I'm not wasting more quinine on him."

"I was covering my raised voice—you can give him whatever you'd like. A sugar pill or something."

"If I had sugar, I wouldn't waste that, either. But yes, I can give him a bicarbonate of soda."

"Unbutton his shirt," Sammy said. "You need to check his belly."

Louise didn't need to do any such thing but understood Sammy's reasoning. Keep the conversation going. She reached out to unbutton Oto's shirt, but he slapped her hand away. Sammy spoke sternly, and finally Oto turned away, as if unable to bear her looking. His belly was thick, but hairless, with a pink, ropy scar running from his navel, across his ribs, and to his back. It was an ugly wound that nobody had bothered to suture.

The nurse in her rebelled at that. She was less concerned with how unsightly it looked than knowing it must cause him discomfort being improperly healed. Someone had done this man wrong.

"So you *didn't* tell your brother?" she asked again.

"Of course I didn't. I know nothing, I saw nothing. Some Americans may or may not have run off when the Japanese came—I can't be sure

"Are the guards letting you come and go?"

"No," she said. "I had a bit of trouble getting out. They'll never let me leave at night."

Oto said something. He gestured with his hands and started to button up his shirt.

"Now he thinks you're done and just trying to humiliate him. He's going to kick you out if you don't come up with something better than malaria."

"What are the Japanese most afraid of here?"

"Parasites," Sammy said without hesitation. "Japanese bathe more than Americans—they keep themselves clean—and they worry about the local vermin: tapeworms, biting insects, and the like. I'd say our friend here is more anxious than most. He's from Osaka, not the countryside."

Americans shared the fear of tropical parasites. One of the first things she'd heard upon arriving in Manila was of a spider called a *chupa-ojo*, so named by the Spaniards because it crawled onto your eyeballs while you slept, anesthetized them, and sucked out the juices. You woke blind, your eye sockets shriveled like prunes.

Miss Frankie had first told her of the *chupa-ojo*. When Louise scoffed, Frankie told her to prove that it didn't exist.

"There's some strange striations on his back," she said, poking at Oto's shoulder blades. She made her tone worried. "I'm concerned he's infected with greater bone worms."

"What the devil is that?"

"Nothing. But if it *did* exist, it would be something you'd want to get rid of at once. Especially if you already had a natural fear of parasitic infection."

"I'll tell him."

"And tell him if his scar is still hurting him, it's probably because the worms release a chemical toxin that impedes healing."

Sammy spoke while she pulled Oto's shirt back down and pointed at various random spots on his back. He tried in vain to look over his shoulder at what she was indicating. When she poked, he winced, as if it had actually caused pain, and said something worried to Sammy. He shook his head in answer.

"Do you have a bowl?" Louise asked. "Good. I want Oto to give me a urine sample. I'll take it back to the hospital to check."

"And what will you find?" Sammy asked.

"Whatever I need to."

"Right."

Sammy gave Oto the bad news. Soon the thickset soldier was tromping down the stairs with a rice bowl in his hand. At first she thought he would just lower his trousers and do it right there. Some of the villagers would urinate in front of her, and maybe Japanese soldiers would, too. But this one apparently didn't want to expose himself in front of a foreign nurse. Little did he know that she'd already seen him bathing naked at the cascades.

"Okay," she said to Sammy. "I've got to get out of the hospital for an extended period of time tonight. How will I do that?"

"You've set it up perfectly already."

"What do you mean?"

"Oto shouldn't be up and about until you've treated him. He should stay here on his mat moving as little as possible."

"That's right," she said, catching on. She gave a solemn nod. "Bone worms can migrate. Very dangerous."

"The two guarding the hospital are no more clever than Oto," Sammy said. "There's a reason my brother left these men behind. I'll bet we can fool them, too. You tell Oto you need me to come with you to translate when you speak to the others, and you'll do whatever tests you need to do on Oto's urine until nightfall. Then you come back to check on Oto. That gets you out in the dark with medical supplies."

It was a good plan, assuming nothing went wrong. The obvious flaw was having to depend on the gullibility of three Japanese soldiers, but other things could go wrong, too. Captain Mori might return, for one thing. Or Kozlowski might die from his wounds before she reached him. Or they might be beyond her abilities to treat.

Oto came in holding the bowl in front of him. He had his hand on his back and was grimacing, as if in real pain. She didn't doubt his sincerity. Some people would believe whatever a medical professional told them. Tell a man he would be dead by sunrise, and there was a chance he would oblige, even if he'd come to you with nothing worse than a toothache.

Louise took the bowl. "He's not drinking enough water. His urine is too dark."

"Probably that fear of parasites again."

"Tell him he needs to drink more. It's bad for his kidneys."

"I'm not telling him that," Sammy said. "It makes the whole thing sound trivial. You're worried about a long-term risk to his kidneys when he's infested with bone-eating worms?"

"Okay, true. Tell him to lie down. That will . . . um, keep the worms from moving around."

Oto did as he was told. He may have been instructed to guard Sammy Mori and keep an eye on the village, but he'd been easily tricked into abandoning his orders.

"Your leg feels fine?" she asked Sammy.

"The muscle is wasted away from disuse, but it doesn't hurt. You're the nurse. Can I walk on it?"

"You're not at that much risk. Don't trip or run or do anything stupid. Of course, if you're seen walking without your crutches, everyone will know you don't really need them."

Sammy said something to Oto, who was lying on his back with his hand over his eyes, as if in great pain, or perhaps he was merely on the verge of panic.

Oto nodded. *"Hai!"* Then something else in Japanese.

"Oto says my crutches are around back, against the building," Sammy said. "He says I can go with you to the hospital."

Louise had him hold the bowl of urine while she fetched the crutches. Captain Mori didn't seem to be trying especially hard to keep his brother from escaping. Was that because there was nowhere to run to, or was Sammy's brother subtly encouraging an attempt?

Stumpy was still outside waiting, and his half tail wagged furiously to see her. Louise had the sudden thought he was trying to tell her something important, that Fárez wanted her to come back or that Mori and the rest of the enemies had returned to Cascadas. But his thinking wasn't so deep as all that. He nosed at her pocket, and she remembered that she'd been hauling around the ham bone all this time.

"Oh yeah. I promised, didn't I? Well, you earned it."

Louise patted him on the head and fished out the bone. He snatched it and trotted off. Not in any direction where they'd spotted other dogs, she noted. Stumpy had no intention of sharing his prize.

She thought about bringing the bananas, but that would be tricky to manage while carrying the bowl of Oto's urine. Besides, there were bigger worries now. She'd rather not add one more thing for the guards to fight with her about. Carrying the bowl of urine, she led Sammy through the village, along the dikes between rice paddies, and toward the hospital.

The two soldiers at the hospital were agitated when they saw Louise and Sammy. She'd been gone for some time, and they seemed angry at this. They yelled at her, yelled at Sammy. He shouted back, and for a moment he looked not so different than his brother. Certainly nothing like the calm, poetry-reading man who'd never advanced beyond the rank of corporal. The two soldiers quieted down and listened.

"All right," Sammy said. "They're convinced about the worms. I think. Come on, let's go inside."

"They won't make you stay out here?"

"I'm not asking permission. Anyway, we have details to work out."

There was shock from the hospital residents to see Sammy again. Some of the response was warm, whereas others gave grudging respect. One man called him "our Jap," and another relayed a dirty limerick and called it his "haiku." Sammy took all this in with a good-natured smile. Only Frankie looked upset to see him again. Her mouth pinched together, as if she'd eaten a rotten orange.

Louise dumped Oto's urine into a bedpan, then told the others what had happened and her plan for getting to Lieutenant Kozlowski. Dr. Claypool opened his eyes and listened attentively, raising Louise's hopes that he was on the mend, but he didn't speak up.

"And you'll do what with him?" Maria Elena asked, her voice doubtful. "Stitch him up yourself right there in the jungle?"

Louise glanced at Dr. Claypool, who still didn't respond. "If I have to."

"You know what I don't like," Frankie said. "It's this man." She hooked her thumb at Sammy. "Why did you bring him into it?"

"I had no choice," Louise said, "as is obvious to anyone." Her patience was like an old slip that had been washed so many times it was nearly transparent. "Do you seriously think that Sammy is going to sell us out? That he'd pretend all of this so he could lead the enemy to the lieutenant?"

Frankie's stare hardened. "Well, why not? Anyway, that's not my worry. They're watching him, that's what. He's been arrested, he's a prisoner. Using him only puts us in more danger. And when he's caught, Kozlowski will be caught, too, and all of us for helping. And that means we'll be punished."

"So what are we supposed to do? Leave the lieutenant to die?"

"Better him than us," Frankie said.

This brought angry retorts from many of the men, including some who hadn't seemed entirely pleased to see Sammy arrive, and who'd listened with worried expressions while Louise explained the plan.

"Wait, that's not what I meant," Frankie said hastily. She glanced at Maria Elena, as if hoping to find an ally, but the young nurse looked away, her lips pinched. "Everyone calm down. I didn't mean it like that."

"How exactly *did* you mean it?" Louise asked.

"Don't try to put words into my mouth. Why did Kozlowski run off? That was his choice. He and Fárez and Zwicker and the rest of them could have chosen to be prisoners, but they didn't. So they went out to do whatever it is they're doing, still trying to fight the war and all of that." She waved her hand vaguely. "Fine, but why do they have to put us at risk, too? Huh? Why? We surrendered, we have to stay here and deal with the Japs. We didn't ask to be dragged back into it."

"That's enough," Louise said. "I'll be out there, not you, and I'll make sure I take all the blame if things go wrong."

"Me, too," Sammy said. "They'll be angriest at the traitor. Not the American nurse."

Dr. Claypool made a little sound. He tried to lift himself up. Louise and Maria Elena helped him into a sitting position.

"You have to bring Kozlowski here," he said in a voice that was barely above a whisper. "What if he needs blood? What if he needs his spleen out? You're going to operate out there in a nonsterile environment? Too risky. Then you have postoperative care, pain management."

"You gonna do all that, Doc?" a man asked. "You look terrible."

"I *feel* terrible. But I'll manage." He turned his eyes to look at Louise, who let the skepticism bloom fully on her face. "And good old-fashioned nursing once that's done. He'll need that, too. It's a doctor's job to keep a man from dying, but it's a nurse who brings him back to life."

"Even assuming you can operate," she said, "how would we get Kozlowski in here?"

"Someone else will have to figure that out," Claypool said. He looked spent by the effort, and Maria Elena helped him lie back down.

He closed his eyes. "Take care of everything else, and I'll find a way to do the surgery even if it kills me."

"That's hardly comforting," Louise said.

Nevertheless, she was thinking hard. At the moment, the whole scheme seemed like a box of puzzle pieces, all mixed up, but she thought she could at least get the borders in place.

"It will have to be tonight," she said at last. "If we wait until Mori returns with his secret police and his Sakdals, we'll never manage. The first step is to retrieve the lieutenant and bring him in for surgery without the enemy catching him."

"You've got Oto out of the way," Sammy said. "But what about the two guards outside?"

"Do you think you can convince them to be treated for bone worms?" she asked.

"Have you treated those men before?"

"The small one had dysentery," Louise told him. "He seems better now. The other one had a leg wound that I rebandaged."

Sammy nodded. "That's Yamaguchi. He got that in Sanduga. Shot by one of the injured men we left behind. The other one is Terasaki. He's clever enough. But I think they'll buy it—if you treated them already, that helps. What are you thinking?"

"I'll bring the guards inside, set up a curtain like I did before to keep them separated from our boys, and put them under for a few minutes. We get Kozlowski, do the surgery. Then the guards wake up, congratulations, men, you're cleansed of worms, and so on."

"It could work," Sammy said. He didn't sound entirely convinced.

"That only solves the first problem," Maria Elena said. "After that what do we do? How do we keep the lieutenant hidden?"

Yes, that was the rest of the puzzle, wasn't it? Get the borders filled in, and the middle was still a jumble of pieces of various shapes and colors that Louise couldn't yet arrange.

Sammy gave Maria Elena a quizzical look. "Hidden?"

"We have a roll call every morning and afternoon," Maria Elena explained. "The building is guarded at all times. Maybe we get him in, but how do we get him out again? How do we keep him safe while he's recovering? The Japanese inspect the building once a day, and there's that young man who works with Mori. What about him?"

"Fujiwara," Louise said. "I know what you mean. He's a clever one, he watches and notices."

"I have the answer to that part," Sammy said. All eyes looked to him. "Kozlowski won't be discovered, because you Americans have one advantage that we Japanese do not." He smiled. "You all look the same, don't you?"

Chapter Twenty-Five

Mori pored over a crude map by the light of a smoking oil lamp. The map was made by a clever Sakdal named Diego, a boy of sixteen or seventeen who had once worked for the Americans in Sanduga, hauling their goods, bringing them supplies. Then the work had dried up, and he approached the Japanese with valuable information.

Mori had added Diego and several other Filipinos to his collection of locals since marching into the mountains. Which was good, because he'd lost Sakdals to enemy gunfire. The other Filipinos grew jittery, but money and fear drove them forward.

Diego had worked as a cargador in Manila off and on since he was twelve, before the Japanese invasion sent him scurrying to his home village. He seemed to have developed an excellent sense of direction while working in the city. His map of the surrounding hills had proven accurate so far and helped locate the Americans and the handful of Filipino gunmen with them. In a few simple pen drawings, he'd identified hills, rivers, possible redoubts for the Americans, as well as the elaborate trail system through the mountains. He'd pointed to certain spots of the map and crossed his arms in an X, shaking his head.

Do not go there.

"Mountain people, sir," he said in English. "Many, many mountain people, sir."

"You mean the Negritos?"

"Amerikanos no go, Haponese no go, sir." Diego traced a callused index finger along one of the trails on the map. "Here fight, sir. Here Amerikanos run, here Haponese find, sir."

Diego's English accent was light for a Filipino, which initially led Mori to believe he spoke better than he did. Mori also appreciated the respectful tone with which the boy ended every sentence. But the more he talked to Diego, the more he discovered a gap between what the boy thought he knew of English and what he could actually communicate.

"What do you mean? This is where we first located the enemy, or where we will find them now? And what about the ones we shot who escaped into the brush? Where are they? Or is that what you mean? Is this where they escaped?"

"Yes, sir." Diego tapped his finger on the map. "Here, sir. Here Haponese go, sir."

"When? Now? Or is that where we had the firefight earlier?"

"Yes, sir."

"That is where we *went*, or where we should *go*?"

"Where you go, sir. Where you go, sir."

Mori clenched his teeth. He thought he understood, but he wasn't sure. There were two other Sakdals who might have translated for him, but they were off scrounging in the bush for the injured American who'd broken off from the others. Until they returned, he was left with Diego's excellent map and wretched English.

"Captain Mori, sir?" a voice said in Japanese outside the door to the shack. Fujiwara.

"Come in," he said, relieved to be free of the tortuous conversation. Fujiwara came in and bowed, and Mori waved Diego away. The young man trotted off.

"He seems bright enough until you try to get information from him," Mori said.

"Do you want me to call him back, sir? I can try in Tagalog."

"Never mind, I've got it." Mori showed Fujiwara the hand-drawn map. "It seems clear enough. He's saying the partisans are holed up here. See where the trail crosses the river? That's above us, I think."

Fujiwara bowed again but looked uncomfortable.

"What is it, Lieutenant?" Mori asked. "Is something wrong?"

"It's Colonel Umeko, sir. One of his men called and demanded an immediate report."

"Call him," Mori said. "Explain the situation. I'll be in direct contact in a few days."

"You are to call him yourself, sir. Many apologies, but I believe he is angry. Shall I fetch the radio?"

Mori didn't like the sound of this. "Go ahead, bring it in."

Moments later Fujiwara was cranking the handle to provide power for the signal. One of the colonel's adjutants responded, snapping at Mori to stay on the line while he fetched Umeko. Mori waited anxiously, sweat beading his forehead. Fujiwara sat next to him on the mat, lips held tightly together, expression worried.

"Mori," the colonel growled at last.

"Yes, sir."

"If this call mysteriously dies, I'll have your head, do you understand?"

"I am confident it won't, sir."

He shot Fujiwara a look. *Don't stop cranking that handle!*

"I want a report on your activities, and I want it now."

"But, sir, I made contact in Cascadas. I've been sending—"

"You've been sending lies! Do that again and your next assignment will be as my official ass wiper. Do you understand me?"

"Yes, sir."

"Good," the colonel said with a grunt. He sounded slightly less angry. "Go on."

Mori explained how he'd found his brother and seized the American field hospital, clearly intended to establish and service partisan activities in the mountains. Several enemies had escaped, and Mori had tracked them deeper into the mountains. Always, the trail was deeper and higher, but he was close now. Close to burning out the entire enemy operation before it could take root.

"And this was your plan all along? You pretended to lose contact in Sanduga so you could go rescue your brother?"

Mori was tempted to spin a tale, how he'd happened into this situation. But he decided to drop all pretense of *gekokujō*. The time for obfuscation was past.

"Yes, sir. Do you know what happened in Nanking, sir?"

"Of course. It was a glorious victory."

"The foreign press reported certain irregularities," Mori said. "Certain behaviors from our own men that might have been a little too . . . exuberant. Some of their information came from a Japanese source."

"Ah yes. That," Umeko growled. "Men were arrested and tortured for it. They invariably confessed. Are you saying—?"

"It was my brother, sir. He sent me a letter admitting his guilt."

"I see. I always doubted we'd find the culprits. Your brother lived with you in America? That would make sense. An English speaker, corrupted by foreign influence."

"You see why I was anxious to retrieve him. He couldn't be allowed to stay with the Americans. He knows too much about our invasion plans, and he's already proven that he can't be trusted to serve the emperor."

"It also makes you look rather bad, doesn't it?" Umeko said.

Of course that was a worry. If one brother was disloyal, why not the other? But at the moment, Mori imagined Sammy falling into the colonel's hands and suffered pangs of guilt. Perhaps Sammy would not be tortured, only imprisoned for a time, then given a gun and thrown into battle on the front line.

You'll have done your duty. That is all that matters.

"Is he with you now?" Colonel Umeko asked.

"I left him with the American prisoners. He has a broken leg and can't march."

"You'd better hope he doesn't try to escape."

"He'll face his punishment. He was disloyal, but he's no coward. Otherwise he wouldn't have written me the letter."

"I suppose."

The line was quiet for a moment, and Mori worried he'd lost the signal. But then Umeko came back on, his voice filled with static. Mori didn't understand and asked him to repeat himself.

"I said you're done. Get your men, and come down from there. Bring the American prisoners, bring your brother. Shoot any locals you've taken prisoner."

"There are a dozen armed men still on the loose, sir. Americans and Pinoys. We have them nearly trapped. If you'll give me a few days—"

"No. You'll come down now. A dozen holdouts and partisans are no threat. The mountain people will turn on them soon enough."

"Why do you say that, sir?"

"The Americans are finished. They can't resupply Bataan and Corregidor, can't evacuate, either. Their strongholds will soon fall. The locals respect the strong and despise the weak. They'll be on our side soon enough, and any last resistance will dissolve like sugar in hot tea. Meanwhile, I need you down here in the city to keep order."

Mori thought the colonel was wrong. The locals might respect strength, but these mountain regions were practically lawless as it was. The last thing they needed were Americans and former Filipino soldiers stirring people up unopposed. Why not crush them now while they were still weak?

But Colonel Umeko was decided. Mori knew better than to defy him again.

"Very well, sir. I'll leave first thing in the morning."

"The morning? Why not now? How far are you from the captured hospital?"

"Only a few hours."

"Close enough. Leave now. Get to the hospital, put your prisoners on the road. Burn the village on your way out to serve as an example."

"Yes, sir."

"And move quickly. I'll give you one day to straighten things out in the village, but I'll have you back in Santa Maria in three days. I'll send trucks to bring you to Manila from there."

"That's . . . fast, sir. It's a long march down from the mountain. The prisoners are sick and injured."

"That is no concern of ours. Those who make it, make it. Those who don't were weak and didn't deserve to live. Am I understood?"

"Yes, sir."

———⋄———

Louise left the hospital with a small bag of supplies. It wasn't as much as she'd planned to take, and there was no scalpel, needle, or sutures. The more things she carried, the harder the questions if she was stopped and searched. So she stuck to bandages, syringes, and morphine—all items she could claim were required to treat Oto.

She still had doubts but was relieved not to be facing a field surgery without training, proper equipment, or even another nurse to assist. If the slightest thing went wrong, if the job was anything other than a crude stitching, a splint, or bandages, Lieutenant Kozlowski would die. Stabilizing him long enough to get him to the doctor sounded much less daunting.

Sammy stayed behind talking to the two guards while she walked back toward the village. He was explaining to them that they'd receive their own bone-worm treatment as soon as possible. Louise wanted to linger and gauge their reaction, but that would look suspicious. Instead she kept walking into the village by herself.

It was dusk when she reached the house where she'd found Sammy. Oto stirred inside, apparently hearing her, and called out in Japanese as she approached. The only part she picked out was "Sachihiro Mori."

"No, Sammy's not here yet," she said. She remained outside. "He'll be here in a few minutes."

And now Oto's tone turned rude, belligerent. She had no idea what he was saying, if he were berating her or ordering her to come at once, or even telling her she was a charlatan, and he knew she'd been lying. But he was furious, whatever it was. No way was she entering alone, and if he came outside she'd run for her life.

Sammy approached a few minutes later. He carried the crutches and walked with only a slight limp. "All right, I think they bought it."

Oto continued to yell from inside. Sammy stopped to listen.

"He's really mad," she said. "Maybe *you* should give him the pill. I'm worried if I go in he'll attack me."

"He's not mad, he's scared. He's begging you to help him, says he doesn't dare get up or the worms will move."

She felt sorry for the gruff Japanese soldier, in spite of herself. All this time Oto had been inside lying on his stomach and worried about some nonexistent ailment. Maybe she could bring him to Dr. Claypool to see if anything could be done about his poorly treated wound. Would Oto allow it?

Louise and Sammy went inside. She spoke in soothing tones as she gave Oto the useless bicarbonate of soda, which he eagerly took, then had him roll onto his side. She reached into her bag and took out a syringe.

"Tell him that this will help him rest while the medicine kills the bone worms."

Sammy translated her words for the soldier, then turned back to her. "Morphine?"

"That's right. I'll give him enough to knock him out. That way we don't have to worry about running into him in town while we're trying to get Kozlowski back to the hospital. I'll try the same thing with the two guards."

"No good," Sammy said. "They're skeptical. They'll take the pills if I do, but there's no way they'll consent to an injection. Not while they're on duty."

"Will they agree to an examination, at least?"

"Probably. How will that help?"

"I don't know," she admitted. "I'm still thinking. Do you know anything else about these men? How they work, I mean?"

"Counting Oto, there are three law police. They need to take shifts to keep two at the hospital at all times. The remaining man will either be sleeping or patrolling the village."

This was the last piece in the puzzle, but she couldn't quite make it fit yet. Anyway, she had time to work that part out. Too many other things to worry about first.

It was getting dark, and Sammy turned on a lamp. Oto glanced at the lamp, but his eyes were drooping shut. Soon he'd be out entirely. For his sake, this whole thing had better work. Captain Mori would be merciless if he learned that one of the three men left to guard the village had allowed himself to be injected with enough morphine to render him senseless.

Louise rose quietly. Sammy started to come with her, but she put a hand on his wrist.

"No, you stay here. Kozlowski is out in the bush somewhere."

"I can help. I won't run off or anything."

"That's not what I mean. I know you won't. Anyway, I wouldn't care if you escaped or not—who would blame you?" She shook her head. "I'm worried about your leg. You shouldn't be walking on it any more than necessary."

"Oto is going to wake up eventually. What should I do when he does?"

"Tell him I'm treating the other two guards—with any luck, he won't go looking. I'll come back here and tell Oto I need you to translate. We'll say whatever we need to in order to keep Oto from following us."

"Sounds risky. A hundred things could go wrong."

"Do you have a better plan?" she asked. When he didn't answer, she took the book of poetry out of her pocket. "Something to do while you're waiting."

Sammy reached for the book. "You are very kind, Louise."

His voice was earnest, the expression on his face solemn. She met his gaze but couldn't hold it.

"Nothing but human decency," she said, her voice pinched. "I'll see you soon."

Louise left him with the sleeping law officer. Night descended rapidly in the tropics, and in the few minutes she'd been inside, the sky had turned from pale gray to soot dark. Louise picked her way through the village largely by touch. She'd brought a flashlight in her bag but resisted turning it on for the attention it would attract. The village wasn't that big, but it took her some time to find Fárez's hiding place. Even when she found the house, she wasn't entirely sure until she'd called out his name and he answered.

"Thank God!" he said in a low voice as he squirmed out. "I couldn't take it anymore."

His voice quavered, and Louise felt for him in the dark. When she found his shoulder, he grabbed her hands with his filthy ones and gripped them so tightly it almost hurt.

"You're okay?" she whispered. "Corporal?"

"I was nodding. Guess you can't see that in the dark, huh?"

Some of the spirit had reentered his voice, and Louise allowed herself a smile. "Lead the way."

Neither spoke again until they were out of the village. Once they crossed the cascades, she told him that she wasn't going to operate on Kozlowski, but bring him back to the hospital for Claypool to look at.

"Then the doc is all better?"

"Not even close," she admitted. "But he thinks he can manage. Even on his deathbed, he'd be a better surgeon than me."

"You took care of Stumpy when you had to cut off his . . . you know."

"Removing a dog's testicle is one thing. Checking to make sure a man's liver isn't bleeding is another entirely."

"All I'm saying is that you'd be better than you think, I just know it."

"I would have given it my best shot," she said, "but I'm happy it won't be necessary. Anyway, getting him into the hospital will allow us nurses to see him through to his recovery."

"How we gonna get him in?" Fárez asked. "We can't just walk Koz past the guards."

Louise was about to answer when she heard someone on the trail behind them. She and Fárez froze. Whoever it was stopped as well.

"Sammy?" she whispered. No answer.

There was no mistake. She'd heard someone, and Fárez had stopped without prompting, too. He'd heard it, too. Louise turned on the flashlight and laughed when she saw who it was. Two eyes glowed back at her.

"Oh, I should have known," she said.

"Come here, you," Fárez said. Stumpy ran to him, tail wagging, and the corporal embraced the squirming dog. "Am I ever glad to see you, buddy. What a good dog."

Louise briefly illuminated Fárez with the light. Now that she got a good look at him, she understood what she'd heard in his voice. He was filthy from top to bottom, with sticks and mud and cobwebs in his hair, and clothes so dirty she couldn't even tell what he was wearing.

"You look like a corpse washed out of a flooded crypt," she said. "And you smell worse than Stumpy. Next stream we cross, you're washing up."

"Can we bring him, miss?"

"Do we have a choice? Not like he'd obey us if we sent him off." The dog nosed hopefully at her pocket. "No, there's nothing there," she told him. "I'm serious, there was only one bone, and you gulped it down, didn't you?"

Stumpy whined.

"This is the army, soldier," she said. "You need to learn how to ration."

Now that the flashlight was on, there was no good reason to shut it off again. They were out of sight of the village, Mori's men were unlikely to be traveling back to Cascadas in the dark, and speed was essential. She only turned it off when crossing wide, flat stretches where the light might be spotted from some distance away.

It was a cloudless night, with a breeze to drive off the bugs and bring cooler air from the highlands. Louise counted herself fortunate. Add one of the country's many delights—torrential rain, mosquitoes, heat, humidity, thick mud—and the journey would have been miserable.

Fárez had strengthened since she'd seen him off, and while he was still hobbling from the muscle wound on his buttocks, he didn't seem to be in pain and didn't slow her pace. She hadn't been joking about cleaning up, and when they reached a stream, she turned off the light for privacy and ordered him to strip down and wash.

While the corporal splashed around, Louise slapped his shirt and pants against a tree to knock off dried mud, then did the same with his boots. This got Stumpy excited, but she silenced him after a single bark. Five minutes later they were on their way again.

"So here's the plan," she said. "I've got the Japanese guards worked up about some nonexistent illness. I'm going to examine the two of them to keep them out of the way while you and Sammy bring the lieutenant inside. Dr. Claypool will operate on him, and we'll slip him in with the other patients to recuperate."

"How will that work?" Fárez asked. "The Japs aren't counting numbers and doing roll call?"

"They do both of those things, and enter the hospital to inspect it, too. Even if we could somehow hide an extra man, we have every reason to think Captain Mori will be forcing us all to march out of the highlands sooner or later. Kozlowski would be found then, if not before.

"But Sammy pointed out something," Louise added. "You know how people are always saying the Japanese all look the same? That one guy is short or tall or with glasses or not, but they all have the same face?"

"Seems that way, yeah. But I heard the same thing about Mexicans when I was growing up. Just meant they hadn't seen enough of us. Same with the Japs, I bet."

"You're right, Corporal. That's a good observation on your part."

"Is it?" Fárez sounded pleased at the compliment. "I figured that much was obvious."

"Anyway, according to Sammy, the Japanese say Americans all look the same."

He laughed. "Now that's just nuts. Americans all look the same?" He chuckled again. "Not one of us looks anything like anyone else."

"But Mexicans do? Japanese do?"

"Yeah, but that's different. That's . . . oh yeah. I see now. Right. You're really smart, Miss Louise, you know that?"

"Do you see my point?"

"I get it," he said. "We got to swap Koz out for someone else and hope they don't see the difference."

"Exactly right. The Japanese have only known us for a few days, and some of that time Mori and Fujiwara haven't even been in Cascadas. And what have they got? Our names, ranks, the number of us, and that sort of thing. But even if all of you men didn't look the same, could they really tell if one of them was suddenly exchanged with another man?"

"Huh. Yeah, could work."

"It has to," she said firmly.

"And who's the lucky guy who you're busting out of there?"

"Sergeant Fisk," Louise said. "He's got dengue, but it's on the mend. I think he's good to go."

"Fisk doesn't look anything like the lieutenant."

"He doesn't have to. Both men just have to look generic enough to the Japanese that they won't miss Fisk or wonder why they hadn't noticed Kozlowski before."

"Kozlowski has that hard look about him, and he's tall," Fárez said. "You sure they won't catch on?"

"Remember what the Japanese are watching for and why they're guarding the hospital. They're keeping men from running away, not trying to stop them from sneaking in. They're more likely to miss Fisk than wonder about Kozlowski."

They continued through the night, and eventually enough time had passed that Louise started to grow worried. Fárez kept telling her they were getting close, but they kept going and going. They entered a thickly forested area, where roots sprawled across the trail and branches had to be pushed out of the way.

"How long did you say?" she prodded.

"This is it. We're here."

It looked like any other place, and she didn't know how he could tell the difference in the dark. A trickling stream ran down the rock face to their left, but they'd passed dozens of them. The trees on the right looked the same.

"You're sure?"

"Pretty sure, yeah. Stumpy, you stay here. Be a good boy, now. Come on, Miss Louise."

They pushed through the brush for about thirty feet before Fárez stopped. "Lieutenant. It's me, Fárez. Where'd you go?"

Louise held her breath, suddenly sure that they'd come too late and there would be no answer. Or that Fárez had taken them off the trail in the wrong direction.

But the corporal was answered by a cough and a weak voice. "Over here. Did you get the doc?"

"No, sir, but I got Miss Louise. She'll see that you're patched up good enough to get back to the hospital."

They found Kozlowski propped against the trunk of an enormous tree with a strangling vine as thick as Louise's thigh wrapped around it like a giant snake. His face was gray when Louise turned the flashlight on him, and he held his hand against his side as if it were the only thing keeping his intestines from spilling out.

But he was alive and conscious, and Louise felt a burn of purpose as she opened her bag. She could help this man. She could save his life.

Chapter Twenty-Six

Sammy started to lose confidence in the plan when Corporal Oto stirred from his morphine haze. Sammy had been reading poetry by lamplight but now shoved the book into his pocket and turned off the lamp, hoping the man would settle back down. Oto kept moving about on his *patati* mat, then cleared his throat.

"Mori, are you there?"

"Assuming you mean me and not my brother, then yeah. I'm here."

"I should get up. The captain will have my skin if he knows I've been sleeping."

"You're sick," Mori said. "You weren't sleeping, you were resting so you could do your job. Anyway, nothing has happened. I'm still here, right?"

"I need to take my shift on guard duty."

"No, you don't. The other two know you're getting treatment. The nurse told you to stay still, remember?"

"Yeah." Oto didn't sound convinced.

Where the devil was Louise? She'd been gone for a couple of hours already. If Oto got up and went to the hospital, the three men would quickly figure out that the nurse was nowhere to be found. They'd put hard questions to Sammy, which he wouldn't be able to answer.

"What about the village?" Oto asked. "Who's keeping an eye on it?"

"Nothing is happening in the village. It's perfectly quiet—the villagers are all asleep at this hour. And the hospital is a few women and a bunch of sick soldiers. Nothing is going on. Relax."

"I'm trying. It's hard."

"I feel like I'm talking to a kid," Sammy said. "Close your eyes and go to sleep. Come on. Those bone worms must still be bothering you. Don't want to get them moving about, do you? They'll migrate away from the treatment, and you'll never get rid of them."

"I should have said something to your brother. It hurts like hell. I kept thinking it was the wound, you know. Didn't want to come across like a shirker."

"You had reason to complain," Sammy said. "The nurse said you weren't stitched up properly. What happened?"

"I was with Colonel Umeko when we came ashore with the Kanno Detachment. American planes bombed us trying to stop the landing. There was some kind of explosion. A big piece of metal knocked me into the mud. I got on my feet and went on with the rest of them, because there wasn't any field hospital."

Sammy allowed himself a mildly subversive comment. "The Americans always have hospitals. Why don't we?"

Oto talked past this as if it hadn't been spoken. "I told the colonel, and he had a medic splash me with iodine and wrap it up. Never saw a needle or stitches, and it healed funny. Nothing to be done for it now, I guess."

Sammy relit the lamp and turned it up slowly to let their eyes adjust. He went to the door and windows to check the mosquito nets. Flying insects piled on the outside of the netting, desperate to hurl themselves at the lamp.

"You could go to the American hospital," he told Oto. "Once the bone worms are gone, I'll bet they'd help you. If it's only been healing for six weeks, they could still do something about it."

"Like what?"

"I don't know, cut it open, stitch it up so it heals right."

"Nah, I'm not going to say anything to the Americans. What kind of complainer would that make me?" Oto pulled himself into a sitting position and chuckled. "May as well whine about my bald spot."

"So you'll live in pain for the rest of your life?"

"Yeah, probably. Rest of my life will be about a month, I figure. The army doesn't care if we live or die, Mori. You know that, right? We serve Japan, we die in the service of the emperor."

"We're arrows in a quiver," Sammy agreed. "If we're recovered after the hunt, so much the better, but the huntsman doesn't cry over the arrows lost in the pursuit."

"Yeah, that's good. Just like that." Oto rubbed at his scar tissue. "You think this is all right sitting up? It won't push the worms out? It hurts to sit too long in one position."

"I'm sure they'll stay put so long as you don't move too much."

"You're a learned man, Sammy. Isn't that right?"

"I've read a few books." His hand felt to the lump in his pocket, where he'd put the book Louise returned.

"They say you know your poets, even write some yourself. A real Japanese. Why'd you do it?"

"Do what?"

"You know, tell the foreigners all that stuff to make Japan look bad. It wasn't even true, most of it."

"It was all true. I only repeated what I saw with my own eyes."

"Oh yeah? So you saw a few bad things. Did you tell the foreigners what the Chinamen were doing to us? They were shooting at us, Mori. Trying to kill us every moment of every day. I was there, too."

"That's what enemies do—they try to kill you."

"Those damn Chinese wouldn't stop fighting, wouldn't stop laying traps. I saw a man with his leg blown off by a mine. It was put there after we'd already cleared the road. Blasted treachery, is what it was."

Something dangerous had entered Oto's tone, a warning like the huff of a viper in the leaves beneath one's feet. Fail to heed that warning, keep stepping forward, and you'd feel its fangs in your calf, the burn of venom entering the blood.

"Another time, they ambushed us from a canal," Oto continued. "We'd cleared the area, we were interrogating prisoners. Three Chinamen came out of the water and started shooting. Good thing their guns jammed in the mud. Only one fired. We got 'em all. Turns out they were men who'd thrown away their uniforms and pretended to be civilians. Can you believe that?"

Sammy knew he should keep his mouth shut, but couldn't help himself. "Men resort to desperate measures when they're defending their homeland."

"You shut up. You don't know what you're talking about. I had friends die in China. Those men in Nanking—are you saying it's their fault what happened? Huh, are you? I'll cut your fucking throat, do you hear me?"

Oto glared until Sammy was forced to look away. For a moment Sammy was torn between two urges. The first was the same one that had made him veer his bicycle in front of the American truck. Goad Oto until he made good on his threat.

The other was to calm the situation, withdraw what he'd said. Go back to where he was before, when Oto and the others had nearly forgotten his treasonous behavior. Keep them calm and sedate so that Louise could help the injured American soldier.

"My apologies, Corporal. I should not have said that."

"Damn right, you shouldn't have."

"I was wrong."

"Yeah, you were."

Sammy glanced back at Oto, whose face was red and his nostrils flaring. He'd sounded so reasonable moments earlier that Sammy had forgotten his earlier assessment. And now Oto seemed in an extended state of agitation. That was no good.

"Sammy?" a voice called from outside. Louise. Bad timing.

"Yeah, hold on," he answered in English. "Don't come up here."

"What does she want?" Oto said irritably. "Tell her to go away."

"Probably only to follow up on your treatment."

"She can do it in the morning. I'm going to get up and do my damn job."

Sammy called out to Louise, "He's in a mood. My fault. Can you get him another shot of morphine?"

"I gave it all to the lieutenant."

"He's here?"

"Not here, but close enough. Fárez has him on the other side of the village. We've got to get him inside to Claypool—he's losing blood."

Sammy glanced at Oto, who was still glowering as he pulled on his pants, then turned back to Louise. "All right. I'm coming out. I have to bring our friend here. He's not going to let me out of his sight."

"Oh, that's not good. Well . . ."

Oto stood and buttoned his shirt. "Why is she still babbling like an idiot? I thought I told you to send her off."

"She's been waiting for you all this time, and she wants one more look at you."

"No point in it."

"Look, you've got to go to the hospital anyway," Sammy said. "If you're going to take your place for guard duty, I mean. She's going to give those men treatment, too. What if you need another injection?"

"It can wait."

"You want to wait on bone worms? They're not even the little ones, either. One big worm can burrow into your toe and grow until it stretches to your pelvis."

"I don't think I have those kind," Oto said, but was that a tiny bit of doubt Sammy heard in his voice?

"And forget it if they reach your brain. You can feel them eating you from the inside. The nurse didn't think I had worms, but I told her to give me a shot anyway. I wasn't going to take a chance. She gave it to me right after you closed your eyes to rest," Sammy added quickly. He gestured. "Come on. You've already had the worst of it. One more shot just to be sure. You're not afraid of a shot, are you?"

"Of course not."

Sammy called out in English, "Use your most soothing tone. I told him he needs another shot, but he's balky."

"I sure hope the other guards are as gullible. That would make our job easier."

Sammy turned to Oto. "She said to walk slowly. The medicine is making the worms sleepy so they can be killed, but sudden movement might still wake them up."

"It all sounds made up to me, this bone-worm business," Oto said, but nevertheless, he walked stiffly and slowly as the two men came outside and down the stairs.

He'd apparently decided not to risk his life on his doubts.

───

It seemed to go well at first. The two guards studied Oto walking stiffly up and agreed to come into the hospital for treatment as soon as the situation had been explained to them. Sammy said he was going to get an injection as well and assured them that they'd have their own private area apart from the Americans and Filipinos.

But then the more alert of the guards, the older fellow named Terasaki, pointed out that they shouldn't all go inside at once. Someone should stand watch at all times.

Sammy could see it unraveling. "You're worried about the Americans?" He let the mockery sound in his voice. "What are they going to do to us?"

"That's right," Oto said, nodding. "These Americans are cowards. They surrendered. They won't try anything."

Terasaki grunted. "You think I'm worried about the Americans? Hah! You said the injection put you under. What if Captain Mori comes back and finds us that way? You saw what he did to that Sakdal. He'll do us worse."

Sammy's brother had given the Sakdals orders to stop harassing the villagers, then punished one of them when he was caught messing around with a village girl. Yoshiko had staked the Sakdal for ten hours in the sun. It was a lesson for Japanese and Filipino alike.

The others fell silent at this. Yamaguchi, the final secret police, wore a mustache that looked like a caterpillar napping on his upper lip and fiddled nervously with it. "That's right," he said. "I don't want to be staked."

"But what about the bone worms?" Oto said.

"He's right, we have to get treated," Sammy said. He avoided looking at Louise, who had cast him an anxious glance as the conversation continued in Japanese. "But we don't want to face Captain Mori, either."

"Captain Mori." Not "my brother." He needed them to see him as just another soldier trying to balance their health against orders from their superior.

"Then what do we do?" Yamaguchi asked. "We've got to get treated, but we got these prisoners to watch. You're the smart one, Mori. Tell us."

Sammy bit at his lower lip and glanced off to one side, as if thinking it over. "Hold on, what if we . . . ? Hmm. I don't know, maybe not."

"Yeah?" Terasaki said. He still looked doubtful.

"Here's what I think," Sammy continued, more decisively this time. "Oto has the worst case—he can already feel the worms, and his life is at risk. He'll get treated, together with you two. Don't want it spreading.

My treatment is precautionary. I'll stand guard while the three of you get your treatment, and then I'll get mine last."

He held his breath as the three men glanced at each other. Oto and Yamaguchi seemed game, but Terasaki shook his head.

"That's no good. You're one of the prisoners."

"You think I'm going anywhere?" Sammy shifted on his crutches to make the point.

"No, of course not," Terasaki said. "You may be a traitor, but you're no coward. You'd never run away, of course not. But it seems wrong, that's what I mean. Captain Mori comes back and sees you there on duty while we're all asleep—it looks bad."

"Don't worry, I'll take the blame. The nurse gave me medical advice in English, and I translated it. You men had no choice."

"Of course we have a choice," Terasaki said. "We can endure the worms until the captain gets back. We'll get our treatment then. I don't even feel it yet, do you?" he asked Yamaguchi.

"I—I'm not sure. Maybe."

"I certainly do," Oto said. "They've been hurting for days, got right into my injury and infected it."

"So get treated," Terasaki said. "We'll stand guard until you're done."

"You're going to risk it?" Sammy asked Terasaki. "They get deep enough into the bone, and they can't be treated except with surgery." He nodded at Louise. "That's what the nurse said."

"Oh, what does she know?" Terasaki said. "She's just a woman. I want to talk to the doctor. Someone drag him out of bed."

It was slipping away. Terasaki dug in his heels the longer Sammy pushed. Any more, and the man's suspicions would bloom into full-fledged disbelief. Fortunately Oto came to Sammy's aid.

"We're wasting time," Oto said. "We'll be finished by morning if we don't sit here arguing about it. Mori and Fujiwara won't need to know how it happened, just that we got treated. Where's the harm in it?"

Still Terasaki looked uncertain. Finally something seemed to occur to him. "All right, but we're holding an inspection at first light. If there's even one prisoner missing, someone's head is going to roll, and it won't be mine." He unslung his rifle and handed it to Sammy. "This is your idea. Your head if it goes wrong."

Sammy nodded. "I take full responsibility for my actions."

Chapter Twenty-Seven

Louise took a risk and increased the dosage of morphine for the third soldier, the one Sammy called Terasaki. He was older than the other two, more alert and suspicious, and she needed him to stay down through Kozlowski's surgery. Terasaki waited until she'd given shots to Oto and the young one with the mustache, then argued some more with Sammy before finally consenting and allowing Louise to approach.

She'd laid out the three Japanese men on *patati* mats toward the front of the building. A hanging blanket served as a makeshift wall to separate them from the rest of the hospital. Terasaki glanced at the blanket, as if more worried about being seen by the American patients than by the shot itself or the supposed parasites it was meant to cure. He watched as Louise tied a rubber tourniquet around his arm to expose the vein but turned away when she stuck the needle in.

"I still say it was too easy," she told Sammy as she put away the syringe. "I'm an American, you're a traitor. Why did they let us do it?"

"Some fears are stronger than others," Sammy said.

Terasaki was already relaxing along with his companions but stared at her, blinking heavily. He let out a long sigh as the drug continued to take hold. She patted his arm and moved to inspect Oto's back, nudging him until he rolled on his side.

"And the thought of a little medically ordered sleep was too much to resist," Sammy said. "Throw in their bluster about not fearing the Americans, and this is the result." He rubbed his stubble and studied Terasaki's glazed expression. "Or maybe we're simply conditioned to obey."

Terasaki closed his eyes. Louise stepped away carefully.

"Bring him in," she said quietly.

Sammy spoke in clipped Japanese as he moved toward the front door, no doubt something about taking up his post outside, in case any of the men were still conscious enough to hear. None of the other Japanese responded.

Louise stood against the wall, watching the soldiers on their mats. So risky. Too little morphine and they'd see what was happening. Too much and she'd kill them. She'd never be able to live with herself if she did.

The door swung open. Fárez and Sammy staggered in, dragging the gray-faced lieutenant with his arms swung over their shoulders. Louise rushed to help.

They hauled Kozlowski behind the blanket to the main ward. There all eyes turned toward them. Two more men assisted, and they soon had the patient up on the operating table.

Dr. Claypool sat on a stool, attended to by the other two nurses. Working in silence, Frankie held him up, and Maria Elena slipped him into his operating gown. When that was done, the two nurses scrubbed his hands with a bucket of water, soap, and a bristle brush. Claypool sat through this with his eyes closed, pale, but breathing steadily.

Louise turned to one of the men who'd helped get Kozlowski up to the operating table. "Sergeant Fisk, are you ready?"

"Yes, miss."

Fisk had been one of the ones struck with dengue but had recovered from that. How about his other wounds? He'd been at Cavite Navy Yard when the Japanese bombed it three days after Pearl Harbor and hospitalized ever since. Louise lifted his shirt to check the burn on his back. The burns were mostly healed, but she wished she didn't have to send him into the bush.

"Miss Maria Elena has a bag packed for you. You need to keep taking your quinine, and I want that ointment rubbed on your back twice a day. Keep the wound clean, you hear?"

"Yes, Miss Louise."

"I mean it. You shouldn't be sent out there. None of you should. Fárez, make sure he gets his ointment."

Fárez nodded. "Sure thing."

"And that goes for you, too," she told him. "You'd better keep changing that dressing on your left buttock, or it won't heal properly."

"Yeah, Fárez," one of the other men said. "You don't wanna keep limping around like Stumpy when his balls were all swelled up."

Some of the men snickered, and Fárez blushed. "Ah, shut up. Come on, Fisk, let's get out of here. Thank you, Miss Louise," he said as he passed her.

Louise joined Dr. Claypool and the patient. There was no room for privacy in the little hospital, and soon the lieutenant was naked on the operating table except for a pair of undershorts, and these Louise pulled down so she could get at the wound. Kozlowski stared at the ceiling.

She used a wet cloth to scrub away the sweat and grime before she did her own washing up. Maria Elena and Frankie brought fresh water and soap and carried away dirty bandages, then set off to get blood to use during the surgery. Kozlowski's dog tags said he had AB blood, which only one of the patients had, and that man was in no shape to donate. They looked around for type O instead, which could be given to anyone. There were a few men with the right type, but their medical conditions also precluded donation. It turned out that Maria Elena herself was the only one with type O who could give.

Louise gave Kozlowski morphine and doused the wound with iodine. Dr. Claypool watched her work.

"What treatment has he had so far?" Claypool asked. His voice quavered, and he looked almost as gray as the patient.

"None," Louise said. "I bandaged it to cut down on bleeding, that's all. How are you doing, Lieutenant?" she asked the patient as Claypool looked over his instrument tray and called for someone to bring him another lamp.

"Getting sleepy," Kozlowski said. "Sure helps with the pain, though. I'm going to be knocked out cold, right?"

Louise glanced at the doctor, who shook his head. "No, Lieutenant. We're not putting you all the way down. In your condition, it's safer if you're conscious. You might feel some pulling and tugging. Might even sting a little. But it shouldn't be bad."

"I can handle it."

"I know you can. You're strong and healthy."

"Not feeling so healthy at the moment."

Louise patted his arm. "You'll do fine. Stay positive."

"We're wasting time," Frankie said, coming over with the blood. "Those Japs will be up, and then we'll be in trouble."

"Easy," Louise said. "We can't rush this."

The morphine was still taking effect, and the whole thing would go much better if Kozlowski wasn't squirming in pain. She set up the IV to give him his blood.

Claypool felt along the man's back. "No exit wound. The bullet is still in there. I can't tell if that's lucky or not. With its trajectory, it might have otherwise come out through the spine. He'd be dead or paralyzed. On the other hand, if it's against the hepatic artery, we might very well finish the job if we fish it out. He'll bleed to death." He eyed the bag of Maria Elena's blood. "For that matter, we'd better not waste what we have."

He held out his hand, and Louise reached for the instrument tray, but the doctor was apparently testing the steadiness of his hand. If that was his question, the answer was "not very." It was going to be a nerve-wracking surgery.

"Well, I don't suppose it's going to improve the longer I stand here," he said. "Let's get started. Forceps."

———◦———

There was a curious way Louise lost track of time in surgery. Nothing mattered, not thirst, hunger, or even a full bladder. Everything stayed focused on the movement of the scalpel, the flow of blood into the vein and out of the wound. The steady movement of hands and instruments. Checking vital signs.

So far no disasters. Claypool found the bullet in the large intestine and extracted it. There was damage to the bowel and the wall of the stomach. An incision widened the wound to get at them more effectively. Louise had only the most general sense that the surgery was moving slowly based on the doctor's deliberate movements.

Finally it was done, and nothing remained but the final sutures. Claypool held himself steady with one hand while gesturing to Kozlowski's open belly.

"You'll have to, Miss Louise. I'm going to faint if I don't sit down."

Louise had witnessed Claypool and other doctors suturing wounds on dozens of occasions. She could see every step in her mind. She'd held needles, tied knots, cut excess thread—everything but done the actual stitching. It turned out it was easier to imagine it than to accomplish the task with her untrained hands. When she finished, she looked at her work with dismay. Sloppy.

Others had come to stand over her shoulder while she worked. They must have been curious to see how a nurse would do performing a doctor's work. Not very well, as it turned out. She shouldn't be embarrassed, she should be relieved that the lieutenant was alive. Yet she couldn't help the flush of shame as she turned to look at the people who'd been watching her. Their expressions were grim.

"I know," she said, "but I did the best I could."

It was only then that she noticed they weren't looking at her. They were staring over her shoulder. Kozlowski's eyes were open, and he was looking in the same direction. The other nurses and Dr. Claypool were also looking at whatever was behind her. Frankie had her hand over her mouth. Her eyes were wide with terror.

Louise turned to see what they were all looking at. A startled cry came to her lips, which she immediately choked down.

Captain Mori was watching her, his face as rigid as a stone statue. His adjutant, Fujiwara, stood at his right shoulder. His eyes were narrowed in a look of perfect suspicion.

"What are you doing?" Mori asked.

"She's performing surgery," Dr. Claypool said. "I'm not well, and I—"

"You will be quiet! I asked the woman."

Louise needed time to gather her composure. She tried to buy a moment. "Dr. Claypool has malaria, and so I took over in suturing the patient."

"Where did this man get his injury?"

The suspicion was in full bloom on both of the Japanese's faces, and she knew what they must be thinking. They'd had a firefight with partisans in the mountains, and wanted to know if this was one of the men they'd shot at. If so, he could be interrogated, tortured until he gave up the location of the others.

"What do you mean, where? This man was shot by Japanese troops weeks ago. Not all wounds heal properly, Captain. We had to perform surgery. That's what this place is—a hospital."

Under other circumstances, she'd have been ashamed by how smoothly the lie emerged from her mouth. Here it felt entirely justified.

And then, with horror, she realized that the tray of instruments, bloody gauze, and the like was still sitting in open view a few feet away. These men were observant. Fujiwara was already eyeing the tray. They'd see the bullet and know that this was a fresh injury.

And then Mori gave her an escape hatch. "Is that so? And in what way did this wound fail to heal properly?"

"I'll show you." She pushed aside the gauze and fished out the bullet. "This is courtesy of the Imperial Japanese Army. We didn't remove it earlier, because it was adjacent to the hepatic artery—that's the blood supply for the liver and pancreas—and we worried if it was in the wrong place, movement would sever the vessel and he would bleed to death. But the bullet was shifting around in there and had to be extracted."

Mori eyed the bullet and let out a grunt. A quick glance to Fujiwara, whose own expression was impassive. It was clear that he had doubts, but he no longer seemed convinced that she was lying.

"You drugged my men. My brother claims it was a medicinal treatment of a parasitic infection, but I don't believe it. They have the look of opium users. I believe you gave them morphine to hide something."

Louise thought about denying it, maybe even trying to convince these two men that they, too, had the same parasites—what had she called them? greater bone worms?—but they'd never buy it.

"It's true," she said. "I drugged them."

Frankie drew in her breath, which drew Fujiwara's penetrating stare.

"I made up a story, and I gave them morphine to render them senseless," Louise said. Fujiwara looked back at her. "Here is why. We had a cache of medicine stored in the village. Beneath your house, in fact. If you look, you'll see it's disturbed under there, because someone had to crawl down and get it. There were medicines we didn't want the Japanese to find, like quinine you'd steal for your own war efforts. Among them was a medication we needed for the surgery. It is meant to thicken the blood so that a patient doesn't bleed to death on the operating table.

"Let's be honest with each other, Captain Mori," she continued, though she was stacking lies on top of lies. "The men you left behind aren't the most imaginative. They wouldn't have let me haul several tins of medication back to the hospital. We needed to do this surgery, and I needed your men not to interfere."

Louise stopped and waited. It was a complicated tale that could break down if they questioned her. What was this blood thickener called? Where was it? How about a demonstration? Where were the dirty tins? But perhaps she'd admitted enough guilt to put them off the real trail. She could only hold her breath and pray that the secret police bought it.

Mori said something to Fujiwara. The younger man responded, and a smile touched the corners of Mori's mouth. He turned to Louise.

"At first light, you will have the men brought outside. All of them. They will line up for roll call while we search your quarters."

"But, Captain, these men are in no condition—"

"Any who resist or refuse will be shot."

Louise kept protesting as the Japanese had each and every person in the hospital brought outside to stand in the early-morning air. Mori ignored her. Some men were so weak, they had to be supported by their comrades. Others could only be carried out on *patati* mats. The air was still and warm, and the birds kept up their chatter.

Several of Mori's men waited outside. They'd fixed bayonets to their rifles, underscoring how serious this roll call was. A few villagers gathered, too, but most were absent in spite of the commotion. Smart not to get involved. Most of the Filipinos on hand were young men with the slouchy air of Sakdals. Louise looked for Sammy but didn't see him. Neither was there any sign of the three Japanese men who'd been on guard duty.

281

Mori read off the names from his list and ordered the men to step forward as they were called. Those who couldn't move on their own were carried. When he got to Fisk, someone pointed to Lieutenant Kozlowski, whom they'd carried out on his *patati*. Mori studied him, eyes falling to the fresh bandages from last night's surgery.

Louise held her breath, waiting for someone to point out that this man looked nothing like Fisk, but the ruse seemed to work, and Mori continued down the list.

Stumpy came trotting in sometime during the roll call. He came up to Kozlowski with his half tail wagging, attempting to lick the lieutenant's face. Louise's mouth went dry. It seemed like a clear calling out of the whole fraud. But the Japanese seemed to see only a meddlesome village dog. One of them kicked at the dog, who growled and dodged the blow. Several more Japanese boots tried to land kicks, but Stumpy danced expertly out of reach.

Mori looked annoyed and said something to Fujiwara, who drew his sidearm. Louise wanted to call out for him to stop, but Stumpy's meddling was at an end. He gave a final, disgusted-sounding bark, and trotted off. Fujiwara saved his ammunition.

Louise heard Fárez's voice in her head after seeing Stumpy's reaction to the Japanese soldiers. *You can't fool a dog.*

The roll call ended. Mori and Fujiwara consulted for a few minutes. The sun rose in the sky, baking them. When Louise tried to see to her patients, she was ordered back into line at the point of a bayonet. She couldn't even give Dr. Claypool water.

Mori and Fujiwara came over to where the nurses were standing. The three women hadn't been allowed to speak to one another, but Louise had managed to keep Maria Elena behind her and partly shielded from the staring, leering Sakdals. Frankie seemed on the verge of a complete mental breakdown.

"You see," Louise said. "We weren't hiding anything. Now, please let me get my patients back inside."

Mori didn't answer but looked over the nurses. His eyes settled on Maria Elena. The young Filipina's breathing picked up. He looked away, glanced past Louise, and studied Frankie.

"We didn't do anything," Frankie said. "I swear to God, we didn't."

"Hush, Frankie," Louise said. "He knows that. May we please carry our men inside, Captain Mori?"

He ignored her. "You," he said to Frankie. "You will come with us."

Frankie let out a little cry. Japanese soldiers rushed in to haul her off. Her legs buckled, and she had to be supported. Louise's heart sank.

For God's sake, Louise thought as the Japanese dragged Frankie away. *Be strong for once in your life.*

Chapter Twenty-Eight

Sammy was forced to concede his brother one thing: Yoshiko Mori was consistent. No favoritism. No special consideration for family.

He was staked to the muddy ground in the middle of a rice paddy along with the three Japanese guards he and Louise had outwitted. They wore nothing but their skimpy *fundoshi* underwear, and Sammy felt his skin burning beneath the rising sun. Sweat trickled down his armpits, and his mouth felt dried out with sand, but there would be no water until nightfall. Ants crawled over his legs, and he couldn't shake them off.

To take his mind off the heat and thirst and ants, Sammy recited a verse about a snail in the morning light. The others looked at him blankly.

"What is that, some kind of poem?" Oto asked.

"It's Issa," he said.

"Who?" Oto said. He was especially dull witted today, with those piggish eyes that looked like those of a man who'd never had an original thought in his life.

"Kobayashi Issa? One of our greatest . . . oh, never mind."

Sammy leaned back and tried in vain to get his aching back some support on the wooden stake. Hard to do with his hands tied behind him. His discomfort was making him mean. He owed these men an apology, not his loathing. They were fools for believing him, sure, but honest fools. A Sakdal had been nearby, armed with a rifle and a machete, supposedly guarding them, but he'd wandered off with a jug of coconut wine a few minutes earlier.

No guard was necessary. Didn't even need to tie the men to the stakes, to be honest; they would have kept their arms twisted awkwardly behind them had they been ordered to do so. None of the soldiers would try to escape their punishment, because it was deserved.

In fact, any anger or frustration they'd shown when Fujiwara tied them up had been self-directed. Terasaki offered to kill himself. Yamaguchi bowed his head as if expecting it to be lopped off with the captain's *guntō*. Sammy's brother had seemed to consider both of these things but finally rejected the offers out of prudence.

Yoshi needed all Japanese on hand. Possibly even Sammy, who would be tried for his crimes eventually but for now was needed by the Kempeitai. He'd overheard two of the returning soldiers speak last night. Something about their colonel, who had ordered the small unit back to Cascadas at once. Why, Sammy didn't know, and apparently neither did anyone else.

Louise's plan had almost worked. Would have if the raiding party hadn't come back in the middle of the night. Yoshi had come back to find Sammy outside, leaning on his crutches as he performed his so-called guard duties while the other three slept off their morphine dose.

They dragged Sammy away before he could figure out how to warn Louise, or even *what* to warn her about. He was anxious for them all, knowing the brutal path that lay ahead of them as prisoners, whether Yoshi figured out what the Americans had been up to or not. But especially for Louise. Pain burned in his chest when he thought of how she'd come looking for him in the village, the risks she'd taken. Pain, and something else.

You fool. You can't fall in love with an American nurse. You're going to die, she's going to die.

Sammy could tell himself that as much as he wanted, but he still ached with worry. What would Yoshi do to her if he found out the truth? Later, as he was staked in place, he picked up enough scattered gossip to believe that she'd outwitted the Kempeitai. Held her nerve and told a convincing-enough story that if the morning roll call turned up clean, she'd get away with it.

And for that, I can endure the heat and the bugs.

But could he endure the dullards who were keeping him company? That was the real trick. Sammy glanced at the other three. Their faces were blank. No doubt their minds were equally free of clutter.

Oto grunted and tried to shift position. Pain flashed across his face for a moment before he seemed to get it under control.

"The American nurse could help you," Sammy said.

"There weren't any bone worms," Oto said sullenly. "So don't keep lying."

"I'm talking about that old wound. Nobody saw to it, and now it's healing badly. It will trouble you for the rest of your life if you don't get it cared for."

"What does that matter? We're all going to die here, you know that, right?"

"My brother won't kill you for this. We'll be punished and let go. Well, *you'll* be let go."

"Die here in the Philippines," Oto said. "And if not here, then on some other war front. It is our duty to die for Japan." His voice was resigned. There was no glory in the thought.

Sammy blinked, surprised at Oto. Not only the way the slow wheels were turning in the man's head, but where was the unblinking faith in the cause of this war? The kind of faith fostered by the indoctrination given to soldiers? "Read This Alone: And the War Can Be Won." In thinking so poorly of Oto, wasn't Sammy guilty of the same sort of dismissive attitude that his fellow Japanese so often exhibited to the Americans? Or how the Americans spoke of the Japanese, for that matter?

"You don't know that," Sammy said. "Soldiers will survive the war. Most of us, I suspect, will find ourselves home again one day."

"I hope so," Yamaguchi put in. "There's a girl in my hometown I would like to marry. So pretty, her face is like the moon."

"A girl," Oto scoffed. "You'll never see her again. She'll never wait for you, and you'll be dead anyway."

"You need to take care of yourself," Sammy told Oto. "If not for your sake, then for the sake of the war. An injured soldier is a bad soldier. The American nurse said the doctor could see you fixed up properly."

"That ugly foreign devil isn't going to touch me again."

"Have it your way." Sammy affected a shrug. "But she's not our enemy. I know that much."

Terasaki turned. He'd been squinting into the sun while the others talked. "You don't *know* your enemies, Mori. That's your problem."

"Maybe I don't."

Sammy's morbid thoughts were reasserting themselves, and inopportune comments threatened to come out. No point to it, but he couldn't help himself. What he wanted to say, what he was *about* to say, was that his true enemies were the makers of war themselves.

They'd never beat the Americans—did these men even have an idea how big the enemy's country was? How vast its lands, how many people it had, the scale of its industry? China was on Japan's very doorstep and was weak, yet they couldn't subdue it. How would they conquer America? And if they didn't, how would they keep the Americans from returning, their fleets rebuilt, their armies huge, organized, and vengeful?

Millions of Japanese would die. Ancient cities would burn. Perhaps the entire nation would be destroyed, its people enslaved for generations to come.

And it would be a self-inflicted defeat. Sammy's enemy wasn't the Americans. His enemy was the men who would destroy Japan. The ones who'd started the war.

Only the arrival of his brother stopped him from speaking these thoughts.

His brother Yoshiko and Fujiwara were leading one of the American nurses. It was Miss Frankie, and Sammy's hopes sank. A coward and a bully. Why was she here?

Frankie's eyes darted around, as if looking for an escape. Looking for someone to rescue her. She briefly glanced at the sweating, nearly naked men staked in the rice paddy, visibly shuddered, and looked away.

"Are we going to stake her?" Fujiwara asked.

"If we need to," Yoshi said. He switched to English. "Tell me what I'm looking for."

"I don't know what you're talking about," Frankie said. "Is there—is there something special you want to know?"

"You tell me."

"I don't know what you want!"

Yoshi switched to Japanese again. "Release Corporal Mori."

Fujiwara's eyebrows went up, and Sammy gave his brother a sharp look, surprised. The adjutant came over and untied the cords holding Sammy's arms behind his back. The first sensation was pain, followed by shooting tingles down his arms as he pushed himself to his feet.

"Why are you letting him go?" Frankie asked. Her tongue darted over her lips. "I thought he was guilty. I thought you were mad at him because of what he said about China."

"What happened last night?" Yoshi asked.

"Miss Louise told you already. That's all I know."

Yoshi gestured to the empty stake. "Two days in the sun. You won't die—you'll get water once a day. Other than that, I think you will find it a very unpleasant experience. You'll be burned, sick, delirious."

"What?" Frankie's face hung slack. "Me?"

"Take off your dress."

"No, please."

"You'll be as exposed as these men here. No more, no less."

"But they're men. They're . . . and I'm a . . . Please, no. Don't make me, please."

Sammy stared at her, willing her to look at him. She could do this. He knew the hatred she had for the Japanese. She could suffer a couple of days in the sun to save Lieutenant Kozlowski's life and spite the Japanese secret police.

Yoshi drew his sword. "Take off your dress, or I will cut it off."

"I'll tell you!" she cried. "I'll tell you everything."

He gestured with the sword tip. "What? Quickly, I have no patience."

"Miss Frankie—" Sammy said, but nobody was looking at him.

"It was all a lie," Frankie said. "The injured man is one of the rebels you were shooting at."

"I knew it."

"If that's what you thought," Sammy said to his brother, "why didn't you question the injured man instead of the nurse?"

"They brought him in last night," Frankie continued. "His name is Kozlowski. He's the whole reason we were up here in the first place. We're a field hospital behind enemy lines. When the men were healed, they'd go off and join the partisans. Some already did. I'll tell you what I know. I'll tell you how they did it."

Frankie talked on and on, giving far more than Yoshiko had requested. She told about Fárez and the others, how Louise was the leader of it all, how Sammy had helped them, even knowing everything the Americans were doing. Her voice was high and excited, and there was a look on her face that wasn't shame, or even fear. No, Sammy thought, it was eagerness. But she didn't have an endless amount of information and was soon repeating herself. Yoshi ordered her to shut up, then translated for Fujiwara.

"I'll ask you again," Sammy said. This time he said it in English for Frankie's sake. "Why didn't you question the lieutenant if you thought he was the guilty party?"

"We've been ordered down from the mountains," Yoshi said. "There was no time to break the man."

His brother had answered in Japanese, but Sammy responded once more in English. "Ordered by whom? This Colonel Umeko people keep talking about?" Sammy stopped and frowned as something occurred to him. "If you're not going after the partisans, why not let the nurses have their patient? If you're leaving anyway, what does it matter? He's one more prisoner of war, nothing more or less."

"He's the leader of illegal military forces in the area."

"Which you're now going to ignore. So what does it matter?"

"Untie the other men," Yoshi told Fujiwara. "We'll need every loyal Japanese to guard the prisoners." To Sammy he said, "You will get dressed and go to the hospital to tell the Americans."

"Tell them what, exactly?"

"We leave first thing in the morning, and we will march all the way to Santa Maria in the lowlands. The men will be prisoners of war. The nurses will be relocated to the internment camp at the Santo Tomás camp for civilians in Manila."

"They can't march that far," Sammy said. "They're sick and injured."

"Nobody will stay behind. They either move or they die."

"You mean you'll kill them," Sammy said in English. "They either march or you shoot them. That's what you mean, isn't it?"

"Tell them. And take this woman with you." Yoshi finally changed back to English to say this last part.

Frankie's face fell. "I don't think I should go back. Not with your brother. He'll tell them what I said."

"That isn't my problem." There was a malicious element in Yoshi's voice. "Go!"

———— ◦ ————

Sammy didn't tell the people at the hospital everything that had happened, but he told them enough. Captain Mori knew about Kozlowski. A colonel with the Kempeitai had ordered Mori and his men to march their prisoners out of the mountains. If they were unable to go, they would be killed.

The men and women of the hospital listened without commenting, but the fear was a fresh wound on every face. They all knew this meant. Not everyone had made it in the flight from Sanduga to Cascadas. Now they were expected to travel all the way to the lowlands, marching at the whim of the Japanese soldiers and driven along by Sakdals.

Sammy glanced at Louise as he spoke. She was looking through the room, her eyes settling on one man after another. Doing a silent diagnosis, he thought. This man would make it; this man wouldn't. This soldier may or may not survive, depending on the pace set by the Japanese. That was Louise, always thinking about her patients, counting them all equally.

"There's one other thing," Sammy said. "If you have any thoughts, any plans for trying to mitigate this disaster, don't say them in front of Miss Frankie."

"Me?" Frankie said, her tone outraged, her expression indignant. "I have no idea what you're talking about."

Sammy wasn't fooled. He knew what she was about to do. He'd watched her face on the way back to the hospital and sensed her wicked mind hard at work. There was a fishhook ready to impale Frankie, and she meant to wriggle free before it did. He waited for her to make an attempt.

"You're the one who spilled the beans," she said to Sammy. "You told your brother everything. The moment you were alone, you said it all. Treacherous right to the end. Of course we never trusted you. We knew you'd do it."

Sammy didn't say anything. His eyes met Kozlowski's, where the man lay in his bed; then he glanced at Dr. Claypool, sitting still and gray, and Louise, who studied his face.

Nobody in the room said anything. A few men whispered, and there were hard looks at Frankie. She looked around, eyes widening.

"What, you think it was me?" Frankie said. "This *Jap*"—the word sounded vulgar coming out of her mouth, not a casual term, as so many used it, but a profanity—"went right to Mori and told him everything. Of course they threatened me, said they'd tie me naked to a stake, but I wasn't going to breathe a word. It was him." She pointed at Sammy. "I heard him with my own ears. It's his brother, of course he told him. They stood around discussing it. I heard everything!"

"And the entire conversation was in English?" Louise asked.

"Yes! They both speak it, don't they?"

"Sammy looks dehydrated and sunburned, like he was staked out in the sun himself." Louise's voice was calm as a judge's about to deliver a verdict. "But apparently not. Apparently he was talking to his brother in English, and you happened to overhear it all."

If there had been any lingering doubts on the faces of the patients, they were gone now. Instead, angry mutters and poisonous glances, all directed at Frankie.

"He's a liar!" she shouted. "You're not going to believe him, are you? As God is my witness—"

"Shut your mouth," Kozlowski said. "Someone stick her in the corner so I don't have to look at her."

Frankie resisted, still proclaiming her innocence. It took two men to get her there. Kozlowski, injured and wincing in pain as his morphine seemed to be wearing off, told her to shut up or he'd have her subdued. That finally silenced her.

Once she was put in her place, Sammy and another man moved Dr. Claypool's and Kozlowski's cots to the other side of the hospital, as far from Frankie as could be managed. When that was done, Sammy and Louise joined the doctor and the lieutenant in a private conference. There was much to discuss before nightfall.

Chapter Twenty-Nine

Louise and Sammy sat down next to Kozlowski's and Claypool's cots where they'd been moved to the front door of the hospital. She studied Sammy's face, her admiration growing as she thought about what he'd done for them. Far more than she could have asked or expected.

Kozlowski spoke first, using a low voice that perhaps the nearer patients would pick up on, but not Frankie, sitting sullenly in the far corner. "Why did your brother leave you alone with us again?"

"Because he knows I won't try to escape," Sammy said.

"He doesn't know you very well, then, does he?" Kozlowski said.

"He knows me well enough. Whatever we plan, I won't be running."

Kozlowski shook his head. "I don't get you, Mori. Why not? You think you still owe them loyalty?"

"You can't go back," Louise said. "Come with us, you'll be treated well. Won't he, Lieutenant?"

"Damn right."

Sammy shook his head slowly. "No. I'll help you, but I won't run. That's a step too far."

"Are you sure about this, Sammy?" Dr. Claypool asked.

"Yes, sir."

A thoughtful look came over Kozlowski's face. "Okay, I got it. I don't agree, but I understand."

"You do?" Louise asked.

The lieutenant winced as he propped himself on one elbow. "Reporting crimes against mankind, helping a wounded man get treatment—that's the stuff of a man's conscience. This is another matter entirely."

"That is right, sir," Sammy said. "I won't desert."

"He's a good soldier," Kozlowski explained to Louise, who was still baffled. "The captain knows it in his heart, and that's why he let his brother come here. He knows he'll return."

Louise was anguished knowing everything that faced Sammy if he went back. "You don't have to do it. Nobody will think less of you if you come with us."

"I will. That is enough."

"In that case," Dr. Claypool said, "you should go back now, before they wonder why you're missing."

"They don't need me. They don't *want* me. My brother isn't going to come looking for me, and if he does, I'll go with him."

"That's not what worries me," the doctor said. "We've got planning to do, and we can't have you knowing what we decide."

Now it was Sammy who looked confused. "Why not?"

"You've done enough," Louise said. "If you're not coming with us, then you have to leave for your own good."

"You're all weak and sick, and you need my help. I can stay here until morning or until they come and fetch me."

"What we need is for you to save yourself," Louise said. She touched his arm. "Sammy, please. Go to your brother. Do what he says, bow your head, take your licks. Whatever it takes to stay alive."

"It will be a long war, Mori," Kozlowski said. "Some of us aren't going to survive it. Maybe you'll be one of the ones to die. But for God's sake, don't throw your life away. What we do will be desperate, and one way or another the Japanese will be furious when we make the attempt. You can't put anything more on your head than you already have."

Sammy looked back and forth between the three of them. He looked confused at first, uncertain, then rose to his feet and held out his hand for Lieutenant Kozlowski.

"Thank you, sir."

Kozlowski returned the handshake and a solemn nod before settling back onto his cot. "Good luck, buddy."

"And you, Doctor," Sammy said, shaking Claypool's hand as well. "Thank you for your work. It was very kind of you to treat me."

Claypool managed a smile. "Miss Louise would have given me hell if I hadn't."

"Yes, I know." He turned and gave her a solemn bow. "Thank you, Miss Louise."

She was sick with worry for him, knowing this might be the last time she ever saw him. There was sadness in his eyes of a depth she'd never seen before. And something else as he looked at her, something that took her breath away.

He loves me. And I—

"Please don't look at me like that," she said in a soft voice. Both Kozlowski and Claypool had averted their eyes.

"I am prepared to wade into the river. I have composed my *jisei*. It is on my lips already. When the time comes, I will speak it and cross to the other side."

"Don't say that. Stay alive, for God's sake. It will be over someday, and you'll have a whole life ahead of you."

He looked into her eyes. "I will try. I promise that much."

"Go!" she urged. She touched his hand. "Go," she repeated more gently.

He nodded and turned toward the door. Moments later he was gone. A long silence passed. Louise's heart thudded in her chest.

"So you want to escape," Claypool asked Kozlowski.

"I want to *try*," he said. "Half of us will die if they march us out of here. You and me among them, Doc."

Louise turned away from the door, forcing herself to stop thinking about Sammy. She had spent some time calculating earlier and had an answer to Kozlowski's implied question.

"I count five who are goners," she said, "including the two of you. Two more are suffering malaria or dysentery who could go either way. They're weak and dehydrated and might not survive a long, hard march. And Ocampo lost both his feet—how could he possibly make it?"

"We have to make the attempt," Kozlowski said.

"We'd be on the run," she said. "Some men would die anyway."

"Then we'll die free men." There was firmness in Kozlowski's voice that belied his weak, pale expression. "Not on a death march at the hands of the Japs."

"And what about the healthier ones? The nurses?" Louise needed him to understand how the ledger would balance if they tried to escape. "Let's say we get away. The sick ones will slow us down. Captain Mori will come after us. He'll catch us again anyway. Some men and women who'd have had a chance as prisoners will suffer. He might even kill us all."

"What are we supposed to do?" Kozlowski said. "Shut up and let the Japs kill us all?"

"The Japanese were called out of the mountains," she said. "Mori must be obligated to go. That's why he's leaving now, before he's found Fárez and the rest. I'm worried if we all escape, he'll have reason to stay, even if it means disobeying orders."

Kozlowski gripped the edge of his mat, face a grimace. It looked part frustration, part pain as his morphine wore off.

"But what if we don't all escape?" she asked. "What if it's only some of us? I'm talking about those of you who are going to die in a death march. You escape, the rest of us stay behind as prisoners. Mori looks and figures you won't survive without medical care, so it doesn't matter."

"And Mori would be right," Claypool said. "You'd need to escape, too. We'll need your help to stay alive."

Louise shook her head. "No, not me. I lied to him, I tricked his men. It's too personal now, too risky—he'd come after me. You can take another nurse maybe, but not me."

"If you're suggesting Frankie . . ." Kozlowski growled.

"I'm not. I'll take Frankie with me. Clarice left with the partisans. That leaves Maria Elena. She's a Pinoy, and I don't trust those Sakdals to leave her alone. They'll split her into a different camp in Manila, assuming she makes it that far." Louise licked her lips, considering. "But I think if you go, hide nearby until the Japanese are gone, you might have a chance with Maria Elena looking after you. The rest of us will go to the internment camp."

Kozlowski rolled onto his back and put a forearm over his eyes. Louise thought he was too overcome with pain to continue and she'd have to deaden his senses with morphine, but moments later he removed his arm and looked at her again.

"Okay. It's a plan. We escape tonight."

"That's not a plan," Claypool said. "That's an objective. We've got guards at the door, no chance of knocking them out with morphine again, and no Sammy to help us. How are we going to get past them?"

"I've got an idea for that, too," Kozlowski said. "Thanks to Miss Louise, there's a back way out of here."

Frankie was making noise again, complaining about being stuck in the corner while they'd let Sammy go. She'd saved these men's lives. How dare they treat her worse than a filthy Japanese soldier? When she saw Bledsoe climb onto the operation table and prod at the ceiling with his fist, her eyes widened.

"Are you all nuts? You can't climb onto the roof. They're going to kill us."

Kozlowski nodded at Louise. "Better tell her the real plan."

The "real plan" was code to get Frankie out of the way. Louise had already whispered what was to be done to both Maria Elena and Seaman Bledsoe. Bledsoe was a strong young sailor, another victim of the Cavite Navy Yard bombings. Now that his wounds were mending and his malaria was on the retreat, he was the strongest patient in the hospital. A quiet, serious young man, he could be counted on to help subdue Louise's fellow nurse.

Louise sat down next to Frankie. "Listen to me. You know that Mori is going to march us out of here, right? We're headed for the lowlands on foot, then we'll be interned."

"We'll be better off that way. We should have turned ourselves in a long time ago."

"I said on foot, Frankie. You know what that means for these men. Some of them will die."

"Then we never should have come up here in the first place. It was stupid, we should have given up in Manila when we had the chance. Then we'd be safe. The Red Cross would see to us, and the Japs couldn't do anything about it."

Her voice was climbing again. The Japanese soldiers outside the door would hear if she kept carrying on. Louise clenched her jaw, so angry at Frankie now she wanted to wrap her hands around the woman's throat and choke the silly hen until her face turned blue.

There was movement to one side. Maria Elena, with a small bottle and a sponge. Bledsoe came down from the bench, glanced at Dr. Claypool, who nodded. Maria Elena slid in from the other side. Frankie glanced at both the sailor and the Filipina nurse and seemed to understand all at once. She tried to stand.

Bledsoe knelt in a swift motion and pinned Frankie's arms to her side. At the same moment, Louise took the sponge from Maria Elena and pressed it over Frankie's mouth and nose. The nurse struggled and tried to cry out, but that only drew ether from the sponge into her lungs. The room stank with an odor almost like spilled gasoline, a smell that would linger for hours. Louise turned her head to breathe in as little as possible. Frankie's violent struggles soon came to an end, and she went limp.

Louise rose to her feet, breathing hard from the struggle. "I feel bad for her, in spite of everything she's done. She's going to have a hard time of it when she wakes up."

"You mean she'll be sick?" Maria Elena asked.

The Filipina nurse sat down next to Frankie with the sponge and the bottle of ether. She'd add a couple of drops periodically to keep the woman unconscious until the escape was complete.

"She'll wake up vomiting thanks to the ether, but that's not what I mean." Louise shook her head. "I don't know what's ahead of us. Maybe Mori will kill us all in revenge, or maybe it will be nothing more than the internment camp. Either way, Frankie is going to suffer more than the rest of us."

"She'll *whine* about it more," Maria Elena said. "That's about all."

"No, I mean she'll suffer. She'll stagger out of here hating us, hating herself. All that complaining only makes it worse. When we get to the camp, those of us who can pull together will survive better than those who wallow in misery."

"Good," Maria Elena said bitterly. "I hope she rots."

And then she seemed to remember that the rest of them would be rotting next to Frankie and looked away, face ashamed. Louise forgave the outburst. She was struggling with the same anger. It was unhealthy and could not be indulged in, or Louise would sink into the same mire that had ensnared Frankie.

Bledsoe climbed back on the bench, stretched for the ceiling, and tore at the thatching. It was slow going at first, but as he got deeper into the grass roof, it turned damp and rotten. Soon he was pulling out big chunks of it. He grinned when he broke through and stuck his arm in up to the shoulder.

"Yeah, that's the night air," he said. "I can already feel the mosquitoes landing on my arm like a thousand bloodsucking Jap Zeros." He pulled back out and went back to work tearing out grass to expand the hole.

"I have a question for you, Miss Louise," Kozlowski asked from his mat as Bledsoe worked. "When you negotiated with Mori about the fence, did you see this happening?"

"What do you mean?"

"You wouldn't let him force us into building a fence. That left the back of the hospital unguarded. We can walk right out of here. Was that your plan all along?"

"Not at all," she said honestly. "I was only trying to protect you men. Not one of you was well enough to be digging a trench or putting up a fence, or whatever else Mori was going to order you to do. I was afraid of losing patients, that's all."

"It worked out in the end," Kozlowski said. "Now we've got an escape route."

"So long as they don't have a guard posted around back," Louise said.

"There aren't enough Japs to look everywhere. And three of Mori's men were staked in the sun today. Even if they are on guard duty, they won't be very vigilant."

"What about Sakdals?" she asked.

"At this hour? Drunk on *lambanog.*"

After that, the lieutenant seemed to withdraw into his own thoughts, only looking up when Louise started laying out the supplies she'd be sending with the escapees. Only the basics: morphine, quinine, bandages. A little food, but not much. They had little and could carry less.

Bledsoe proclaimed the hole big enough to escape through.

"Give me names, Miss Louise," Kozlowski said. "Who goes?"

She named the sick and injured men, starting with Kozlowski himself and Dr. Claypool. Seven men in all, plus Maria Elena. The doctor nodded weakly at her assessment.

Kozlowski pulled himself into a sitting position with a grimace. "Okay, boys. You heard Miss Louise. Time to get out of here."

Somehow they got the men to their feet. Bledsoe climbed out to the roof, and then three others hoisted the escapees up to him, one after another. Kozlowski took Louise's hand when it was his turn.

"Thank you. It was an honor and a privilege. Don't forget us."

It was so much like Sammy's final good-bye that her heart felt like it would break. *Don't forget us.* The words of a man who didn't think he would survive.

"You're a good nurse, Miss Louise," Dr. Claypool said, waiting his turn. "The best I ever had."

She spoke quickly, before the lump in her throat choked off her voice. "Don't go far. None of you has the strength. Just wait, hope they leave, then come back to the hospital. Don't push too hard if you can help it. Not one of you should be out of bed, let alone—"

Claypool stopped her with a low chuckle. "Thank you for the medical advice, nurse."

She felt herself blushing and stammered an apology. To her surprise, the doctor embraced her, and she clenched the older man in return, feeling for a moment that she was back in her father's arms when he hugged her before she shipped off to join the nursing corps.

When he pulled away, Louise looked around to see that Kozlowski was already gone. Claypool went next, and finally arms reached down from the ceiling to grab Maria Elena and hoist her up. She was slender and disappeared quickly through the hole. Louise ached not to have even said good-bye, but then Maria Elena's face appeared.

"Thank you," Maria Elena said. "Please take care of yourself."

When Maria Elena was gone, Louise sniffled and her eyes stung. But she wasn't the only one with tears in her eyes. Some of the strongest men in the room were sniffling or turning away to hide their faces.

Louise wished she could afford to cry. Fárez, gone—no word from him since he'd vanished into the mountains. Sammy, gone. Kozlowski and Claypool, gone. Her only friend among the nurses, Maria Elena, gone.

No time for tears. With the departure of the Filipina nurse, Frankie would soon be waking up and complicating matters. Louise had to get organized first.

"All right, everyone," she said. "You're still the walking wounded. Captain Mori will be here in a few hours, and assuming he doesn't kill us all, we've got to get ourselves down from the mountains in one piece. That means we've got work to do."

Chapter Thirty

Night seemed to last forever, yet at the same time, morning arrived with terrifying speed. Louise had everything packed up, her men dressed and ready to go. Even Frankie was cooperating for the moment, but although she was sick after waking from the ether, it hadn't stopped another angry outburst when she'd learned what had been done.

When Captain Mori threw open the door and barked for them to line up for bows and roll call, everyone fell silent. There was fear on every face.

Louise's heart was pounding. "I'll go first."

"Koz left me in charge," Bledsoe said. "I'll go. If that fellow loses his temper, better me than you."

"Stay here," she said firmly. "We've got a better chance if it's me facing him when he figures it out."

Louise stepped into the hot morning air. Steam curled above the rice paddies and lingered above the trees on the surrounding forest.

The Japanese soldiers were lined up in their uniforms with their rifles at the ready. Bayonets fixed. Packs on their backs. Not one of the Kempeitai looked eager to be facing a long march out of the mountains. Mori and Fujiwara stood in front of them with their typical haughty expressions. Behind them, the Sakdals, sullen and slouching.

The villagers had gathered, too, perhaps curious to see the conquerors march off with their prisoners. They'd have been smarter to stay indoors until the Japanese were gone. Even the village dogs had come out to see what the commotion was about. At their head was Stumpy, wagging his half tail and looking about eagerly, as if searching for Fárez or one of his other human friends.

Louise almost didn't see Sammy at first. Her former patient stood to one side, leaning on his crutches, with a crude bamboo splint on his leg. Good. She'd have liked to see that cast still on him, but even a few sticks would give his tibia a better chance of making it down without re-breaking from the repeated stress.

Stumpy trotted through the crowd, as if he belonged in the center circle. He approached Sammy, tail wagging. Sammy pushed him away with a crutch, a scowl on his face, though Louise knew it was an act. One of the Sakdals pitched a stone at the dog, who danced expertly aside and barked. Mori spotted the dog and looked annoyed.

You silly thing. Get out of here.

In any event, Louise didn't need the Japanese angry when she made her plea, so before Stumpy could get any more stones thrown at him, she walked up to Mori. She bowed low, as she'd been taught, and kept her expression respectful. She did not look at his sword, though it was hard not to think of it as he rested one hand on the hilt.

"Thank you, sir, for your kindness."

"Get them out here," Mori snapped. "We have no time for this. I want bows and roll call in five minutes. Then we march."

Louise waved behind her without turning away from the captain. Bledsoe came first, leading the limping, slowly moving soldiers out of the hospital. They came out, stood in front of Mori and Fujiwara one at a time, and bowed low and respectfully. Fujiwara watched them through narrowed eyes. Suspicion seemed to be blooming on his face already, even as men kept filing out.

As the men bowed, Louise kept talking. "You have treated us well as prisoners, sir, and I have no doubt you will allow us time to arrive safely at our destination."

"We will move at the pace required."

"Some of the more seriously wounded and sick would not survive too rapid a pace."

"Nevertheless, they will make an attempt. Some may fall along the way. This is a war, men die."

"As a nurse entrusted with their care, I did what I could to save those who wouldn't survive a rapid march. The men who stand before you will obey your every command. There will be no resistance, I promise you."

The captain glared. "What are you talking about?"

Fujiwara said something to him then, and Mori whipped his head around, took in the dozen men lined up with their little bundles of food and medical supplies.

"What is this?" Mori demanded. "Get the rest of them out here at once."

"I am sorry, sir."

"I'm warning you, woman. If my men go inside, they go in with bayonets." He reached into his jacket pocket and removed the list of names and ranks of the hospital patients and slapped the rolled-up paper onto his palm. "Get them out here. Every last one of them."

As Mori spoke, Fujiwara was giving instructions in Japanese to the secret police. Their faces turned grim. Three of them lowered bayonets and moved to block the dozen Americans, as if expecting resistance. Sakdals hurried to join them. The other three Japanese moved toward the hospital door. Their bodies were tensed, expressions grim.

Louise bowed low, her head and neck exposed. "Mercy, please."

Mori grabbed her hair and yanked her head back. "Get them out here!"

"I can't. They escaped in the night to save their lives."

306

"What?" He jerked her head.

"I'm sorry!" she pleaded. "They would have all died on the road. They'll all die in the jungle, too. Please, the rest of us—"

He threw her to the ground, and her words died as she struck her head. By now the three Japanese soldiers were inside, crying out their findings. Bledsoe and the other soldiers made as if to surge to Louise's aid, but they were blocked now by an equal number of Japanese and Sakdals, all armed. It would be a slaughter if they tried to help. The Americans wisely held back.

Louise tried to stand.

"No. Stay down." Mori was above her now, his sword drawn.

"Please, I promise you we'll cooperate, I only—"

"Quiet!"

He pulled back his sword as if to strike, and she closed her eyes. This was it; this was when she'd die. Mori consulted with Fujiwara for a moment.

"So, your men escaped through the roof," Mori said. His sword was still clenched in his hand. "They then escaped into the jungle by walking out through the trench and past the fence that was never built." He sounded disgusted. "Your men were too sick and weak for labor, so we made a pact, you and I. You would guarantee their cooperation, and I wouldn't force them to work."

"I treated your men, too," she said. "They had malaria, dysentery. That was the arrangement. I'd treat your men, and you wouldn't work my patients to death. That's what your march means. It's working them until they die. It's a death march. They wouldn't have made it. They're only going to die in the jungle with some dignity. You'll arrive with all of the prisoners who would have survived anyway. There's no difference."

Mori seemed to consider this, and for the first time Louise felt a twinge of hope. He wasn't a monster; he could be reasonable. There was something of his brother in him.

"Very well, nurse. I'll take my prisoners and march them down."

"Thank you."

"The one who betrayed me, however, must be made an example of." He pointed at Louise with the tip of his sword. "You will not be accompanying us. You will die here."

Frankie screamed. There were shouts from the Americans at this. But they couldn't move against the lowered bayonets of the Japanese Kempeitai, now six in number and backed by the Sakdals.

"Put your head down and die with dignity," Mori said.

"Please."

Fujiwara said something, to which Mori responded. "I told him you won't be forced," he told Louise. "You either put your head down willingly, or your men die in your place. All of them. Will you do it?"

"Yes," Louise said, her voice so soft even she could barely hear it.

She was light-headed to the point of passing out. Her bowels felt hot and loose. This was no joke or test. It was her death.

You can face this.

Men had already done it by the thousands, and more died every day the war continued. Women, too. She could die to save the dozen men and the nurse who remained. Her body felt like someone else's as she knelt and exposed her neck.

Suddenly a grunt. The sound of bodies hitting each other. Shouts of alarm from all around. She looked up as two men grappled in front of her. It was Sammy and Captain Mori.

Sammy still had one of his crutches in hand and hit his brother with it as he held him close with his free hand. Mori tried to use his sword, but it was pinned between the two men. Fujiwara drew his sidearm and shouted.

Other Japanese were yelling, Sakdals making noise, too. Bledsoe cried for Louise to get out of there. Every dog in the village erupted into barks.

All Louise could think was to stand up and try to separate the two men. Sammy was flailing about so furiously with the crutch that his brother would have no choice but to defend himself with the sword if he could get it free. And there was Fujiwara with his pistol. The man was trying to get an angle.

Louise moved toward Mori, thinking to pull him away, even as she cried out, "Sammy, no! Stop!"

Fujiwara now leveled his pistol at *her*. He seemed to have found his target. The look on his face held no mercy. There were cries from every direction. Dogs barking furiously.

Mori got his sword free. He lifted it above his head. Sammy began to raise the crutch to block it. Louise was just out of reach of both men and couldn't get there in time.

Mori swung his sword. Louise didn't know if the captain was swinging at his brother or trying to slice through the wooden crutch. It didn't matter. Sammy didn't get the crutch up in time, and the sword came down with great force at the point where Sammy's shoulder blade met his neck. There was a sickening crack, like a cleaver meeting a butcher's block. Sammy hit the ground as his brother was wrenching the sword free.

Mori staggered backward, eyes wide in horror. Blood spurted from Sammy's wound. His eyes were blinking, looking up, and his hand went to his shoulder. He didn't seem to feel anything yet.

A hand grabbed Louise's arm—Fujiwara, she thought—but she twisted free with a cry and fell down next to her injured friend. She put her hand over the wound and attempted to stop the flow of blood. It was too much, a ruin of his shoulder and chest. Mori's sword blow had severed muscle and bone and cut into chest and lungs. Blood streamed through her fingers, so much of it.

Sammy's eyes fixed on hers. He beckoned her down. "Please," he mouthed.

Louise put her ear at his lips.

"A narrow river with a deep channel." Sammy drew in a ragged breath, and Louise didn't think he would say another word. What came out next was barely whispered. "Cross it once and—"

A final, sighing hiss escaped, and then he was still. His eyes remained open, unblinking. Whatever was next, however he had finished his death poem, nobody would ever hear it. Louise pulled back with a sob. She was covered with Sammy's blood.

Captain Mori's face was a mask of anguish. The sword slumped in his hand until the tip dragged the dirt. Sammy's crutch lay at his feet. Mori looked up from Sammy and fixed Louise with a terrible, vengeful look.

She rose and stood, rigid and still. He lifted his sword, and she didn't move.

Stumpy came up while Mori was steadying his weapon. He paid the captain no attention but nuzzled at Sammy's hand. A whimper. The half tail wagged hopefully. He nosed harder. There was something desperate in the way his half tail kept wagging harder and harder until his entire backside was shaking back and forth. This time the whimper sounded pitiful, almost a mournful cry.

"Get away from him, you filthy—" Mori's English trailed into a single, polysyllabic string of Japanese rage. He came at the dog with his sword.

Louise was too shaken to react. Could only stand frozen as Mori swung his weapon.

Stumpy leaped out of the way. The sword whooshed past his ear. Stumpy barked defiantly.

Still yelling in Japanese, Mori came after the dog. He swung again and, when Stumpy came under the sword to force another miss, lashed out with his boot. He caught the dog on the haunch. Stumpy yelped but came up growling and snarling.

The dog darted in and under before Mori could ready his sword again. He clamped his teeth on the back of the man's leg. Mori cried out in pain. He twisted around, trying to hook the attacking animal with his sword. Once again, Stumpy danced clear. He retreated a few paces, barking furiously.

Fujiwara aimed his pistol at the dog. He was next to Louise, and she lowered her shoulder and jostled him. The gun went off. She was so close the sound was like hands slapped hard over her ears. But the shot went wild.

Two more shots chased Stumpy off. Bullets tossed up dirt around him but didn't hit. Then the dog was in the midst of the Sakdals, who kicked at him and swung their rifle butts, jeering and laughing as they tried to kill him. The other dogs were barking crazily, like rioting inmates in an asylum, and tore off after Stumpy toward the village as he fled.

Moments later the commotion was over. The dogs had vanished, uninjured. Sammy lay dead in a pool of blood at Louise's feet. The American prisoners remained pinned against the hospital at bayonet point. Mori still held his sword. He stared at Louise.

A long moment stretched even longer. At last Mori reached slowly into his shirt pocket and removed a faded handkerchief. Moving deliberately, he stroked it along the blade to clean it of blood, then sheathed the sword, folded the bloody handkerchief, and returned it to his pocket.

"Warn your patients, nurse," Mori said as he took a step back, favoring the leg Stumpy had bit. "The first man to step out of line loses his head. We leave now."

Chapter Thirty-One

February 3, 1945—Santo Tomás Internment Camp, Manila

Louise tucked herself on the floor with her hands behind her head as explosions rocked the compound. Planes rolled overhead, and the sound of bombs rumbled from elsewhere in the city. The women in the dorm-style room had turned over beds and formed makeshift bomb shelters.

She held two Dutch children, eight and six, who had come trembling into her arms when the excitement started. Like many children in the internment camp, they had lost parents, and after three years, probably remembered little of their life before Santo Tomás. Sometimes, Louise envied them.

Five minutes earlier, she had been watching Manila burning through the windows of a hallway in the converted university, but when the electricity went out and the bombs started to fall, she retreated to the room she shared with thirty other women and children.

Japanese voices sounded in the corridor, high and excited. The camp guards. The sound of breaking glass. Rifle fire. Was this it? Had the Americans come?

Then it was quiet. For several long minutes the sounds of war retreated except for the distant rumble of artillery and bombs. Heavy breathing in the dark, whimpers, and whispered conversation. The silence was broken at last by an excited conversation in mixed French and English from the hallway outside. A fist pounded on the door.

"They're here!" came a muffled voice through the door.

Louise joined the others in pushing into the corridor, down the stairway, and into the warm night air outside. It smelled of burning fuel. Flares lit up the front gate.

Her heart pounding, she joined the mob of refugees waiting. The gates gave a terrific screech and collapsed inward. A hulking metal tank clanked through on its treads. A searchlight swept over their faces. Soldiers jumped down from the tank.

And a voice called out in English. "Hello, folks!"

American soldiers stepped in front of the searchlight. Louise shouted in joy and relief, her voice joined with dozens of others. Those who'd remained fearfully inside the building came spilling out now, crying and weeping. People clasped their hands and prayed while couples embraced. Wounded American soldiers who'd been tortured and then interned with the civilians dropped to the dirt.

Others crowded the newcomers, Louise included. She hugged the soldiers, one after another. So strong and muscular—it was a shock after these three years of steadily reducing rations to see and feel men so healthy. Some of the soldiers stared at her in shock and outrage as they saw what she looked like. What all the internees looked like.

One of the men handed her a chocolate bar. She turned it over in trembling hands.

"Well, lady, ain't you gonna eat it?" the man asked cheerfully. He had a wide, pleasant face and a Texas twang.

She broke off a tiny piece and popped it in her mouth. An ordinary chocolate bar, but the taste of it was enough to make her swoon.

"Go on, then," he said, grinning. "You can eat it all."

"I would like to, but I'm afraid it will make me ill."

Several men entered the building in front of them to ensure that the Japanese had truly fled and were not waiting to spring an ambush, and now a familiar figure emerged from the midst of the soldiers still warily entering the camp. It was Lieutenant Kozlowski.

Louise stared at him, stunned, unable to move. His face was older, more settled, his eyes carrying the hard expression of a warrior who had survived battle and killing and the death of both friends and enemies. But then he spotted her, and a smile broke on his face, sweeping the years away.

"Louise!"

She embraced him, laughing. He joined her in laughter, sweeping her up, but that died as soon as he set her down. His expression turned grim.

"My God, you weigh nothing."

She turned away, ashamed. She felt bony, starving. Her dress felt like a sheet draped over a collection of sticks. These days, she could press her hand against her aching belly and feel her backbone through it. She felt old—she *was* old. Only twenty-six, but her body was aching, suffering beriberi, her joints in constant pain, her hair falling out.

"Those damn Japs," Kozlowski muttered. "Starving you to death."

"They fed us early on," she said. "But they don't have much to eat themselves anymore."

"You're too easy on them. Cowards and thieves."

There was some truth in his words. Japanese had stolen vegetables when the internees planted gardens on the campgrounds. They'd stuck their bayonets into cans of food delivered by the Red Cross. They'd prohibited Filipinos from passing in food to help the starving inmates. But she wouldn't dwell on that now.

"Come on," he said. "I'll get you some good army chow."

"Only a little," she said. "My body can't take anything rich."

Nevertheless, by the time morning dawned, she'd eaten too much for her own good and was rushing to the bathroom. There, she joined dozens of others fighting cramps, vomiting, and diarrhea. Some didn't make it in time and soiled themselves.

When she felt better a couple of days later, she sought out Kozlowski to arrange for medical supplies to be brought in. He'd been promoted to captain and was organizing the relief of the camp even while the battle for Manila still raged elsewhere in the city. She found him in a makeshift office with a Japanese war calendar still hanging on the wall, though most everything else had been torn down. The mats had been tossed out, the floor swept, and an American-style desk and chair brought in. Kozlowski led her outside while she gave him her list of needed goods.

"You'll want penicillin, too."

"What's that?"

He grinned. "There have been some developments, Miss Louise. Miracle drug—wait until you see how it works."

Food was the biggest medicine the army had brought, but they continued to lose internees. The next two weeks would be critical. She shared her thoughts for how to safely distribute food as shrunken stomachs became accustomed to the new rations.

Kozlowski glanced up at the sky at a pair of American fighter planes rumbling just above the tree line, then turned back to her. "I saw some other nurses—evacuees from Corregidor and Bataan. Didn't see Frankie. I guess she didn't make it, huh?"

"She's still alive," Louise said grimly. "But you won't find her working the medical detail."

Kozlowski shook his head. "Imagine that. So many good men and women dead, and that poisonous snake manages to survive."

"I said she's alive," Louise said. "I didn't say she survived."

"Is there a difference?"

315

Just then, Frankie came walking out. She was muttering to herself, rubbing her hands together. Louise's hair may have thinned, but Frankie's was almost gone, only tufts here and there like clumps of dying weeds. She had no friends in the camp, and though Louise had gently told her to take better care of herself, she had ignored this and it showed. Most of her teeth were gone, leaving lips sucked around shrunken gums. She wore no shoes, not even *bakya*, and her feet had the leathered, horny look of an old Filipina peasant.

"Louise?" Kozlowski said. "You were saying about Miss Frankie? Where is she now?"

Louise blinked. "That's her."

"Where?" He looked around at the internees walking across the grounds, and his eyes swept over Frankie without seeming to see her.

"Right there!"

"I see two young girls, that mixed-race fellow smoking over there, and an old woman."

"The old woman is a thirty-five-year-old nurse. That's Frankie."

"My God."

He gave a violent shake of the head and looked away from Frankie, who had reached the open front gate and turned to follow the inside of the fence, as if the grounds were still closed and she were forbidden to leave them.

Again, "My God."

"Yes, well." Louise paused. "I hope she gets better." Another pause. "The war has been unusually hard on her."

"It has been hard on all of us. You're probably curious about the others."

"Very. Can we take a walk outside? Is it safe?"

"Not safe at all," he said cheerfully. "Can't you hear the shells?"

She listened. "They sound far away."

"For now. They'll be pounding us here soon enough."

But Louise couldn't stand being cooped up any longer, and the compound didn't seem safer than anywhere else in the city, so she told him she wanted to risk it. That was, if he felt he could leave for a few minutes to escort her on a walk.

"I don't see why not. Come on."

They left through the open gates, where troops were digging fox-holes lined with sandbags and armed with machine guns. More soldiers had arrived on Jeeps. As they walked into the city, Kozlowski told her how he'd survived the last three years.

After escaping the hospital in Cascadas, Kozlowski and the others holed up in a small valley about a mile from the village, staying still and hidden for three days until they thought they were safe to move. Two of the patients died, in spite of Maria Elena's best efforts. Later, after they'd made contact with Fárez and the mixed band of American and Filipino partisans, Dr. Claypool had died of malaria.

"Maria Elena did everything she could," Kozlowski said, "but it wasn't enough. The jungle, the humidity, and the miles of walking were too much for the doc."

"I'm sorry to hear that," she said. "Is Maria Elena okay? Did she make it?"

"Last I saw her, yeah. Stuck with us all this time—I can't believe we were going to leave her in Manila during that initial evacuation. Just because she was a local. She only got better at her job. Miss Clarice grew up a lot working with her. Getting away from Frankie helped."

"So Clarice made it, too."

"She did."

It warmed Louise's heart to hear about the two nurses, and she urged Kozlowski to go on. He and Fárez had stuck with the partisans for three years, occasionally losing men to disease or Japanese bullets. They gained others after the fall of Bataan, and Filipinos joined them as the enemy starved out their villages or introduced oppressive measures.

At one point Kozlowski counted more than a hundred men in his band. It wasn't enough to launch an uprising, but they kept up a regular harassment of the Japanese and punished Sakdals and other collaborators. They pinned down a good number of enemy troops that might have been used elsewhere.

Kozlowski established contact with the Americans after MacArthur's return and was ordered to report for duty. They slapped a fresh uniform on him, awarded him a brevet promotion to captain, and gave him a key role in the liberation of Manila.

"What about Corporal Fárez?"

"He's fine. Walks with a limp—you can't regrow your butt, it turns out—but it doesn't hold him back."

"Where is he?"

"Still running with the partisans, but soon enough he'll be back in uniform for the duration. That fellow deserves whatever promotion he gets." Kozlowski glanced at her. "You, too. You know army nurses have rank now?"

"I heard that."

"No more Miss Louise for you. It's going to be Lieutenant Louise Harrison. Unless they send you back to the States. You've suffered enough for one person."

"I'll stay until the war is over unless they kick me out."

Kozlowski's face turned grim. "That may be years."

"It sounds like Hitler is about to fold," she said. "That's something. The Russians and Americans are going to overrun Germany. Once that's over, we can turn all our attention to Japan. That should bring about the end of the war."

"Maybe," he said dubiously. "These Japs fight like the devil himself. They won't surrender. We're fighting island by island out here, and we haven't come close to Japan yet."

What a depressing thought. So much misery. So many dead, so many still to die.

Kozlowski seemed to be worrying over the same thing, but suddenly his face brightened. "Guess who we picked up last month? Stumpy! Yeah, that guy had been hanging out in Cascadas the past three years right under the nose of the Japanese occupation."

"Really?" she said, laughing.

"Sure thing. He recognized us, all right, and practically jumped into Fárez's arms. Better Fárez than me. Smelled pretty ripe and he's as mangy as ever. Otherwise, fine. Little gray around the muzzle, is all. But I'll tell you something." Kozlowski grinned. "There were eight dogs in Cascadas with stumpy tails."

"What? Really?"

"I always thought he lost his tail in an accident, but I guess he was born that way. Remember when you had to treat the dog's . . . illness? Cut one of 'em off, didn't you, but Stumpy managed just fine."

Louise put her hand over her mouth to stifle a laugh.

"Did you ever hear what happened to our Japanese buddy?" Kozlowski asked, voice turning serious.

Her heart fell. "Sammy Mori."

"Yeah, right. Mori. Haven't thought about him for a while, but that talk about Stumpy reminded me. I figure he had a hard time of it once he was back with the Japs, but . . . well, it's a war, and anything can happen. Maybe he came out okay."

"Then you don't know?"

"Know what?" His face fell as he took in her expression. "What is it?"

Louise told him what had happened: Captain Mori's fury at learning of the escape, his demand that Louise bow her head to be executed, Sammy throwing himself at his brother to stop it and dying as a result.

So many months and years had passed, so long maintaining her poise. She'd needed to stay strong. Every time weakness threatened, she'd thought about the people she'd lose if she failed, if she collapsed in on her fears and doubts like Frankie had. First her soldiers, then the

Michael Wallace

internees after she was brought to Manila. She'd faltered inside many, many times but never let it affect her outward behavior.

And now she broke. Thinking not just of Sammy, but the others she'd lost, the pain she'd seen on so many faces. The cries of hungry children and the terror of cruelty at the hands of the enemy. And now she was here, outside the walls that had been her prison, in the open air with palms swaying gently above her. So beautiful and ugly at the same time. Tears welled up in her eyes, and she couldn't stop them.

Kozlowski held her for a moment. When he pulled away, his own eyes were damp.

"But Sammy saved your life, didn't he?" Kozlowski said, his voice rough. "Killing him must have shocked the violence right out of his brother."

"And Stumpy." Louise laughed through her tears. "He bit Mori on the leg after Sammy died. They all tried to kill him. Stab him, kick him, shoot him. Stumpy ran off, mocking all of them."

"When this war is over," Kozlowski said, "I'm going to find Fárez. Find that mutt of his. We'll get Stumpy a medal, wait and see."

Something changed in the tenor of the blasts that had been reverberating dully through the air and ground as they walked. The enemy artillery was changing targets. Kozlowski cocked his head with a frown.

"Come on," he said, all business. "We're safe for now, but I'd rather be inside when the shells start to fall."

Louise nodded. "I've got work to do anyway."

They turned around. Captain Kozlowski held out his arm, and Louise took it.

As they passed back through the gate, Louise's eyes spotted a captured Japanese flag with its rising sun and splaying rays. An American soldier was using it to wipe the mud from his Jeep. Another man rested his stocking feet on a pair of Japanese steel helmets while he polished his boots, a cigarette dangling from his mouth.

320

Seeing the remnants of the Japanese soldiers made Louise think about Sammy Mori again. He'd died with his beloved poetry on his lips. A death poem. Had he written it himself? She thought he had. But how had it ended?

A narrow river with a deep channel. Cross it once and—

He'd died before he could say the rest. Over the past three years, she'd tried to put in the word or words that would complete the thought. The river must represent death. The channel narrow, but deep. The poem must end with something about crossing the river and never returning. But that seemed too direct, and Sammy told her such things had a surprise or a twist.

Maybe the end of the poem was about the people who watched your back as you crossed. Wishing they could speak to you one last time. Knowing they never could.

Or maybe it's not about death at all. Maybe I'm the one who crossed the river.

Three years ago, a few short weeks had passed in the mountains while a war raged around them. Louise had met a sensitive Japanese soldier, and something had bloomed between them, unexpected amid so much cruelty and death. It meant something. It had to mean something.

Author's Note

I was fortunate to once visit the ancient Japanese capital of Kyoto. Like everywhere I visited in Japan, the city was clean, the people friendly and impossibly polite, the society well ordered. But even in a country filled with great beauty, Kyoto stands apart. Every corner seems to have a temple or shrine or garden with a sublime beauty that will make you catch your breath.

I had been reading about the Pacific theater of World War II in preparation for writing this book, and as I traveled through Kyoto I wondered how the same people who'd built the Zen Buddhist temple of Kinkaku-ji—the Golden Pavilion—could be responsible for such atrocities as the Rape of Nanking and the Bataan Death March.

A similar question could be asked of the Germans, of course. That two cultures such as the Japanese and Germans could be synonymous with culture and civilization and law-abiding behavior and yet have inflicted so much cruelty and suffering on other people raises troubling questions about human nature and should make us all feel humble about our place in history. What happened there can happen anywhere.

I used a number of sources for the Japanese poetry in this book, as well as some of my own tweaks (translation being an imprecise art), but a book that helped me narrow my focus is *The Essential Haiku: Versions of Bashō, Buson, & Issa*, edited by Robert Hass. It is highly recommended for its thought-provoking and humorous translations of master Japanese poets.

About the Author

Photo © 2011 David Garten

Michael Wallace was born in California and raised in a small religious community in Utah, eventually heading east to live in Rhode Island and Vermont. In addition to working as a literary agent and innkeeper, he has been a software engineer for a Department of Defense contractor, programming simulators for nuclear submarines. He is the author of more than twenty novels, including the *Wall Street Journal* bestselling Righteous series, set in a polygamist enclave in the desert.

Made in the USA
Columbia, SC
19 June 2017